THE BULLET TRICK

Louise Welsh

WINDSOR
PARAGON

First published 2006
by
Canongate Books Ltd
This Large Print edition published 2006
by
BBC Audiobooks Ltd by arrangement with
Canongate Books Ltd

Hardcover ISBN 10: 1 4056 1549 4
           ISBN 13: 978 1 405 61549 5
Softcover ISBN 10: 1 4056 1550 8
           ISBN 13: 978 1 405 61550 1

British Library Cataloguing in Publication Data available

Printed and bound in Great Britain by
Antony Rowe Ltd., Chippenham, Wiltshire

For Zoë Strachan

The author wishes to express her gratitude for a Hawthornden Fellowship, which helped in the writing of this book.

Ah, sweet whisperer, my dear wanton, I
Have followed you, shawled in your warmth,
  since I left the breast,
Been toady for you and pet bully,
And a woeful heartscald to the parish priest;
And look! If I took the mint by storm and
  spent it,
Heaping on you in one wild night the dazzle
  of a king's whore,
And returned next morning with no money
  for a curer,
Your publican would throw me out the door.

'Raftery's Dialogue With the Whiskey,'
Padraic Fallon.

Glasgow

The aeroplane wheels touched the runway, jerking me awake.

'I envy you, that's a gift.'

The blonde woman in the next seat smiled. I wiped a hand over my face.

'Sorry?'

'You slept like the dead all the way from Tegel. You're lucky, I don't sleep like that in my own bed.'

Some other time I might have asked how she slept in strangers' beds, but I kept my smart mouth shut and waited while the pilot bumped us into a smooth landing, just another flight. The seatbelt lights turned off and the business types got to their feet and started pulling their bags from the overhead lockers. A mobile phone chimed awake and a man said, *I'll call you back in ten minutes. I'm on a plane.* He laughed. *No it's OK, we've landed.* My insomniac neighbour stood up and I slipped my equipment case from under the seat in front. It felt heavy, but I'd added nothing to it in Berlin, except for the envelope packed tight with bank notes that I hadn't bothered to count.

The queue of passengers edged along the aisle then down the metal staircase and onto the tarmac. No one kissed the runway. I pulled my coat close and kept my eyes on the ground.

A long line of luggage lurched along the carousel but I'd left my broken suitcase along with its contents in a hotel room in Berlin.

The taxi-rank controller was bundled against the weather in a fluorescent jacket that looked regulation issue and an old checked bunnet that didn't. He slammed the cab door on the safely settled traveller in front then turned to me.

'Where to?'

'Glasgow.'

He smiled patiently, a man used to jet-lag and bad English, and asked, 'Where in Glasgow son?'

'City centre.'

He wrote something on his clipboard saying, 'That'll do.' And waved one of the white cabs forward.

The driver asked the same question that his supervisor had. This time I said, 'Do you know anywhere I could rent a bedsit in the city centre?'

He looked at me in the rear-view mirror, seeing the same face I'd splashed cold water on only minutes before in the gents. A nondescript face with a hard cleft in the centre of its brow that might suggest ruthlessness or worry, but nothing that would make me stand out in a crowd.

I said, 'There'll be a bung in it for you.'

And he swung the taxi out of the airport, down into Glasgow and towards the Gallowgate.

I sat in the back and closed my eyes, wondering how I'd got myself into this mess and what lay in store for me in the city I used to call home.

London

The first night I met Sylvie she saved me from dying. The clock has ticked round and the pages have been flipped on the calendar, its numbers switching from red to black and back, shades the same as playing-card suits, and I realise that over a year has passed since Sylvie and I first met.

In those dim days I was known as *William Wilson, Mentalist and Illusionist.* Conjuring was throwing off the shackles of the dinner suit and velvet bow tie. It had slipped off the family viewing prime-time TV slot and into the clubs, gone underground, kicked around with freak shows and circuses, and now the feeling was it was ripe to hit the big time again. I was one of the many who thought they might just be able to shake the profession back to life, if only I got the right break. Like a gambler waiting on the right cut of the cards.

I'd left Glasgow for London seven years ago and had been toiling through the British circuit ever since, long enough to almost recognise what town I was in, long enough not to care. I was a warm-up act for a whole trough of comedians and stand ups. The guy nobody came to see. I'd performed in the King's, the Queen's, the Prince's and the Consort; done my stuff in the Variety, the Civic, the Epic and the Grand. I'd released doves across the ceiling of the Playhouse and watched them crap on the heads of the crowd in the Cliffs Pavilion. In Liverpool a woman fainted on stage and was dragged into the wings. In Portsmouth a row of

3

sailors chased an usher through the aisles. In Belfast I slept with a girl in the Botanic Hotel.

I'd had professional excitements too. A TV scout who thought he might get me a slot that could lead to a series, an independent production company who proposed a documentary about my act. But in the end it seemed they were bigger failures than me. At least I could put a show on the road.

My agent was Richard Banks, Rich to his friends. He represented a slough of comedians, a couple of afternoon quiz show presenters and me. Rich had been an operator since the days when variety was king. In the fifties he'd mopped up the ENSA boys, the sixties had seen him branching into teenage pop and by the seventies he was a regular supplier of what he liked to call talent to piers from Brighton to Blackpool. A couple of his stable had even made it as far as *Saturday Night at the London Palladium*. Then entertainment had improved and Rich had moved on, signing a new generation of stand-ups to his fleet. Rich was realistic and adaptable but he was loyal too, after all, as he said, 'Loyalty costs nothing William.'

Though you can bet if it did Richard would have included it just above the VAT in his agent's fee. He brought loyalty up early in our relationship. He had an office in Crouch End. I'd popped in on spec, part because I was passing and part to remind him of my existence. I'd tried and failed to work a James Bond/Moneypenny routine with Mrs Pierce, Rich's steel-grey coiffured and steelier-eyed secretary. Now she just glanced at me from behind her word processor and said, 'Mr Banks has someone with him, but he won't mind if you go through.'

The man in the visitor's chair was a sprightly seventy with a boyish face that should have been in black and white but was red-cheeked, purple-veined and rheumy-eyed. He'd leaned back in his chair, his pale hair flopping away from his forehead, a brilliant advert for toupee tape. His upside-down smile was tight. We both knew my unannounced entrance was his cue to leave. Rich introduced us and I remembered the name from long ago, though I still couldn't recall what I'd seen him in.

'Wilson, not a very stagey name,' he said over my shoulder to Richard as he shook my hand, trying and failing to squeeze my knuckles. I mugged a wince, just to please him, and his eyes sparkled.

'Times change,' said Rich, getting to his feet.

'They surely do.' The aged theatrical nodded his head and looked slowly round the room at the black and white photos of yesterday's stars that mingled with the portraits of Rich's current stable. Perhaps he was searching for a picture of himself, perhaps at his age you get used to looking at places as if you're never going to see them again. 'Well, Rich, it's been lovely but I can't sit gabbing to you all day.' He raised his mug, pinkie outstretched, and knocked back the last of his tea with a loud slurp. 'So what's this one? Another comic?'

'Conjurer.'

The elderly gent rose slowly, his thin body looking too young for his old man head, and pulled on a spotless gabardine I pegged as at least fifteen years old.

'Conjurer, eh? Known a few of them in my time.

5

None of them made it big, but they were nice boys.'

I leered at him.

'I'm not a nice boy.'

'No,' his eyes glanced me up and down, 'I didn't think so. Still, nice or not I'd give the last ten years of my life to have six months at the age you are now. Bet the offers never stop coming in for this one, eh Rich?'

Rich gave a noncommittal smile and the old man laughed, suddenly spry as he gathered his hat, scarf, gloves, briefcase and a carrier bag of groceries, fluttering apologies to Richard for taking so much of his time. He winked at me on the way out and said, 'Never mind dear, we all have our dry spells.'

I gave him a wide-boy grin and held the door open. When he was safe in the outer office, chatting to Mrs Pierce with a familiarity she'd never have tolerated from me, I took his seat, wincing against the warmth stored in the cushions and said, 'Nobody loves a fairy when they're forty.'

Rich gave me a long stare, as near to a frown as I've seen him come, then he gave me a lesson.

Stuffed at the back of his filing cabinets were the profiles of men with a million mother-in-law and darkie jokes, female impersonators, ventriloquists, crooners and jugglers. He plonked the files on the desk in front of me and I flicked through them for form's sake. Each file had a photograph paperclipped to its top left-hand corner. Outmoded hairdos, polyester dinner suits, big bow ties and grins that had once seemed alive, but now looked desperate, caught in a mad moment twenty or so years ago.

'I keep them on the books,' Rich said, 'there's no harm in it. They don't take up much space and it's nice to be nice. After all, put together, these kids made me a lot of money at one time. And anyway, who knows when some post-modern ironist is going to suddenly discover one of these has-beens was a genius? But just remember son, it's like they say in the financial ads, your shares may go down as well as up. So,' he tapped his nose like a tipster revealing a cert, 'remember, loyalty costs nothing.'

Once upon a time Rich had thought I might be in the new wave of conjurers, 'the post-Paul Daniels brigade' he called them. These days we weren't close, but he let me call his answerphone direct. The evening this story starts was the first time in weeks he'd called me back.

'It may not be the big time William'—Richard hailed originally from Southend. He had a voice as loud as a McGill postcard, all whelks, beer and fat ladies flashing their drawers. I held the receiver an inch or two from my ear; there was no premium in adding deafness to my problems. 'But there'll be some interesting people there. You never know who you'll meet.' I'd made some noncommittal sound, and Rich had gone on with his spiel, selling it to me though he knew I'd take it. 'You'll have fun. It's a police retirement night.'

'Lovely, just what I need. The filth interrogating me on how I do my act.'

'Is that any attitude to have towards Her Majesty's finest? Anyway they'll love it, William. These guys are into lies and misdirection big time.' Rich paused and I could hear him dragging on his cigarette. 'Tell you, here's an idea, pick on the weediest one and do some funny business with his handcuffs.' His laugh caught in his throat and there was a pause as he struggled to catch his breath. I wondered if he was lying down on his office divan.

'That's wonderful advice, Richard: pick on a weedy looking polis, the one with the Napoleon complex. I'll remember that. So who am I opening for?'

'You know these events, William. They're not name in lights occasions, but they have the benefit of equality, there's no headline act.'

'OK, am I on first or second?'

'My understanding would be first.'

'So who am I preceding?'

'A fine duo known as The Divines.'

'Tell me they're mind-readers and not strippers.'

'They're billed as erotic dancers.'

'Really pitching me high, Richard, support act to a pair of lap-dancers.'

'Don't knock it, William. I've seen these girls, they need a lot of support if you get my drift.'

'What's the bottom line?'

'Peachy, you could write a symphony about their bottom lines.'

I was beginning to understand why Richard had so few female artistes on his books.

'What's my fee?'

'Two-fifty. Hey, who knows, maybe you could buddy up with the girls for the night? Make some of their clothes disappear?'

'A real novelty act.'

Down the line more smoke was sucked into lungs. 'Don't be so bloody Scottish. Tell you what, if you get laid I'll waive my ten percent.'

8

I said, 'You're a prince, Richard.'

And heard his laugh collapse back into coughs as I hung up the receiver.

*   *   *

That evening a bomb scare on the tube shut down main stations and the flatmate of the girl who filled in as my occasional assistant informed me that Julie had got a proper acting job. When I asked her if she fancied taking over instead she'd laughed and said, 'After the stories Julie told me? You must be joking,' and hung up still laughing.

I wondered if I could get a volunteer from the audience, but half-cut coppers waiting for a skin act didn't seem promising recruitment material. Hurtling beneath the city in a carriage, pressed amongst jaded commuters who would rather take their chances than be rerouted and nervous tourists bracing themselves for an explosion, my mind drifted towards the dog track. A quick change of underground line and I could be there in time to place a bet on the third race. There was a young dog in the running that I fancied, it was untested enough to have high odds, but could do well if the conditions were right. I was onto a sure two-twenty-five from the gig once Richard had shaved his commission off the top, but if luck was on my side I could win a lot more. I thought about the money I owed my bookie and the demand for rent that the landlord had slipped under the door that morning after he'd got tired of battering on it. Next time he'd send one of his sons with a key and a couple of helpers to give me a hand shifting my gear onto the street.

We pulled into the station where I needed to switch line if I was going to abscond and I almost got to my feet, but I'd never missed a show to go gambling yet. Only addicts took a bet on their job.

*   *   *

The club turned out to be a private members' place in Soho. I found the street, walked three blocks, then realised I'd overshot it and had to retrace my steps. The entrance was at street level, an anonymous green door with no sign or brass plate to distinguish it, just a number beside an unmarked buzzer. I pressed the buzzer and somewhere in the building a mechanical droning announced my presence.

There was a brief pause, then a bustling beyond the door and a Judas hole slid back with a crack. A pair of green eyes painted with emerald glitter and fringed by false eyelashes appeared behind a tiny wrought-iron grill. They stared at me unblinking, like an exotic anchorite.

I said, 'Joe sent me.' And the Judas hole slammed shut. When it became clear that the door wasn't going to open I buzzed again. This time when the hatch slid back I gave my name and when that got no response added, 'I'm the conjurer.'

'The what?'

The voice was cockney, younger than I'd expected and full of scorn. I gave her the benefit of the William Wilson grin and said, 'The magician.'

The eyes looked me up and down, and found me wanting. The voice said. 'That's funny, I thought you were a bloody comedian.' And buzzed me in.

'You're late.'

The door led straight into a tiny entrance hallway divided by a counter into a reception and cloakroom. Black carpet ran across the floor, ceiling and walls. A harsh neon strip revealed fag burn melts and ooze between the jet pile. I guessed a TV design guru wouldn't approve, but once the lights were down it would suit the musty come-alive-at-night feel of the place.

The green eyes belonged to a large pale girl, squeezed into a red and black dress whose lace-up bodice was losing the struggle to control her bosoms. She was the kind of girl old gentlemen like to pinch: ripe and big, with skin that fitted like skin should. Once you got past the hardness of her stare she'd be a fine pillow against the world. Her hair was a mass of white-gold curls, piled high and tumbling on the top of her head. A soft blush of down brushed her cheek. The overall effect was voluptuous, blowsy and somehow Victorian. My grandmother would have called her a strumpet, but I thought she looked too good for this place.

The girl lifted a flap on the counter and put it between her and me.

I smiled and asked, 'All on your own?'

I was aiming for avuncular, but it sounded like a line that Crippen might have used. The girl ignored me and switched on the Tiffany lamp on the counter, then started to dim the overheads.

'What's in the case?'

'My props.'

'Have you got a rabbit?'

'Aye, but he's invisible.'

She gave me a disgusted look that suddenly revealed the teenager beneath the makeup.

11

'Bill's upstairs chatting up the tarts.'

I guessed she was used to creeps and thought of saying something to show her I wasn't one of them, but couldn't come up with anything other than, 'Maybe I should go and introduce myself.'

She shrugged with a look that said she expected nothing less and pointed towards a set of swing doors.

'Changing rooms are through the bar and up the stairs.'

*   *   *

The bar was a larger, more dimly lit version of the foyer. A disco light bounced a coloured spectrum half-heartedly against the walls and from somewhere an eighties chart hit, that I dimly remembered from a stint I'd done at a holiday camp in Kos, was blasting across a tiny dance floor. A few men who looked too serious to consider dancing sat drinking at dimpled copper tables. I might be late, but the party wasn't swinging. They dropped their voices and followed me with their eyes as I passed. They would be hard men to entertain, hard men full stop. I gave them a nod and they kept their gaze level, each man's stare a mirror of his companion's even look. I thought of a school of fish, each in tune with the other, slipping as one through a dark ocean. I wondered if Rich had meant two-fifty before or after his cut. I always forgot to ask.

*   *   *

At first glance Bill looked vintage doorman.

Broad-shouldered, squat-nosed and tuxedoed. He was leaning against a dressing-table, arms folded, long legs crossed. The door to the room was half-closed but I could see two slim girls reflected in the mirror behind him, one Asian, the other a Jean Harlow blonde. The blonde girl was the shorter of the two, but they looked strikingly alike, monochrome sisters, hair styled into the same short curly bob, jeans and T-shirts not identical but similar enough to be interchangeable. I was no connoisseur of ballet, but I thought I might be able to tolerate watching them dance.

Bill leaned back slowly, giving me a good glimpse of his long profile, and said in a public school mockney that made me suspect he'd got his broken nose at a hunt meeting, '. . . everyone has a good time'.

I banged my case against the banister to avoid hearing the rest of his instructions and he pushed open the door gently with the toe of his smart black shoe, revealing a quick flash of metal segs. The toe was slim, but I suspected it would be steel capped.

Bill's move was smooth and unhurried but his expression flashed from smile to wary then to smile again as he spotted first me, then my equipment case with its motif of gold stars, and guessed who I was.

'Mr Magic, we were just wondering when you'd appear.'

'We thought you might come in a puff of smoke,' cut in the blonde girl.

I said, 'There's time yet.'

And we all laughed.

Bill straightened up with the elegance of a sneak

13

thief.

'Meet Shaz,' he put his arm around the Asian girl's waist, 'and Jacque.' His free arm snaked around the small blonde. Bill squeezed his captives who staggered slightly on their high heels. He smiled. 'Lovely. Well I guess we should leave you ladies to powder your noses.'

He kissed them twice, continental style, then closed the door gently behind him and fished out a white hanky, absently wiping his mouth before folding it back into a perfect triangle and returning it to his breast pocket. He held his hand out to me.

'Mr Williams.'

'Wilson.' I didn't like the way he'd wiped the feel of the girls' flesh from his lips. I wondered if he would wash my handshake from his palm. I thought I might his.

'Mr *Wilson*,' he let the emphasis hang on my name as if he was amused I'd bothered to correct him. Letting me know it didn't matter to him who I was, or perhaps that in his world one name served as well as another. 'The girls have commandeered our only dressing room, but there's a few cubby holes on offer if you need to change or,' he paused, smiling, 'fix your makeup.'

'Are you trying to tell me my mascara's run?' He gave me a quick sharp look, then laughed. 'I'd appreciate somewhere to go through my props.'

Bill showed me into a shabby bedroom equipped with two single beds draped with orange and brown floral covers and polyester valences that had long lost their bounce. He leant against the doorjamb. Leaning in doorways seemed to be Bill's thing. He watched as I laid the suitcase on one of the beds and unfastened its clasp.

14

'You based in London, Mr Wilson?'

'Ealing.'

'Travel much?'

'When required.' Bill might just be making casual conversation or he might be looking for a travelling man to deliver a parcel or two. I set a pack of playing cards on the bed and changed the subject. 'So how's business? Club keeping you busy?'

'Busy enough. Keeps me out of mischief. Speaking of which,' he turned to go, 'anything I can get you before I start mingling with the invited guests?'

'I could manage a white wine.' I slapped my stomach. 'I'm on a bit of a health kick.'

Bill smiled.

'I'll have a bottle sent up.'

I turned back to my case. In truth there was nothing I needed to do to prepare, but Bill still lingered in the doorway.

'A word of warning on tonight.' I looked back at him. 'These guys are here for the booze and the girls, for most of them you're an unexpected bonus.'

'Nice to know you think I can improve on booze and girls.'

Bill's smile looked like a threat.

'The inspector who's retiring is nicknamed the Magician. I think you're more in the way of an in-joke.'

'Good to be in.'

'Just remember this isn't a kid's birthday party. If I were you I'd keep it short and snappy.'

'Don't worry, I know my place.'

'Good, always best to make sure everyone

understands each other. I reckon they'll be ready in about half an hour, so take all the time you need.'

'As long as it's short of thirty minutes.'

Bill smiled.

'We don't want people getting impatient.'

*   *   *

I'd expected the door girl to bring up the wine, but when the knock came it brought a familiar face.

'Sam?'

'The one and only.' Sam Rosensweet smiled. He slid himself and a tray holding two glasses, a corkscrew and a bottle of white wine into the room. 'How you doing?'

'Great.' I got to my feet and slapped him on the back. 'Good to see you, man.'

'Hey!' Sam raised the tray in the air, like a ship's waiter serving through a squall. 'Watch the merchandise.'

I pushed the lamp on the small bedside table to one side and Sam settled the tray in the gap. 'So how are you?'

Sam started to work the corkscrew into the bottle's cork and grinned.

'Never better.'

'Nice threads.'

He glanced at his suit.

'Yeah well,' Sam pulled the cork from the bottle and poured us each a glass. 'When in Rome.' He handed me my drink. 'How about you, William? Still a slave to the gee-gees?'

'You know me, always the animal lover.'

He shook his head.

16

'I'm not sure following form quite qualifies you as St Francis. Won't keep you warm at night neither. You want to quit all that and get yourself hooked up with a nice bird.'

'That's good advice coming from you.'

Sam grinned.

'You know what I mean. How's old Fagin? You seen him lately?'

'He set me up with tonight.'

'Aha.' He sat down on the single bed opposite me and took a sip of his drink. 'That's where you're wrong. You've got old Sam-I-Am to thank for this particular box of tricks.'

'Yeah?' I tried to look grateful. 'Rich didn't say anything.'

'Well he wouldn't would he? Wants to make sure of his 10 per cent, greedy sod.'

'Cheers, Sam.' I raised my glass in a toast, then put it to my lips and took a sip. Its cheap sourness cut through the chill. 'Thanks.'

'No worries, you and me go way back.'

'And . . . ?'

Sam laughed.

'You may not be a whizz with girls and horses . . .'

'You can add dogs to that.'

'Ah, William.' Sam shook his head, looking like a priest caught between sorrow at the sin and the satisfaction of being able to squeeze a few more 'Our Fathers' from the sinner. 'Despite all your weaknesses, when it comes down to it, there's no flies on you. OK there might be a bit more to tonight than meets the eye. But you just sit tight and it'll all come out cushty.'

Sam was a young comic who had also been

17

under Rich's tough love care. We'd spent a long summer season together until he'd decided he could do better under new management. I'd not seen him for a year, maybe longer. In that time he'd grown leaner, but in a sleek way. He chinked my glass and knocked back the last of his wine.

'I'd better shift myself. Bill's got a jealous streak. He's already suspicious about why I suggested you.'

'You mean you and him . . . ?'

'Yeah,' Sam's face lit up. 'You wouldn't think it to look at him would you?'

'No, you wouldn't.'

'Yep, he's a mean queen-killing machine. For me to so much as look at a bloke is to condemn him to a cement overcoat.'

'Maybe you should open the door then, let him see there's nothing to worry about.'

Sam laughed.

'Your face, William. Don't worry. I'm just having you on. Now he's seen you he won't be worried.'

'What do you mean?'

Sam got to his feet and moved to the door.

'That's what I love about you William, always able to laugh at yourself. I'll catch you after the show eh? Bill likes me to stay in the wings when he's got business on, but we'll grab a drink, the three of us, when you've done your set.' He gave me a last grin and I thought I could see a new, tougher Sam beneath the comic I'd known. It was hard to imagine this new shiny version bothering to parry some of the heckling I'd seen the old Sam spar with. He said, 'Don't let me down. I gave you a big build.' Then shut the door gently behind him.

*   *   *

I sat for a moment, after Sam's footsteps had faded down the stairs, wondering what I had got myself into. Then I took the bottle by the neck, slipped into the hallway and tapped at the door of the girls' dressing room. A female voice said, 'Oh, for fuck's sake!'

There was the sound of another woman laughing then the Asian girl opened the door. I held up the bottle of wine. 'I thought you might fancy a wee drink.'

Shaz leaned in the doorway, her left hip jutting towards me, right arm swinging the door slowly against her body. 'We've got our own thanks.'

Through the slim gap I could see the blonde sitting at the dressing-table, intent on her reflection. Both girls were wrapped in long cotton dressing gowns, their makeup bright and showgirl thick. The door started to close on Shaz's smile. I slid a foot into the room, and her smile died. She said in a calm voice, 'Jacque, will you phone down to the bar and tell them we've got a wanker up here?'

Jacque looked up from the dressing-table. I held a hand up in surrender, but kept my foot where it was.

'No, look, don't, I've got a proposition for you.'

Jacque's voice was weary.

'In case you haven't noticed we've got all the work we need right now, love.'

'That's right,' the other girl was calm but there was an edge to her voice that had been absent before. 'We're going to have our hands full.'

19

'It'll be an easy score for one of you.'

'There's no such thing, mate.'

'Oh, ask him what he wants Shaz.'

I looked beyond the gatekeeper at the girl in the mirror.

'Purely business.'

She kept her gaze on her reflection; concentrating on pencilling a beauty spot on her left cheekbone, level with the corner of her eye. She frowned at the pressure of the pencil against her skin.

'Nothing up your sleeve?'

I smiled and pulled back my cuffs.

'See for yourself.'

She gave her reflection one last look, then put down the pencil and swivelled round in her seat. Her face looked sharper than the image in the mirror, or perhaps she was getting tired of our conversation.

'Just ask him in, Shaz.'

Shaz bit her lip.

'As long as he understands whatever he wants it'll cost. We're not here for charity.'

'I think he knows that.'

'Of course I do.'

The tall girl leaned back, leaving me a narrow space. I slid by, ignoring the warmth of her body beneath the fabric of her robe.

*   *   *

If I hadn't known that we were all hired for one night only I might have thought that the girls had inhabited their dressing-room for weeks. The flex of a set of hair tongs snaked through bottles of

20

makeup, a slick of foundation pooled on the scarred dressing-table. An almost empty bottle of white wine and two glasses sat amongst the debris. Their discarded outdoor clothes lay bundled on the bed. A white envelope stuffed with notes jutted from the pocket of a sports bag. It looked like they were on a better rate than me, but then they were the main act while I was just an in-joke.

Shaz closed the door then leaned against a paint-chipped radiator on the far wall, keeping her eyes on me.

I made a brushing gesture to my nose and after a moment's hesitation she glanced in the mirror and dusted away the frosting of white powder that lingered round her nostrils, breathing in sharp, as if trying to inhale any stray grains that had caught in the air.

'You know that's the Old Bill down there?'

She resumed her position, her expression blank. 'What's it to do with you?'

'As little as possible.'

The other girl glanced at me through the mirror, stroking a fluffy pink makeup brush against her cheekbone. 'The Old Bill sent young Bill up with it.'

The tall girl flashed her a sharp look and I wondered if they really were sisters.

I smiled.

'Very nice.'

Jacque turned back to the mirror, wetting her finger and smoothing an imagined ruffle in her eyebrow.

'Hadn't you better tell us what it is you want?'

I opened my arms like an old-time ringmaster and said, 'Which one of you lovely ladies would

21

like to be my assistant?'

Jacque laughed. Shaz shook her head then reached over and took the bottle from me, tilting it to her lips.

'You must be mad.' She passed it to Jacque, who tipped a measure into her glass. 'Bill would go crazy if we came down early. It'd spoil the big surprise.'

'Is he your manager then?'

The word 'manager' came out wrong and both girls shot me a frown. Jacque's voice was flinty.

'We *manage* ourselves.'

'I didn't mean it to sound like that. I'm in a bit of a bind. The trick I want to do relies on the help of a lovely lady and the audience seems to consist entirely of ugly coppers, so there's no point in asking for a volunteer.'

The blonde girl aimed a weary look at me.

'You rely on a pair of tits to stop the punters noticing if you make a balls-up?'

'Not quite how I would have put it . . .'

'But, yes?'

'Glamour's an element of the show, yes.'

'Ask chubby downstairs, I bet she'll do it for fifty.' Shaz laughed.

'She'd do it for twenty.'

Shaz giggled again when I asked if they were related and put her arm around the blonde girl, posing as if they were about to have a portrait painted.

'You might not have noticed, but we look a bit different from each other. Ebony and ivory together, sometimes in harmony.'

She ruffled the blonde girl's curls and I thought maybe I understood what they were to each other.

22

'Hey, multiethnic Britain, no reason why you couldn't be related.'

'Only through drink.'

Jacque slapped Shaz's hand lightly and set to repairing her hair. I gave the room a last glance, taking in the scattered clothes and makeup, the rumpled bed with its tired candlewick and said, 'If you ladies want to make a quick escape I'd recommend you pack up your gear and leave it at the door.'

Shaz had started painting her nails the same flame red as her lipstick. She looked up at me.

'Don't worry. You may be the magician, but there's not much you could teach us about vanishing acts.' I could tell from the rumble of male voices that reached me as I went down the stairs that the lounge had grown busier. I searched out the door girl; it turned out her name was Candy, though I doubt she'd been christened that. The girls had been right. She was eager to help me in a surly kind of way. I explained what I wanted her to do, then went back through to the lounge. Bill wasn't the only one required to mingle with the invited guests.

*   *   *

The disco lights glowed hazily through the sheets of cigarette smoke that shelved the air. The room smelt of alcohol, testosterone and sweat. There were about twenty of them. They'd ignored the booths that lined the walls, choosing to congregate in the centre of the room, knotting together like a fragile alliance that daren't break ranks for fear of treachery.

23

I sloped over to the bar, ordered a double malt and looked for Bill. I soon spotted him talking to a small man seated at a centre table. Bill was angled away from me, but he had the peripheral vision of a sniper. He turned and met my look, holding up three fingers, indicating he'd be with me soon. I nodded and raised my glass to my lips, letting the whisky do its slow burn down my throat, surveying the crowd.

A casual observer would have got an impression of cohesion, a solidarity of spirit. But as I slid amongst them the divisions started to come into view like the fractures in a jigsaw. They showed in the tilt of the men's bodies, a half-turned back, the block of a shoulder. Their clannishness crossed age boundaries, but it showed in the style of their dress, the cut of their hair.

Near the centre of the room was a tight knot of dark business suits, the type you see crushed into the tube early in the morning reading copies of the *Telegraph*, though commuters generally had fewer buzz cuts and broken noses. Grouped around them were louder tables where the camaraderie seemed stronger. These guys were quickest to their feet with the fresh rounds. Their colour was higher, cheeks shinier. These were the ones to watch, men out of their depth who wore their smart casuals with the self-consciousness of people used to wearing a uniform. I spotted a glass or two making their way from them to the suits. The exchange seemed one way, but perhaps I'd just missed the reciprocating rounds. Furthest from the centre tables were the men I labelled Serpico wannabees. These guys were dressed with a scruffy trendiness that spelt money. Their laughter had a superior edge. If I had walked into a bar in a strange town and seen this assemblage, I would have gone in search of somewhere else to drink.

The room had gone from silent to the edge of boisterous. I had a special routine for macho crowds. An unfunny string of jokes Richard had encouraged me to buy as an investment from one of his down-on-their-luck comics. I hated them, smutty schoolboy gags that no one finds funny but everyone laughs at, all lads together. I silently rehearsed, then amused myself by deciding which line of crime these men would be best suited to.

The man sipping lager near my left would be perfect old-time bank robber material. No finesse, just a sawn-off shotgun and a stare that said he was mad enough to use it. The sly-faced weasel next to him would surely be a pick-pocket. The broad-shouldered grunt behind Bill's companion would be ideal for strong-arm stuff. I identified conmen and drug dealers, pimps and burglars, then turned my mind to the man Bill was talking to. He was compact for a policeman, surely just within the height regulations. Mid-fifties, dressed in a slate-grey suit, with a blue shirt and a pink tie that matched his eyes. What would he be? It was obvious. The Boss, the mild-mannered gang leader who wore conservative suits, drank VSOP brandy and executed his enemies with a nod of the head.

Bill began making his way towards me, shaking hands, squeezing shoulders, smiling a crocodile smile that was all teeth. He patted me somewhere near my elbow in a gesture an anthropologist would probably describe as dominating, then offered me another drink.

'No thanks, one helps, two hinders.'

'Maybe afterwards then.'

I wanted to escape before the girls started their act, but I smiled and said, 'If you like. So who's the birthday boy?'

'Detective Inspector Montgomery, the man I was talking to. Him and my dad went way back, he made himself useful at a difficult time.' Bill smiled dryly. 'I used to call him Uncle Monty, so I've got a personal interest in his send-off.'

'Young to be put out to pasture.'

'Law enforcement pays.' Bill smiled knowingly. He drained his drink, putting the empty glass on the bar. 'They've had their official party with wives and WPCs, testimonials and all that stuff. Tonight's the real celebration. Just go with it.' I nodded and Bill smiled, satisfied I was cool with whatever was going to happen. 'Right, let's get the music turned off and give you a big build.'

'Why not?'

Bill nodded to the barman. 'Crowther, switch that racket off.'

Crowther was already busying himself freshening Bill's glass. He hesitated, unsure of which order to obey first, then did them both at once, laying the drink on the counter with one hand and killing the sounds with the other. Bill ignored him, turning the swizzle stick in his brandy and soda.

'Remember, keep it brief. Forty-minute set max—thirty would be better.'

He took a last slug of his drink and made his way towards the small dais to present me. There was no calling for attention, no tinkling of teaspoons on glasses. Bill just stood there and the room grew quiet. I glanced at Montgomery. His face wore a small smile. The kind Stalin was reputed to wear after a good week. Bill's voice cut through the silence.

'Gentlemen, this is a special evening, the retirement of James Montgomery, one of the finest police officers it has been my pleasure to know, and I'm sure yours to work with.'

There were murmurs of agreement and *Hear hears* from the men at the tables. A couple of those near to Montgomery leaned over and patted him on the back. Montgomery nodded, whatever his attributes modesty wasn't one of them. I wondered how sincere Bill was, why he was giving the address and not one of the squad.

'I know you had a posh gathering on Wednesday with the Chief Constable, so you'll have heard your quota of speeches for a while.'

There was laughter at this. Someone shouted, *too true.*

'So tonight for your delectation and entertainment we have The Divines.' There was a cheer from the audience and the sound of deep nervous laughter from some of the men.

Bill held up his hand for silence. 'A pair of very beautiful young . . .' he hesitated as if searching for the right word. 'Dancers.' More laughter. 'But before we meet them we have a very special guest. It's well known that Inspector Montgomery is a worker of wonders. Indeed, he's got so many illusive convictions he's been christened the Magician. So, in tribute to Inspector Montgomery's well-earned retirement I'd like to ask you to put your hands together for William Wilson, mentalist and magician.'

Half-hearted clapping scattered across the room

27

and suddenly I thought that maybe I should start doing kids' parties. At least some of them might believe in magic. There was a fraction of hesitation, then the barman put on the CD I'd given him and mysterioso music drifted across the room. I walked up onto the stage and stood there silently for a moment with my head bowed, hands folded in front of me, letting the soundtrack do the work, then slowly raised my eyes, keeping my stare level, my mouth serious, wishing I had a lovely assistant to flash her legs and take some of the heat off me. The music died and I cast my gaze across the room, grave as Vincent Price's Van Helsing revealing the presence of vampires.

'Welcome.' I paused, making eye contact with as many of the audience as I could. 'Gentlemen, there are mysteries beyond our control, wonders that even the greatest scientists are powerless to explain. Tonight I am going to look into the unknown and explore some of these strange and perplexing phenomena.' The crowd stayed silent, I stepped off the dais and approached a thin man sitting towards the front of the gathering. 'Sir, would you mind standing up for me please?' The man got to his feet. He was tall and lank, with receding hair and a good-natured drink-fuddled face.

'What's your name, sir?'

'Andy.'

'Nice to meet you Andy.' I shook his hand, staring him in the eyes and slyly unfastening his watch. 'Let me ask you Andy, do you believe that there are powers we don't understand?'

'I believe in the DPP.'

The crowd laughed and I smiled indulgently.

'I see that you're a married man, Andy.'

He nodded unimpressed.

'How did I know that?'

He held up his left hand with its gold marriage band.

'Quite right, the powers of observation.' I smiled round the room, giving him his moment of reassurance, then raised my voice. 'But this evening I am going to reveal to you things that the powers of observation would be powerless to divulge.' I made my tone more conversational. 'Andy, I would imagine that in your profession well-developed powers of observation are essential?'

Andy nodded.

'That's true.'

'A good memory for a face?'

He nodded again.

'I believe so.'

'Have we ever met before?'

He shook his head slowly, cautious as a man on a witness stand.

'Not to my knowledge, no.'

'You've never arrested me?'

'Not to my recollection.'

'So you would be surprised if I could guess your rank?' He shrugged.

'Possibly.'

'Come a little closer would you please, Andy?' The man looked around at the audience smiling. I said, 'Don't worry, the force is with you.' And he stepped forward an inch. 'May I place my hand on your shoulder?' He hesitated and I stage-whispered, 'No need to be coy.' The audience laughed, the volunteered man gave a brief nod and

29

I reached up, resting my hand gently on his right shoulder. 'I would say, Andy,'—'that you are'—I paused again—'a sergeant.' I removed my hand and he nodded to the crowd, who gave me a brief scatter of applause. I bowed, keeping my expression restrained. 'I suppose that's vaguely impressive. But maybe I could guess that from your age and the fact that you look fairly intelligent. So let me go a little further.' There was an *oooh* from the audience. The man stepped back, clowning a slight mince. The men at his table laughed and I shook my head in mock exasperation. 'Calm yourself, Sergeant. I've told you that you're married, but as you've confirmed we've never met before so there's no way I could tell you the name of your wife.'

A voice came from the audience. *Not unless you saw it written on the wall of the gents.*

Andy shouted, 'Oi, watch it.' Taking the joke in good part.

I held up my hand for order.

'I see a good-looking woman . . .' The crowd *ooohed* obligingly again and I traced an S in the air, making it sexy like the cartoon outline of a woman's body. 'Her name is . . . Sarah . . . no not Sarah, something similar, Suzie . . . Suze . . . Susannah.' The man's face was pleasingly bemused. He nodded and the crowd clapped. I held up my hand, silencing them. 'You have children . . . two lovely daughters . . . Hai . . . Hail . . . Hailey and Re-e-e-e-Rebecca.' Andy was smiling now, nodding his head to the room. Again the applause and again I held my hands up to stop them. 'You also have a dog?' This was dodgy, dogs die more often than the wife and kids, but the

30

group photo I'd lifted from his wallet with the names of its subjects obligingly written on the back in neat pen looked pretty recent. Andy nodded. 'Your dog is called . . .' I hesitated a beat beyond the audience's expectation and the room grew still, half-hoping I'd make it, half-hoping I'd fail. 'Your dog is called, "Peele!"' The small audience erupted into applause and I bowed, relieved to find policemen as gullible as the rest. 'How're we doing for time, Sergeant?'

Andy looked at his wrist, and then looked at me.

'Has anyone got the time?' There was a confusion of murmurs as the men I'd selected each noticed their missing wristwatches. 'Ach, it's fine, I've got it here.'

I pulled up my left cuff to reveal the half-dozen watches fastened round my wrist. As things go, they were a good audience. I fed them more facts from filched wallets, keeping the action brief and cheeky, then kicked into the finale.

'Now, I know you're keen to see The Divines.' There was a stamping of feet and a jungle-drumming of hands against tables. 'Let me assure you are they are most definitely divine. But first I've got another young lady I'd like you to meet. Welcome to the lovely, the delicious, the truly scrumptious Miss Candy Flossy.'

Candy slunk in doing her best impersonation of a vamp. She would have looked prettier if she'd smiled, but she was doing me a favour. I grabbed her by the hips, putting myself behind her bulk and doing a leer over her shoulder for the benefit of the audience.

'Candy's agreed to help me out.'

There were a few wolf whistles and catcalls.

You can help me out anytime love.
You can touch my truncheon.
Feel my new extending baton.
Try on my handcuffs.
Play with my helmet.

And I thought that perhaps they weren't such a pleasant audience after all.

There are many ways to cut a lady in half. If you have the resources you can fashion jazzy coffins fixed with bewilderments and employ a girl who can contort herself so well it's a waste to put her in a box. But my brand of the effect relied on a not-so-innocent-looking buzz-saw of the type you might see in an old-fashioned sawmill. It was an appearance of mere penetration where others managed dismemberment. But the kind of audiences I entertained were amused by it.

I steeled a serious tone to my voice and said, 'My final trick is so dangerous that only a very few members of the magic circle are initiated into its secrets. Should my concentration be disturbed at any point during its execution,' Candy shuddered and I put my hand on her shoulder, 'this young lady might lose one of her lovely limbs,' I hooked the hem of Candy's dress with my wand and slid it upwards. She smacked my hand away before I'd revealed more than her calves. I gave the wand an impatient slap. 'I'm sorry. My wand has a life of its own. But I'm sure you'll agree, gentlemen, that any injury to these fine pins would be a tragedy.' There was a gallant rumble of agreement from the tables. 'Therefore I'm going to ask you for silence while we prepare to amaze you.'

They were men more used to giving directions than receiving them, but they quietened down a little, the drinkers at the bar lowering their voices as they gave their orders to the barman.

I dipped them a brief bow, then made a show of pulling the saw's fake chain, at the same time surreptitiously pressing the button that started the sound effect. The noise was as deafening as a motorbike stripped of its silencer. I'd warned Candy, but she took a step back. A show of nervousness was good, but only if she didn't bolt. I grasped her firmly her by the arm and hissed, 'Remember what I told you, it's all show.'

The big girl's breasts quivered, she glanced towards the bar and Bill gave her a nod.

She whispered. 'You promise it won't hurt?'

'Do you really think I'm going to slice you in two in front of the filth? No, course not. It's all smoke and mirrors sweetheart.' Candy winced, but she let me sit her on the table then swung her legs up, modestly holding her skirt to her, but still revealing a flash of fishnets that drew some whistles from the audience as she sank slowly onto her back. I though I saw tears trembling in her eyes. I gave her a wink and locked a small box around her waist, turning to the policemen and shouting over the noise, 'Those of you who do a lot of shift work might like to know that this doubles as a chastity belt.' I started to move the saw, knowing that from their angle it would look like I was cutting through the girl. Candy's eyes were leaking now, but her smile was a little braver. I twisted my face, trying to look like the kind of crazed personality that might indeed saw a woman in half, but ran a finger reassuringly down her waist. I let the saw complete its journey then did an evil, *heh, heh, heh* to the audience. Candy

33

looked up at me, unsure whether it was working. I winked again willing her to keep silent.

There was a wave of applause and then the catcalls started.

I know which end I'd like.

Come round to my place and do that to the Missis, that's the only half of her I need.

Now, mine's talks out of her arse anyway.

I unlatched the box, grabbed a giant silk flag painted with red and black flames, shielded Candy with it while she detached herself from the equipment and got to her feet. I waved the flag three times and forced her into a bow.

'Shit, he's put her back together again,' said a boozy voice from somewhere in the audience.

I slipped twenty quid into her hand and she went off to tend to her coats, while I took a final bow.

*   *   *

Bill slid into a booth with a good view of the dance floor. I slipped in opposite him with my back to the action. The mirror angled on the wall above Bill's head caught the room in a convex swirl, flinging it back in a distorted haze of lights and colour. I sipped my drink. A Middle Eastern beat that was all drums and pipes started up. Bill put his glass down and looked beyond me towards the stage.

'You been looking forward to this?'

I shrugged and wondered where Sam had got to. Whatever hopes I'd had of catching the last race of the night were lost.

Two tall black shadows glided across the floor. At first I couldn't make out what they were.

34

Perhaps the audience were confused too, they had fallen quiet, the men at the bar no longer keeping stiff-faced Crowther busy with a barrage of rounds.

Bill laughed. 'Christ, we're going to have a fatwa on our hands.'

He shook his head, amused, looking confident of his ability to stave off any attack. The shadows slid into focus and I realised that Shaz and Jacque had draped themselves in burkahs. They stood nun-black, with just a mesh of fabric to see through, swaying with the music, twirling round in a dance that looked traditional, but was probably made up. It was impossible to see what their bodies were doing beneath the robes, but I bet it would be lithe and smooth. The only part of them uncovered was their feet, tripping soft and dainty against the dance floor.

Together the girls raised their right hands and with a delicate move unhooked the grilles that veiled their eyes. The sparkles glistering from the makeup that jewelled their eyelids caught the light, even flashing into our dull corner. Shaz's was pure emerald, Jacque's switched between sapphire and diamond. For the first time since the pair had stepped onto the stage the men made a noise, a low cheer.

The girls danced on as if alone, swirling the burkahs, though now I suspected these were of thinner material than standard. They floated above the girls' ankles, revealing painted toenails beneath black mesh and anklets of silver that clinked and trembled with each step.

Bill glanced at his watch, then suddenly, as if the girls sensed the audience's attention was wavering, they reached out, each grabbing the other's dark

35

garment by the hips. There was a slight pause, a hesitation of Velcro and the dancers' legs were revealed, smooth and stockinged, diamanté garters competing with their eyes in the sparkle stakes.

The men roared. Bill took a drag of his cigarette and turned away from the dance floor.

'Not quite what I expected.'

I nodded towards the group of policemen.

'They seem to be enjoying it well enough.'

'That's the main thing.'

In the mirror above his head the girls twirled some more, their veiled faces and covered bodies incongruous against the flesh of their exposed thighs shimmying above the dark stocking tops.

Bill seemed to have lost interest.

'You were better than I expected.'

'Cheers, but you weren't seeing me at my best.'

'Even better then.'

Out on the dance floor Shaz had torn Jacque's top off to reveal a black brassiere, beaded fringes all a-twinkle. Jacque did a shimmy to the audience that made her bosoms shiver, then turned to her friend and returned the favour. Shaz's bra was identical but silver-white. Their act was tacky, but it worked.

I said, 'It's tacky but it works.'

Bill made a face, 'I guess you could call it tacky, but I thought you had something, with the right girl you might get somewhere.' He looked back at the dancers. Jacque had wet her finger and placed it on Shaz's thigh. She drew it back quickly as if scalded. 'Let's face it, you'd get nowhere lumbered with that fat tart.'

'She was OK.'

'She looks all right now, but those pale blondes

wash out pretty quick.' The girls were playing with the front fastenings of their bras now, teasing the crowd. Jacque leaned into the ringside table and let a burly man unclip hers. Her breasts fell forward and she rubbed them teasingly across his baldpate. 'I watched you boosting those guys' watches. You've got nimble digits there. Ever get you in trouble?'

'Once or twice, as a kid.'

'No convictions though?'

'I learned to make it work for me.'

'All the same, you were taking a chance with these coppers.'

'You think so?'

'No, not really, but you know what they can be like, there's some touchy buggers amongst them.'

'You get an instinct for them in my game.'

Bill took a sip of his drink.

'I suppose you do. It's amazing how you know things.'

'It's just a trick Bill.'

'I realise that . . . but all the same. You were spot on every time. Maybe there's more to the trick than you think.'

It had happened before, people mistaking dexterity and good observation for something else, but I hadn't expected it from Bill. He passed me a cigar. We both lit up and sat silent in the smoke-scented gloom of the booth. Bill's body was relaxed, his smile easy. A careless observer might have thought us old friends having a casual conversation. I mirrored his calm pose and waited for him to get to the point.

Sam skirted the dance floor, keeping clear of the boisterous bevy of men and inserted himself into the booth beside Bill. He nodded towards The Divines.

'Very *Tales of the Unexpected.*'

Bill turned towards him.

'A bit arty for me.'

Sam raised his eyebrows in mock exasperation. 'There's a surprise.' His face grew serious. 'Have you asked him yet?'

Bill paused like a man trying to make up his mind. I half expected Sam to cajole him, but there was a silence between the three of us almost as loud as the beat of the music and the laughter of the policemen. At last Bill sighed and put his cigar in the ashtray.

'There's something I'd like to know.'

He played with his glass, not taking a sip from it, just looking into the brown liquid as if the answer might lie amongst the bubbles. Curiosity and the dangerous faint hope of an easy score kept me in my seat.

'Go on.'

'I'd like to know what Inspector Montgomery had on my dad.'

The sentence hung in the air, a bridge between Bill's world and mine. A bridge I wasn't sure I wanted to cross. Eventually I said, 'So why don't you ask him?'

'It's not as simple as that.'

'Sorry to hear it.' I reached for my jacket. 'I'm in the entertainment game. Complicated isn't my scene.'

'Hasty.'

Bill raised his index finger and I found myself hesitating.

Sam said, 'At least hear him out. If you don't

like what he says then no hard feelings.'

My half-finished drink sat on the table before me; the cigar Bill had given me still stretching tendrils of smoke into the air. I sighed.

'OK, go ahead.'

Bill's smile was dry.

'Policemen and businessmen: it's no secret that sometimes one hand washes the other.'

'Yet somehow no one gets clean.'

He shrugged.

'It's ancient history now. My dad and Inspector Montgomery had an arrangement, as I said, Monty helped my dad out at a very difficult time; he owed him and old loyalties die hard.'

'So?'

'My dad died three months ago.'

'I'm sorry for your troubles.'

Bill took a sip of his drink.

'He was only sixty-eight. It was unexpected.'

'Natural causes?'

'You're not in murder central now, Jock, this is civilisation. He had a heart attack. It was instant.'

'So where do I come in?'

Sam's smile was tense. 'It's really just a matter of . . .'

Bill interrupted him.

'You save me the unpleasantness of laying my hands on an elderly policeman.'

Bill ordered more drinks. Out on the dance floor the music had changed to an R'n'B beat. The girls still had their stockings and panties on, but now they'd each equipped themselves with high heels and were stalking around the men waving purses in front of them, getting the audience to pay up if they wanted them to go further.

In the booth Sam said to Bill, 'William's straight up. Tell him the whole story and he'll help you out. Won't you, William?'

I shrugged.

'See?' Sam smiled. 'I told you he was the boy for the job.'

Bill shook his head.

'What does it matter? We'll be gone soon.' He took another puff of his cigar and resumed his story. 'I said that Monty and my dad went way back?' I nodded. 'Well, they didn't like each other. In fact, I'd go as far as to say they hated each other's guts, but they helped each other out. I asked my dad why once and he changed the subject. I assumed it was just business.' Bill gazed out over the dance floor, but I got the feeling he wasn't seeing the half-naked girls still teasing the drunken policemen. 'Last week Monty shows me an envelope and says my dad paid a lot of money to keep its contents quiet. If I keep up the payments I can keep it quiet too.'

'So what was in it?'

Sam interrupted. 'He didn't say.'

Bill gave Sam a stern look.

'He was enjoying himself. Said it was something my dad wouldn't want me to know, but now that he was dead it was up to me to decide whether I wanted to or not.' Bill took a swig of his drink. 'My dad was no angel, but . . .'

'But you don't think there would be anything diabolical in his past.'

Bill shrugged.

'We all do bad things. Who knows? But I don't think so, no. He straightened out a lot after my mum went. He did what he had to do,' Bill glanced

40

over to where Montgomery had Shaz on his knee. 'But my dad always knew where to draw the line.'

I looked for a telltale drunken glaze in Bill's eye, but his grey gaze looked clear. I wondered why he was telling me all this.

'Maybe you should sleep on it.'

'This is the last night this place is open. I've sold it.' He grinned. 'I'm getting out, bought a yacht. Me and Sam are going to have a taste of the easy life before we decide what to do next. Tonight was meant to smooth the way. My dad had to duck and dive to make a living, but he gave me a good education and a good inheritance. I'm cutting old ties and that doesn't mean sending some copper hush money every month, no matter how far him and my old man went back.'

'So buy it from him and burn it.'

'That's one option.'

He looked at me.

Bill's plan started to dawn but I said, 'Where do I come into all this?'

Sam said, 'It's in the inside left-hand pocket of his suit jacket.'

I remembered Montgomery's smile, sharp as a broken razor-blade and reached for my coat.

'I'm sorry gents, you picked the wrong conjurer.'

Sam's voice was injured.

'Come on, William . . .'

Bill silenced him with a look.

'Leave it out Sam. He does it voluntary or not at all, that's what we agreed.'

'But . . .'

Sam shot me a glance like a man betrayed, but Bill put his hand gently on top of his lover's. His voice was soft.

'Get William a bottle of Moët from behind the bar would you, Sam? Help compensate him for his extra time.'

I said, 'There's no need.'

Sam gave it one last try.

'Go on, William. I've seen you do harder than that. Think of it as a bet.'

Bill's voice was harsh.

'Just get the champagne will you.' He paused and smoothed a bit of finesse into his tone. 'Please.'

Sam got to his feet and left the table without looking at me.

'Thanks for the drink and the cigar.' I pulled on my jacket. 'I don't need any extra compensation. Good luck with your new life. I'd like to help, but I've got worries of my own.'

Bill glanced towards the bar, making sure Sam was out of earshot, then he reached into his pocket and pulled out the bundle of IOUs it had taken me months of hard losing to accumulate with my bookie. His voice was low and sympathetic, like a nurse about to stick a needle into a particularly tender portion of flesh. He said, 'Are any of them financial?'

$$*\qquad*\qquad*$$

Pick-pocketing is not as easy as some people would have you believe. The greatest defence is a crowd, where a little bit of physical contact won't be unduly noticed, a packed subway or a busy lift. The second-best defence is distraction. Luckily for me the biggest distraction in the world was right in front of the inspector's eyes, sex. Jacque made her way up to our booth, there was a slight stagger to her walk and I could see a glaze in her eyes that might have been drink, drugs, an attempt at detachment, or maybe all three. She shook the full-looking bag in front of us. It was all notes.

Bill said, 'Leave it out, Jacque.'

But I took out my wallet and dropped in a fifty.

'I'd like to buy Mr Montgomery a retirement present.'

Jacque tucked my fifty in tight with the rest.

'You could have saved your money, that lot out there have already paid for him.' She looked back over her shoulder. 'Ta all the same.'

Back on the dance floor there was a cheer as the girls peeled off the remnants of their costumes. They were shaved and vulnerable in amongst the suits and studied casualness of the men. Bill said, 'I guess this is where I leave you to get on with it. Sam and me'll be upstairs in my office when you're ready to deliver.'

Jacque and Shaz were on the floor, the men crowding round them now, shielding them from my view.

I asked, 'Will they be OK?'

Bill said, 'They're whores. OK doesn't come into it.' A second cheer went up. Jacque was standing in front of Montgomery, loosening his tie. The men beside him had pulled back. I watched the men's eyes as Jacque worked her way down the Inspector's body, sliding his tie between her legs. I finished my drink and made my way towards the bar as if in search of another. When I passed the knot of men I reached over and grabbed Jacque by the waist, pulling her towards me.

'Any chance of a private dance, doll?' Montgomery got to his feet as I'd hoped he would, pushing me to one side. I lurched to the right, still holding the sweat-slicked girl in my grip, and dipped his pocket, feeling the envelope, sliding it out quick and sure, tucked between my thumb and index finger, then crabbed it in my hand and conveyed it to my own pocket, pushing the naked girl towards him as I did so. 'Hey, no harm meant pal.' Making my accent thick and drink-addled.

One of the men gave me a shove, 'Stupid bloody Jock.' But the scene was quick to resume itself, Jacque flashing me a sharp confused look that might have spoken of suspicion or regret or perhaps just of disgust. I gave her the briefest of smiles, and then went to deliver my prize.

Glasgow

My first months back in Glasgow I never once let daylight touch my face. I slept more than seemed possible and woke groggy-eyed from half-remembered dreams. It wasn't hard for me to hide during the day. Apart from those mornings when train timetables heaved me from my pit, unshaven and blinking, to stagger with my suitcase into the predawn, I've rarely ever left my bed before noon.

I perfected my practice method early in my career, around the age of nine, when I stumbled on *The Boy's Own Guide to Conjuring* in the local library. I can still see the front cover of the book. A boy with dark hair cut in a side parting, dressed in a red school blazer and grey shorts, pulls a rabbit from a hat. On a table suspiciously swathed by a green cloth, reclines a copy of *The Boy's Own Guide to Conjuring.* The boy on its cover is pulling the same rabbit from the same hat and the same book rests face up showing the same image, though it is more of a smudge now.

If I positioned the mirrors on my mother's dressing-table at a particular angle I could achieve the same effect, myself repeated over and over into infinity. It gave me a strange feeling to see all of these other Williams shadowing my actions. I felt that when I stepped from the glass these other boys did the same and moved on in their own worlds where everything was an inverted image of mine and these Williams were the braves or bullies of their school.

It was a solitary pleasure. Every day when I got home I'd set the panes of the mirror at exactly the right angle, like a precocious teenage masturbator, then set to work. Under my command the army of other Williams stumbled through the same tricks until we had mastered one to perfection. I was the prince of illusion. And even though these doppelgängers might have been tougher or more popular in their worlds than I was in mine, in the world of mirrors it was my decrees that held sway.

In time, the reflection aged into a thirty-three-year-old trickster, standing before dead-eyed hotel mirrors murmuring the patter beneath his breath. Sometimes I'd forget to whisper and my voice would boom across the empty room and into the lifeless hotel corridor.

It was these practice sessions rather than companionship or money that I missed most in Glasgow, because, although I was used to making my fee stretch and sleeping alone in anonymous

45

rooms, I never adjusted to abandoning the ritual of rehearsal.

The bedsit the taxi-driver had taken me to faced south; it would have got the afternoon light if it weren't for the shadows cast by the building opposite. When I got there I resolved to stay put and think things out. But that very first night the walls started to close in on me like a torture chamber in a bad Hammer Horror movie and I found myself putting on my shoes and coat and setting out into the darkness.

I didn't go far, a walk of a few blocks, counting the turnings, though I knew the way. I hesitated outside the Tron Theatre looking upwards at its spire, and for an instant thought I saw the form of a hanging man dangling from the window below its turret. It sagged there, still and dark beneath the pointed hat of the building. But perhaps I was just remembering that this was the district where they hanged criminals in the old days, because when I looked again there were nothing but shadows clinging to the walls.

I skirted the building, keeping my eyes on the pavement, then turned up a side street. Across the road a tattoo parlour glowed iced-neon blue. I thought of my own tattoo. Four aces splayed above a laughing skull in a top hat. It had hurt like a napalm burn but I'd thought the pain worth it. Now I'd happily slice it off. I leaned against the aluminium grille that screened the door and reached into my jacket for my fags. Above my head a sign twirled *Tattoo/Artist, Tattoo/Artist, Tattoo/Artist,* then reached the peak of its revolutions, hesitated and twisted back in the opposite direction *Artist/Tattoo, Artist/Tattoo,*

Artist/Tattoo.

Opposite, the glass front of the theatre bar shone into the street. I could see the audience crowding into the space. Even from here I could sense the halftime buzz, the disagreements and posturings as they discussed the show. For an instant I thought I glimpsed Sylvie amongst the crowd, but I'd grown used to such sightings and ignored the leap in my stomach. The girl turned and I saw the angle of her jaw was wrong, her face so different it seemed impossible I could have imagined any resemblance.

I was lighting my fag when a slim shadow edged into the doorway, blocking my exit. He was a thin spider of a lad, his jacket even older than mine, hair longer and danker; he stank of piss and neglect. We faced each other across the lighter's glow and I wondered if I was looking at my future self, Old Scrooge meeting the ghost of Christmas future. I killed the flame and pulled out my cigarettes, offering him one to negate the image in my head. Then I ruined the effect by saying, 'Piss off son, I'm not looking for company.'

The boy took the cigarette impatiently, without thanks and slid it behind his ear. He reached towards me, gentling his nasal whine down till it was close to a keening. 'There's a lassie round the corner does the business, thirty quid a time.'

'Fuck off.'

'She's clean.'

His smell penetrated the nicotine. I took the lit cigarette from my lips and threw it to the pavement. Red flakes of ash scattered as it dropped towards the gutter. The junky watched it fall. I waited for him to bend towards the dowt, but he had the single-mindedness of a true scaghead. His eyes fixed mine; his hand touched the edge of my lapel in a tentative stroke.

'I'll set you up with her for a fiver.'

'Fuck off.'

I shoved him away, but his hands were persistent, patting my body now with all the efficiency of a drunken border guard.

'Come on, mister.'

He was the first person to touch me in an age. His voice was soothing, coaxing. Revulsion shivered through me, and this time my shove was harder. My only intention was to get him off me, but the boy was frail. He lost his footing and staggered backwards. For a second it seemed he might regain his balance, but then his heel slipped on the kerb, gravity won and he pitched backwards hitting his head against the cobbles with a gunshot crack that sounded across the street. I saw him lie still, felt a sickening realisation, then stepped towards him. My move was reflected across the road in the bright lights beyond the plate glass. In the mirror world of colour and warmth a girl stood up, pointing towards me. A man followed her aim, shook his head and raised his pint to his mouth.

I took a step towards the boy, leaned forward to feel his pulse, then heard a shout. The silhouettes of two policemen stood outlined against the bright lights of Argyle Street. Suddenly I was on my feet and running, my boots clattering against the pavement. I glanced behind me just before I turned the corner, hoping I'd see the junky move, but seeing only one of the police bending over him and the other one haring towards me. I outran him so easily I guessed he wasn't putting his whole

48

effort into the chase.

For a week and a half I stuck to my room, only venturing down to the licensed grocers at the foot of the close for essentials. I lived on morning rolls, ham and crisps, washed down with milk or strong lager occasionally braced with blended whisky. The *Evening Times* was my oracle. I forced my way through drownings and arson, robberies and knifings. I knew of every murder and act of violence reported in the city. I dreaded sight of my crime, but was never relieved to find it absent.

Eventually the walls of my room started their old trick, shifting until they took on the proportions of a coffin. I decided there'd be more space in prison and ventured out, as nervous of a hand on my shoulder as a teenage shoplifter on their first spree.

It was a week before I saw him. A pathetic figure slumped in an Argyle Street doorway, the grey remnants of a hospital dressing still stuck to his head. He didn't give me a glance until I shoved a tenner into his hand, then the look he gave me was pure love.

London

Bill's office was three storeys up, at the top of the building. I gave a sharp rap at the door and Sam unlocked it, grinning. Bill was talking in a low voice to someone on the telephone. He motioned me inside and pointed towards a chair, still talking to whoever was on the end of the line. Sam locked the door behind me. I sat at one side of the desk,

Bill at the other, one of his endless chain of cigarettes smouldering in the ashtray beside him. Sam leaned against the wall behind Bill, looking pleased with himself.

The office had probably last been decorated sometime around the coronation. There were hints of how the place had looked then in the bright rectangles around the walls where pictures had once hung. The wallpaper had been plain white intersected by regal bands of red flock. But the flock had darkened with age. It was balding in places, scored and chipped in others, and the once-white background had developed the faint toffee tint that old men and paper take on after decades of soaking up nicotine. The carpet had been chosen to match the walls, a plain red pile that had been good and might still be OK if someone took the time to run a Hoover around. Bill's desk looked like you could take to sea in it, a grand mahogany structure too big for the small space. Bill had either recently been turned over or he was serious about moving. The room was pretty much stripped. What was left was a guddle of cardboard boxes, slouching half-full bin bags and discarded files. An empty safe yawned behind the desk. High above Bill on a set of almost cleared shelves was propped a picture of the young Queen Elizabeth in full sparkle mode, looking glam and only half horse.

Bill's voice was soft and serious.

'Yeah, just tell them I've had to go out. Unavoidable circumstances.' He put the cigarette to his lips. 'Everyone paid, everyone happy?' He paused, listening to the person on the other end of the line. 'Well, Crowther will take care of them.

50

Just wait till the last have gone and lock the door behind you. Nah, don't worry 'bout the clearing up. Not our problem any more. Yeah, cheers, Candy, good luck.'

Bill put the phone back on its cradle and I held the envelope out to him.

'Mission accomplished.'

For a brief moment his face was still. I wondered if he was already regretting telling me as much as he had, then his mouth creased into a grin.

'OK, good.' He turned towards Sam. 'You got William's fee?' Sam reached into his pocket, pulled out a white envelope and handed it to Bill. 'Cheers.' Bill slid it across the desk towards me. 'I think this'll cover your trouble.'

'Thanks.'

'Fair exchange.'

He weighed the packet I'd given him in his hand and for a second I thought he was going to open it, but the moment passed and he laid it carefully back on the top of the desk.

'OK, I guess there's no need, but I'll say this anyway: tonight's little adventure stays strictly between us.'

Sam raised his eyebrows. I ignored him and said, 'Already understood.'

'Good, because only three people know about it: you, me and Sam. So if word gets out I'll know where it came from.'

I tucked the fee into my pocket. Sam put his hand on Bill's shoulder.

'You bought a captain's hat and a cat o' nine tails for that new yacht of yours?'

Bill laughed gently.

'Yeah, point taken. OK.' He held out his hand.

51

We shook and Bill palmed the IOUs to me. He gave me a quick wink. 'Good doing business with you.'

'And you.'

I meant it. I'd arrived that night deep in debt and left with cash in my pocket. I got to my feet taking my props case in my hand. Bill came out from behind his desk.

'I'll show you out the back way. Save you going past that lot.'

Sam stepped to one side and Bill unlocked what I'd thought was a cupboard door in the wall behind him.

I said what had been bothering me ever since I'd slipped the envelope from Montgomery's pocket.

'There's always a chance he's got a copy of whatever it is.'

Sam grinned and suddenly he was the same comic I'd spent countless bar-room nights with.

'Bill will molicate him if he has.'

I laughed but Bill's nod of agreement was serious.

'He's treading on thin ice as it is. He knows the score. I got it from him gently this time, for the sake of whatever there was between him and my dad, next time I won't be so patient.'

'And if he notices and comes up here?'

'Five minutes and we're gone.'

'Good luck.'

I was already halfway through the door when the knock came from the hallway. Bill tensed, looked at me and put a finger to his lips.

'You in there, Bill?'

We froze, silent as kids in bed hearing their dad come home from the boozer.

'Good going, but you only got half the story

there, Billy boy.'

There was a hesitation in the policeman's voice that made me sure he was lying.

I whispered, 'He's bluffing, I can tell.'

But Bill shook his head. He shouted, 'Hang on a second.'

Sam said, 'You promised me, Bill, no argy bargy.'

Bill's whisper managed to be furious and pleading at the same time.

'Jesus fuck, Sam, he's taking the piss now.'

Sam's voice was low and determined.

'I know he is and you're right to be angry, but I swear, Bill, you hit him and I'm out that door with William.'

Bill shot me a dark look and I said, 'I think he means at the same time as me.'

Sam shook his head.

'Bloody hell, William, get a grip.'

The knock came at the door again.

'I know you're in there, Bill. This is the one chance for you to find out the truth about your mother.'

Sam took the envelope from his lover and shoved it into my hand.

'Look, let him search the place—he'll find nothing. This'll be safe as houses with William.'

I hissed, 'This is nothing to do with me.'

Bill's voice was low and determined.

'Don't worry; I'll make it worth your while.' He smiled. 'And if you open it I'll know and you'll have your balls to play with to prove it. Now go on, it's abracadabra time, this is your cue to disappear.'

Bill put his hand on my shoulder and pushed me

firmly from the room, Sam gave me a last smile over his lover's shoulder, then the door was closed behind me and the key turned softly in the lock. The landing was dark and damp. There was a small wash basin to my left, and next to it a steep set of stairs leading downwards. I stalled for a second silently cursing, the envelope in one hand my case in the other, trying not to breathe for fear the small man would hear. Through the door I heard Bill's voice, welcoming as a warm brandy on a cold night.

'Inspector Montgomery.'

I started to creep my way down the stone stairs, hearing Montgomery say something, and perhaps a second man with him or maybe just Bill, responding to the policeman's words. I wondered if I should wait, wondered if there was anyone I should call. Then padded softly on, careful of the flaking whitewash against my velvet suit. I reached the ground, pushed open the exit bar and stepped out into the night, the envelope containing Bill Senior's secrets pressed tight against my chest.

*   *   *

My mobile woke me the next day, buzzing 'The Sorcerer's Apprentice' from under the pillow. The ringtone had been a present from an ex-girlfriend. I'd never liked it, but I guess I didn't get gifts, even sarcastic ones, very often. I retrieved the phone, wondering whether keeping it under the pillow would give me a brain tumour and why my alarm had gone off so early, then realised it wasn't the alarm.

'Hope I'm not disturbing your beauty sleep?'

Richard's voice was too loud for ten in the morning. I said, 'I was working last night.'

'I know. Did you have a divine time?'

'Is that why you're calling?'

'Just a friendly enquiry.'

I reached for my gregs, put them on and watched the world come into focus, then got out of bed and walked naked into the tiny cupboard that served as my kitchen. Rich's interest in my non-existent sex life was starting to grate.

'Do you want to get to the point?'

'I'll take that for a no then.'

'No, I had a drink with the proprietor though.'

'Ah yes, young burglar Bill.'

'You know him well?'

'Knew his father.'

I filled the kettle and plugged it into the wall. Rich shouted, 'You're breaking up.'

'Sorry.' I walked back into the small bed-sitting room and asked, 'What was he like?'

'A swine. Why'd you want to know?'

'Just showing a friendly interest.'

The envelope containing the money Bill had given me was on the coffee table. I poured it out; a thousand in twenties, not bad for a couple of hours' work, but I had a feeling it was money I was yet to earn. Montgomery's manila envelope lay under the cushion on the sofa. I slid it out and looked at its seal. It wouldn't be so difficult to break, but somehow I was happy to leave it alone.

Rich's voice came loud down the wire.

'Listen, have you got a passport?'

I ruffled the notes through my fingers.

'Somewhere, why? Someone want to buy it?'

'I've got something for you—Berlin.'

'Berlin?'

'Yes, Berlin, capital of Germany, once divided city now happily reunited.'

'I know where it is. I'm just wondering what about it?'

I've got a contact, who has a contact there, who knows a man who needs a conjurer for his club. Bijou little place, the Schall und Rauch, means Smoke and Noise, just up your street, William.'

'Maybe. How much are they offering?'

'A bit of enthusiasm would be nice. I said Berlin. It's a top entertainment spot son. The home of cabaret. Remember what Germany did for the Beatles.'

'If I remember rightly one of them copped it there.'

'The money's OK. I managed to squeeze them for 10 per cent over the usual to cover your subsistence, plus they'll pay for your flight and fix you up with accommodation.'

It sounded like the best offer I'd had in months, but something made me hesitate.

'I don't know, Richard. It's a bit out of the blue.'

'Remember what they say about gift horses.'

'Don't take one from a Trojan?'

'It's up to you, but there's nothing much on the cards for you over here right now.' There was a short pause while we both silently mourned my early promise. 'I spoke to the boy in Berlin and it all seems kosher, they've got a website and all that jazz.'

'Your faith in modern technology is touching.'

'Got to move with the times, Will.' There was another pause while I took a sip of my coffee and Rich sparked up; I heard him draw the smoke

56

deep down into his lungs and reached for my own pack of cigarettes. When he spoke again Rich's voice was brisk. I imagined him sliding his next client's folder, complete with mug shot, onto the desk in front of him. 'It's up to you, old son. You've got an hour to decide. No skin off my nose either way.'

I looked at my one-room rented flat, the unmade bed, the scattering of books and CDs, the pile of unwashed laundry, the red demands propped on the window ledge. There was only one thing I had to ask.

'When do they want me?'

'That's the attitude. They're in a rush. Someone let them down. Get yourself there by tomorrow show time and the job's yours.'

I agreed to let Mrs Pierce arrange my flight then sat for a while looking at Bill's secret. I decided it was nothing to do with me. Then I did a very stupid thing. I wrote a short letter, went out to the post office, bought an envelope big enough to hold Bill's, sealed it securely and got it weighed and stamped. Then I addressed it to the safest place in the world and put it in the postbox.

Back home I put the kettle on, smoked another fag and started to pack.

Berlin

The man who ran the cabaret was a German called Ray. He was the opposite of Bill, a soft-bellied doughy-faced rectangle of a man. He had blond hair shot through with grey flecks that looked too artful to be natural. And a tense smile hedged beneath a shaggy moustache I was willing to accept as German fashion, but at home would have made me think he was a gay man on a retro kick.

I put out my hand and he took it hesitantly, giving it the briefest of shakes.

'How was your journey?'

'Fine.'

Ray nodded. 'Good.' He looked me up and down. 'I'd hoped you'd be able to perform in our opening number with the rest of the ensemble but . . .' He shook his head sadly and smiled like a man who had faced enough disappointments to know that he would face many more. 'Never mind.'

'Try me.'

He shook his head.

'We will manage. So, I guess the first thing is to show you around the theatre.' I followed him from the tiny ticket office and out into the auditorium. 'This is our hall.'

Ray paused, waiting for my reaction at my first glimpse of his kingdom.

I'm used to the abandoned atmosphere empty theatres take on during the day. Deserted by audiences they lose their sheen. When the house lights go up the grandest chandeliers can look cobwebbed, the finest gold-framed mirrors age-spotted and marred. The red velvet seats where theatregoers dream themselves onto the stage night after night reveal frayed gold trim and balding nap. But I knew that, like the leading man who arrives grey-stubbled and sour-breathed, or the femme fatale who dares to bare her pockmarked face to afternoon rehearsals, come curtain-up great theatres are ready to wow them all the way to the gods.

Still, I had my doubts about the Schall und Rauch. When I'd called him back to accept the gig Rich had built the revue into something between the Royal Festival Hall and the Hot Club of France. I'd known he was exaggerating, but I hadn't realised how much.

The auditorium smelt of mildew, tobacco and wet coats. Its dirty pine boards were still littered with the debris of last night's performance. Small tables, spattered with red candle wax and equipped with bentwood chairs, were regimented across the hall in diagonal rows. The formation was an optimistic attempt to create an unimpeded view of the stage, but it made me think of a desperate army making its final stand.

The safety curtain was up, the unoccupied stage littered with random props, a large ball, a tangle of hula-hoops, and, somewhere near the back, a trampoline. The stage was deep, its rake steep, but it was the ceiling that revealed this had once been a truly impressive building. High above our heads plaster cherubs toyed with lutes and angelic trumpets amongst bowers of awakening plaster blooms. Remnants of white paint still illuminated some of the chubby orchestra, but most of them had sunk into the same mouldering grey that covered the rest of the ceiling. In its centre, half hidden by the lighting rig, was a chipped but still elaborate ceiling rose marred by a half plastered hole where I guessed a massive chandelier had once hung. Cracks fractured out from the damaged rose and into the outskirts of the ceiling. Not all of them were linked, but they gave the impression of being connected, like irrepressible tributaries sinking underground when the earth turns to stone, but always resurfacing.

'Have a seat,' Ray pulled out a chair and lowered himself into it, 'see what it's like to be one of the audience.'

I drew up a chair, turning at the hollow sound of foot-steps on the wooden floor. A slim, dark-haired girl strode in and started to wipe the tables, putting debris of crumpled tissues, abandoned leaflets and empty fag packets into a tin bucket as she worked. I smiled but she looked past me to Ray, shooting him a sour look. Ray attempted a smile.

'So, what do you think? Maybe not as big as you're used to, but it has a certain charm?'

The girl saved me from answering, calling something in German across the hall. Ray answered quick in a tone that might have been friendly or harsh. She turned away from him, reciting a few words in a singsong voice, then tucked the cloth into the back of her jeans and walked towards the exit. Ray shook his head, 'Women, the same across the world, impossible and irreplaceable.' He smoothed the grey moustache slowly, like he was calming himself. 'I know your agent negotiated a few days of freedom before you start . . .' I could feel it coming, the not-quite-deal-breaker the management hits you with to soften you up for the rest of the betrayals. 'But in this business we have to be flexible.'

He paused and I gave a noncommittal smile. On the stage behind him a well-built man in cut-off sweats started going through a warm-up, easing into some stretches, then lifting his leg high in a balletic pose. I nodded towards him and said, 'I'm

60

not sure I could manage that level of flexibility.'

Ray frowned then turned to look at the man.

'Acrobats aren't worth the trouble. You invest in them, break your back helping them, then they go and do the same, only they break their backs for real. Kolja is talented, but acrobats have short lives; he'll be walking with a stick or teaching sports in a kindergarten before he's thirty.'

'Seems harsh.'

Ray shrugged his shoulders. I could imagine him sending a ten-year-old to drown a sack of kittens with the same shrug.

'It's a fact. These kids go to circus school. They know the odds, but still think they'll live forever. That is natural too.'

On the stage Kolja stopped his stretch to watch us. I thought I saw amusement in his face, but he turned away too quickly for me to be sure. Perhaps Ray saw it too, because he leaned back and shouted something in German towards the athlete. The young man made no reply, but his mouth set into a stiff smile as he punted himself down from the stage.

'There's no time for you to go to your lodgings now. He'll put your luggage in the dressing room.'

I got to my feet.

'I'll do it myself.'

Kolja walked past without glancing towards us, leaving me standing awkwardly by the table. I sat back down and lit a cigarette. Ray shrugged. He sounded tired.

'He's proud of his muscles, let him use them. Come on, let's finish our business, then perhaps you'll do some preparations.'

'Perhaps.'

Ray smiled and led me through to his office.

'So this is my sanctuary. Anytime you need to find me, you start looking here.'

Ray's sanctuary was cramped. A workbench ran the length of the far wall, hidden beneath stacks of paper and some surprisingly new computer equipment. A small window above the bench looked into the ticket-booth where the girl who had been clearing the tables was now busying herself behind the desk. Beyond her I could see the empty foyer and an open door leading out into the courtyard. The wall behind me was covered in a mosaic of photographs, some expensively framed, others carelessly sellotaped to the wall. I looked at a smartly mounted photograph of a man in full evening rig placing his head inside a polar bear's mouth. The man had removed his top hat for the act, and now flourished it in his right hand. His own grin was just visible through the jagged teeth of the bear.

Ray saw me looking and said, 'My grandfather.'

'It's an amazing picture.'

'More amazing than you can know. Outside the ring my grandfather was as soft as butter. People said he let his children run wild, but when it came to animals he was in charge. He ruled lions, tigers, polar bears even, for thirty years, with no injury to himself or to them.'

'A brave man.'

'Yes, he knew the risks.' Ray turned his attention to his desk, sifting through a pile of papers looking for something. 'The moment after that photograph was taken the bear attacked him, perhaps the flash provoked it. My grandmother was his assistant. She was standing by the cage, as she did every night, with a loaded pistol. She shot the bear, but it takes more than a single bullet to kill a creature like that.' He glanced back at the photograph. 'It's something we should all remember. Even if you're not placing your head in a bear's mouth, show business is a risky occupation.' He smiled. 'It's a sad photograph. Let me show you one that will make you smile, then you can meet our stage manager and go through your requirements.' We rose and Ray walked me into the theatre's small foyer. 'Look.'

Pinned behind glass was a large poster featuring a publicity shot Rich had insisted on three years ago. It was a while since I'd looked closely at it and blown up poster size it was clear that the intervening years had been crueller than I remembered. The suit I was wearing no longer fitted, and either the photographer had employed an airbrush, or I'd grown a deal redder and a trifle more craggy since we'd met. The man in the picture looked younger, leaner, sharper than I ever recalled being. It was even possible that he had a little more hair than me. I stroked my hand across my head wondering if I was about to add baldness to my list of worries. Ray's expression was hidden behind the grey moustache, but his voice sounded anxious.

'What do you think?'

I looked at the red lettering scattering superlatives across the poster. My German might be non-existent but I could guess the meaning of *Fantastisch!* I turned to the posters hanging beside my boastful image and it suddenly became clear why Ray had decided I was unsuitable to join the ensemble. Schall und Rauch's cast shone from the picture fresh and smiling, the outlines of their bodies impressive beneath the tight fabric of their costumes. The recognition that Ray was right stung, but another more pressing worry had suddenly presented itself. Painted in shiny blue letters below the image was the legend, *Cabaret Erotisch!*

*   *   *

The stage manager turned out to be the girl I had first seen wiping the tables. She slid wearily from the ticket booth, brushing back tendrils of not very clean hair that had escaped from the loose roll twisted at the back of her head. She looked as if she hadn't slept in weeks, but the look suited her. Suddenly, despite the rundown theatre and the reminder that I lacked the basic equipment to qualify for an erotic entertainment, Berlin didn't seem such a bleak prospect. Ray introduced her as Ulla; I held out my hand and she shook it gently. Her palms were cold and dry and slightly calloused. I tried to keep the wolf out of my face and asked, 'Do you do everything round here?'

Ulla frowned.

'I do my job.'

Her English was slightly more accented than Ray's. I liked it better. She was easier on the eye too, even when she was frowning. I slipped the duster that still dangled from her jeans pocket into my own.

Ulla led me through a door marked *Privat* and towards the changing rooms. Her silence should have been a relief after the journey, but I wanted her to talk to me. I reached into my pocket and drew out the old duster now tied in the centre of a ream of rainbow-coloured silks, presenting them to her with a flourish and a half bow.

'There was no time to buy flowers.'

Ulla accepted the string of scarves without smiling.

'The clowns present me with flowers all the time.'

'And now you think every bouquet is going to squirt water in your eye?' She ignored me, gently detaching her cloth as she led the way through the backstage labyrinth. 'I hope I'm not disrupting you too much.'

Ulla handed back my crumpled silks without looking at me. I followed her gaze and saw the object of her attention. The buff athlete detailed to deliver my case was striding our way, a large cardboard box tucked casually under his arm. He stopped when he reached us and Ulla raised her face to his in a swift but tender kiss. I stood awkwardly while he whispered something into her hair that made her laugh then shake her head, glancing quickly towards me. Kolja turned the corners of his mouth down, gave her waist a quick squeeze with his free hand, and then continued along the corridor. Ulla's eyes followed him briefly and then turned back to me.

'Kolja has moved in with the twins, so you can have his dressing-room.'

There seemed no point in protesting that I was used to sharing. After all, I seemed destined to disrupt Kolja. The room Ulla had assigned me was like a slim prison cell bereft of even a barred window. I sat in the only chair and looked at the photos of Kolja stuck to the mirror.

65

He was a good-looking lad. Here he was on stage balancing an upside-down fellow athlete on one hand. Here he was again, stripped to his bathing shorts posing with both hands resting on his waist, his pumped-up arms a perfect complement to his inflated trunk. Did Kolja need these mementoes as reassurance of his athletic prowess? Or did he just like looking at himself? I wondered why he hadn't taken the photographs to the twins' cell with him. There were a lot of them, but not too many for Kolja's muscular arms. Perhaps he'd been in too much of a rush or maybe he didn't think I'd be around long enough to warrant the move. Whatever the reason I hoped I hadn't upset Kolja. He looked like he could destroy me with a flick of his wrist.

Outside I could hear exchanges of greetings as staff and performers started to arrive for that evening's show. I imagined I could smell the winter damp settled on their coats. I pushed the noise away, tried to ignore the resentful stares of all the different Koljas and concentrated on preparing my act.

*   *   *

Ray's moustache trembled a little when he saw me leaving the theatre half an hour before show time, but he knew better than to interrupt a performer before their act. Folk have strange rituals and who was to say mine wasn't walking out before I walked on?

There was a stall in the courtyard selling soup that was all noodles and dumplings. I bought myself a bowl, added a beer to go with it and sat on a wooden bench in sight of the theatre entrance, watching the audience arrive.

Unless you're a children's entertainer, your audience doesn't believe that what you're doing is truly magic. They want showmanship. Anyone can feel the satisfaction of teaching their hands to twist the rope until it unravels the way they intend. It isn't so hard to jump the right card from the deck, or snap a shiny silver coin into your fingertips. The skill lies in making these moves into a performance.

I was always in the smart-suited-cheeky-chappy conjuring brigade, bounding on stage and spinning a line as I spun through my act. I'd long ago consigned mime to a box marked 'puppets and face painting'. I lacked the nimbleness for a dumb show. And all those exaggerations of the face and form, the Marcel Marceau smiles and grimaces, made me cringe. Sitting outside the theatre in Berlin I began to think how important words were to my act and began to hope that it was true all foreigners understood English these days.

The arriving audience looked young, bundled against the cold in dark coats livened by bright hats and scarves. I watched them drift in and wished I was one of their number, out for the evening with a pretty girl, looking forward to a show. I got up and returned my empty dish and half-drunk beer to the stall. It was time to get focused.

*   *   *

Inside I bought another beer, deposited myself on a seat near the back and watched an old woman in a black dress going between the tables trying to sell the contents of her tray of clockwork toys. She wasn't having much luck. I signalled her over and blew twelve euros on a small tin duck. I turned his key and let him clack between the ashtray and my beer.

Then the lights dimmed, the audience grew quiet and high on a platform, way above the stage, a woman with the black hair and red lips of Morticia Adams grinned and stroked the ivories of her baby grand into something soothing that spoke of the sea. She reached out her right hand, never letting the music fail, and caressed a huge hollow drum as it descended past her to hang mysteriously over the stage.

The ensemble from the poster ran from the wings, the females in thigh-skimming dresses, the men in close-fitting shorts. Kolja jogged on last, his face shuttered and his muscles specially inflated for the occasion. The troupe waved to the audience, acknowledging their applause then stood still, like a starship crew ready to be teleported, as the glowing drum descended all the way down to the stage, trapping them within its bounds, silhouetting their forms against its pale walls. One by one each dark outline peeled off its clothes to reveal the black shape of their naked body, then they started to rotate slowly, forming a living magic lantern. Each disrobing received a polite round of applause that was rewarded with a pose as the artistes took turns to fold themselves into new shapes, slipping from athletic to romantic, from Charles Atlas to Rodin's *Kiss*. There were no unfortunate bulges, no regrettable slips of decorum, and I guessed that the nudity was

68

an illusion, each person contained in some tight-fitting body stocking. Kolja was the easiest to spot. His was the widest chest; the thickest thighs. It was he who held two seemingly naked girls on his shoulders, balancing their weight like a set of human scales. He too who got the loudest applause as he flexed his physique through a catalogue of muscleman positions. Overall it was a good effect, an innocent erotic, about as naughty as an Edwardian postcard.

The first of the performers to appear solo was a lithe lycra-clad girl with a blonde ponytail, who seemed to be in love with her hula-hoop. The audience sat still in anticipation as she twirled the hoop around her body, letting it rotate her waist, chest, neck then suddenly drop to her ankles in an act of obsequiousness that seemed sure to kill its gyrations, but was merely a prelude to a snaking dance up her body and onto her right arm. Her hand snatched a second hoop, rival to the first, which proceeded to do its own dance around her curves. It seemed this girl couldn't get enough of the hoops. She lifted them one by one from a pile as high as herself until she had screwed her little body into a spiral of weaving plastic. The small audience went wild and my tiny tin duck clacked like there was no tomorrow.

I was hoping for Kolja, but the hula girl was followed by a trio of juggling clowns. They cavorted onto the stage dressed in bright baggy shorts and outsized shirts. The tin duck drew me a sad stare, I took a sip of my drink and nodded back at him. The crowd were clapping them on but the jolly jesters looked too wholesome to amuse me. I've always preferred Kinky the Kid-loving Clown, a hard-drinking funster who has his full makeup tattooed on.

Somewhere a violin started to play a waltz and onstage the trio began tossing their batons gracefully in time to the music. I could see where it was going. The tempo increased and so did the speed of their pitches until the music sounded like a fiddler devil's crossroads challenge and the clowns were flinging their batons like missiles, ducking to put their partner in the frame, turning the cat's cradle of their throws into a crisscrossing sequence it was impossible to anticipate. The speed increased, a baton or two was lost, after all a trick must never look too easy, then, just when the audience were getting used to their expertise, the entire volley was turned on the smallest of the three, who caught the batons with his hands, arms, legs and feet, looking askance at the final club before catching it deftly in his mouth. The audience cheered. The troupe acknowledged the applause with a series of synchronised back-flips, then the runt ran offstage and returned brandishing three buzz-saws and a manic smile. I got up and made my way back to the wings. I left the duck on the table. It would be nice to think that someone in the audience was rooting for me.

*　　　*　　　*

The clowns finished their not-so-funny business then flip-flopped offstage accompanied by music that was an improbable mixture of oompa and punk. The crowd clapped and stamped to the rhythm and the irrepressible funsters cart-wheeled back on for an encore, throwing buzz-saws at each other with calamitous abandon before finally running unscathed into the wings.

The little one buzzed his saw at me as he sped past. I muttered, 'Buzz off'. And he flashed me a wicked grin saying something in German that might have been *Good luck* or *Fuck you.*

Two stagehands dressed like ninjas jogged on to clear the clowns' debris and deposit my equipment. The mysterioso music I'd given Ulla reached its fifth bar. I took a deep breath and strode out from stage right as the stagehands exited stage left. The clown's applause still trembled in the air. I measured it, gauged the warmth of the crowd, pretty hot, and realised that for once I wasn't the warm-up.

I lifted a flimsy transparent perspex table above my head, twirled it like a baton then waved my hand Mephisto-like below it and snapped a set of oversized playing cards into view. Beyond the edge of the stage there was nothing but black punctuated by the candle flames glowing out of the darkness. God looked out into the firmament and saw nothing. Then he snapped his fingers and created the world. I gave the slightest of bows, and got on with it.

*   *   *

Have you ever seen a film of an ocean liner ready to embark on a long voyage? People were so loath to leave their loved ones that they stretched streamers from the decks to the quayside. The nearly-departed held one end, the soon-to-be-strangers on the shore, the other. As the ship moved off the streamers would grow tense, taut, then break.

That was the image I had of my audience's attention, slender strips of colour connecting them to me. I wanted to keep them at the moment the ribbon was at its tautest, and never let it snap until my final bow.

The music died and I slid into my set, I was halfway through the first trick when I heard the whisper of conversation. The fragile strands connecting me to the audience snapped and it was as if I was a lonely soul on the top deck holding a bunch of limp streamers without even a breeze to give them a flutter.

There was a clink of glass on glass as drinks were refreshed. A jarring note of laughter where there should have been the silence of suspense. I did the only thing I could do, kept the smile on my face and stumbled on until the moment came for the house lights to be raised. Now I could see the faces of my audience, too many of them in profile. I stepped forward, feeling like a man on the scaffold, and asked for a volunteer.

Later, Sylvie would show me this was the wrong way to go about things. But that evening even the old lady who sold the tin toys stopped her rounds and waited for my humiliation. I paused three beats beyond comfort, unable to spot a dupe amongst the crowd, putting all my will into not begging. The stage lights seemed to flare again, the audience bled out of focus and even the candles seemed to lose their glow. A bead of perspiration slid down my spine. Then a young woman got to her feet and I knew everything was going to work out fine. And so it did, for a while.

The girl bounded onto the stage with so much

confidence I suddenly thought the audience might assume her to be my accomplice. I shouldn't have worried. Even on that first night, though I was the one with the tricks and the tail-coat, everyone wanted to see what Sylvie would do.

*   *   *

My volunteer was a slim girl in high-stacked boots and an old-fashioned shirtdress that showed off her figure. Her hair was sleek, cut close to her head, and her lips were painted a vampire red that glistened under the stage lights. She turned to face the audience. Her stare was confident, her mouth amused and I realised I should never have chosen her for my dupe. I swallowed, arranged my features in the semblance of a smile then went into my patter.

'So, gorgeous, what's your name?'

'Sylvie.'

She had an American accent, all Coca-Cola, Coors and Marlboros, a bland corporate voice that could have come from almost anywhere.

'And what brings you to Berlin?'

Sylvie shrugged and looked out into the darkness beyond the stage.

'Life?'

The crowd laughed, and I smiled, though I didn't see the joke.

'So, would you like to help me with a trick?'

'I guess so.'

Again her voice was deadpan and again a ripple of laughter worked its way through the audience. I might not be getting the jokes, but I was grateful. The clatter of glasses and conversation had ceased and all eyes were on us, the audience rooting for Sylvie, waiting for her to upstage me.

I turned her towards me, looked into her grey-green eyes and grinned.

'OK then, let's get on with the show.'

The shell game is an ancient trick also known as Chase the Lady, also known as Thimblerig. The man who first taught me prefaced his lesson with a warning.

'This is a trick as old as Egypt—older, I don't doubt. It has saved many a man from starvation and landed many another in debt or jail. The wise man is always on the showing side, never on the guessing.'

My old teacher was right, but it isn't big news that it's better to be the sharper than the sharper's dupe, so my variation had an extra distraction to twist the ruse.

I fanned three brown envelopes in my left hand, and raised a picture of the crown jewels in my right, holding it high in the air so that the audience could see it. I'd thought that the royalist kick might go down well with the Germans, after all, they were related. I slid the photograph into one of the envelopes, making sure that Sylvie and the audience could see which one it was.

'Sylvie, how would you like to win the British crown jewels?'

Her voice was dry.

'The real thing or this photograph?'

I feigned an outraged look.

'This rather fine photograph.' Sylvie laughed and the audience joined her. I kept the note of injury in my voice. 'What? You don't find it exciting?'

She shook her head matching my mock

74

offence—'No'—and turned to leave the stage.

'Hey, hold on.' I touched her shoulder and Sylvie twisted back towards me on cue, as if we'd been rehearsing for weeks. 'What about if I were to offer you . . .' I leaned forward and snapped three 100 euro notes from somewhere behind her ear. It was the kind of cheap move a half-cut uncle could manage after a good Christmas dinner, but for the first time that night I got a round of applause.

It's hard to convey the look that Sylvie gave me. A smile that acknowledged we were in this together and a glint of sympathy cut through with something else, an urge to please the audience that might amount to recklessness.

'Yes,' she said in her cool, who-gives-a-fuck stage voice. 'Yes, that might make a difference.'

I slid the money into the envelope alongside the maligned picture and sealed it tight.

'Now, Sylvie, examine these envelopes for me please.' I passed all three to her. 'Are they identical?'

She took her time, turning each one over in her hand, scrutinising their seals, drawing her fingers across their edges. At last she turned and nodded.

'Yes, they're the same.'

'Now . . .' I feinted a soft black velvet hood into my hands. 'How do you feel about a little S&M?'

Sylvie made a shocked face and someone in the audience whooped.

*   *   *

Sylvie's fingers were strong as she secured the hood over my head. She tied the cord in a bow at the nape of my neck, then smoothed her fingertips

75

over my face, pressing them against my eyelids for a second. I felt the prickle of total darkness and breathed in the faint peppery mustiness that the velvet bag always held, pulling the fabric towards me as I inhaled, letting my masked features appear beneath the velvet.

'I want you to take these envelopes and shuffle them in any way you wish.' The audience laughed. I wondered what she was doing and asked, 'All done?'

'Yes.'

'Now, I'm going to ask you which envelope the money is in. You can lie, you can tell me the truth, or, if you choose to be a very unkind girl, you can keep silent. The choice is yours.' The audience were quiet, willing my destruction. 'OK, Sylvie, I want you to present me with each of the envelopes in turn. But because I can't see anything you're going to have to provide me with a commentary, so name them please as you hold them up. Let's call them . . .' I hesitated as if thinking hard. 'Number one, number two and number three. OK, in your own time.'

Sylvie waited a beat, then in a loud, clear voice said, 'Number one.'

I lifted my head, breathing in again, hoping my covered features looked blunt and dignified, like an Easter Island statue.

'Is it in this one?'

I waited. Sylvie didn't respond.

'Ah, I thought you might be one of those girls who like to torture men.'

No one in the audience would have noticed, but Sylvie gave a short intake of breath. She recovered quickly and said in her calm, even voice.

76

'Number two.'

'Is it in this one?'

This time she answered me.

'No.'

'Aha, you're not an easy girl to work out, Sylvie. I've got a suspicion that you might be rather good at lying.'

The stage was so quiet that I might have been standing there alone. I felt the warmth of my own breath inside the bag, then Sylvie said, 'Number three.'

I waited. This time it was my silence that ruled the stage.

'OK, if I'm wrong you go off with a week's wages. Is it in this one?'

There was an instant's hesitation and then Sylvie answered me.

'No.'

It was the hesitation that told me. I took my chance, snatching the hood off then grabbing the final envelope, ripping it in two and drawing out the money and the photo. The audience applauded and I raised my voice above their clapping, 'Thank you Sylvie, you've been a wonderful assistant. People from Scotland have a reputation for being mean, but it's a cruel slur and to prove it I'm going to make sure that you don't go off empty-handed.'

I presented her with the photograph of the crown jewels. Sylvie held it close to her head and bowed prettily to the audience. We exchanged a quick kiss, and then I watched her slim figure descend into the darkness and the applauding audience beyond.

I thought that would be the last I saw of her.

Glasgow

The past is like an aged Rottweiler. Ignore it and it'll most likely leave you alone. Stare into its eyes and it'll jump up and bite you. It was no more than coincidence that an old face came out of the darkness, but it felt that by living half in the past I had invoked old times to slip from the shadows.

I'd decided not to favour one bar above the rest. Glasgow's got a hostelry on every street corner and a fair few in between, so why confine yourself to one pishy pub when you have the choice of plenty? I'd long been a travel-ling man so I travelled from one shop to the next, moving on before I could be hailed and hassled by any Jimmy/Bobby/Davie deadbeat who lived his life propped against the bar. I was a sailor on drink's high seas, while they were merely landlubbers.

I favoured places with no mission other than to empty your pockets, fill you full of bile and kick you into the street at closing time. I had no time for quizzes and karaoke, pub grub and Sky Sports. Anything more entertaining than a puggy machine and I was out of there.

I had thrown my noose a little wider that night. From the outside it looked like my kind of place, trad dad, no theme, no music, no enthusiastic throng of patrons slapping each other on the back or measuring up for square goes.

The illusion hung together when I went inside. The only decorations were drink advertisements, but my radar should have gone on alert: they were for long-abandoned classic campaigns—My

Goodness, My Guinness; Martini & Rosso; Black and White Whisky—there was even a green fairy sparking out of a cup under the power of absinthe. The bar was a square island in the centre of the space. I was pushing the boat out. It was my third pub, fourth pint. I was going to make a night of it. See if I could get to the point where I'd lost count.

I kept my head down, my attention caught by the red carpet, busy with an abstract design which seemed to shift out of focus then arrange itself into a mosaic of grinning devils. I wondered what other people saw in the pattern. Flowers? Vast cities? Angelic girls? The thought preoccupied me and I'd approached the bar before I realised this wasn't the kind of place I'd thought it was.

The revelation lay in the beers. As well as the compulsory piss-poor Tennents Lager there was a variety of real ales and a pretentious clanning of single malts. It was a spit-and-sawdust theme pub, an ersatz recreation of the traditional Scottish howf, but lacking the essential ingredient—misery.

But even a poor pub is hard to leave. I ordered a pint of lager and stood leaning against the slop-free bar, counting the green tiles that covered the gantry wall. My pint was three-quarters down in the glass and I'd reached 150, estimating and adding together the fractions of divided tiles, when I felt a hand fall in between my shoulder blades. I tensed, steeled myself for a confrontation, turned and came face to face with Johnny Mac.

My first instinct was to walk away, but the thought came and went and I was still standing there. It was seven years since I'd last seen him, but Johnny hadn't changed much. There were a few creases round his eyes I didn't remember and maybe his hairline had withdrawn a little from his temples. But he was still scrag-end thin, his dark hair still unfashionably long, but just short enough to ensure his curls lost none of their bounce. When we'd hung around together, long second-hand coats had been the fashion. I'd worn an old herringbone tweed that smelt when it got wet and Johnny'd more or less lived in an olive-green army greatcoat that had served as a second blanket on his bed at night.

I probably wasn't one to judge, but Johnny didn't seem to be following fashion any more. The old greatcoat was gone, replaced by a navy parka with a small rip in the sleeve that appeared to have been mended using a bicycle repair kit. Beneath the parka he wore a T-shirt with a diametric pattern that meant nothing to me. His jeans were scuffed, splattered with the same paint that decorated his worn-out trainers. Johnny's mouth bent into a wide grin and I noticed a gap where his left incisor used to be.

'I thought it was you. God, I don't believe it.' He draped an arm around my shoulder and pulled me into a hug that was traitor to his west coast of Scotland origins. 'Hey, Houdini, long time no see. How's tricks?'

The barman caught Johnny's eyes, and saved me from answering. Johnny slacked his grip, letting me pull free as he leaned in towards the bar and started to stumble through a round of drinks. He was pissed, but only the meanest of pubs would refuse him service. Anyone looking at Johnny Mac would know he'd be no trouble drunk or sober. He finished the order with a nod to me.

'And whatever he's having.'

'No, nothing for me, I was just on my way.'

'Dinnae be bloody daft.'

'No, Johnny, I've got to be off.'

The barman was used to these friendly altercations. He wiped his hand on a towel, waiting for me to be persuaded. Perhaps he was on profit share because when Johnny demanded, 'Give him a pint,' he poured me another lager.

'We've got a table over there.' Johnny nodded towards a far corner of the pub.'

'I told you, I can't.'

The words came out harsher than I'd meant. The bar-man glanced back at us, maybe wondering if he'd pegged Johnny wrong and there was going to be a fight after all. The drink cleared a little from Johnny's eyes and he seemed to see me properly for the first time.

'What's the problem?'

'I've got to be somewhere.'

He glanced up at the hands of the bar-room clock ticking beyond a quarter past ten. His voice grew less insistent. 'Aye, well spare me ten minutes. We've not seen each other in an age. How long has it been? Six years?'

'Something like that.'

'Mebbe longer.' Johnny picked up his pint of heavy and sucked the head off it. A rim of foam stuck to his upper lip; he wiped it away and took another pull looking at me over the brim of the glass. 'So what've you been up to?'

'Nothing much.'

'Still practising the black arts?'

'No, I gave that up. It's a mug's game.'

'Never thought I'd hear you say that, Billy boy.'

I raised my drink to my lips, hiding my

81

expression behind the glass and taking a long gulping swig, all the quicker to finish and get out of there.

'Aye, well, it's true.'

Johnny seemed to have forgotten he had a round of drinks to deliver. He stood there waiting for me to tell him why I'd given up my calling. I let him wait. Johnny Mac had never been good at silences.

'I ran into your mum in the town the other week.' Johnny hesitated waiting for me to say something then broke the pause again. 'She said you'd been not well.'

'I don't know where she got that from.'

'You're all right then?'

I held my arms out.

'See for yourself.'

Johnny looked dubious.

'That's good.'

I forced my face into a smile.

'I'm doing fine, you know what my old dear's like. I get a cold and she thinks I'm on my bloody deathbed. She's aye been like that.' I strained the smile wider. 'Like the man said, reports of my death were much exaggerated.'

Johnny nodded, his eyes still on my face.

'Glad to hear it.'

From across the room I caught sight of a slim, dark-haired woman in her late twenties. Even before she started making her way towards us I knew she was with Johnny. Johnny's dark curls and quick smile had given him his pick of women, but he'd always gone for good Catholic girls, fresh-faced Madonnas who refused to sleep with him. Johnny had left his faith at the schoolhouse gates, but in those days it seemed that the tenets of the church were destined to rule his sex life. Johnny's girl was clear-skinned and sober, but her eyes were amused. She slid her hand round his waist, his grin reappeared and I reckoned that after a certain age even good Catholic girls started to put out.

'There's men at that table complaining their throats are cut.'

Johnny slammed his forehead with the back of his hand.

'I'm sorry, Eilidh love. I ran into William here and he kept me talking.' He flashed me a look. 'He's a right chatterbox this one.'

Eilidh smiled. She was the staid side of fashionable, her hair long and simple, brushed into a side parting. It was her smile that kept her from being homely. Her smile and her eyes, a violet blue I'd have thought was painted on if I'd seen her on a movie poster. I wondered what she did for a living. Johnny liked them saintly. I took in her low-heeled brown boots, her coordinating skirt and jacket, just a shade away from a suit and guessed teaching or social work.

'Will you join us?'

I shook my head. For some reason I was having difficulty meeting her look.

'I'm sorry, I can't.'

Eilidh didn't try to press me, simply shook her head in mock exasperation and leaned past Johnny to take the three remaining pints in hands that looked too small to span the glasses.

'It was nice to meet you, William.' She smiled at Johnny. 'I'll give you ten minutes then you'd better come over.'

Johnny gave her a kiss that threatened to topple

the pints.

'You're a wee doll.'

'I know,' Eilidh smiled again. 'One hundred per cent pure gold.'

Johnny watched her careful walk to the table, 'Who would have thought I'd end up henpecked?'

He looked more proud than bowed. I followed his gaze, watching the slim figure depositing the drinks on the table.

'She's a good-looking girl.' Johnny gave me a stern look that was half mocking but fully meant and I added, 'My womanising days are over.'

'You're a broken man right enough. You shouldn't give up yet though. Ye canny whack the love of a good woman. As long as she's your own.'

'Aye, point taken.' I drained my glass and held out my hand. 'It was good to see you again, John.'

'You too. Maybe we can meet up for a drink when you've got more time.'

'I'm not in town for long.'

Johnny gave me a look that said he knew me for a liar, but he didn't try to argue. Instead he reached into his pocket.

'Look, I'll give you my number. It'd be good to catch up.' He pulled out his wallet and flicked through its contents. 'Fuck, I never have any cards when I need them.' The thought of Johnny Mac with business cards amused me and I smiled in spite of myself. 'Here,' he took out a bit of paper and scribbled a couple of telephone numbers and an address on them. 'Now you can get me at work, home or on the move. Mobiles, eh? They were yuppies—only when we were knocking about.'

I glanced at the scrap of paper and saw a half-familiar address. I pocketed the note, intending to

84

drop it in the street when I got outside.

'No, no.' Johnny shook his head he knew my game. 'I went to the trouble of writing that down, the least you can do is keep it safe.'

I fished the paper out of my pocket, found my wallet and slipped it in.

'Happy now?'

'Not really, but it'll do.'

'Catch you later then, Johnny.'

'Aye,' he said. 'Make sure you do or I'll hunt you down.'

I made my way into the street. Eilidh gave me a wave as I passed her table. I looked straight ahead and pretended not to notice.

I wasn't surprised that my mother and Johnny Mac had run into each other. However hard it pretends to be a city, Glasgow is just a big village. I'd known it wouldn't be long till someone recognised me, and news of my return filtered along the M8 to the pensioner bungalow in Cumbernauld. That was one of the reasons I'd only held out a month after my return before phoning her, that and the brown envelope from another time that she was keeping safe for me. Mum came through the day after I phoned, as I knew she would.

The clock outside Buchanan Street bus station is a fey sculpture, a working clock frozen fleeing towards the entrance on long aluminium legs. I wondered what had come first, the image or the title, 'Time Flies'—too bloody true.

On reflection the bus station probably wasn't the best place to hook up. It had been renovated a few years back, but no one had bothered to maintain it since and the building was shrugging

85

off the revamp. I arrived early, or perhaps the bus was late, so I took a seat on one of the cold perforated metal benches that sit on the edge of the concourse unprotected from the elements, smoked a cigarette and watched the buses sailing in and out of their slots, sliding across the forecourt like reckless ocean liners on speed. A bus left the far stand, the faces of its passengers blurred behind fogged-up windows. As it revved into top gear a second coach sped into the concourse from Buchanan Street, slicing towards the departing bus. They faced each other like reflections in a mirror and I tracked their course, tensing myself for impact. Just when collision seemed inevitable one of the drivers, I'm not sure which, peeled back and they cruised by with a quick exchange of salutes, one two-fingered, the other a single digit.

A woman of around my mother's age sat at the far end of the bench. I gave her a reassuring smile and said, 'They should set that to music.' She shot me a sour look and shifted away from me. I muttered, 'Stuck up old cow,' just loud enough for her to hear, then threw my cigarette butt onto the concrete, walked to the edge of the stand and looked out into the forecourt. The wind had full reign across the open space. It blew down from the Necropolis, through the infirmary, across the motorways and round the high rises until it could reach its goal and whip loose grit into the inadequate shelter. I rubbed my eyes. There was an illusion waiting to present itself on the edge of my mind.

'Excuse me, Jim,' an old man stood at my left hand. 'Could you help us out with my fare to

86

Aberdeen?'

I searched in my pocket for some change, the illusion still shifting angles in my head.

'There you go.'

I put fifty pence into his palm. He glanced at the coin before folding it in a firm grip, like a child scared of losing his pocket money before he made it to Woolworth's.

'I need to get away frae this godforsaken city and back to civilisation, see?'

'Aye, well, I hope you make it.'

'This is a bad place, son; Sodom and Gomorrah had nothing on London. Land of bloody heathens.'

'You're not in London,' I said, distracted away from my vision of collisions and vanishing buses.

'I know that, I'm no bloody daft.'

'Fair enough.'

I was through with illusions, magical and philosophical. I pushed the calculations from my head and turned towards the benches, but they were full now. The wind was growing sharper, cut through with a dampness that meant it would rain soon. I leaned against the wall of the shelter and the old man shifted with me, muttering something I couldn't make out. The wind was bitter, but it wasn't strong enough to carry away his tang. I wondered when he'd last had a wash. Maybe it'd been in London. I pulled out my half-empty pack of cigarettes.

'If I give you a fag will you go away?'

'That's what you bloody yuppies are like.' The old man's voice was getting higher. 'You think you can bloody buy and sell everyone. Well Jackie McArthur's no for sale.'

The people on the benches turned towards us. I

didn't care, maybe it would be the last time I'd be the entertainment. I held the pack towards him.

'Aye fine, you can have one anyway, if you lower the volume.'

Jackie took a cigarette.

'Bloody fucking metropolitan yuppies. No room for a working man any more.'

Perhaps he really had come all the way from London. He seemed to have the measure of the place.

Another bus slid into another stand, but the Cumbernauld service was still missing in action. The people waiting on the benches started to shuffle into line. I looked back towards the clock in the main hall and saw a short moustached man in a navy-blue fleece walking towards us. He wore a silver ticket-machine strung round his neck like a badge of office. The woman at the top of the queue began counting her change, getting the correct fare together. She looked up as the conductor passed, but he ignored her, walking by the waiting queue towards my new pal Jackie McArthur.

The ticket-collector cocked his thumb at Jackie.

'Move it.' The old man looked up, his fight chased off by the uniform and moustache. The ticket-collector moved a little nearer, putting his face close to the old man's. 'I said, bloody move it.'

I counted to ten, but when I finished counting the old man was still mumbling and the ticket-collector was still puffed before him like a bantam facing a flyweight.

'There's no need to talk to him like that.'

'This isnae vagrant central.'

Jackie started muttering, 'Nae place for a

working man any more.'

I tried to keep my voice reasonable. 'He's only waiting on a bus.'

'No, he's no, he's just in here for the heat.'

'Then he's bloody kidding himself isn't he? You'd get more heat off my granny's fanny and she's been dead fifteen years.' Someone in the queue laughed and the conductor flushed.

'You watch your mouth. There's ladies present.' He turned to the old man. 'Where are you headed?'

'Away from London, son. City of fools and killers.'

'He's going to Aberdeen.'

'Where's your ticket?' The old man patted the pockets of his jacket and the official raised his voice, enunciating slowly. 'I said, where is your ticket?'

The man stopped his search and the collector's eyes sparkled. He adjusted the settings on his machine. 'That'll be fifteen pounds please, sir.'

Jackie looked confused. He put his hand into his pocket and pulled out the fifty pence I'd given him. He turned to me his voice high.

'I told you already. I dinnae have the money.'

The cogs of the ticket-machine rasped as the collector cranked it backwards.

'Well fuck off and stop wasting our time then or I'll be forced to call the cops and have you done.'

I took out my wallet.

'Look, I'll bloody pay.'

I pulled out a tenner. The old man took it gently from me, smiling, and I noticed how well his horn-yellow nails coordinated with the nicotine tint of his fingertips.

The ticket-collector's voice was nasal and sharp.

'It's fifteen pounds please, *sir.*'

'Give me a moment.'

I patted my pockets for change echoing the old man's search, but that morning I had resolved again to live within the bounds of the bru and never to touch the tainted money hidden in my props case beneath my bed. I remembered too late that the tenner was the last of my cash. I looked towards the queue.

'Look, this old boy's a bit confused, he's four-fifty short of his fare to Aberdeen.' I hesitated, not really wanting to go ahead with what I knew I was about to do, but sure that I wouldn't be bested by the bully. I scanned the faces before me. Third in line stood a skinny red-haired girl in a green coat. She looked like a student, but the coat was new, her bag mid-range expensive. Others were looking away, keen to remove their better nature before it was called on, but the skinny redhead was half out of the line, watching us. I bet she had some money on her. Even as I caught her look in mine, her hand went shyly to her pocket. I held her gaze and said, 'You *want* to help this old man.'

The order freed her and she stepped forward, calmly unzipping her handbag.

Jackie took off his bunnet and started to sing.

The northern lights of A-a-berdeen are home, sweet h-o-o-me to me.

A couple of people in the queue started to grin, but the girl continued to reach for her purse. I kept my eyes on her, smiling but willing her to speed up.

Then suddenly everyone in the queue was laughing, the girl looked up confused, a flush burning her cheeks.

Jackie was tilting a small bottle of whisky to his lips. He finished his swallow, raised the ten pounds to his mouth, kissed it, then lifted the note in the air and began jigging back into the station, towards the exit.

The northern lights of Aberdeen are where I want to be.

'Remember, son,' he shouted over his shoulder, more lucid than a drunken, dancing tramp with money in his hand should be, ''member and keep away from London. It's full of killers and fools.'

'Aye, that's good advice for your money,' said the ticket collector. 'So do you want this ticket to Aberdeen?'

'What do you think?'

'I think you should bugger off.'

Jackie's song echoed from the exit.

I've been a wanderer all my life and many a sight I've seen, But God speed the d-a-a-a-y when I'm on my w-a-a-a-y to my home in Aberdeen . . .

I hesitated, caught between the impulse to run after the old man and an urge to thump the ticket-collector. I said, 'Who the fuck do you think you are?'

He shook his head, and started to walk towards the waiting queue. I made to follow him, then a small figure caught my eyeline. I turned and said, 'Hi Mum.'

*　　　*　　　*

We wandered down past the Stalinist façade of the concert hall and into the city. I reached towards my mother's carrier bag but she pulled it away from my grasp. The last time we'd met I'd taken her to an Italian restaurant I'd read about on the flight from London. This time I didn't even have the price of a cup of coffee. The change hung between us as we walked towards the cafe of her choice.

I've drunk coffee in Starbucks from Manhattan to Inverness and never yet enjoyed the experience. We queued, ordered, Mum paid, then we waited to see what we'd paid for. Perhaps it said something about the indomitability of the human spirit that no matter how hard the coffee corporation tried they couldn't guarantee service with a smile. Our server looked like he'd had a rough night. His skin had a veal-calf pallor and there were red rings round his eyes that told of late nights and smoky rooms. He clattered our cups onto their saucers, swilling milky coffee over the side.

I lifted the tray and said, 'Ever thought you were in the wrong job?'

'All the time, pal.' He leant forward and whispered low enough to exclude the other customers. 'I'd prefer one that didn't involve dealing with wankers.' Getting things off his chest seemed to cheer the boy up. He smiled, resuming normal volume. 'Mind and have a nice day.'

I started to answer, but Mum put her hand on the small of my back. She should have been a nightclub bouncer. There was no arguing with that steady pressure. I bit back my words and we made our way to the only seats available, two stained chairs set round a table littered with a debris of sandwich wrappers and dirty cups. I slid the tray between the mess. Suddenly I wanted a pint.

Mum set our cups on the table and started to fill

the empty tray with the rubbish. A plastic sandwich pack sprang open and her mouth grew tight as she forced it shut.

'Do you have to pick a fight with everyone you meet?'

I watched her hand the tray to a passing employee with the smoothness of a fly-half passing a rugby ball. One minute the guy was loose-limbed and unburdened, the next he was laden.

'Bad manners annoy me.'

Mum folded a napkin and placed it between the saucer and the cup to soak up the slopped coffee. She rubbed a paper hanky over the spills of the previous customers, then put her carrier bag on the table between the lattes.

'It's me that's the pensioner, not you.'

'Aye, sorry.'

She smiled to show me the reprimand was over then reached into her handbag and pulled out an envelope with her address written on it in my handwriting.

'I'd best give you this before I forget.'

'Oh, right.'

I took the envelope from her, feeling the cord that seems to stretch from my guts to my groin tighten.

'You said it was insurance documents.'

'That's right.'

I slid it into my inside pocket wondering if Montgomery's envelope would be my insurance or a bait to my downfall.

'Your dad always said you had a good head on you, underneath all the carry-on.'

'Thanks, Mum.'

'I brought you a couple of things.' She unfolded

the plastic bag and pulled out a three-pack of navy socks. 'I thought you could probably do with these.'

'Thanks.' I lifted them up trying to look interested in the 80 per cent wool, 20 per cent acrylic mix. 'Great.'

'They were on sale in the Asda. How are you for pants?'

'Fine.'

'I almost bought you some, but I minded the last time I got them you said they were the wrong sort.' I vaguely recalled a set of piping-trimmed Y - fronts I'd be scared to get run over in. 'I brought you this as well.' She handed me a blue shirt still in its cellophane wrapping. 'I got it for your dad, but he never got the chance to wear it.'

It was the kind of shirt that would look good with an off-the-peg from Slaters, a shirt for a nine-to-five man, the kind of shirt I never wore.

'It'll mebbe be a bit big for you but I thought you could wear it under a jumper.'

I took it in my hand smoothing the slightly brittle cellophane.

'Aye, it'll be grand in this weather.'

'That's what I thought. Keep the chill out.'

We sat in silence for a moment. Neither of us touched our coffee.

'I bought it for your dad to wear to Lorna's wedding, but he went before that came round.'

I bowed my head. Every time there was a crisis Mum would begin to reminisce about my dad's death, as if reassuring herself with the knowledge that the worst had already happened.

She lifted her teaspoon and began to peel back the skin that had started to form on the top of her drink. 'Almost two pounds each these coffees and we've not even touched them.' I lifted my cup and took a sip. 'I almost had him buried in that shirt, but in the end I dressed him in plain white. I don't know why, blue always suited him better. White just seemed more appropriate for a funeral.'

'There's no point in fretting over it now. I'll wear it under a jumper.'

'Aye,' she laid aside the teaspoon and looked me straight on. 'Or mebbe you should keep it in the packet and save it for your own funeral.'

'What's that meant to mean?'

'Look at the state of you, son.'

'I'm fine.'

'You don't look it.'

'Well, I am.'

I sat up a little straighter hoping improved posture would convince her. But I knew what she meant. I'd looked in the mirror before I left my room and seen my face puffy from the night before, my skin pale from days spent indoors, my cheeks jowlier than they'd been in Berlin. 'Why are you here, William?'

'That's a nice question.'

Her face wore the same stern look she'd used to coax the truth from me when I'd been a wee boy.

'You're not in trouble are you?'

For a second I wished I could tell her everything. The thought almost made me laugh. It was like an urge to put a finger in an electric socket or the impulse to jump under a subway train. I knew it would be fatal but the temptation still beckoned. I took a sip of my coffee, looked her in the eye and said, 'Of course not.'

The straight stare worked no better than when

I'd been a kid.

It's nothing to do with drugs is it? Your dad was always worried about you being in showbiz. I told him you were a sensible laddie but he said it was high risk for drugs. I mean look at Elvis.'

She smiled at my dad's folly, agreeing with him all the same.

'It's not drugs, Mum, honest.'

'Honest?'

She took another sip of her drink, uncertain but wanting to be reassured.

'Honest.' I tried to keep the irritation out of my voice. 'You need to keep a clear head in my line.'

'Aye, I suppose so.'

How's Bobby?

Her face brightened.

'He's grand. Mrs Cowan's laddie's going to take him out when he comes in from school.'

'I didn't know they were letting dogs into school these days.'

It was a poor joke but she did me the grace of laughing.

'You know what I mean. Though mind you, he's as clever as some folk I've met.'

'More intelligent than Mrs Cowan's laddie that's for sure.'

'Ach, you're terrible, William. He's doing his standard grades now.'

'That's good.'

I sipped my coffee, pleased the conversation had moved to neutral ground. I should have known better. Mum let me relax, then hit me again with the old verbal one-two.

'Is it a girl, son?'

I kept my voice level.

'There was a girl, Mum, but there isn't any more.' She smiled. Romance was a good problem.

*   *   *

We left Starbucks and walked down towards the town. Mum wanted to see where I was staying. I said it was being painted, but promised to take her when the renovations were over. She asked me about the colours the decorators had chosen and I lied my way through an addled spectrum that had her shaking her head. We wandered into Marks & Spencer's where she clucked at the prices and tried to patch my misery with reduced-price knitwear.

'It's not my style, Mum.'

'You're getting too old for style, son. Feel that, it's lovely wool.'

'I'd never wear it.'

She reluctantly let go of the sleeve of the jumper she'd been holding out for my inspection.

'It's a nice shade. It'd go well with your complexion.' I thought it looked the colour of dog sick. But I smiled and said, 'Where do you want to go now?'

She straightened the hooks on the hangers, making sure they were all facing in a uniform direction.

'I still think these are a bargain.'

'Not if they stay in the cupboard.'

'I suppose not.'

Across the racks a smartly dressed shopper stared at us. She looked away as I caught her eye and I wondered if she was the store detective or just a nosy cow with too much time on her hands. I glanced to check Mum's back was turned then mouthed *Fuck you*, clear and silent. Mum dug me sharp in the ribs.

'What?'

'You know what. I brought you up better than that.'

'Sorry. She was staring at us.'

'Well, let her stare.' Mum steered me towards the exit. 'And you a bally magician. Did you not know I could see you in the mirror?' She started to laugh. 'Mind she was a nosy torn-faced auld besom.' We were both laughing now. Mum wiped her eyes. 'Honestly, you'll be the death of me.' She looked the most cheerful she'd been all day. 'Come on,' she handed me her shopper. 'It's an hour before I need to get the bus. Will I take you for a wee drink?'

*   *   *

The pub was a converted bank. Mum admired the ceiling and gasped at the size of her glass of wine, but she kept a brave face when the barmaid told her the price of the round and managed to pay up without flinching. I carried the drinks over to a corner booth with a good view of the room. It was still early in the day and the last of the sun was filtering soft yellow through the frosted windows of the old bank. The nearest I've come to religious experiences have been in pubs in the late afternoon. A few office workers were scattered about the place, self-medicating with cheap bottles of wine and two-for-one lager offers. I'd always said I'd kill myself before I worked in an office. I wondered if I was destined to join their ranks, or if I'd stick to my principles.

Mum folded her coat on the seat beside her, took a sip of her wine and asked, 'Why do you not come back with me for a wee while William? Just till you get on your feet again.'

'You've not got the space.'

'That couch folds out into a bed. It's comfy, I slept on it when your dad was not well.'

'And where would Bobby sleep?'

'He's not allowed on the couch.'

'Aye right, I bet he's sleeping on it right now.'

'Just for a wee while, William.'

'I'm fine where I am, Mum.'

She gave me the same look she'd given me when I'd said I was giving up university to concentrate on my conjuring.

'I wish I could believe that. What's wrong son?'

'Nothing, I'm just having some time out.' I drained the last of my pint. 'It's a popular twenty-first-century lifestyle trend.'

'For those that can afford it maybe.'

My empty wallet burned in my pocket. I cursed my warped conscience for making deadweight out of the money I'd brought back from Germany. It had been seeing me through my slow decline in the pub and the bookies' shop. I'd lost count of the times I'd resolved never to touch it again, though I never went so far as to give it away. 'Do you want another drink?'

'No,' she started to gather her things together, 'Bobby frets if I leave him on his own for too long.'

We retraced our steps back towards the bus station. On Buchanan Street the clock was still caught mid-flight, its long legs poised on exactly the same spot, but its hands had ticked round the hours. The Cumbernauld bus was already at its

99

stance, a new conductor issuing tickets to the waiting passengers. Mum glanced at the queue, making sure she still had time to board, then turned back to me, her face serious.

'William, I know things aren't right with you just now, but remember whatever's bothering you it'll never be so bad you can't share it with your old mum.'

I gave her a hug. It was hard to remember there'd been a time when she'd been taller than me and able to set everything right. She fished in her handbag for her purse, took out a twenty-pound note and folded my hand over it, squeezing it tight.

'Ach, Mum, you don't have to.'

'Wheesht. Just for just now. You can pay me back later.' I leant down and gave her a kiss on the cheek. 'Remember, whatever you do your mammy'll always love you.'

I said, 'I know that, Mum.'

Knowing I could never grieve her with what I'd done, I waited till the bus moved off, then turned and made my way back to the Gallowgate.

*   *   *

It was late that evening when I returned home from the pub lightened of the twenty my mum had given me. The envelope had been burning against my chest since I'd slipped it into my jacket pocket; now I was anaesthetised enough to face what it might hold. I sat down on the bed, took the envelope in my hands and slit its seal for the first time since Bill had handed it to me over a year ago. Inside was a map. I unfolded it, revealing a

100

small red biro ring around a lakeside portion of a country park. I took off my glasses and rubbed my eyes, then slid my fingers inside and drew out the only other thing in the envelope: a photograph.

Two young men stood grim-faced and weary at the edge of a lake. It was dusk or dawn on what looked like a brilliant summer's day, but this was no holiday snap. One of the men was Montgomery, younger, with more hair and less gut, but still recognisable. The other man was taller, broader and more powerfully built. I hadn't seen him before, but I took an educated guess and decided that he was Bill senior, the father of Sam-loving-gay-gangster Bill. Montgomery held an edition of that day's newspaper in his hand. There was no blood, no violence, no murdered corpse or bruised face, but there was something horrid about the image that forced my eyes to stay on it. This photograph had caused me a lot of grief in Berlin. In a way it was responsible for everything that had happened there, and I had no idea what it meant. I reached into my pocket and felt for my lighter. It would be an easy matter to burn the photo and have done with the whole business.

I turned the lighter over an over in my hand, then discarded it and slid the image and the map back into the envelope. I got a piece of tape from my props box and stuck it to the underside of my bed. I could think of a better hiding place later. Perhaps by then I would know what I was hiding and what to do with it.

Berlin

When I left the theatre that evening Sylvie was standing in the yellow sliver of light cast by the open stage door. She raised her head and smiled, like a diva about to embark on her opening number. Which in a way I suppose she was. I hesitated for a second, then she shaded her eyes against the brightness. I let the door swing to and the beam of light slipped silently away, leaving us alone in the gloom of the car park.

There are some conjurers I know who claim their art helps them when it comes to women, and perhaps it does, but it's never worked like that for me.

'Hey.'

Her voice was slightly deeper than I remembered, made hoarse by the damp and the cold.

'Hi.' I hesitated, wondering why she was there. 'Thanks for volunteering tonight.'

Sylvie's expression was hidden by the dark, but her voice sounded like it had a smile in it.

'You're welcome.'

'Aye, well, you saved my skin.'

'Always a pleasure.'

Men's-mag wank fantasies fluttered across my mind. I put my suitcase down and asked, 'Are you waiting for someone?'

'Yes.'

Her slim silhouette looked vulnerable against the night shadows. The car park had a bleak abandoned feel, but there were still a half dozen or so cars scattered in the parking bays. Their headlamps were dead, windows dark; anyone could be sitting in them, watching, waiting for me to leave the girl on her own. My mind glimpsed the image of her face, caught in the half turn of a laugh, snapped at some celebration, her smile at odds with the stark appeal for witnesses. I pushed the picture away and bit back the urge to ask if she'd be OK. She was the captain of her ship, I of mine. Besides, I had the feeling she might laugh.

'I'd best get going. Thanks again, enjoy the rest of your evening.'

I unlatched the handle of my case, ready to trundle my burden to the nearest taxi rank and on to my hotel.

'Aren't you going to ask me who I'm waiting for?'

Then, of course, I knew, but wanted to hear her say it anyway.

'None of my business.'

She took a step forward and the wank mags did another quick flit.

'I was waiting for you.'

I let go of the case, not ready to reach towards her, but wanting my hands free all the same.

'I'm flattered.'

I could see her face now, her bright expression somehow open and unreadable at the same time.

'You don't know what I want yet.'

The unease was back. I glanced towards the abandoned cars wondering if a movement had drawn my eye there.

'I naturally assumed it was my body.'

Her smile grew wider.

'You Irish guys are all the same.'

'Scottish.' The brow beneath the smooth fringe pinched and I added, 'But my granddad was Irish if that helps.'

'I bet you'd say you were Klingon if it helped.'

'Assuming they don't have national service.'

She laughed.

'You're funnier off-stage.'

'So I've been told.' Somewhere beyond in the dark a tram hissed across the wires. She shook her head and I saw raindrops jewelling her dark helmet of hair. I waited for her to tell me what she wanted, then, when she didn't speak, said, 'So what can I do for you?'

'Shall I tell you over a drink?'

'I thought you'd never ask.' I glanced at my suitcase. 'Do you mind if we swing by my hotel so I can check in and dump this bag?'

She smiled showing perfect American pearly whites. 'Maybe we could have a drink there?'

'Why not?'

I returned her smile, but kept my teeth hidden, thinking Casanova himself couldn't have managed things better, forgetting that she hadn't told me what she wanted.

*   *   *

In the hours since I'd arrived the district had changed. It was still busy, but the pace had slowed. We were at a crossroads of the night. The traffic of homeward-bound theatregoers and late-night diners was cut through with the young club crowd for whom the evening, like everything else, was still young. Sylvie led me along a street lined with bars and restaurants and I caught glimpses of couples and clusters of friends caught in the bright lights, smiling. I could almost have imagined myself in London and yet I was most definitely abroad. Maybe it was just post-show tiredness made worse by a slight sense of dislocation, but everything looked too good, too clean, too nice for me to relax. It felt like the scene in the movie just before the bad guys come blazing in.

We waited for a tram to clang its way around a corner then I stepped from the pavement and into the road.

'Hey, hasty.' Sylvie put her hand on my arm and nodded at the red pedestrian light.

'Sorry.' I grinned and stepped back onto the kerb. 'Where I come from traffic lights are for the aged, the infirm and homosexuals.'

The light switched to green, we crossed together and Sylvie asked where I was staying. I told her and she said, 'It's pretty close, we can walk from here.'

'Any good?'

Sylvie shrugged her shoulders.

'I've never put in any time there.' She flashed me a smile, her heels brisk against the concrete. 'I love new hotel rooms, don't you?'

'I've spent too much time in them.'

'I haven't.'

We'd turned away from the bars and cafes into a side street dominated by the skeleton of a half-constructed building. Blue plastic flapped in the structure's frame and I thought of a giant ghost ship travelling through the night, sails slapping against the squall. Sylvie stepped onto the kerb of the unfinished pavement, and our pace slowed as she teetered along its edge, pausing occasionally to steady her balance like a tightrope-walker on the highest of high wires. I walked beside her, my suitcase's wheels grumbling against the roadway's newly surfaced tarmac. Sylvie stretched out her arms, seesawing with exaggerated concentration, then placed the tips of her right fingers against my shoulder to steady herself.

'If I ever make it big I'll live in a hotel. Clean sheets every day, a minibar full of cool drinks, room service, cable TV, a shower with fuck-off water pressure . . .'

We reached the end of the pavement. She wavered, swaying slightly like it was a long way down; I took her hand and she jumped lightly from the verge, landing in a small curtsey. I said, 'And a cooked breakfast every morning.'

'A cooked breakfast whenever you wanted. Midnight, if you felt like it, *and . . .*' She hesitated making sure she'd got my full attention before adding her pièce de résistance '. . . free toiletries.'

We were back on a main street now. A young couple crossed our path and went into a bar, his arm around her shoulder, hers around his waist.

'See if you were in Glasgow at this time of night the streets would be full of drunks.'

'Yeah? Why?'

'I don't know. That's just the way it is.'

'Where I come from only big-time losers are drunks.'

I felt myself bridle.

'Is that right?'

'Yep, just the guys that are too fucked-up to score crystal meth. Getting drunk's for pussies.'

'Lucky pussies. Where is it you come from?'

'Let's just say I come from here, now.'

106

'The here and now?'

'You better believe it.' The heels of her boots gave a final clack then she stopped before a doorway. 'Here we are, Hotel Bates. It doesn't look very lively.'

I glanced at the shuttered windows, the fastened storm doors and sleeping neon sign. 'The guidebook said this was a twenty-four-hour city.'

'It is, but only where it pays to stay open late.'

I rang the bell and watched, straining my ears for the sound of a porter's footfall, then pressed the bell again, unsure whether it was ringing somewhere deep within the house or if it had been disconnected sometime around the porter's bedtime. I stopped and listened.

'Did you hear something?'

Sylvie shook her head. I started to bang my fist hard against the door. But my blows seemed to be absorbed by the thick wood; all I was going to end up with was a sore hand. Behind me, three notes chimed like an incomplete scale on a cracked xylophone. I turned towards the sound and saw Sylvie switching on her mobile, her face illuminated by the phone's green glow.

'Perhaps we should call them.'

I glanced at the address Ray had given me.

'I don't have their number.'

But Sylvie was already keying the buttons on her mobile. She nodded towards a hand-painted sign above the porch. Somewhere beyond the bolted door a phone started to ring. We waited twenty peals then Sylvie broke the connection, retapped the number and we waited twenty more. I swore under my breath. Then Sylvie said the words that every single man and many a married man who's just met an attractive young woman longs to hear.

'I guess you'd better come back to my place.' Then she added the caveat we all hope is just for form's sake. 'There's a spare bed.'

*   *   *

I'd imagined Sylvie living somewhere compact and modern, an apartment as bright and uncluttered as the bars we had passed. But it was obvious when she opened the door that the years had been unkind to Sylvie's flat.

The hallway's unpolished lino and beige wallpaper could have dated from before Soviet times. There was a stack of unopened mail spewed across the hall table and an old slack-chained bicycle propped against the wall. The bicycle sported a man's battered leather jacket on its handlebars. It looked triumphant, like a redneck truck with roadkill strapped to its bull bars. The apartment had the rundown temporary feel of a place that's sheltered a succession of tenants and received no care in return. Sylvie gave the mail a quick uninterested glance.

'Well, here we are, home sweet home.'

'Great location.'

She laughed.

'We like it.'

I wondered if the other half of the 'we' had anything to do with the leather jacket. Sylvie started to take off her coat.

'Coffee?'

'I think I can do better than that.' I unzipped my suitcase and drew out the bottle of duty-free Glenfiddich I'd stashed there. 'I knew there was a reason I was dragging this bloody bag around with me.'

'Looks like good stuff.'

'I thought you said alcohol was for pussies?'

'I said in America alcohol is for pussies. We're in Europe now.'

'Ah, America, that narrows it down.'

Sylvie gave me a look.

'Nosy boy.' She draped her coat over the mystery man's jacket, then took my raincoat and hung it, snug, embracing hers on top of the pile. 'You go introduce yourself to Uncle Dix and I'll fetch us some glasses.'

'To who?'

She walked through to the kitchen and I positioned myself in the doorway watching her peer into cupboards as if she wasn't quite sure what she was looking for.

'Uncle Dix.'

She looked up, giving me the benefit of those perfect teeth again and pointed across the lobby.

I muttered, 'Casanova my arse.' And walked into the dimly lit lounge hoping to discover that Uncle Dix was a cat or maybe a small dog of the non-yappy variety.

*   *   *

Whoever had decorated the room had been in a hurry, or perhaps they just hadn't had enough paint to go round. The walls and ceiling were ransom-note red, the paint applied in uneven swathes, a choppy red sea, pink-foamed and unpredictable, or the interior of a burst blood vessel.

There was a small anglepoise lamp pointing up towards the ceiling, and a half dozen or so tea lights guttering towards extinction on an unused hearth. The walls sucked the light into them making the shadows in the room dark and crimson like arterial spatters at a murder scene.

The man I supposed must be Uncle Dix was sitting on a brown leatherette easy chair. The chair had a rip in its arm that had been mended with gaffer tape. Whoever had mended it probably hadn't expected the repair to last. They'd been right. Uncle Dix plucked gently at the tape's edge, as if testing the sticking power of the glue, then, when the strip succumbed unfurling towards him, he smoothed it gently back over the rip, sealing it tight against his next mild assault. There was no TV flickering in the corner, no interrupted book or newspaper placed on his lap, just a deep ash-tray half full of dead rollups on the coffee table beside him. Uncle Dix was either a man with something on his mind, or a man giving his mind a rest.

*   *   *

We age people on much more than their faces. We check out their clothes, the condition their body is in, the company they keep. We look at their hair, the way they talk, all of this in the first few seconds of meeting and without even knowing we're doing it. I'm pretty good at calculating people's ages. It's part of the job. I coughed, the man on the chair moved his gaze from the torn arm towards me, and I decided he could be anywhere between thirty-nine and sixty. He gave me a long, uninterested stare. The kind of look a man gives his shopaholic wife's latest purchase.

'Hi, I'm William.' I stuck my hand out. He waited a beat beyond politeness then shook it softly without rising from his seat.

'Dix.'

His voice had the rusty quality of old keys and broken locks. It was hard to make out the colour of his hair in the gory gloaming of the room, a steel-grey that might be black. His face was studded with stubble, which I guessed was two days' growth drifting into the third night. He wore a pair of loose jogging trousers and a half-buttoned shirt beneath which I could glimpse tendrils of chest hair. Dix looked unkempt, unwashed and was carrying about half a stone too much weight, but I had a sneaking feeling he was the kind of man that women find attractive.

I lowered myself onto the couch, wishing Sylvie would hurry up.

'Sylvie's just fetching some drinks.'

Uncle Dix kept his eyes on my face but his hand had gone back to its plucking. Once again there was a brief pause before he spoke, like the hesitation between the wires in a long-distance phone call.

'You're back.'

Against Dix's hoarse whisper Sylvie's voice sounded like the clear chime of a Sunday morning church bell. 'Sure looks like it.'

Sylvie held three mismatched glasses pinched in one hand with my whisky swinging negligently by its neck from the other. She placed herself cross-legged on the floor between us, putting the bottle and glasses on the coffee table, keeping the

111

overfull ashtray at the heart of the arrangement. I sensed some disagreement, past or maybe just postponed, between the two and it crossed my mind that I might yet find a hotel willing to take me in. Sylvie said, 'William's homeless.'

And shot me a dazzling smile. I unscrewed the bottle and started to pour three measures.

'Temporarily homeless.'

'His hotel locked him out.'

Uncle Dix turned his eyes towards me. They were puffed and bleary, but they could see OK. I wondered again how old he was and watched him take a sip of whisky. He made a grimace of approval, took another sip and said, 'Bad luck.'

It sounded like an ill-omened toast. I raised my glass.

'Prost.'

Sylvie lifted hers in response.

'Bottoms up.'

Dix's hand left the gaffer tape, went into his pocket and re-emerged with his rolling papers. I took my own cigarettes out and offered them round. Sylvie shook her head, but Dix took one and put it behind his ear for later.

'Not a very auspicious start to my first night in Berlin.'

Maybe it was the whisky, maybe it was the cigarette, or the company, but Dix seemed to be coming out of his fugue. He snapped a couple of cigarette papers from their packet and asked, 'You just arrived?'

For the first time I noticed an American tinge to his German-accented English. I wondered if he'd spent time there or if the inflection came from living with Sylvie. For all I knew he'd picked it up from MTV. I wondered how long they'd been together and what they were to each other. The sound of my name broke me from my thoughts.

'Will was the star of the show I was at tonight.'

I took a sip of my drink and nodded the compliment back to her.

'You were the star.'

Dix put his hand back into his pocket rooting for something. He looked distractedly at Sylvie.

'They gave you a job?'

'Not yet.'

Dix started to feel behind the cushion at his back, he gave an annoyed growl and there seemed a danger he might shift from his seat, then Sylvie reached under the coffee table and pulled out a bag of grass. Dix gave as close as he would get that night to a genuine smile, took the bag from her and untied the knot in its neck. The odour of fresh skunk flooded the room. I asked Sylvie, 'What do you do?'

'I'm a dancer.'

'What kind?'

'What kind you want?'

'She dances good.' Dix finished loading the joint. He sealed the papers with his tongue before lighting up and taking a couple of long drags. He passed it across the table to me. 'Here, it goes good with whisky.'

Sylvie laughed.

'Goes good with everything.'

'Cheers.' I took a long toke, pulling the smoke right down into my lungs then coughed against its goodness. 'Quality stuff.'

My voice had taken on the same dry essence as Sylvie's uncle's.

'The best.' He nodded.

I took another couple of drags. I could feel it working on my bones, better than any massage.

Dix squinted at Sylvie through the smoke.

'You should dance for him.'

Sylvie got to her feet, I noticed again how slight she was, how upright her posture. She leaned towards me, taking the spliff, then threw her head back, sucking down a long drag of the joint, twirling her small body into a pirouette. She tumbled out of it laughing, 'You should try this, Will, it surely ups the high.'

'If I get any higher I won't come down.'

Dix repeated, 'You should dance for him.' He looked at me. 'They need any dancers at your place?'

'I don't know. I could ask around.' I looked at Sylvie. 'You don't have to.'

'But I'd like to.' She walked over to a CD player and started flicking through a handful of discs on the floor beside it. 'I need the practice.' Sylvie lowered her voice into a parody of an artist. 'I'm *between* engagements.'

'She quit her job.' Uncle Dix smiled proudly. 'Told them to stick it up their ass.'

Sylvie looked up from the CD in her hand, 'That kind of job you can get anywhere.'

Dix shrugged his shoulders; he was already rolling another spliff.

I asked, 'What's your line of work?'

He looked at me and I wondered if he didn't understand the phrasing of the question, then he grinned and said, 'I mind my own business.'

'Dix can turn his hand to anything.'

Sylvie found the disk she was looking for and

114

slid it into the machine. She kicked off her boots, bent into a couple of stretches, knocked back the last of her whisky, and pressed Play>. The CD started with a lazy saxophone solo. Sylvie was already backing away, shaking her hips to the contra-beat, moving upraised arms against the melody, rolling her eyes as if in ecstasy as she reversed onto the bare floor in front of Dix and me. She eased her hips into a long weaving roll like a Hawaiian girl who'd had some soma slipped in her coconut milk. Then the rhythm changed to a percussive beat and Sylvie cartwheeled backwards into a handstand that was slow and sexy, showing the length of her leg, a flash of secret seam. She drew herself up to her full height, raising her arms till she was posed like JC on the cross and shook into a rhythm that was old and elemental. Sylvie smiled as she altered her moves to meet the tempo, pointing her toes like a ballerina, high-kicking like a burlesque showgirl then dropping to the floor in avant-garde writhings impossible to classify. Dix nodded his head and I fought an urge to look at my feet. At last the music ended, Dix and I clapped and Sylvie broke her final pose, slumping back onto the ground looking like she hadn't broken sweat. She smiled and said, 'That was my audition piece.'

*   *   *

I woke in the morning with a dread of my forthcoming performance, a sore head, dry throat and only a vague recollection of the night's end. I rolled over, hoping against hope to see Sylvie's dark head beside me, but the rest of the bed was empty, the sheets rumpled as if I had been thrashing about, though the stiffness in my back suggested I'd slept like the dead.

After Sylvie's dance it had been my turn for a party piece. Sylvie had produced a pack of cards and asked me to give them a show. I'd palmed them for the deck in my pocket and given my hosts a simple routine. She'd been full of gasps and exaggerated wonder but Uncle had kept his cool, looking like he'd seen it all before. After a while he'd asked, 'So are cards just for tricks or can you play serious games?'

'Like what?'

'Like poker.'

He inclined his head, his face so card-sharp straight it was hard not to laugh. I guess the grass had started to work on me by then. I pushed down the giggles and said, 'Sometimes.'

'Any good?'

I folded the deck into a fancy weave.

'Too good to play you for money when I'm accepting your hospitality.'

'Ah, that good.' He took the pack from me and riffled them into a neat shuffle. 'I'd like to see you play all the same.'

'Fine by me if we make it a friendly stake.'

Dix looked amused and I wondered if he thought I was after his grass or his girl, if indeed she was his girl, but then Sylvie went to her bag and threw a couple of matchbooks onto the table and the moment passed. I picked one up and started to strip the flimsy paper matches from it. The cover was glossy black, printed with a gold image. A woman dressed only in knickers and crisscrossing fishnets had tumbled into a fancy

116

cocktail where she now sat, laughing. Her bosoms were as round and as buoyant as the bubbles floating from the glass. Her long legs kicked happily beyond its rim, her arms raised in a *ta-da* showgirl gesture. The cover read *Ein Enchanted Nachtreview.*

Dix broke into my thoughts. 'You do the casinos a lot?'

I shook my head, not wanting to get into it, my hand going to the small scar near my left eye.

'In my younger days.' I watched as he dealt a hand. 'But casinos are trained to be suspicious.'

Dix laid the last card on the table and left the pack face-down, next to the ashtray. 'They don't like you to win too much.'

I picked up my cards and sorted them quickly into suites. 'It wouldn't be good business.'

We played a couple of hands, aces low, in more or less silence. I called canny, watching the cards, memorising sequences, noting who had what and what had gone before. The first two hands I won were calculated luck. But by the third I had the measure of the pack and though my voice stayed smooth and my movements were slow and gentle my strategy was full-on edgy.

Dix didn't have my grasp, I'd spotted any luckies that chance dealt him and without a monster hand he had the odds of a borstal boy with a yearning for Eton. He lost with the same calm disinterest that had characterised his moves all night, but I thought his lazy eyes betrayed a brighter keenness than they'd shown before. The whisky was a quarter lower than when we'd started. I poured my hosts a measure each, slipping a small tot into my own glass. Catching Dix looking at me over his

117

deal, I wondered if he'd noticed that since the game began I'd been drinking less and inhaling so light it barely counted. Sylvie was beginning to look bored. She spread her cards into a careless fan. I said, 'Sylvie, I can see your cards.'

And she pressed them flat against her chest, like a colonial lady startled into a heart flutter.

'That's how he does it, X-ray vision.'

'Hey, no, honey,' I affected an American old-timer accent. 'I just know when to hold them, know when to fold them, know when to walk away and know when to run.'

Dix ignored our banter. His voice had the rusty edge to it again.

'I think there's a story you're not telling us. If it was me I'd forget this trickster stuff and do the casinos.'

I levelled my stare at him and put my cards down with a flourish, winning the final hand and leaving the others with the old stains of coffee cups where their stake used to be. Even without a penny of gain it was a good feeling and I spoke to remind myself of my priorities.

'I'm a performer.'

Dix pushed the rest of the matchstick jackpot towards me. 'Your choice man, but it seems a waste. With all these matches you could start a really big fire.'

'Could do, but then things might get a bit hot.'

He nodded. 'I understand. But you got a gift, seems a shame to waste it. There are a lot of good casinos in Berlin. We could go to Alexanderplatz right now and clean up more than you'll make in a week of hiding aces up your sleeve.'

I reached over to Sylvie and palmed a gold coin

from behind her ear, presenting it to her with a small flourish, showing Dix's slight on my knack didn't faze me. Sylvie giggled but he looked unimpressed.

'Maybe you don't want to play the casinos, I can understand that.' He raised a hand absentmindedly to his eye and for the first time I noticed a fading rack of small bruises on his knuckles. 'But there are a lot of bored rich men in the world, you find a trick to entertain them, something special, some private show, then you'd collect big money.'

'Maybe we'll do that one night.'

'You let me know.' Dix's stare was serious. 'Right now you're wasting your talent. Think about it. You have the audience watching you, maybe a pretty girl by your side and what do you do? Wave your wand and make her disappear or cut a piece of string in two then put it back together again.' He shook his head at the futility of my act. 'You've got quick hands, a fast memory,' he grinned, 'you can make people see things that aren't there. That's a hell of a skill. You change your mind you tell me. I've got good connections in this city.'

I nodded then squared the cards and slid them back into their box, not wanting to hear any get-rich-quick schemes or remember the kind of trouble my nimble fingers could get me into.

'So "Uncle", is it an honorary title or a real one?'

He shrugged.

'Of course it is an honour.'

Sylvie replaced the dead candles on the hearth with fresh ones and we lit them with my winnings. The talk moved on and so did the night while we continued making a dent in Dix's grass and killing

119

the whisky, until everything faded.

*   *   *

I hauled myself out of bed, realising I'd gone to sleep in my contact lenses again. Vanity would send me blind. My trousers and shirt were in a bundle at the bottom of the bed. It looked like an alien had come along and zapped me off for an anal probe, leaving my clothes shrivelled on the ground behind me. I listened for noises, coughed into the silence, then dressed and went into the hall, trying to remember which door led to the bathroom.

The bathroom was kidney-shrivelling cold. I was midstream when I heard a noise behind me and glanced over my shoulder. Sylvie stood in the doorway wrapped in a thin floral robe. She rubbed her eyes and said, 'Don't mind me.' Then turned on the tap and started to wash her face. It's hard to be nonchalant while peeing, but I did my best.

'Sleep well?' I did a final shake over the pan and zipped myself away.

'Not so much sleep as pass out.' She patted her face dry with a grey-looking towel. 'How 'bout you?'

'The same.'

Sylvie hung the towel back up and did a quick shuffle, hopping from foot to foot.

I said, 'Cool dance.'

And she made a face.

'Very funny, you finished there?'

We swapped places and she seated herself, holding her long dressing-gown around her thighs. She had thick woolly socks on her feet, but I had

120

the impression that other than that she was naked under her robe. A thin trickling filled the room. I did the gentlemanly thing and looked in the mirror. I needed a shave and my breath probably stank, but the night hadn't left too much of a mark on my face. Thoughts of the show were still bothering me. I would have to get away soon. Somewhere on my own where I could start thinking how I might tailor my act to this new audience. Behind me Sylvie sighed.

'That's better.'

I looked towards her then looked away quick, catching her blotting herself dry. My contact lenses eased away from my eyes, letting the world blur to the state where everything looked fine. I splashed my face with cold water.

'Dix has a razor and stuff if you want to use it.'

'I'll be OK.' I held up my toilet bag. 'You forget I've got all my worldly possessions with me.'

'There's a lot to be said for that.'

Sylvie put the toilet-lid down and sat on it, looking at me as I brushed my teeth.

'Yep.' I spat out the foam and rinsed my mouth. 'Just an old jakie, footloose and fancy-free.'

'A jakie?'

'A tramp, a hobo.'

'But you've got ties in the UK right? A house and kids and all that shit?'

'No house, no kids, not even a budgie; indeed no loved ones of any description.'

'No family?'

'Well there's me old mum, but we don't see much of each other.'

'Wow.'

I reached for the towel then remembered its

121

greyness and dried my face on the hem of my shirt. Sylvie's expression was blurred but I thought she was smiling.

'All done?'

'My normal regime includes a mudpack and a seaweed wrap but I suppose I'll have to make an exception today.'

'Hungry?'

'Hank Marvin.'

'What?'

'Starving.'

She laughed and pushed me playfully from the room.

'Well here's the deal. You let me get ready and I'll let you take me out for breakfast.' She started to close the door behind me. 'You know, a girl needs a bit of privacy sometimes.'

*   *   *

Sylvie took me to a small Turkish cafe on the corner of her street. The aged proprietor smiled when he saw her and they exchanged greetings in a quick slick German while he settled us at a small pavement table. The old man shouted something through the door of the cafe and pretty soon a young waiter appeared with a tray carrying tiny cups and a tall curvy coffee pot. He handed me a menu printed in English. Sylvie snatched it away good-naturedly, ordering for both of us, saying something that made the waiter laugh then glance at me shyly before he went back inside to prepare our breakfast.

I massaged my temples above my right eyebrow, wondering why my hangovers always concentrated

122

there. Perhaps it was some congenital weakness that would only be diagnosed after I suddenly dropped dead. I wondered if I'd die on-stage, collapsing in the middle of a trick, everyone thinking I'd done it for comic effect. Folk said it was the way Tommy Cooper would've wanted to go. I'd never met him but it seemed like a nightmare exit to me. The sound of embarrassed laughter and the audience whispering to each other that they couldn't believe what an old ham you'd become.

We sat there, bundled against the cold. Sylvie poured, steam curled from the spout and the rich scent of thick sweet coffee began to lift my hangover. We both lit up, adding cigarette smoke and warm breath to the mix.

'You've got a good grasp of the lingo.'

'I went to school here.'

'Careful, Sphinx, you're telling me things about yourself.'

She smiled.

'There's no big mystery. It's just, who needs the past? Dix says we should let go and he's right. What's the point in looking back? We live for now.'

'Where is Dix? Still in bed?'

'Why?'

'No reason. Nosiness. I wanted to say thanks.'

'I'll tell him thanks for you.'

'Thanks for that.' We both laughed and I said, 'No, I mean it, thanks. I would've been walking the streets last night if it hadn't been for you.'

'It was no problem.'

'Well, I owe you one.'

She put her elbows on the table and propped her sharp little chin against her fists. 'Wanna pay me back?'

I remembered for the first time that she'd been waiting for me for a reason. My voice was cautious.

'If I can.'

'Will you see if there's any jobs going for dancers at your place?'

'Sure.'

The waiter brought out two sticky pastries and Sylvie dropped the subject, telling me instead about her Berlin, shops and cafes not listed in the guidebook, streets to search out and a couple to avoid. She talked quickly, taking distracted puffs at her cigarette between bites, laughing often and making me laugh in response. She spoke with her mouth full, somehow still managing to look good. The waiter came out to check whether we wanted anything else and Sylvie ordered a second round of coffees. The two of us lingered on at the pavement table though it should have been too cold to sit outside. We smoked more cigarettes and discussed the passers-by, people with places to go, each of us pretending to be shocked by the slanders the other concocted about perfect strangers.

Eventually the thoughts of that night's show, which had been tugging at my mind since I woke that morning, became too uncomfortable to ignore. I stubbed out the last of my cigarette and pushed my empty coffee cup to one side.

'I'd best get going.'

'People to do, things to see?'

'A show to fix.'

She smiled.

'It wasn't so bad.'

'Wasn't so good either.'

'You'll fix it. You just need to work out an

124

angle.'

'I guess so.'

We swapped mobile numbers and I promised again to ring her if anything came up. It crossed my mind that I might phone her anyway, but then thoughts of Uncle Dix intruded. *Uncle Dix,* where did people get off with these weird names? Styling himself like some Weimar pimp. I bet even now he was cursing the late night and getting ready for some second-rate lecturing job. No, I probably wouldn't phone. I gave her a last wave then strode onto the street and hailed a taxi to take me to my hotel.

*   *   *

It was early in the afternoon when I stepped out and started to walk towards the theatre.

I'd been in the shower when the phone had rung. I'd assumed it was a wrong number, then when the ringing persisted thought it might be someone from Schall und Rauch. I'd answered half-draped in a towel, wondering why it was I seemed to be naked whenever the phone rang, though I was sure I was clothed most of my waking hours. I picked up the receiver, saying, 'Ja?' Assuming whoever it was would appreciate the effort.

'William? That you?' My agent evidently thought he should shout even louder when talking to someone abroad. 'What's with the Ja? You gone native? You'll be singing 'Tomorrow Belongs to Me' and sieg-heiling next.'

I started to rub myself dry.

'Times have changed Rich. They don't go in for

125

that anymore.'

'Once a Nazi always a Nazi. Anyway, where have you been?' He didn't give me a chance to reply. 'Don't you ever check your bloody messages?'

For the first time I noticed the red light flashing on the hotel-room phone. 'You could have rung my mobile.'

'I tried that. Dead, wasn't it?'

'So where's the fire?'

'Have you seen an English newspaper today?'

'No.'

'Well get yourself a *Daily Telegraph* then phone me back.'

'A *Telegraph*, you been checking your stocks and shares, Richard?'

'Just do it. I'll speak to you in five.'

The line went dead. I looked at the receiver, shook my head then phoned down to the front desk and asked them to send out for a copy of the paper. I'd finished my interrupted shower and was just retying the towel around my waist when the knock came at the door. I tipped the porter, locked the door behind him, sat down on the bed and turned the pages.

It was the photograph that I saw first, a picture of a younger stern-faced Bill that might have been a police mug shot, or might just have been a poor passport photo. There was a picture of the club too. An outside shot that looked vaguely dated, though I wasn't sure why. There was also, chillingly, a small photograph of Sam onstage from what must have been a long while ago. He looked younger, hopeful, his head thrown back in a laugh. I'd seen him laugh like that often.

I turned to the text though the headline had

126

already given me the substance of the news, *CLUB SHOOTING SLAYS TWO*. The building's new owners had gone on a tour of inspection and found Bill and Sam in the office, each lying in a pool of his own blood. The verdict so far was murder and suicide, the finger pointing towards Sam. My balls climbed up towards my belly. I laid the paper down on the bed, poured myself an unnecessarily chilled Famous Grouse from the minibar, downed it, then read on.

The article was big on photographs and low on facts, though it mentioned a jail sentence Bill had served for extortion and referred to his father, calling him a businessman in a way that would leave no one in any doubt of which side of the law he favoured. The whole family was pictured, the biggest space reserved for his mother, Gloria. Montgomery had promised to tell Bill the truth about his mother. Bill had said she was gone. If I'd thought anything of it, I'd assumed death or divorce. The newspaper revealed that she'd gone missing some time in the seventies, her fate never discovered, though after all this time the obvious conclusion was that she was dead.

I'd shut the adventure at Bill's Soho club in a neat trunk in the corner of my mind. I visualised the trunk. It was an old seaman's chest. The wood dry and peeling with age, banded with thin strips of black steel. There was a strong padlock clamped tight in its metal hasp. I unlocked it, opened the lid and started to examine my situation.

I thought of Montgomery standing outside the door and Sam thrusting the envelope into my hand. I thought of the envelope lying unopened somewhere in my mother's bungalow in

Cumbernauld. I was sure Sam was innocent, a victim. He wouldn't be the first person to pay the ultimate price for falling for a bad boy. Maybe they were both victims. If Sam hadn't insisted on a peaceful approach perhaps Bill would have been more on his guard. But then maybe the business with Montgomery had been settled amicably after all. Bill was a gangster. Who knew how many enemies he'd made? There might have been a queue lining up to settle old scores before he and Sam sailed into the sun.

If Montgomery had had anything to do with the shootings I didn't want him to have an inkling that I'd been on the scene when he'd shown up. That meant not alerting any of his chums in the police. If he hadn't had anything to do with the killings then I was of no practical use to any investigation. Whatever way I looked at it, I was best sitting quiet and letting people who were used to this kind of thing get on with it.

The phone buzzed back into life.

'You found it yet?'

'Yes.'

'Whadda you think?'

'I don't know. Tragic.'

'Yeah, yeah, young lives cut short and all that, but that wasn't what I meant. What do you know?'

My voice was defensive.

'Nothing.'

'Don't be so touchy. I know you wouldn't get mixed up in anything heavy, William. Silliness with drink and women, yes, the odd dabble with drugs possibly, but heavy stuff, no.' The line went quiet while my agent took a long drag on his cigarette then exhaled and resumed his monologue. 'So you feel no sudden urge to go and present yourself to the police?'

'No.'

'Good, 'cos it would fuck up your Berlin gig that's for sure.'

'Yeah.' I made an effort to keep my voice casual. 'That's what I was thinking.'

Hundreds of miles away in Crouch End Richard grunted into the phone.

'You know what bum boys are like, William, unstable.'

'You seem to know a lot about it.'

'Well I would do working in this trade wouldn't I?' He sighed. I've got nothing against poofs, William, but they're a race apart.'

Disgust at Rich, myself, the whole sorry business suddenly filled me. I snapped, 'You knew Sam, don't you feel anything for him?'

Rich's voice was sharp.

'I'll do my mourning on my own time, William.' His tone softened. 'Look, I'm not saying it isn't sad and I'm not saying he deserved it, but Sam always was reckless. You remember the way he walked out of that summer tour.'

'It's hardly the same thing.'

'Maybe not, but he wasn't what you'd call steady. I mean what was he doing hanging around with the likes of Bill in the first place? Get yourself mixed up with that sort and you take what you get.'

'I suppose so.'

'Anyway don't be surprised if you're called back to Blighty to answer a few questions.'

I drew the towel closer round me.

'How d'you make that out?'

'All those bloody coppers on a police balls-out?

129

Only a matter of time before one of them drops you in it.'

'I'd not thought of that.'

'No, well that's why you're schlepping around Krautland while I sit in a nice warm office with Mrs Pierce putting the kettle on.' He took another asthmatic pull at his cigarette. 'Speaking of Krautland, how's the gig going?'

'Bloody awful.'

'Pull your finger out and sort it then. I've told you before, you need a bit of glamour. Fix yourself up with a nice Fräulein to saw in two and you'll be laughing.'

'It's just teething problems, you didn't tell me the erotic nature of the club.'

Richard laughed.

'Didn't I?'

'No you bloody didn't.'

'Oh well, keep your hand on your ha'penny and you'll be fine.'

'I'll do my best.'

'That's the boy.' I heard the quick tap of computer keys and knew the phone call was coming to an end. My agent's voice took on a self-consciously compassionate tone. 'I'll get Mrs P to find out when Sam's funeral is and send along a nice wreath.'

'Thanks, Rich.'

'Don't worry, son, it's coming out your wages. Now you put all this from your mind and concentrate on making magic magical. OK?'

'OK.'

'Good boy.'

He hung up with his usual abruptness. I sat on the bed for a while, staring blankly at the wall,

130

then tied the towel around my waist, went to the wardrobe, took my mobile phone from my jacket pocket and turned it on. The screen glowed lazily awake. Richard's unanswered calls were logged like accusations. But slid in beside his familiar phone number was a number not featured on my address book, a British number I didn't recognise. The mobile suddenly sprang back into life. I dropped it on the bed and stepped backwards, giving a small groan and looking at the tiny machine with all the horror I'd show a crawling, disembodied hand. My instincts were against it but on the third ring I reached out, pressed the call accept button and raised the phone to my ear.

A voice said, 'Hello?'

And I hung up. Almost immediately the mobile resumed its buzzing. I turned it off, went through to the en suite, filled the sink and dropped the phone into the water. Tiny bubbles rose from it, almost like the phone was breathing its last. I'd heard the police could trace locations through sim cards, but I had no idea if it worked overseas. Maybe I was overreacting. Maybe Sam had done for Bill then killed himself. Maybe I was safe as houses in Berlin, and maybe it hadn't been Inspector James Montgomery's voice I'd just heard at the end of the line.

Glasgow

For all of the warnings drink seemed a pretty slow killer. Not like a knife in the guts or a bullet through the head. Looking at the men that lived in

131

the pubs around the Gallowgate it appeared you could reach sixty or seventy on a diet of whisky, beer and bile. But perhaps the drinkers I took for pensionable were raddled thirty-somethings and it wouldn't be long before I looked the same. I stared in the mirror and whispered, 'Bring it on.'

Already my waist had thickened; there was a scaliness between my fingers that itched more at night. My skin had the porridge pallor of a prisoner after a six-month stretch. I'd abandoned vanities like deodorant, cologne and contact lenses. My specs added three years, though they were a mite flash for my current circumstances. I wondered if I should get a new pair, ones that didn't mark me out as a man who had known better days. My hair was longer too. I could go a full fortnight without showing it the shampoo. And there was no need for mousse or gel or any other crap. I just swept it back with my fingertips and left it as nature intended—which seemed to be a dirty brown flecked through with dandruff. Add to that the new old clothes I'd bought at Paddy's Market and, all in all, I was managing my decline pretty well.

When I was a boy my heroes were two great escape artists, Harry Houdini and Jesse James. I borrowed library books about them, read up on their exploits and stared deep into black and white photographs of two men so skilled they could only be killed by cowards. In my fantasies I was the cowboy magician, no bonds could hold me and I was swift enough to sidestep a punch in the guts or any bullet in the back.

I jammed so many yales and mortises my father decided we were under siege and called the police.

But in time my picking grew smooth. I freed tethered dogs, opened padlocks to sheds, gates and lockups. I released jangles of bicycle chains and liberated telephone dials from locks designed to frustrate teenage sisters. I bought a pair of trick handcuffs and taught myself to unfasten them with a dismantled hair clasp stolen from my mother. I hung about the locksmith's shop, begged adults for old keys. My fingers were twitching to try their skill on a safe, but round our way there was nothing that worth securing, so I kept on the alert for a gang of thieves on the lookout for a nimble-fingered boy. They wouldn't need to promise me lemonade streams or big rock-candy mountains; all I wanted was a chance to click that dial to the right combination. I'd be their creature and if we got caught, no great matter, I'd unlock the prison and set us free. But no wily crew ever spotted my talents and once mastered there was no drama in solitary achievements. Jesse had his pursuers, Houdini his audience. So of course I decided to organise my own great escape.

Ten-year-old boys have more access to padlocks and chains than adults might think. I invited the kids in my street to collect all they could find, and leave the keys behind. We met down by the railway line in an abandoned signal box that had once been boarded shut. They came with dog leashes, belts and skipping ropes. They came with rusty iron links that had hung round gates for years. One boy brought a pair of handcuffs he said he'd found at the bottom of his parents' wardrobe. I gave a short speech, and then chose the prettiest girl in the group to come and tie me up. She was too shy, but the boys obliged, setting on me with cowboy whoops and primitive yells. I flexed my non-existent muscles, like I'd read Houdini had done, and kept my face straight, though the bellows and rough jabs from the boys all eager to bind me as secure as possible made me want to struggle. Eventually I was trussed. Some of the strapping was slack but at its core was a tight tangle of metal, a firm pressure through my clothes and onto my flesh. My hands were cuffed behind my back. I felt a strange excitement in my stomach. The boys stepped away, I put on a deep voice that demanded they leave me for fifteen minutes precisely; the audience hesitated and my vulnerability entered the room. I gave them a strong hard stare. Then Ewan McIvor, the tallest of the group, said, 'He's a fucking weirdo.' Neil Blane picked up the refrain, 'Weirdy Wilson.' And it became hard to make out individual insults beneath the melee of abuse. *Stupid fucking poof . . . silly cunt . . . weirdy bastard . . . Jessie . . . fucking spazmo . . . Joey Deakon . . .*

Ewan pushed me to the ground and the others joined in with quick kicks and jabs, then almost as suddenly as it had started the assault was over. They turned and ran whooping out into the sunshine, slamming the door behind them.

It wasn't completely black in the hut. Light filtered in through cracks in the untrue slats, but it was dark enough to give the old signalling equipment a sinister aspect. I bumped up onto my bottom, brought my hands round in front of me and grasped the small metal pick I'd hidden beneath my tongue. Then I got my second shock of the adventure. Police handcuffs are not as easy to unfasten as the trick set I'd been practising on.

134

It was dinner-time before my mother noticed I was missing. Neighbours' children were interrogated and my fate soon discovered. My father shook his head, borrowed a pair of bolt cutters and set off to release me. The summer nights are long in Scotland, and it was not quite yet gloaming when he found me. But the shadows inside the signal box had spread their fingers until the little space was black. The darkness had crept inside my clothes, filtered into my nose and mouth, and slunk into my ears until I was unsure whether the rustling noises and groans came from the trees and grasses outside or from some creature inside the box with me.

My father ruffled my hair, and slowly cut my bonds, scolding and comforting in turn, finally releasing me, piss stained, snot crusted and tearful, into my mother's custody. That was the first time I learned a fact that has haunted me throughout my return to Glasgow. I can't stand to be locked up and I was never destined to be an escape artist.

*   *   *

After a few of my usual consolations I decided I was finished with pubs for that morning, so I bought myself a picnic and went down to the Clyde to drink it. In Berlin the rivers and canals were part of the centre of the city, there was bathing and boating, tourist barges and river taxis. People sunned themselves and played tennis and frisbee by the banks of the Spree, and though there were rainy days I only ever went there when it was sunny, so my impression is of brightness and good times.

It was damp down by the Clyde. The concrete

walkway was deserted but there were signs others had been there before me, rusting beer cans, dead bottles of Buckfast, old porno magazines splaying already splayed women in the breeze. There were a few boats moored by the riverside, but the water was lead-grey dead, if I'd had any thoughts of drowning myself I would have ditched them for the day. The water was too cold to consider it. It would swallow you with a slurp and no word of pardon afterwards.

I walked along by the edge for a while trying to keep my mind empty. I didn't bother trying to conceal my carry-out from the early afternoon. It swung from my hand in the kind of thin plastic bag licensed grocers seem to think sufficient for transporting lager, though every drinker knows they'll bend and snap before you've walked a mile.

An old man with Struwwelpeter hair lay skippered in the shadows beneath Jamaica Bridge. He'd made a nest from an army-issue sleeping bag supplemented by a bundle of rough-looking blankets and some dismantled cardboard boxes. A tattered tartan trolley stuffed with newspapers lay toppled on the ground beside him. The old man mumbled something and I leant beneath the bridge's supports and passed him a can of lager. It was more a plea for karma than any kind of sympathy, but the old tramp tipped his hand to his forehead and whispered 'God go with you son' in a voice raw with phlegm and cold. I nodded and said, 'And with you.' Though I thought any god had probably given up on both of us a long while back.

I found a bench, tucked my supplies neatly beneath its seat and settled myself down with my first tin, pulling the collar of my jacket up. It was pretty bitter down there by the river, but there was a distant gleam somewhere across the sky and it was no longer impossible to believe that spring was somewhere in the beyond. I took a sip of the beer. The liquid was warmer than the air outside, but it was better quality than the stuff I'd been supping in the bar. These old tramps were obviously men of discernment. Who knows what I might learn if I joined their ranks?

Berlin

The sound of Montgomery's voice had sent me out into the street cursing Bill with his public-school vowels and his gangster pretensions that got people killed. This whole escapade was nothing to do with me.

There was money in my pocket; I could catch a flight that afternoon if I wanted. I fished out the scrap of paper Sylvie had written her number on. It took me a while to find a phone box, and then it took me a while to follow the instructions in German, but eventually the phone at the other end started to ring. Sylvie picked up and I asked her, 'Still looking for a job?'

'You found something already?'

'How do you fancy working with me for a while as my assistant?'

I left the phone booth with her shriek of excitement still ringing in my ears and started to walk towards the theatre, wondering what was inside the envelope I had sent home.

Glasgow

Seagulls were cackling above the Clyde. They made low, swift, argumentative swoops towards the water, maybe remembering times when they fished for their supper, instead of splitting restaurant rubbish bags and vying with urban vermin for abandoned takeaways. I wondered why they chose to live in this city when there were swathes of white sandy beaches and clear seawaters up north on the coast, but then who was I to judge? I raised my can to the sky and said, 'Go on yoursels. Away and shite on as many heads as you can.'

A posse of neds sloped down the walkway towards me. I lowered my eyes and tilted my head so they wouldn't catch me following their progress. The last thing I wanted to hear was the immortal line, 'What the fuck're you looking at?' A prelude to a Glasgow kiss or worse. There were five of them, dressed in trainers and shell suits, each with their hood up, hands in pockets. They had an excited bouncing walk, their heads bowed towards the ground, torsos nodding in rhythm with their feet. I could hear their keyed-up voices growing louder as they got closer and cursed myself for choosing this deserted spot. If they wanted to they could hold me down, fillet me and leave me for the seagulls. I slid my can into my pocket and kept my eyes fixed on the further shore, watching them with my peripheral vision. Their voices were high and nasal, tossing some recent adventure between them.

'You pure gave him a doin'.'
'Split his head like a coconut.'
'A jammy coconut.'
'Jammy donut.'
'Fuckin' jammy fanny.'
'Fucking mental, man.'

One of the boys glanced at me. I saw a fine spray of rust-red droplets across his nose, like a delicate dusting of freckles. His face was as pale as mine, but instead of the graveyard grey of my complexion, his was the milk white of youth before the acne sets in. In another life he might have been a model or a movie actor. Our eyes locked and the boy peeled his top lip into a sneer. I thought *fuck, here we go* and got ready to spring into the kick-off. Then one of his companions gave a shout of sheer joy, and I saw a Miami-blue launch cutting through the water churning two great wings of white spume in its wake. The boys' heads turned, following its progress, then they began to run, keeping it in their sight. I saw one of them lift a stick and throw it towards the water, knowing he had no chance of hitting it, but wanting somehow to be part of the boat.

I took my can out of my pocket, noting that my hands were trembling. All the same I wondered at the quick stab of fear I'd felt. They were only boys and I had done worse than any of them would ever accomplish.

Berlin

The theatre doorman was slumped behind a newspaper in his booth at the stage door. I rapped gently against the glass and he snorted awake, harrumphing like an old dog who's lain by the fire too long.

Early in my career I learnt the importance of cultivating that all-powerful alliance of janitors, cleaners, ushers and doormen, the people who can lose your fliers and cut your rehearsal time to the minimum or allow you free access to the building and gift you gossip that might solve all your disputes with the management. I gave the doorman one of my best smiles and he gave me a hard stare that suggested he'd seen my type before and hadn't been impressed. The newspaper started to go up again. Still smiling, I rapped on the window.

'Guten Morgen,' I nodded towards a poster of the younger brighter version of myself. The doorman looked at it blankly then returned his gaze to me. His eyes had taken on a deliberate vacancy. The smile was beginning to ache, but I'm a pro, I kept it strained in place and asked, 'Do you speak English?'

The doorman's stare was cold. I fished out the bargain imprint German phrasebook I'd bought at Heathrow, but there was no entry for, *I'm a conjurer performing here tonight; please let me in so I can do some preparation.* I stepped next to the poster, pointing at it, then at myself, sure he was buggering me about but not willing to lose my temper.

'That's me . . . Das ist . . .' I pointed at the poster again. 'Ich bin . . .'

The doorman grunted and lifted the newspaper. Then something caught his attention, he straightened in his seat, smoothed back his hair and a small smile touched his lips. I followed his gaze and saw Ulla dismounting from her bicycle. She was wearing the same scuffed jeans she'd had on yesterday, but her hair was tied back in a neat ponytail and her shirt was clean. She looked like an advert for shampoo or sanitary towels or some other product that required a fresh, feminine, sporty beauty.

'Morgen.'

Her smile took in both of us, but I thought the doorman got the lion's share of its warmth. He returned her greeting then said something indicating me. Ulla laughed and the two talked for a few minutes that seemed like an age, leaving me stranded beside the image of my more promising self. At last the guard buzzed open the main door and let us into the building. I gave him a cheery *Danke* as I passed, but the newspaper was already back in place, shielding his face from the light of the corridor.

Ulla's smile seemed all used up but her voice was apologetic.

'Sorry, I should have given you a pass yesterday.'

'No problem, you got me through Check Point Charlie.' She gave me a sharp look and I cursed my stupidity. 'Sorry.'

There was a fork ahead in the corridor. Ulla hesitated, probably waiting to see what direction I chose so she could take the other.

141

'So you have everything you need?'

'More or less, but I could do with an intro to your chippy.'

She looked confused.

'My what?'

'The theatre joiner, carpenter, the man who makes the sets.'

Further down the hallway a door opened and Kolja stepped out. He stood silently watching us, dressed in his sweats again, his chest naked and shining. Ulla smiled and raised her hand in greeting. I muttered 'Big poof' under my breath and she turned to me.

'Pardon?'

'Nothing.'

She explained where to find the props department then walked off to greet Kolja. My eyes did an involuntary drop to her taut denim-clad rear. Whatever my trials, whatever my vicissitudes I always retained my aesthetic sense. It was a comfort of sorts. I looked up, saw the athlete watching me and raised my hand in a greeting I knew would go unanswered, then went in search of my quarry, wishing buffed-up krauts and a clumsiness with women was all I had to worry about.

The joiner had worked for a while in Newcastle and was keen to use his English. We discovered mutual acquaintances amongst the Newcastle theatre crowd, swapped experiences of brown ale, and then I explained what I wanted. He looked at my designs, asking a couple of questions, nodding to show he understood the answers and promised to have what I needed ready for the following week.

Sylvie was small and lithe, pretty, witty and clever. With her help I would build an act that would astonish this city. As for the other business, I couldn't really believe it had anything to do with me. I'd stay here, work out my contract, and if there was any trouble I'd deal with it when it appeared.

Glasgow

I bent my empty can in two, scuttled it beneath the bench, then broke the seal on another and took a big swig. The Clyde was a still, battleship-grey, a shade lighter than the drear of the sky, a shade darker than the drab of the concrete. The only splash of colour came from the septic yellow label on an empty bottle of tonic wine rolled in the verge. There was an extra note to the dampness now. It would rain soon.

Dealing with trouble later was a stupid strategy. If anyone asked me now I'd say always meet trouble halfway. At least then you might have the advantage of surprise.

It had grown cold by the river. I wondered how people managed to stay alive sleeping under the bridges in the green damp. Did their skin give in to verdigris and decay, their bodies mistaking this preparation for the grave for the real thing?

Somewhere in the city a clock struck three. The four cans had hit home and the fifth might just get me near to where I wanted to be. My legs felt as leaden as the landscape. I got up and gave them a shake, trying to shift the stiffness, then started to wander back the way I had come, taking occasional pulls from my last can as I went.

The bundle of rags that was the old man I'd given the beer to still nestled at the foot of one of the wide stone pillars of the bridge. I hesitated, listening to see if I could hear any wisdom in his mumbles. But if he was saying anything it was lost in the rumble of early evening traffic from the road above.

Fuck listening. Confession was meant to be good for the soul and here was someone I could talk to without fear of judgement or retribution. I'd honour this old king of the road with a portion of my most precious worldly possession, my final can. I'd tell him what had brought me to this, and perhaps he'd share his decline with me.

I eased myself down towards his nest.

I'd be the new uncrowned prince of decay. He'd bequeath me his sores, his scabs and scaly skin, the lice that played amongst his beard. I'd learn what itching was. I'd be the itchiest itching tramp that ever frightened a schoolchild or tapped on a restaurant window. There was a strong smell beneath the bridge, but drink and cold are kind to the nasal passages; it didn't bother me.

'Hello, pal, how're you doing?' The bundle of rags lay motionless, but I could see the electric aureole of grey hair escaping the blanket. 'There's a wee sip of lager here if you want it.' It was still cold, but the pillar gave a bit of shelter from the wind. Outside it started to rain. 'This is a rare spot you've found yourself.' The old man was silent. 'Not feeling like a blether? Aye well, that's fair enough.' I got down from my haunches and sat on the ground with my knees pulled up to my chest.

144

'Do you mind if I share your wee space just for the now?' I took another sip of lager. If he was asleep it meant I didn't have to share. 'Just tell me if you do and I'll piss right off.' I thought perhaps he shifted, but maybe it was just a stray breeze finding its way beneath the shelter, ruffling at his hair. 'You're me.' I sought for the words to explain what I meant. 'You are the way I'm heading. But just 'cos you're me disnae mean I'm you.' I took another sip from the can. 'You had your own road here I guess. I hope it wasn't as bad as mine.' I laughed. 'Jesus Christ, man, I could tell you a story.'

The rain picked up a little outside. It was warmer under the bridge than I'd expected. It was true; these old jakies knew a thing or two. The can was almost empty. I'd have to move soon, walk back up to the real world of cars and traffic, find myself a pub and grab a final pint or two. Yes it was a damn sight cosier down here out of the wind and the rain. I closed my eyes. It wasn't such a bad place to stop for a while. I listened to the whirling cackles of the seagulls and the even rumble of the traffic. My last thought was that I could almost be beside the sea. Then I shut my eyes and gave myself up to the warmth and the black.

*　　　　*　　　　*

It was a white light that woke me. A pure searing cocaine white that peeled open my eyelids then forced them shut. There was a man behind the beam. His voice was stern, but there was a weary quality to it that made me think the sternness was an act.

145

'Come on, you know you can't sleep there.'

I shrank back, shielding my face with my hands, like a disgraced businessman trying to hide from the camera flashes of the press. Behind the bright light I could make out the figure of a policeman. My specs were skewed across my face. I straightened them and whispered, 'Montgomery?'

But that was a nonsense. He hadn't worn a uniform and anyway he wasn't as big as the man that was reaching towards me and rattling my arm in a shake.

'Come on, rise and shine.'

I tried to get to my feet but my legs were locked. The policeman dipped his torch and I levered myself onto my hands and knees, trying to remember how to work my limbs. I was beginning to recall where I was. There was bitter taste in my mouth and an explosion of bright spots behind my eyes.

'Look at the state of you.'

For the first time I noticed the second policeman to my left. He reached over and prodded my companion with his torch. It was a gentle businesslike prod. The old man remained motionless, his wild halo of hair the only part of him visible above the blanket.

'Give old Leonardo a shove will you.'

The smell was strong now, a mix of shit, urine, decay and something else, a rusty iron scent I almost recognised. I pushed down the nausea in my chest, leaned over and shook my companion softly by the shoulder.

'Come on, pal, I think it's time to move on.'

I thought the old man stirred, but then he started to slip slowly, oh so slowly sideways. I

146

reached out to steady him, felt a wetness soaking the rough weave of his blanket, felt him slump against me in a sickening softening lurch.

I said, 'Are you OK?'

Then the torches caught him in the centre of their beams, and I saw the face that rested on my shoulder, a John the Baptist head, bearded and bloody, mouth lolling open, sweet sticky redness glazing his frozen face. The whole petrified tableau framed in the white light.

I scrambled to my feet and felt a hard grip on my arm, helping me rise out of the filth. The policeman wasn't acting anymore. His words were caught in a sigh that was pure anger.

'Jesus fuck! What in Christ's name have you done?'

*   *   *

The police doctor who examined me was quick and businesslike. He prescribed a hot drink and pronounced me fit for interview. My clothes were put into plastic bags and I was issued with a white jumpsuit. I knew enough from the movies to ask for a solicitor and no one tried to talk me out of it. The cell was cold. I took the blanket off the bunk and draped it over my shoulders, then a wave of nausea hit me and I bent over the toilet. The orange police tea came up in a quick warm flush of liquid, followed by a painful gagging that only managed to cough up a thin streak of yellow bile. I'd corrupted the crime scene with the rest of my stomach contents when I realised what I'd been sleeping next to.

I rolled back onto the bed clutching the jaggy

brown blanket around me, not caring who else might have sweated into its coarse weave. I was shivering now. I pulled my knees up to my chest; the damp of the river still seemed to cling to me. I rubbed the blanket between my fingers. It had an animal smell, the odour of all the men who had been shut in here. I tried not to think about the noise the door had made as it closed, the turn of the key in the lock. Would it square accounts to do penance for a crime I hadn't committed in lieu of one that I had? I could feel sleep coming to claim me. How could I doze while I was at the centre of a murder? It was my last coherent thought before darkness claimed me. But then, the same thought had been in my head every night all of these long months.

*   *   *

I woke to the sound of the key turning the tumblers in the lock. Someone had set up a workshop in my head, but beneath the hammering in my skull and the filth of my own body I felt sharper than I had all night. I wondered what time it was. I'd handed in my watch at the front desk and the neon-lit cell gave no hint of how long had passed. The door opened and a concrete-faced policeman half-entered the room. 'Here's your solicitor, Wilson. Are you going to behave for her?' I swung myself upright on the bunk and nodded my head. 'See that you do.'

He turned and said something to the person standing behind him, then withdrew still holding the door open.

A slim dark-haired figure walked into the room

148

and I said, 'Ulla?' Feeling all the sharpness go out of me. And then I saw that she wasn't Ulla. I sought for where we had met. Desperation plucked the images from my brain. The ersatz theme bar that had been trendier than I'd realised. My old university buddy. A pair of violet eyes, and her name came to me. 'Eilidh.' The woman gave me a blank look. 'I'm a friend of Johnny's.'

Recognition clouded her face.

'Yes,' she said. 'William.'

The policeman stuck his head back round the door. 'Everything OK?'

Eilidh gave him a professional smile.

'It's fine.'

The door closed behind her. I'd thought I was immune to embarrassment but Eilidh's presence made me want to pull the manky prison blanket over my head and hide until she'd gone. I attempted a smile.

'I seem to have got myself into a bit of a scrape.' Eilidh's mouth twitched in a quick spasm.

'You're looking at a murder charge. What we need to establish is how are you going to plead? Guilty or not guilty?'

'I didn't do it.'

'OK.' Her voice was coolly neutral. I imagined she'd been brought up on tales of wrongful convictions, the Guildford four, Birmingham six, Maguire seven. Perhaps these injustices had even been what had turned her towards law, the chance to save innocent people from becoming victims of the judicial system. But then none of these people had been accused of beating an old defenceless man until his head resembled a rotten strawberry.

'No,' I made my voice firm, 'I really didn't do it.'

'OK.' The cool neutrality remained. She'd be one of the first to be dismissed from the hypnotist's audience. 'Take me quickly through what happened.'

I started with the walk along the Clydeside, giving the old man a can, my drinking session on the bench, and finally my urge to share my last drink with the old tramp.

'You don't believe me do you?'

Eilidh glanced up from the jotter she'd been scribbling notes into.

'It's not me you have to convince.'

*   *   *

The interview room was painted a pale shade of blue I supposed was designed to keep people calm. It seemed to work. There was a dead feeling in my chest where there should have been panic. Two plainclothes men were waiting on us, a red-haired, red-faced invitation to a heart attack and a large sandy-haired man with a broken nose and ginger moustache that would have looked good on a seventies' footballer. The sandy-haired man introduced himself as Inspector Blunt and his companion as Inspector Thomas. He placed a thin sheaf of papers on the table and asked, 'Anyone want a glass of water?'

I nodded, surprised to find that the words wouldn't come out.

Blunt looked at Eilidh. She smiled. 'Yes please.' And I got the feeling that they had faced each other this way many times before. The policeman fetched four plastic cups from a Water at Work cooler in the corridor. Thomas turned on the tape,

150

introduced himself to the machine, then got us to do the same. My voice sounded weak and untrustworthy. I reached out to take a sip of water and toppled the cup across the table. Blunt saved the tape recorder. Eilidh took out a paper hanky and mopped up the splash. No one offered to get me another drink and I guessed there was no point in asking to fetch one for myself.

The whole thing felt like a formality. The policemen behind the desk looked like they'd met too many men who had tried to drown their troubles in drink, and when that hadn't worked had tried to stab them away instead, to think that I was anything else. Blunt glanced at my written statement then looked up at me.

'Right, Mr Wilson, I'm not really getting this. You're unemployed, you decided to have a wee drink down by the River Clyde and then you fancied a bit of company, so instead of phoning a pal, or even taking yourself to a pub where you might run into someone you knew, you went to offer,' he glanced at the paper in front of him, 'the deceased, Mr Michael Milligan, a swig from the last of your can?'

He looked at me for confirmation and I nodded miserably.

'Mr Milligan seemed asleep and it came to you that this wasn't such a bad idea so you bedded down with him, under Jamaica Bridge, for forty winks?'

I nodded again.

'Except it turns out he wasn't asleep was he?'

'I didn't know that when I sat beside him.'

Red-faced Thomas spoke for the first time. His voice had a weedy treble tone that seemed out of kilter with his broad frame.

'You snuggled up beside a corpse and never noticed?'

'I didn't snuggle up with him. I was drunk. I fell asleep.'

Thomas's face grew redder. If there was ever trouble down at Blochairn fruit market he'd be able to go under-cover as a cherry tomato.

'Drink isnae an alibi.'

'It's not a bloody crime either.'

Inspector Blunt sighed; he looked at the statement again then turned his weary eyes on me.

'According to your statement you saw five youths going along the walkway at around the time the assault might have taken place.'

I nodded.

'You're suggesting that they're responsible for Mr Milligan's murder?'

'I don't know. It's a possibility.'

'You can see the difficulty I'm having with this, Mr Wilson?'

'I can see it's a bit unusual.'

'It's unbelievable.'

I glanced at Eilidh for support, but she stared ahead, her jaw sternly locked.

Inspector Blunt leaned forward and the tiredness seemed to have gone from his face.

'I think you did go for a walk by the Clyde and I have no doubt you had a drink on one of the benches down there. I'm even fairly confident that we'll find someone who saw you doing that very thing. But I don't think you went to kindly offer Mr Milligan a bit of hospitality. I think the opposite is true. You were angry and frustrated and that poor old man was in the wrong place at

152

the wrong time.'

'I didn't do it.'

'What did you use? A hammer?'

I stood up, balling my hands into fists.

'I didn't bloody use anything.'

Eilidh put her hand firmly on my arm and I sat down. The fat policeman looked like he was enjoying himself. His weedy treble piped up.

'You seem to have a bit of a temper there, Mr Wilson. Have you ever been in this kind of trouble before?'

'No.'

I lowered my head so he wouldn't see the lie on my face.

There was a sharp knock at the door; a uniformed officer came in and whispered something softly into Blunt's ear. The inspector glanced swiftly at his watch then addressed the tape recorder.

'11.57 p.m., interview suspended, inspectors Blunt and Thomas leaving the interview room.'

He leant over and switched off the machine.

Eilidh spoke for the first time since she'd accepted the glass of water.

'Can I ask what's going on?'

'You can ask.'

'My client has a right to know of any developments.'

'At the moment my guess is your client knows more than the rest of us.'

He rose wearily and shut the door behind him. The policemen's departure left me with a strange mingling of hope and unease.

'What do you think it is?'

Eilidh's tone was professional. 'It might be

153

nothing to do with your case. Or it might be new evidence of some sort.'

'Would that be good or bad?'

She gave me a thin look.

'It'd depend on what the evidence was.'

We sat in silence for a while. Movie lawyers always passed their clients a packet of cigarettes as soon as they sat at the interview table but my guess was that Eilidh probably didn't even smoke. The headache was back, pressing at the usual spot above my temples. I wondered if I could ask Eilidh for a painkiller. I glanced at her profile; it was set in a grim expression that made me wonder how this would affect my mother if it went wrong.

'How's Johnny?'

'John is fine, but it's best if we concentrate on what's happening here.'

The realisation that she couldn't tolerate Johnny's name on my lips stung and my voice came out high and querulous.

'I've done nothing.'

'You were found sleeping next to the body of an old man who'd just been battered to death. The cut on his neck was deep enough to almost decapitate him. Your finger-prints were on a beer can in his possession and you have his blood on your clothes. The police are within their rights to question you. Indeed they'd be remiss not to.'

'I didn't do it, Eilidh, I was drunk and stupid, but I didn't touch the old man. I wouldn't do a thing like that.'

She shook her head and glanced at her watch. Then an officer came to accompany me back to the cells.

I sat in the cell for a long time. My waiting was punctuated by deliveries of tea that I drank and food that I felt too sick to eat. From time to time the sound of footsteps would raise the faint hope that I was about to be released, and a more definite dread that some drunken hard man was about to join me in my cell. But perhaps it was a quiet night in the world of crime, or maybe the stripy-jumper team were on a win that evening, because I was left alone to work through what had got me there.

The policeman who eventually came to collect me kept his face blank. I didn't bother questioning him. I would find my fate out soon enough.

Eilidh was waiting for me in the same interview room where we'd sat earlier. I wondered if she'd been on duty for the whole time that I'd been locked up and how she man-aged to look so fresh in the middle of the night.

'They think they have the boys who did it.' Relief made me drop my head into my hands. Eilidh squeezed my shoulder for a brief second and I felt her warmth through my police-issue jumpsuit. 'They're setting up an ID parade and want to see if you recognise them.'

I lifted my head from the cradle of my hands, feeling the blood rise to my face.

'So I've been promoted from arch murderer to star witness?'

'Be thankful.'

'Oh aye, I feel like I've won the bloody lottery.'

It was early the next morning when I eventually left the station. They'd left me to sweat it out for a few more hours in the cells but the policemen's demeanour towards me had subtly changed. They still thought me a nasty, smelly alcoholic fuck-up, but they didn't think I'd killed the old man. Eventually my clothes were returned. They were caked in grit from under the bridge and there was a streak of blood on the front of my jumper where the old man's broken head had slumped against it. I threw the jumper into the corner of the cell, then lifted it and bundled it beneath my arm. I would dispose of it myself; I didn't want to leave anything that could be stored up for future convictions.

The boys had looked diminished in the harsh light of the identity parade. A couple of them looked like they'd been crying, another like he had drifted into a trance. One of them was full-on cocky. I wondered if he really didn't feel any fear or if he was psycho or maybe just a consummate actor. I stood behind the viewing mirror and indicated each of them by number. The boys looked young now that the energy of the assault had left them, and I remembered the way they had careered after the boat. Even if I hadn't recognised them I would have been able to spot the accused. They were the youths who had spent a night coming down in a police cell, the ones who had sat with their social worker or mother and answered questions about the killing of an old man. If I hadn't recognised them the parade would have been a travesty, but I knew their faces as well as I knew my own. After all, I'm expert in the art of recall.

156

I collected my personal belongings at the front desk, expecting a hand to reach out and a firm voice to tell me another matter that had come to light that they needed to talk to me about. I'd signed for my watch, wallet, keys and the little bit of cash I had left, when the officer at the desk produced a white envelope with my name written on it in a plain modern hand.

'Miss Hunter asked me to pass this on to you.'

'Miss Hunter?'

His voice was brisk.

'Your solicitor.'

I waited until I was outside before I opened it. I'm not sure what I expected; an apology for not being convinced of my innocence? Inside were five brown notes, fifty pounds in cash. I slid the money back into the envelope and looked at the note that had been tucked beside it. *Johnny asked me to give you this.* I shook my head then stuffed it in my pocket and went to look for a quiet bar.

Berlin

It's worth repeating—tricks don't make a conjurer. Anyone with time to spare and a mind to it can cobble together a stock of sleights. You meet them in bars: men that can fold a napkin into nothing, or rip a ten-pound note to shreds and restore it just before its owner hits him between the eyes. These are the guys who get you to pick a card any card and reveal with their back turned and their eyes closed which one you chose. There are granddads and Lotharios across the globe can pinch a coin out their baby's ear, science bofs and businessmen who try to milk charisma from a loaded deck. But without an act these men are as much diversion as a karaoke amateur.

The key lies in performance. A true conjurer is as hungry for applause as he is to master any deception. He schemes and worries, composing new ruses to thrill the crowd, working variations on his theme—smashing, breaking, vanishing; elephants, Mercedes, aeroplanes, whole buildings —until it becomes a trial to find anything worthy of being at the centre of his illusion. He guides the audience's eyes, forcing them to glance away from the stage at exactly the right moment. They follow the hand he wants them to follow, see what he wants them to see. The hours spent perfecting a sleight mean nothing if the trick isn't done with style.

The master conjurer is a psychologist deserving of a professorship. He can anticipate greed and tell when sex will give things a twist. He knows from the angle of your head, the hunch of your shoulders, the set of your eyes whether you are a liar. He can spot the easy touch as well as any conman can. He can chase the lady and cut the cards, he can summon up ghosts and put genies back in bottles, he can throw the dice and roll out sixes every time. He can rap tables, vanish loons, hang himself and come back for more. He can saw a lady in half, stick her together, then run her through with knives; and if he spills a drop of blood nae matter, he can zap it into one of God's white doves. A successful conjurer can challenge gravity, defy nature, escape any restraint and sidestep death—as long as he's on stage.

*   *   *

I'd long given up the illusion that I'd ever near the top of my profession, but for some reason in Berlin in the face of trouble I got an urge for that to change. Maybe it was a secret wish to impress Sylvie and Ulla, maybe it was an urge to make something of myself before I ended up like Sam, or maybe it was just anger at being pulled into something that had nothing to do with me. Whatever the reason, the confusion around me seemed to concentrate my thoughts and sharpen my wits into ambition until I became determined to produce an act that would stun the city.

*   *   *

Sylvie was a quick learner. We rehearsed by day and each night I ran on as the clowns bounded off, ready to haul her from the audience when the time came for her to play my shy conscripted volunteer.

At first it was a simple routine. Sylvie stood blinking prettily against the glare of the stage lights, wearing one of the succession of sweet thin dresses she'd equipped herself with from the Flohmarkt. She wore no slip beneath it, allowing the bright lights to reveal the outline of her body to the audience below.

I'd welcome her gallantly, then ask if she had a piece of jewellery I could use in a trick. Sylvie would shake her head, softly whispering no, putting her arms behind her back, resisting just a little when I grabbed her wrist and held up the hand wearing the cheap cut-glass ring that shone brighter than any diamond ever dared.

My new assistant was a better actress than I could have hoped. When she gasped that the ring was her only reminder of her dead grandmother, I thought she was overdoing things but the audience gasped with her. Perhaps Berliners, with their history of loss and separation, valued keepsakes even more than most.

I slid the ring from her finger then held it to her mouth, telling her to blow through it and make a wish. Sylvie closed her eyes and puckered her lips like a child about to blow out the candles on her fifth birthday cake. She puffed a morsel of breath through the ring and I folded it fast away. Sylvie opened her eyes; I put my hands on her shoulders, turned her towards the crowd and in a deep voice that echoed all the way to the back stalls and left no one in any doubt of what a prick I was, asked her to open her mouth and take the ring from beneath her tongue.

Sylvie's eyes opened wide, she touched the inside of her mouth with her fingers, then slid into a rehearsed panic sobbing a stream of German, almost pushing me across the stage with the force of her fury. That first night there was a rumble in the crowd. I almost laughed to see them buy the ruse but managed to keep my tone pure pompous as I held up my hands and said 'I think you may have swallowed it.'

There was a grumble from below and Sylvie repeated the line, slowly, in German.

'You think I swallowed it?'

I faced the auditorium and smiled a full-on

evil smile.

'Don't worry, this has happened before and it's always worked out OK in the end.'

Then strobe lights flashed across the stage, the band creaked into a tune that was as near to manic as they could get and Sylvie leapt into an escape, but fast as she was, she was no match for me. I grabbed the girl by the waist, whirling her onto a table that had lain unnoticed at the back of the stage. Sylvie screamed, I laughed again. Then roughly buckled her down beneath thick leather straps, until she was struggling like a silent movie star tied to the railway tracks, and I was gloating over her like a moustachioed villain. I slapped a napkin over her front and, donning a handy operating gown, whizzed the table fast on its casters to centre stage.

Sylvie's cries ripped across the hall and I half-expected the audience to storm the stage, but they were quieter than they'd been all night. I could feel their attention, but couldn't tell whether their silence signalled interest or disapproval. I grabbed a scalpel from my top pocket, held it high so they could catch its quick sharp glint, eager as a shark's grin, then I stabbed her hard in the solar plexus.

Fake blood from the gel packs concealed in the napkin's lining spurted red and unforgiving over my gown, face and hair. I spluttered against its bitter tang and laughed like a crazy man. An echoing ripple of laughter came from the audience. They were with us now.

Sylvie lay frozen beneath my hands. Her sweet dress was ruined, her sleek mane stuck to her head with theatrical gore. She wiped a hand across her face and asked in German, 'Have you found

161

it yet?'

I shook my head.

'Not yet, but don't worry.'

Then shoved my hand roughly into the red stuff, seeming to lose first one arm then the other as I delved shoulder deep into her open wound, pulling out latex guts and organs, tutting at her liver, marvelling at the contours of her still beating heart, yohohoing as I hauled her intestines the full length of the stage like a reeling routing sailor tearing down the rigging. The audience laughed, delighted with this Grand Guignol conjuring. I pulled a succession of impossible objects from her slim form, a bottle of champagne, a waxen head I'd found in Costume, a bicycle wheel. Each one received its own slick comment and was welcomed with applause. At last I found the ring. I spat on it then rubbed it clean against the hem of my operating gown and held it triumphantly in the air. On a rig high above the hall the lighting engineer turned a spot to face a glitter ball. Bright diamonds of white light bounced across the stage then glimmered into the beyond, embracing the auditorium, dancing across the faces of the crowd as if the gleam from Sylvie's ring were dazzling the whole world.

It was as heavy-handed as the *ta-da* at the end of a poor symphony but at least the audience knew it was time to clap. And they did, there were even a few cheers. I unbuckled Sylvie, helped her to her feet then stood her centre stage, noticing how the bloody dress clung to her curves and the hand that accepted the cheap glass ring trembled. She grinned at me, blood-spattered and beautiful; I smiled back then put my arm against her shoulders

162

and made her take a bow before giving her a quick peck on the cheek and returning her back into the audience.

Alone on stage I ripped off the gown, wiping my face as clean of the stain as I could in one slick move, and stood, arms outstretched in my dinner suit, drinking in the applause, trying to look like James Bond after a violent victory. There was no doubt about it, the trick had gone down well. But no one could mistake it for a clever conjuring.

*   *   *

I cleaned myself up then waited backstage for what felt like an age. Eventually Sylvie burst into the dressing-room breathless with amusement and made to grab me. I threw a towel at her, ruffling her still sticky hair but keeping her at arm's length.

'Watch the suit.'

She took the towel and rubbed it through her hair still laughing.

'Why'd I bother with makeup and fashion all these years? All I needed to do was throw a bucket of blood over my head and I'd have got all the attention I needed.'

I passed her a packet of facial wipes. I'd had a couple of tilts of the bottle of whisky in the room but I was too thirsty for spirits.

'Bit of a man-magnet were you?'

'You've no idea.' Her laugh was loud and buzzed up. 'They loved us didn't they?'

'I guess so.'

Sylvie smiled, satisfied that I was as pleased as she was, then she turned round and I unzipped her dress. The phoney blood resisted mixing with her sweat, trembling in droplets on her pale back, like tiny worlds caught on a microscope slide. I fought the urge to trail my finger down the damp of her spine.

'D'you fancy going for a pint?'

She laughed.

'A man out there offered me champagne.'

I turned slowly to face the wall, feeling vaguely sleazy as I watched her reflection shrug off the ruined dress in a small shaving mirror above the sink. I took my fags from my pocket and lit one.

'Ten years in this game and no man ever offered me champagne.' I took a long drag. 'You going to take him up on it?'

'No, I think you and me should celebrate together.' She stretched a red hand into my line of vision. 'You got one of those for me?' I gave her the freshly lit cigarette and sparked up another for myself. Sylvie wrapped herself in a soiled robe and drew deep like she was toking a joint. 'Let me catch the next act and I'll assist you in what I suspect is your favourite trick, making beer disappear.'

I said, 'As long as we can watch from out front.' Thinking about the cold lager they served there in tall chill-sweating steins.

'It's a deal. Set 'em up and I'll catch you when I'm decent.'

'That'll be never then.'

She gave the back of my head a light slap as she ran off to the showers.

*   *   *

It was a poorer house than it'd felt from up on

164

stage and I had no trouble bagging a table towards the middle of the room. For once my nod to the waitress produced swift results and soon I was sitting back with a cool beer and a cigarette. I was beginning to learn that there were some things you couldn't touch the Germans on. Good beer and a lax smoking policy in public buildings came pretty high on the list.

The twins, Archard and Erhard, were nearing the end of their acrobatic act, a narcissistic man-in-the-mirror excess of preening and vogueing that had a table of buff queens next to me sitting to alert. Each twin was decorated with the inverse of his brother's tattoos, spiralling green, black and red designs curling out of their tight trousers, across their chests and down their arms, emphasising the swell of their muscles, the sinewy definition of their bodies.

When the twins looked at each other they saw themselves, but I found no difficulty telling them apart. The secret lay not only in the direction of their tats but in the tiny Greek letters, one alpha, the other omega, clumsy home-done jobs, inked into their wrists, telling the world the first and last out of the womb.

I watched as Archard nimbly climbed his brother's torso, and then did a handstand on his image's upturned palms, gently disconnecting his right hand, each acrobat slowly moving his free arm until it was at right-angles to his body. They held the pose and my neighbours clapped ecstatically. It was a good effect. I glanced at my watch just as Sylvie slid in beside me smelling clean and citrus.

'Those are two strong boys.'

165

'You know who to ask if you can't get the lid off a pickle jar.'

'Ah, they wouldn't be my first choice.'

'No?'

'No, definitely make the reserve list though.'

I was about to ask who would be at the top of the list when all chance of talking was drowned by cheers from the next table as the twins took their final bow. The ninja prop shifters jogged on in their wake, bearing a huge plastic sheet. They spread it across the stage, ran off and returned with a full-size bathtub and half a dozen buckets of water. A trapeze was lowered above the bath, then the next turn came on and I worked out the answer for myself.

Kolja's naked chest shone with oil; he stalked across the stage, pecs puffed out, shoulders thrown back, spine straight all the way down to the swell of his muscular buttocks. The bulge on the other side of his white leggings looked unnaturally large. I whispered to Sylvie, 'I see he's packed his sandwiches.'

But she ignored me, concentrating on the vision of Kolja circling like a young Nureyev about to wow the Bolshoi. He stopped, rubbed some chalk theatrically into his palms, casting a superior glance at us mortals below, sneering slightly, as if he didn't even deign to pity us, though I knew the lights rendered everything beyond the stage invisible.

The trapeze looked impossibly high but Kolja sprang effortlessly into the air and grabbed it with both hands, hoisting himself steadily upwards until his chest was level with the bar, he hung there for a moment, letting us admire his silhouette, then

166

swung his legs into the dark, tipping himself slowly up and over into a leisurely 360 degree turn that made his muscles swell. The men at the table next to us sat without touching their drinks, nodding in appreciation as Kolja threw himself into a faster loop and then another, spinning round and through the trapeze, switching hands, making his slim hips follow through, his white leggings shining against the black backdrop of the stage, his speed increasing until he no longer looked like a man, just a twirling birling blur in the centre of the stage.

I nudged Sylvie, thinking she'd be amused by the body culturalists' captivated stares. But she put her hand on my arm, staying my elbow. I turned to look at her and saw her lips parted, her tongue pressing against her teeth. I downed the dregs of my beer and signalled for another.

Up on stage the trapeze was descending with Kolja astride it now, he sat motionless for an instant above the bath, then somewhere a needle hit shellac and a slow number started up.

> In the heat of the night
> Seems like a cold sweat
> Creeping cross my brow, oh yes
> In the heat of the night

The stage lights switched to a cool midnight blue, Kolja swung to and fro, clutching the supporting rope, making his muscles swell in the deep indigo, then he fell suddenly backwards into a turn that made my stomach slide and Sylvie give a quick short gasp.

167

> I'm a feelin' motherless somehow
> Stars with evil eyes stare from the sky
> In the heat of the night

Kolja caught the bar of the trapeze, holding his body rigid above the tub, ignoring but somehow basking in the audience applause. Then he swung himself into the water, all the time holding tight onto the U of the trapeze, drenching his legs, torso, chest, emerging dripping, his costume clinging. The men at the next table went wild and Sylvie joined in their applause.

> Ain't a woman yet been born
> Knows how to make the morning come
> So hard to keep control
> When I could sell my soul for just a little light
> In the heat of the night

Kolja continued, oblivious to the audience. He swung himself up and over, submerging then resurfacing, sparkling with droplets as if it were all for his own amusement.

> In the heat of the night
> I've got trouble wall to wall
> Oh yes I have
> I repeat in the night
> Must be an ending to it all

Then finally he slipped from his swing and into the tub, sinking his head beneath the water, releasing himself from the audience's gaze. He broke the surface and lay looking up towards the heavens and into the beyond like a man with serious troubles on his mind. The music carried on.

> Oh Lord, it won't be long
> Yes, just you be strong
> And it'll be all right
> In the heat of the night

The last bar crackled to its close, the scene sank into dark. Then just as quick the stage lights came up, Kolja tumbled from the tub and stood, arms outspread, water cascading from him onto the plastic sheeting, warming himself in the audience's ovation. I turned to look around the room and saw Ulla standing below the glow of the exit sign. For an instant our eyes met, then she turned away.

Maybe it was the music or maybe it was the beers hastening my descent from the euphoria of my own applause, but suddenly, watching Kolja take his bow, I felt a swift sharp stab of melancholy.

I caught Sylvie's eye, she laughed, still clapping, and leaned across to me.

'Now that's what our act needs, a bit of sex appeal.'

I wondered at the 'our', but when the floorboards began to vibrate with the force of the audience's stamping feet, I realised she could have a point.

*   *   *

Dix was wearing an expensive charcoal-grey suit that could have been Armani, Versace or fucking Chanel for all I knew. It made him look like the

169

younger, richer brother of the stubbly unwashed man I'd last seen slumped in a torn chair in Sylvie's flat. He raised his beer and saluted me.

'To your new partnership.'

His smile was amused. For some reason it annoyed me.

Sylvie filled her glass with white wine from a deceptively dainty jug and said, 'To our new partnership!' Half draining the large glass, then refilling it.

I chimed 'New partnership', putting my stein to my lips and taking a long hard pull, remembering that three had never been my favourite number.

*   *   *

This was Sylvie's and my fourth bar, Dix's first. He was sober, but had the air of a man in the mood to indulge others' foolishnesses. He signalled for more drinks though his own was still fresh. I hid behind my glass, smiling between each swallow, counselling myself not to turn into Tartan Willy on the rampage.

Sylvie was no longer the anxious supplicant who'd lain beneath my hands earlier in the evening. Her hair shone glossy and smooth around a face powdered to pale ivory, only her red lipstick recalled the bright stain that had coated her body. Sylvie's stylised makeup was at odds with the plain black satin dress she'd changed into. It was a good combination, something like a whore on a murder charge. She took another inch out of her glass and asked, 'Successful evening?'

Dix smiled, keeping his own counsel. I didn't bother to ask what had required a suit and sobriety until 2 a.m.

*   *   *

The two of us had left our previous bar about thirty minutes before, Sylvie urging me to hurry up or we'd miss the show. I necked the last of my beer, Sylvie linked her arm through mine and we reeled into the street, silly with sudden air, drink and new friendship. Sylvie's straight spine seemed to straighten mine and we walked fast and tall like a soldier boy and his bride on their wedding day.

I recognised the club from the matchbooks Sylvie had substituted for a stake on our first night. The sign shone from above the doorway in sharp pink neon, Ein Enchanted Nachtreview, and the same festive lady lounged in the same triangular cocktail glass, spilling electric pink bubbles into the air from her careless toast.

Perhaps I wouldn't have noticed Sylvie's pace slowing as the Nachtreview came into view if our arms hadn't been entwined, but though her conversation still sparkled as bright as the neon, I could feel her growing alert, her attention shifting from my orbit towards the door of the club. I matched my pace to hers, until her steps faltered, then stopped.

'Wait a second. I just want to see who's on guard duty.'

She peered into the gloom. The bouncer moved into the lee of the doorway, cupping his hand around his cigarette, squinting against the lamplight.

'Perfect.' She slipped her arm from mine and started to walk briskly across the road. 'Come on.'

At first I thought she'd misjudged things. The bouncer stood barring the entrance, arms locked behind his back, expression like a breeze block, impervious to the cute way Sylvie's smile flashed on and off, as she spieled out a patter peppered with one of the few German words I knew—*bitte.*

I tried to look sober, wondering what I was doing in a country where I didn't even know the licensing laws.

'D'you spracken ze English?'

'It's OK, William, Sebastian and I are old friends.' Sylvie dropped her voice soft and low. 'Bitte, Sebastian.'

I reached into my pocket, folded forty euros in the cushion of my hand then put my arm round my new assistant's waist and palmed the notes to her old friend. He looked at me uncertainly then opened the door, shaking his head more in sorrow than in anger. Sylvie touched his arm as she passed and he muttered something that sounded like a warning. But entering the club had revived Sylvie's reckless mood. She laughed and reached back towards the doorman, kissing him on the cheek. I waited for Sebastian to change his mind, but he laughed too, wiping away her lipstick and reissuing the warning, his sternness lost in the moment. I nodded my thanks and he gave me a quick appraising glance as he moved back into the shadows, a mix of sympathy and contempt. The kind of look you give a dupe.

*   *   *

I'd been in larger sitting-rooms, but whoever designed the club hadn't allowed size to contain their style. The ceiling and walls were rose-gold peeling away to red below, and the curved coral-quartz bar shone with more champagne than a Soho clip joint. At the far end of the room was a small stage where a long-legged girl in a sailor suit that would have sent Lord Nelson spinning was sitting demurely on a bentwood chair, singing about how her mama thought she was living in a convent.

Sylvie took a table near the stage and I slid in beside her, making sure I could monitor the sailorgirl's act for professional reasons. I glanced back to the entrance where the bouncer still lingered, following our progress through the glass as if unsure of whether he had done the right thing.

'What was that about?'

Sylvie shook her head dismissively.

'Nothing.' She looked around. 'What do you think a person has to do to get a drink in this place?'

Up on stage the sailorgirl was walking round the chair. Now that she was on her feet I could see just how short her skirt was. I wondered if she realised she'd forgotten to put her knickers on. Sylvie followed my gaze.

'She's a classically trained ballerina.'

'I suspected that.'

Sylvie raised her eyebrows then peeled her lips back into a dazzling smile as the prospect of more alcohol approached.

The waitress's uniform was deep pink edging sweet pink, it hugged her form, dipping and swooping around a wolf-whistle of a body. I gave her my stage show grin and she smiled back, taking all those clichés about Botticelli angels, wrapping them up and tying a bow on them. Then she clocked Sylvie and her expression glazed to strictly business. The waitress kept her eyes lowered as she took our order, then returned to slide our drinks onto the table without a smile.

I put my hand on the waitress's arm and said 'Dankeschön', looking her in the eyes, making my tone soft and soothing.

She hesitated, glancing at Sylvie as if trying to decide whether she was worth a murder sentence, then murmured, 'Bitteschön', and turned her back on us.

I lifted my lager and peered at the girl on stage through its liquid lens.

'Do you think I should check this for arsenic?'

Sylvie shot a look of venom towards the departing waitress.

'Why?'

'You don't seem too popular around here.'

'Don't worry, things have a way of rebounding on bitches like her.'

'Bad karma.'

'Something like that.'

Up on stage the naughty nautical shifted her rear making the pleats on her skirt bounce. The singer straddled the chair and I shifted my eyes from the shadows beneath her pelmet-lengthed skirt towards her face while she belted out the last verse of her song.

> You can tell my papa, that's all right,
> 'Cause he comes in here every night,
> But don't tell mama what you saw!

174

She tipped her sailor's cap at the audience, smiled at the scattering of applause and left the stage, darting a quick look at our table.

Our waitress took her place; she'd changed into a stage costume and was smiling now, flanked by two equally jolly and equally busty girls. The trio were dressed identically in short shorts, low-slung halter-necks and cheekily angled bowler hats. They each dragged a chair on with them and started to go through a routine that must have been hell on the thighs. I had no illusions, Germans didn't need to plunder their past for their own amusement, this was aimed at tourists hungry for a taste of Weimar decadence, but there was something about the way the flesh at the top of the girls' legs trembled as they went through their steps that appealed to me.

The fascination seemed lost on Sylvie. She mooched a cigarette, and started talking loudly about the costumes she was designing for herself. Up on stage the trio were doing a syncopated wiggle while beside me Sylvie fought for my attention with descriptions of satin corsets and nipple tassels. Travel was certainly expanding my horizons. Sylvie's voice rose a notch and I put my hand on hers. She smiled warmly at me, triumphant at wresting back my attention.

'What do you think?'

'I think you'll get us thrown out.'

She shot me a hard look, then suddenly she was on her feet, waving towards the doorway, and that was when I saw Dix.

*   *   *

175

Dix was as stone calm as he'd been at our last meeting, but Sylvie's high was edging on a fever. She described the evening, acting out both of our parts, not minding that Dix only nodded where she laughed, but then she was laughing enough for all three of us, her eyes darting between Dix and me, as if unsure of whether she could hold us both on her leash while there were so many other distractions around.

'You have to come tomorrow, Dix, it's an ace trick, they loved it.'

'OK.' Dix looked beyond Sylvie at the girls on stage, following their legs, his face unimpressed, as if he'd seen the act before and didn't find it much improved. He turned to me. 'So, William, did they want to see a magical trick or did they want to watch you cut her open?'

'Is that not a bit sick?'

Dix's face wore a serious expression, but it was hard to see his eyes behind his specs.

'Perhaps, but that doesn't mean it's not true.'

Sylvie's smile was eager; her teeth shone white against the nightclub gloom.

'They want to see you murder me, William.'

'Aye, the greatest show on Earth.'

Dix looked me straight in the eye, his voice mellow, and I thought that perhaps he meant what he said. 'There are people who would pay a lot of money to see it.'

'Sick people.'

'Rich, sick people.' He stubbed his cigarette in the ashtray then levelled his stare to meet mine. 'Better they see a trick than the real thing.'

'Better they get treatment.'

He shrugged.

'Maybe it could be treatment of a sort. Get it out of their system. Seriously, we should talk about it. You're a conjurer. We find the right sick people and make it look real enough—it could be a good way to get rich.' His gaze held mine. 'Remember, William, we're all sick in some way.'

'Speak for yourself.'

'You're a dying man, William.' Sylvie leaned forward with an intensity that might have been sincerity or maybe just drink. 'From the moment we're born we start to die.'

I lit a fag and said, 'All the more reason not to hasten things along.'

Sylvie slid the cigarette from my fingers.

'You'll not want this then?'

And for the only time that evening we all laughed together. But even as we laughed, Sylvie grinning at me through the smoke of my lost cigarette and Dix almost managing to look avuncular, I started to wonder if this was the only late-night place in the district or if there was a quiet bar somewhere that I could slope off to. Sylvie and Dix began slipping between English and German. I listened for a while, keeping my eyes on the girls up on stage, then stood up and made my way unsteadily across the room.

The saucy sailor was perched on a stool by the bar in a pose that made the best of her long legs. I guessed she'd grown too tall to be a ballerina, but I had no problem with her height. I looked up to tall girls. The barman was wiping glasses at the opposite end of the small bar. I feigned interest in the matchbooks tumbled in a round fishbowl on the counter next to the dancer, picking one up and

177

reacquainting myself with the champagne bather, wondering how drunk I was. I swung onto a stool, grasping the edge of the bar to steady myself, realising I was pretty blasted. But a man fit enough to get his leg over a barstool still has some hope. I treated the sailorgirl to the full force of the William Wilson grin and said, 'Great song.'

Close to, the girl's thick stage makeup grew malicious. Face powder had drifted into the fine lines around her mouth; it rested in the creases that framed her dark eyes and hung amongst the fine down coating her cheeks and upper lip. She looked ten years older than she had on stage, but she was still out of my league. She gave a slight nod of the head, but there was no trace of the smile that had glittered throughout her performance.

'Thank you.'

Her accent was Greta Garbo, Marlene Dietrich and Ingrid Bergman all coiled into one well-tuned set of vocal cords. The barman gave me an amused look, then turned his attention to the glass he was cleaning, holding it up to the light, making no move to serve me.

I said 'Ein Bier, bitte', pleased my German was coming along, then turned to the girl and gave her my best chat-up line.

'Can I buy you a drink?' She hesitated. I followed her gaze to the table where Dix and Sylvie were deep in conversation, then caught her eyes in mine, forcing her to look at me instead. 'Singing must be a thirsty business.'

It was nowhere near hypnosis, just a cheap use of her good manners, but it worked.

'OK, that would be nice.'

I wondered if she'd put on any underwear, and

if my new status as exotic foreigner would add to my pulling power. The ballerina said something to the man behind the bar then turned back to me.

'You're from London?'

'Via Glasgow.' She looked uncertain and I said, 'Scotland—wind, snow, rain, tartan, haggis, heather, kilts, all that crap.' She nodded and I added, 'We don't wear anything under our kilts either.'

She laughed, pretending to be shocked, hiding her mouth behind her hand geisha style.

'Then we have something in common.'

'Aye, cold arses.'

The girl giggled. I appreciated the effort.

'My name's William, William Wilson.'

I stuck out my hand and she took it in her soft grip. 'Zelda.'

The name suited her and I wondered if she'd had it long. The barman returned with something pink and fizzy in a tall fluted glass and said a price that suggested he'd just handed her the elixir of life. I slid a fifty-euro note across the counter and she raised the glass in a jaunty salute.

'Prost!' Zelda took a sip of her drink and gave me a smile that was worth the money. 'You're a visitor to Berlin?'

'I'm working here, performing at Schall und Rauch.'

The smile was genuine this time.

'I know it.' She rubbed away some imagined stain from the side of her face. Her eyes did a quick flit towards Sylvie and Dix then back to me. 'Is Sylvie dancing there?'

There was an enforced casualness about the girl's question that made me wary.

'Sylvie is my lovely assistant.' I smiled and fanned half a dozen of the matchbooks seemingly from nowhere into my hand. 'I'm a conjurer.'

Zelda clapped, but it wasn't my trick that had made her sailorgirl eyes wide.

'Sylvie isn't dancing any more?'

The edge to her tone might have been gloating or maybe just surprise. I played it safe for Sylvie's honour's sake.

'There's a lot of dance in the act.'

'Ah.' The glass went to her lips and I began to wonder if I had enough cash to buy her a second drink. 'You can't have been together long.'

'This was our first night.'

'So you are celebrating.'

'Got it in one.' Zelda glanced towards the table where Dix and Sylvie were leaning intently towards each other, their faces serious. I asked, 'You know each other?'

Zelda smiled a small tight smile.

'A little.'

'Come and join us then.'

The smile grew tighter.

'Dancers need a lot of sleep. One drink is enough.'

I took a sip of my beer.

'There's a saying where I come from, one's too many, a hundred's never enough.'

Zelda drained the last of the pink stuff from the flute.

'You seem like a nice man.' She hesitated. 'Sylvie's a good dancer, good company . . .'

'But?'

Zelda shrugged her shoulders.

'There is always a but.'

180

Yes, I thought, *and yours is very nice,* but kept my opinion to myself and put a tease into my voice.

'And in Sylvie's case?' She hesitated and I said, 'Remember, I'm going to be working with her.'

Zelda held her empty glass in front of her, studying its stem, all the better to avoid meeting my eyes.

'Things happen when Sylvie's around. Sometimes they're fun.'

At last she met my gaze, telling me that what she said was true, she and Sylvie had had fun together.

'But sometimes not so much fun?'

She held my gaze.

'Sometimes not so much fun, no.' She smiled. 'We were friends. I mean it well.' She glanced back at the table where Sylvie was deep in conversation with Dix. 'You know how it is in this business, friendships change with shows, and Sylvie . . . well, she has loyalties that make it difficult for anyone to stay her friend for long.'

I nodded, encouraging her to go on, while wondering if the poison had been personal or professional. Zelda lifted a small bag from the seat beside her. A gentleman would probably have eased her descent from the high stool, but I hesitated and she slid off elegantly without my help, her skirt shifting up her slim thighs to reveal that she was still naked beneath. Now that she was standing Zelda was taller than me, but I still held her eyes in mine.

'So Sylvie quit?'

Zelda glanced way from me.

'She quit, yes.'

The glance told me some of what I wanted to

know. Whatever reason Sylvie had left, it hadn't been voluntary. 'I don't suppose you care to go into details?'

Zelda looked at something beyond my left shoulder. I turned and found Dix at my elbow. He smiled, said something soft to Zelda in German then turned to me.

'Another drink?'

'Sure.'

He looked at the dancer and she shook her head. 'I must go.'

I took the stein Dix slid towards me and thanked him, mentally cursing his timing. The sailorgirl was buying a pack of cigarettes from behind the bar. I leaned in towards her.

'Perhaps you'll come and see my act?'

'Perhaps.'

'I'll drop by with a couple of tickets.'

'OK.' Zelda's smile was cool and detached and told me not to bother. Maybe the disappointment showed on my face because she leant over and gave me a kiss on the cheek and whispered, 'Be careful, William.'

Her perfume smelt sweet beneath the faint tang of performance sweat.

'Hey,' I grinned. 'Of course I will. After all I'm a stranger in a strange town.'

This time there was no responding smile. She glanced towards Dix as he made his way back to the table with the drinks and said in a low tone, 'Then perhaps you shouldn't make life stranger still by mixing with strange people.'

I watched as her slim form swished away from me. The bouncer opened the door, she gave me a last smile then turned away, lifting her skirt, giving me a quick naughty flash of her naked rear, then the door swung to and she was gone. I finished my pint at the bar, ordered another round and went to rejoin Sylvie and Dix.

* * *

Dix had set up a fresh jug of wine for Sylvie, but his own glass was empty. I placed a beer in front of him and he shook his head.

'It's sad, but I have to go.'

'Dix is a busy, busy man. He has cards to deal and deals to shuffle.'

Sylvie's words were slurred, but she was holding her own against the drink.

Her mention of deals and shuffles made me think about the casino at Alexanderplatz that Dix had mentioned on our first meeting. But I hadn't placed a bet since I'd arrived in Berlin and was hoping to keep it that way. Anyway, even if I had fancied a flutter I wouldn't want to do it in Dix's company, even before his talk of rich perverts who could make our fortunes.

'Up on stage the bouncer had donned a red-sequinned waistcoat and bow tie. He smiled shyly then somewhere a karaoke machine started up and he launched into 'Those Were the Days, My Friend'. He moved his body with the music, jerking against the beat like a blind piano player belting out a Motown number. Tension constricted his voice, making the words come out high and off-key. He should forget the strong-arm stuff. If there was ever any aggro all he needed to do was sing at the troublemakers.

Dix pulled on an expensive-looking coat just as

the bouncer swooped into an alarming pitch change. I nodded towards the stage.

'You picked a good time to get going.'

Dix shrugged.

'It's necessary.'

He laid his hand for a second on Sylvie's sleek head, and then raised it in general farewell. There was something saintly in the sparseness of the gestures that irritated me.

I gave him a glib, 'See you, then.'

And he leaned in for a final word.

'Remember what I said, we should talk, we could make money together.'

Dix stroked Sylvie's hair again but she turned away, as if his decision to leave had already removed his presence and any need for goodbyes. She grinned at me without a last glance towards Dix as he walked out of the door.

'Poor Sebastian, he surely loves to sing.'

The bouncer was belting out the chorus now.

> zose were ze dayze, my friend,
> I thought zyd neffer end

His German accent so thick I wondered if he'd learnt the words phonetically. But whatever skill his performance lacked, it had sincerity. A small tear coursed its way down a cheek layered over with powder and rouge. Sebastian's brimming eyes were spiked with mascara, his mouth painted cherry-red. He looked like a corrupted oversized Pinocchio, cast out into the world and destined never to be reunited with Gepetto. A mad puppet set up on stage to remind us that all of our gods are dead.

Sylvie's voice held an indulgent superiority.

'I like Sebastian, even if he is a violent, tuneless, poor excuse for a bouncer.'

Her voice was growing loud again. Sebastian's eyes flicked towards us. I wondered if he could hear what she was saying above the music, but he kept singing, throwing his body into his same spastic dance. He slid off his suit jacket and I realised that his shirt was just a front secured by thin straps crisscrossing over his back and around his waist. Sebastian was on the da-da-da-da-da-das now. He unfastened the straps and let the bib shirt go flying towards the bar. His chest was hairless, his nipples unnaturally red or rouged with the same jammy gloss that coated his lips.

'Bring back the dancing girls.'

Sylvie shook her head.

'You ain't seen nothing yet.'

Across the room a heavyset man excused himself from his companions and started to make his way awkwardly across the room.

'I've seen enough—look, folk are leaving.'

Sylvie kept her gaze on Sebastian and put her hand on my elbow. I glanced towards the door, wondering if there was a general exodus, and saw the large man veering in our direction, rolling like a sailor who'd lost his sea legs. Sylvie's eyes were still fixed on the stage.

'Wait for the money shot.'

'Do I have to?' Sebastian leant forward, grabbing his trousers by the waistline, then there was a ripping sound, the Velcro seams gave and he was standing before us in a pair of pink and black lacy panties, suspenders and stockings. 'It's a fucking freak show.'

185

'Don't worry, William. No fucking involved.'

Sylvie's laugh halted abruptly. I felt a pressure at my back. The fat man's hands were resting against my chair as he leaned in towards Sylvie.

'Hey Suze.' His breath stank of beer, smoke, strong spices and belly rot. 'Long time eh?'

Sylvie looked up at him, her eyes panicked but her voice free of all recognition.

'You're mistaken.'

The man smiled apologetically at me, drink making his grin lopsided, his other hand resting on Sylvie's chair now. He smoothed it across her back, gracing me with a wink.

'Maybe you could spare her for a while. Fifteen minutes,' the grin flashed again. 'Probably less.'

'She's told you pal, you've got her mixed up with someone else.'

The fat man raised his hands.

'Hey, no mistake, I never forget a face,' he smiled, 'or a mouth, or a cute ass, or a . . .'

I got to my feet, pushing his hand from the back of my chair. Up on stage Sebastian raised his arms ready to conduct the audience in the chorus, grinning against the sadness of it all, swaying stiffly like a human metronome.

'The lady's told you, she's not interested.'

'Hey—if she tells me to go I'll go.' The fat man's grin was moist, his broad face smooth and pink like a slab of boiled ham. 'There's enough to go round, first or second, I don't care, you take your pick.' He laughed. 'You take your prick, then take your pick.'

Sylvie said, 'When was the last time you saw your prick, you fat fuck?', just as I shoved the heel of my hand into the centre of his barrel chest. It

186

wasn't a hard push, but the man was drunk. He staggered backwards, jarring against the table behind us, spilling drinks in a smash of ice and glass undercut by the sudden protests of the drinkers. It looked like he was going to hit the ground, but the fat man's rolling gait had taught him his centre of gravity and he regained his balance, pitching like a skittle that refuses to go down. The grin was back now, broader than before. Up on stage Sebastian faltered. The man shrugged his shoulders, palms raised upwards to show there was no problem. I righted my fallen chair and he turned back to me, his voice hurt.

'Why fight about a whore? She's anyone's for the asking.

'Not yours.'

He shrugged.

'Enjoy her. She's a good fuck, for a whore.'

Sylvie sloshed her wine in his face. The fat man shook his head like a Labrador shaking itself free of water after a swim. He put his face close to Sylvie's and spoke in English for my benefit. 'You best watch out, Sweetheart, word is your boyfriend's in debt to the wrong men, and my guess is it's you who'll have to pay.'

He put a hand on her breast and squeezed.

When I thought about it later I wasn't sure whether my anger was sparked by the squeeze or because the man had referred to Dix as Sylvie's boyfriend. But at that moment there were no coherent thoughts in my head, just the blinding red of rage.

I hit him a punch that connected with his jaw and a bolt of pain shot up through my knuckles. The room boomed as Sebastian dropped the mike.

I grabbed my injured right hand in my left and the fat man made to get me in a hug. Sylvie started throwing glasses. One skated across the stage. Its rumbling progress was picked up by Sebastian's abandoned mike and blasted across the room. The second flew towards the fat man. He ducked, but too slowly to avoid a glancing blow; beer splashed into his eyes and his big hands flew towards them. Sebastian clambered from the stage. Everything seemed to slow except Sylvie. She kept on moving, grabbing her bag and coat, pushing me towards the door.

'Forget it!'

We staggered towards the exit, no one making any move to stop us, except for Sebastian, who was off the stage now, his progress hampered by the patrons. I looked behind me and saw him leap a table, more threatening than a man in women's underwear should be.

We clattered up the basement steps and out into the street. I followed Sylvie blindly, chasing the sound of her heels until at last I realised there was no one behind us and stopped, leaning forward, hands on knees, taking deep gasps of the night air, wondering if I would ever breathe normally again. Sylvie heard the echo of my footsteps fail. She turned and laughed, then resumed her siren flight, her heels ringing against the pavement. I took a deep draught of air and ran on, realising I was no longer fleeing Sebastian. Sylvie darted away from the main drag, down a darkened alleyway and I followed, caught in the chase. For a second I thought I'd gone the wrong way. The lane looked deserted. Then Sylvie laughed again and I saw her, hidden in the shelter of a goods entrance. Her smile shone out from the darkness and the fat man's words flashed through my mind. Her voice was low and teasing.

'You fought for my honour, William.'

'Was it worth saving?'

Her voice dipped an octave.

'Come here and find out.'

I walked slowly down the alley until I was facing her. We stood not touching for a moment then I put my hands gently on her hips and we leaned into a kiss that started gentle and grew deep. I broke the clinch, moving my mouth down to her neck, feeling her hand beneath my jacket, warm against my spine. Sylvie pressed herself into me, digging her hipbone hard against my erection.

I asked, 'What about Dix?'

She stroked her hand down the length of my groin. 'This dick?'

'Your uncle or whoever he is.'

I breathed kisses against her neck, wondering why I was raising objections.

'Don't worry about Dix. He's been in trouble before. He'll get out of it again.'

I wondered what she meant but then her hands moved to my fly, pushing all thoughts away. Her fingers slid inside my trousers, releasing me. I had her dress open down the front now. Her breasts were small and round, soft and firm at the same time. I lowered my mouth and Sylvie arched her back, pushing herself towards me but never letting off the pressure down below. I moved my own hands beneath her dress, pulling at her tights, not caring if I tore them. She whispered, 'Fuck me.' And I steered her against the wall, tugging her knickers down, feeling her soft wetness. I glanced up and saw her pale, smooth face, her mouth slightly open. A shadow hung beneath her cheekbone, the same shade as a bruise. She looked young and vulnerable, defenceless beneath my rough hands.

Something inside me shifted and Sylvie whispered, 'You OK?'

I whispered, 'Shit.' Sylvie's hand started to move, trying to revive me, but I knew it was no use. I pushed her away more roughly than I'd intended and she jarred her head against the doorway.

'Sorry.'

My voice grated in the darkness.

'It's OK.' Sylvie rubbed the back of her head then started to button her dress. 'It happens.'

'Did I hurt you?'

'I'm in for a hangover tomorrow anyway.'

'I didn't mean to hurt you.'

'Hey, William, it's OK. It was an accident.'

I looked away and we started straightening our clothing, our awkward modesty at odds with the moments before. There was a sound of voices from the mouth of the alley, a couple of youths walked towards us and I realised the madness of what we'd been about to do. One of them said something to Sylvie as he passed and she answered him back in a short guttural phrase that made me think of Glasgow. I asked, 'What did he say?'

'Nothing.'

'Was he being funny?'

She ignored me, righting her dress. I groped through my scant vocabulary for an insult to throw at them. 'Shitzders.'

The boys looked back over their shoulders shouting something back at us, but not bothering to rise to the insult. Sylvie's voice was tired.

'Shitzder? That isn't even a word.'

'They got the message.'

'I guess they did.'

We were back on the main street now. Glass display cases shone at the edge of the pavement boasting of the fine objects for sale in the adjacent department stores—handbags, jewellery, shoes, accessories for your accessories—everything shiny, everything expensive. Two disembodied heads on impossibly long necks gazed out from one of the glass cubes, tiny hats teetering on their Marcel waves. Their stares were superior, as if they found the hatless passers-by rather common, too encumbered by flesh. Somewhere across the city I could see the illuminated sign of the Mercedes Benz building rotating slowly in the night sky. Hidden beyond it the half-ruined spire of the bomb-blasted memorial church would be shining out a warning against war.

Up ahead the lights of a taxi rank glowed into view, a row of white Mercs waiting for business. We walked to the top of the line, I opened the door and Sylvie got in.

'Want a lift?'

'No, I'll walk, sober up a bit before I get to the hotel.'

Sylvie gave me a last kiss, her eyes glassy with tiredness, drink and almost-sex. Her smile shone from the cab's shadows. 'You gonna be OK?'

'Don't worry.'

'See you tomorrow?'

I nodded my head then slammed the door, not knowing if she could see my face in the darkness of the street.

Glasgow

Not so long ago, in the days when Glasgow was ship-building capital of the world, particular pubs opened before dawn to kill the drouth of the nightshift. While rich men slept and children rested safe in bed, while mothers readied themselves for the day and posties sorted through their sacks, the nightshift looked at the clock and licked their lips. And not far from the factory gates pub landlords polished glasses, checked the levels in their optics and made certain that floors were swept, tables wiped, the cash register drawer running smooth on its rollers. Then they looked at the clock, unlocked the door and waited, for men who had toiled through the watch hours with the vision of a pint shining golden before their eyes.

I made my way from the police station with Johnny's money warm in my pocket. Drink had got me into this trouble and it seemed that only drink could release me. I hardly saw a soul, just a lone dog-walker, who crossed the road at the sound of my footsteps. The armies of men that once filled whole streets at shift's end are long disbanded. But the early morning pubs are still there, if you know where to look.

There's a licensing law demands these bars serve breakfasts to mop up the drink. And so they're always steeped in the smell of discount bacon, black pudding the colour of blood-soaked shit and gangrenous battery-farmed eggs. Everything fried in ancient lard, set grey since yesterday and melted each morning until it is hot enough to fry any cock-roaches that might have burrowed in for a midnight feast.

I pushed open the door and stepped back into the night, though I knew it was a little past 7 a.m. The bar was busy. A couple of student types sat in a corner using the beer to ease the come down from whatever had kept them up. A businessman sank a predawn brandy. A guy in a brown leather jacket that went out of fashion sometime around 1983 studied the racing form, putting little crosses next to the horses he fancied, taking quick sips of a beer I'd seen him top up with vodka. No one looked like a shift worker. No one was eating the breakfast. No one talked because no one was here to be sociable. The jukebox pounded out some ancient hit even though no one was here for the music.

Everyone was here to drink.

I stepped up and ordered a pint. I was filthy, unshaven and there were still traces of the old man's blood spattered across my trousers. The barmaid sat my beer on the counter without looking at me. I waited for her to put her hand out for the money and when she didn't, set one of Johnny's notes on the counter. She peeled it from the dirty bar without a word and slapped my change back into the beer spills and fag ash crumblings. I was too tired to care. I gave my pint a full second to settle then raised it to my lips.

The beer tasted stale enough to be the contents of the slop tray. But I sank a third of it in one deep swallow then used my change in the cigarette machine. I lit up, finished my drink then ordered another, looking at the men around me and realising I fitted in fine.

I was into my third when the old man's battered face flashed into my mind's eye and with it the memory of another face exploding in a spray of blood and brain. I took my glasses off and rubbed my eyes. A voice behind me said, 'That's your last for the morning.'

I turned and saw Inspector Blunt, still wearing the same suit he'd had on during my interrogation.

'You arresting me?'

'Naw I'm telling you.'

'What are you now, the bloody beer police? Lager patrol?' I took out a cigarette and lit it. 'You're not in your station with your wee fat pal now, so fuck off and annoy someone else.'

'Is one sight of the cells not enough for the day?' Inspector Blunt turned to the woman behind the counter. 'Mary, no more for him, understand?' The barmaid glanced up from the pint she was pouring and nodded. He turned back to me, his ginger moustache looking dry and alcohol hungry. 'You're going to be needed if this thing comes to court, until then I don't want to see or hear anything from you.'

'That makes it mutual then.'

The barmaid set a nice smooth pint of best beside him. 'On the house, Mr Blunt.'

'Cheers Mary.' Blunt took a cigarette from my pack and lit it with my lighter. 'If we got a productivity bonus I wouldn't be bothered, but we're a bit pressed right now so I'd like to avoid any unnecessary paperwork.' He picked a bit of tobacco from his tongue. 'Bloody cheap fags. Get over whatever it is that's bothering you, because right now you're going in one of two directions, the jail or the morgue. Now piss off. And remember, this is my local.'

I looked around at the tired décor, the deflated men, the uneasy chairs, then back at the police inspector supping his first pint of the day at eight in the morning and said the worst thing I could think of.

'Aye, it suits you.'

*   *   *

I got back to my room, stripped, double-bagged the clothes I'd been wearing in black bin bags and put them in the lobby. I stood in the shower until the water ran cold, and then I stood there until the cold seemed to burn. After that I lay on the bed, looking at the ceiling, thinking. I'd not been doing enough thinking lately.

Blunt was right. I was headed down whatever I did. There was no point in hiding a skin that wasn't worth saving. It was time to set some things to rights, and then maybe I should make sure I had some company on the low road I was set to take.

*   *   *

The Mitchell Library is a wedding cake of a building overlooking the motorway that cuts a swathe through the city. I stood on the bridge and looked down into the ravine of speeding cars. I'd heard that some people claim their loved ones were mesmerised into throwing themselves from bridges like these by the moving lines of traffic. But I found it hard to believe. No one can be hypnotised into doing anything they don't want to do.

195

The Mitchell's computer hall was busy. I got a ticket, then found an empty berth and sat there amongst the students and school kids, the pensioners and unemployed, the asylum seekers and researchers. The room was quiet save for the clicking of fingers against keyboards, but I could almost feel the electric buzz of thoughts firing around the room. Everyone beyond their bodies, absorbed in their own project, back in the depths of ancient Rome, their family tree, legal precedent or who knows what? There was a mix of ethnicity I'd not met elsewhere in the city and suddenly I missed London.

I logged onto the system, then scrolled through the internet, chasing Bill Senior until I thought I might have an idea of where else to look, then I got a librarian to direct me to where the microfiches of old newspapers were stored and struggled with the small plastic slides until I worked out how to use them. After a while I realised that I might be getting somewhere.

*   *   *

It was past three when I left the library and caught a bus over to the West End to pay back one of my debts.

The work address that Johnny had given me was on University Gardens, a short Victorian terrace that had once housed lecturers but was now converted into university offices and seminar spaces. I worked my way down the doors until I came to the number Johnny had given me. The outside of the building was covered in scaffolding that looked like it had been there for a while. I made my way up the entrance steps, past the neglected scrub of front garden and into the hallway.

Inside there was a fusion of damp, floor polish and books that hit me a smack of nostalgia for a time I'd almost forgotten. The foyer was as dark as I remembered, a notice-board on the wall covered in a confusion of posters and notices for classes, assignments, student theatre shows, political meetings and books for sale. I had a sudden memory of saturating campus with starry homemade advertisements for my new brand of magic. The scent of nostalgia was overlaid by the smell of turps and paint, the stairway swathed in spattered dustsheets, and suddenly it made sense why Johnny had given me this address.

A man in white overalls was balanced near the top of a long ladder in the stairwell reaching up towards a barely accessible slant of the underside of the stairs. I walked up towards him, the steps creaking under my weight; I could feel a corresponding creak in my chest that hadn't been there when I'd used these buildings fifteen years ago. The painter peered down and I said, 'Can you tell me where Johnny is, mate?'

The man's roller continued moving white on white across the wall; he was doing a fine job.

'Johnny?'

'Aye, he said he was working here, I think he's probably one of your guys.'

'Oh, John.' The man pointed his roller upwards. 'Second floor, first room on the right, chap the door afore you go in: they might have the ladder in front of it.'

'Cheers.'

197

I kept on climbing. Johnny's dad had been a painter decorator. I wondered if the firm had fallen to him now. Johnny had been smart enough to do whatever he wanted, but hash and booze had always threatened to hold him back. I'd been no better, spending the best part of my grant in the union bar before leaving halfway through my third year. I reached the second floor, turned right and rapped on the large dark-varnished door. A voice shouted, 'Aye, it's clear.' And I went through. A broad-set, balding man was poised on the top of the ladder at the far side of the room painting the walls a sunshine yellow that looked washed out in the dim light. His apprentice was crouched on the floor, touching up the skirting near the door.

'I was looking for John.'

The older man stopped mid stroke and stared down from his ladder.

'You've found him. What can I do for you, son?'

*   *   *

I glanced at the nameplates on a couple of the doors until a uniformed attendant with a bundle of late-afternoon post tucked under his arm asked if he could help me. I saw myself as he must see me, a scruffy middle-aged waster skulking round a university campus, and gave him a grin to liven up his nightmares.

'Aye, is there a good pub round here?'

The guard directed me to one of my old student haunts, staring at me as if storing up my description for later use. I felt his eyes on my back as I walked down the stairs and supposed he'd reach for his radio as soon as I was out of earshot, alerting the rest of the security squad to the potential menace in range. I looked back up at his worried face peering down from the top of the stairwell and held my right hand up.

'May the lord hold you and keep you.'

Making a sign of the cross with my index finger just to freak him out. Then the front door opened behind me letting in a blast of sudden spring air.

'William!'

Johnny's greeting caught me mid-genuflection.

The guard shouted down, 'Everything OK, Dr Mac?'

Johnny gave the grin that I bet swelled his lectures with swell young female students and nodded up at the guard.

'Fine thanks, Gordon, I'll look after Mr Wilson.' My old friend turned to me. 'You've still got good timing.' Johnny's hair was slightly wet, his face flushed. He smelt of something fresh and sporty. 'I just dropped by to dump this.'

I glanced at the sports bag he was carrying, suddenly feeling tongue-tied, and reached into my pocket for the fifty pounds he'd lent me, handing it over awkwardly.

'I wanted to return this.'

'Aye, thanks,' Johnny rubbed his fingers through his damp hair. 'I hope you didn't mind . . .'

'No,' I tried for a smile. 'It helped to know someone had faith in me.' The weight of the hours I'd spent in the Mitchell that morning, searching out old newspaper accounts of crimes and cruelties, suddenly weighed on me. 'I was just going for a pint, d'you fancy one?'

John hesitated.

'I do but I can't.'

199

I remembered the way that Eilidh had looked at me in the police cell.

'Fair enough.'

'No, it's not that. It's just I promised to get home early. Listen I've some beers in the fridge, why don't you come back with me?'

'I'm not sure that Eilidh would be so pleased to see me.'

John ran his hand through his hair again.

'Don't be daft. If you hadn't dropped by I would have got your number from her and called you.'

'Ach I don't know, John.'

'Well I do. I need a favour and you owe me at least the one.'

*   *   *

John's flat was just off Byres Road, a quick fifteen-minute walk from his office. He was waylaid twice by students and each time used me as an excuse to move on.

'Looks like you're a celebrity, *Dr* John.'

He laughed.

'They always get friendlier towards the end of term—exam time.'

I said, 'I'm impressed.' Realising I meant it. 'What happened?'

John looked at the ground as he walked.

'Nothing much. I discovered that I quite liked philosophy, screwed the nut, passed the exams, applied for a postgrad. And the rest is history.'

'You were free of a pernicious influence.'

'Don't flatter yourself.'

He turned into a close.

'Here we are.'

200

Johnny's flat looked big enough to accommodate six students. But any resemblance to the semi-slums we'd once shared stopped there. The hallway was painted a tasteful parchment shade that made the best of its high ceiling, the walls were hung with bright prints and the floor carpeted with pale sea-grass matting. He led me through shouting, 'That's me back.'

A smartly dressed woman in her sixties stepped briskly into the hallway.

'Wheessht, I've just got her down.'

Johnny lowered his voice.

'Whoops, sorry.'

The woman smiled expectantly at me, perhaps imagining I was a scruffy visiting philosopher.

'This is William, an old friend from university.'

The woman's face lost some of its welcome.

'I think maybe Eilidh mentioned you.'

I nodded.

'All good I hope.'

And the old woman gave me a sharp look that told me not to take her for a fool. She turned to John.

'Grace's had her feed, so she should sleep for a while yet.

'Thanks, Margaret.'

'A pleasure as always.' She took down her jacket from the coat stand. 'Sorry to be in such a rush: book group night.'

John handed her a smart leather bag that had been left by the door.

'I remember. Have a good time.'

'Oh, it's always interesting, even when you don't like the book.' Margaret finished fastening her coat and gave John a quick peck on the cheek. 'You take good care of my grandchild.' She knotted a small silk scarf round her throat, tucking it into the collar of her coat. 'I'll see you tomorrow. And goodbye Mr . . .'

'Wilson.'

'Yes, I thought that was it. I'll probably not see you again so I hope things go a bit better for you.'

I bent into a slight bow.

'Thank you.'

She gave me a nod that said she'd do for me if she saw me again and I smiled to show that I understood.

John closed the door behind her. 'Sorry 'bout that.'

'You can't get the staff these days.'

He smiled, relieved I hadn't taken offence.

'Come on, I'll get you a beer then I'd best check on the wean.'

The kitchen was large and homely with a scrubbed-pine table at its centre. I sat there nursing the bottle of weak French lager Johnny had given me, trying not to listen to him talking to his sleeping daughter on the baby intercom. When he came back he was smiling.

'How old is she?'

'Ten months.'

'Congratulations. Next thing you know you'll be getting married.'

'You always had an uncanny knack for prediction. Date's set for July. Have a seat. My affianced won't be in for a while yet.' I resolved to be gone before Eilidh came home. Johnny reached into the fridge, helping himself to a beer. 'What are you up to right now?'

'Nothing much.'

'Nothing much or nothing at all?'

'Why d'you want to know?' I took out my cigarettes then hesitated. 'Is it OK to smoke?'

'Eilidh's not so keen on it in the house.' I slid them back in my pocket. John looked at me and laughed. 'You'll get me shot, William.' He reached into a cupboard and selected a saucer. 'Here, use this.'

'Sure?'

He opened the window above the sink.

'Course.'

'Want one?'

'More than my life's worth mate. Anyway, you didn't answer my question. Are you working?'

'Why're you so interested?'

'Apart from the usual social niceties? I might have a gig for you.'

Johnny leaned back in his kitchen chair and started to tell me what he had in mind.

Berlin

The Schall und Rauch's joiner had made a fine job of the task I'd set him. The box was perfect; a shiny metallic blue, decorated with a zodiac motif of constellations and multi-ringed Saturns that would shine from the stage and draw the audience's eyes from other distractions.

Sylvie stood on stage in the empty auditorium next to Nixie the hula-hoop girl, while I explained

203

how the trick would work.

'OK ladies, this is a classic illusion, I am going to slice my elegant assistant Sylvie here in half, and you, Nixie, are going to be the legs of the operation.'

Nixie looked bewildered, Sylvie translated and the hula girl's giggle followed a beat after.

'OK,' I wheeled out the box and lifted its lid, 'Sylvie this is where you go, head and hands sticking out the wee holes in this end, feet poking out the other.' Sylvie and Nixie looked at the box. 'OK?'

Sylvie nodded.

'OK.'

'Right, Nixie.' I smiled at the blonde girl. 'Unfortunately, you're not going to get the benefit of the audience's applause, but you are going to get the satisfaction of knowing you've been instrumental in successfully pulling off one of the classic illusions in the conjurer's calendar.'

I looked at Sylvie. She rolled her eyes and started to translate. Nixie listened, her eyes widening, then collapsed in giggles, putting her hand over her mouth as if scandalised at her own amusement.

I asked, 'What did you say?'

Sylvie's expression was innocent.

'I just repeated what you said, you're a very funny man, William.'

*   *   *

There had been no awkwardness between us after our drunken celebrations. Sylvie had simply said, 'Well I guess that got that out of the way.' And I'd agreed, both of us laughing, relieved that the other wasn't offended.

I'd wanted to ask her about the fat man. He'd called her by the wrong name, but Suze and Sylvie didn't seem so different to me and I remembered a quick flash of panic in Sylvie's eyes that could have been surprise, or could have been recognition. I'd kept my thoughts to myself and though I'd pulled the guts out of her at ten fifteen precisely every night for a week since, nothing had passed between us that would have scandalised even the pope's maiden aunt. Still, the memory of Sylvie's body stayed with me, making me glance away from her as I went onto the next bit of my explanation.

'OK, let's go down to the stalls.' The girls followed me, chatting in German. 'So what do you see standing next to Sylvie's box?'

'You make me sound like a puppet.'

I gave Sylvie a look, she translated my question and Nixie replied.

'Einen Tisch.'

Sylvie singsonged, 'A table.'

'Great, back up on stage.'

The girls groaned but they followed me up to where the props were standing.

'Now what do you see?'

'Ahh,' Nixie's voice was full of realisation. 'Eine Kiste.'

I looked at Sylvie.

'A box.'

'Correct. Observe.' I opened a flap exposing the compartment in the tabletop that was hidden from the audience by the sharp black angles on its tapered-under edges, revealing that although the table was only an inch thick along its white-painted rim it was deep enough at its centre to hold a slim woman lying flat. 'You lie in here, Nixie, hid-den from view. I put the box on the table and help Sylvie into it. She surreptitiously pulls her knees up to her chest and you slide your legs up through the flap on the top of the table, sticking your feet out through the foot holes in the box so the audience think that they belong to Sylvie. Then voilà, I wield my saw,' I grabbed the oversized saw lying on the ground next to me and shook it in the air generating a wobbling sound, 'and cut through the bit of balsa obligingly holding the two parts of the box together,' I started to saw through the balsa, letting them hear the metal rasp against the wood, 'until I'm able to separate the two halves,' I pushed the two ends of the fancy coffin apart, 'to reveal a head in one and wiggling feet in the other, making the crowd go crazy.' I held my arms up to the imaginary audience and grinned at the girls, but Nixie was whispering something to Sylvie, shaking her head. I asked, 'Was ist das problem?'

Sylvie sighed.

'The silly bitch says she can't do it. She's claustrophobic.'

Sylvie and I ran through every member of the company, but we already knew that Nixie was the only performer on staff slight enough to fit inside the tabletop.

'So that's it then, fucked again.'

'Hey William, it's not my fault.'

I kicked the trolley that the new box was lying on, sending it trundling towards the back of the stage. 'It was a fucking clichéd piece of crap anyway.'

Sylvie caught the trolley and rolled it back down

the rake towards me.

'You'll work it out.'

I slammed the trolley again, sending it hurtling back the way it came, not watching where it went, simply taking relief in the act of hitting something. It juddered, almost losing its load, then against all odds regained its keel, sailing into backstage.

I said, 'Fuck.'

And moved to retrieve it just as there was a gasp and Ulla came from the wings pushing the trolley away from her. I took a step forward. 'Shit, sorry.'

Ulla rubbed her arm. Her voice was high and annoyed. 'We have to be careful here.'

'Sorry, Ulla, I didn't mean to push it so hard.'

'The stage is a dangerous place.'

'Yeah, I know, sorry.'

Ulla had a pencil stuck in her hair and a sheaf of invoices tucked under her arm. Her frown made a small crease between her eyebrows. I wondered what she'd do if I reached out to smooth it away.

'I came to see if you had finished with the stage. There are others who would like to rehearse.'

'Yeah, you may as well tell them to go ahead.'

Ulla hesitated, noticing our dejection for the first time.

'Problem?'

Sylvie took a step back and looked her up and down.

'No,' She placed her arm around Ulla's shoulders and levelled her gaze at me. 'I don't think so, do you, William?'

My eyes slid down Ulla's body. But I already knew the proportions of the German girl's figure well enough to realise that Sylvie just might be right.

Ulla grasped the simple illusion straight away.

'But this is a very old trick, the audience will have seen it many times before.'

'Not the way William's going to do it.'

Sylvie and I hadn't discussed the razzle-dazzle surrounding the illusion, but her confidence was inspiring.

'That's right, it's going to have that classic Schall und Rauch twist, a super-sexy variation on the theme.'

Ulla looked worried.

'Will I have to wear a costume?'

'No, just something comfortable you can move easily in and,' I felt the back of my neck flush, 'an identical pair of shoes and stockings to the ones Sylvie's chosen.'

'They're going to be darling.' Ulla had extricated herself from my assistant's grasp but Sylvie was determined to hold her attention. 'Bottle-green fishnets with the reddest, highest, shiniest pair of kinky wedges you ever set eyes on.' She glanced at me. 'I'm borrowing them from a fetish shop in return for a mention in the programme.'

'Well done.' I turned to Ulla. 'Will you help us out?'

'I'm not a performer.'

'No performance skills required. All you have to do is lie there, stick your legs through the flap at the right time and wiggle your toes when I ask you to.

Ulla hesitated.

I took a step forward.

'There's no one else.'

She sighed.

'If it is necessary for the show.'

Sylvie swept her into a hug.

'I knew you would!'

Ulla freed herself and I made an effort to meet her eyes.

'Thanks, you're a life-saver.'

I watched as Ulla made her way back down towards the office, and then turned to find Sylvie staring at me. Her voice was full of exaggerated marvel.

'William, you *like* her.'

I shook my head and started to put our props away, hiding my expression in the task.

'I've never gone for bossy women. Anyway, she's taken. She's with Kolja.' I tried to keep my voice light. 'A match made in heaven.'

Sylvie grinned.

'Then they'd better watch out. Those heavenly matches are notoriously vulnerable to temptation.'

Glasgow

It didn't take Johnny long to get to the point.

'I'm organising a benefit and I'd like you to headline.'

I drew on my cigarette, wishing I hadn't agreed to come back with him. I tipped some ash into the saucer, and smiled to sweeten my refusal.

'Sorry, John, I don't do that anymore.'

The smile was a mistake. Johnny leant forward, enthusiasm for his new project shining on his face.

'So you said, but I thought you might be able to come out of retirement, just for one night.'

I wondered where he found the time for benefits between lecturing, exams, visits to the gym and a new baby.

'I'll put up posters, take the tickets, shift props or act as bouncer, but don't ask me to get up on stage. It's just not possible.'

Johnny continued as if he hadn't heard me.

'It's in the Old Panopticon. It's not normally open to the public so a lot of people might come along just to see the venue, but I'm finding it harder to get hold of halfway decent acts than I'd anticipated. You're a godsend, William.'

I remembered this technique from our student days; Johnny's water torture. It involved a relentless dripping at any objections until it became easier to do what Johnny wanted than to resist. I steeled my voice.

'I'm not a performer anymore.'

He shook his head, still smiling, sure that with the right persuasion I'd do it.

'I just don't believe you, William.'

'You'll have to because it's true.'

Perhaps there was something in my voice or maybe Johnny had learnt that it wasn't always possible to force the unwilling to his will. He leaned back in his chair and rubbed his hand through his hair.

'Well, at least give me a reason.'

I said, 'Maybe one day.' Knowing it was a lie. Johnny's face was incredulous, his dark curls stood up in angry little spikes.

'So that's it? First time in years that I ask you to do me a favour and there's no apology, no explanation, just no?'

Sunlight cut through the kitchen window, making a pattern of golden squares between us on the wooden table. I turned my head and looked out towards the backcourts where the tops of sycamores moved with the spring breeze. Sometime earlier in the year someone had planted bulbs in the window box; lilac hyacinths shivered in their pots, sending their perfume into the room. The kitchen would be perfect for socialising. The ideal place to share a meal with friends around the big table, knowing that if the baby woke she was only a few steps away.

I shook my head and kept my voice low.

'I'm not abandoning my career just to inconvenience you, and for the record I did apologise.'

We were interrupted by the sound of a key turning in the front door. There was a pause while the new arrival took off their coat, and then Eilidh put her head into the kitchen. Her hair was pulled back into a roll, but it looked as if the wind had caught it and loose tendrils curled softly around her face.

'Hi.' She smiled at Johnny, then noticed me for the first time. 'Oh, William.'

I got to my feet, hoping my stubbed-out cigarette wouldn't cause a row after I'd gone.

'It's OK, I've got to head.'

Eilidh came into the room, glancing at the saucer, but not mentioning it.

'Are you sure?'

'Positive.'

She looked towards the other end of the table. 'John?'

211

'Let him go, Eilidh. William's got things to do.'

The woman looked between us, sensing tension but unsure of its cause.

'How's Grace?'

John took a drink from his bottle of beer.

'I just looked in on her, she's sound.'

'Good. I'll have a wee peek after I've walked William to the door.'

John shrugged his shoulders. I lifted my jacket from the back of my chair.

'I'll be fine.'

But Eilidh accompanied me anyway. She turned to me in the hallway.

'What happened?'

'John wants me to do his gig, I told him I wasn't able to.'

'Couldn't or wouldn't?'

'Can't.'

She looked up at me then put her hand gently on my arm. Her voice was tender, as if she were seeing me for the first time.

'What happened to you, William?'

Something in her touch and her soft tone forced a pressure behind my eyes. I stepped free of her grip.

'Nothing, I just don't perform any more.'

'It's OK.' Eilidh smiled gently and I wondered if she'd always been able to switch between the hard professionalism she'd shown in the cells and this empathy that seemed able to sheer off my emotional armour with one look. 'I'll speak to John. He's under a lot of pressure and . . . well, you know how he is when he gets the bit between his teeth.' She shook her head. 'Every time you meet us there's a display of bad manners.'

212

I returned her smile; grateful she'd changed the subject. 'Not the night I met you both in the pub.'

'It seemed to me you were a bit prickly then.'

'Possibly.'

'Anyway, I'm glad I saw you. I wanted to apologise for the other day. I should have been more sympathetic. You'd had a terrible experience and I was . . .'

'Sure I was guilty?'

'. . . not as sensitive as I should have been.'

'You've a lawyer's way with words.'

'That's good, I am a lawyer after all.'

'Will I have to go to court?'

'No, not unless one of them changes his guilty plea.'

'That's something.' I put a hand in my pocket and took out my cigarettes, turning them over nervously in my hands, remembering that smoking was taboo. 'Eilidh, if . . .'

I hesitated, not wanting the mother of John's child any where near my quest, but realising she was the only legal counsel I was liable to get. She smiled encouragingly.

'Go on.'

'. . . if a crime happened a long time ago would old evidence still be any good?'

Eilidh raised her head, her interest sparked, and I caught another glimpse of the sharp lawyer who had sat with me in the police station.

'It's hard to generalise, it'd depend what the evidence was, but technology's moved on remarkably. There are cases that were thought long dead being dusted down, re-examined and solved through DNA and the like.' She smiled. 'A lot of worried crims who thought they'd got clean away are dreading the knock at the door. Why?'

The urge to share was strong, but I resisted.

'Just something I was reading.'

Eilidh gave me a look that said she wasn't sure she believed me. But it wasn't an unfriendly look.

'Please think about John's benefit.' She held my red-rimmed eyes in her violet gaze. 'He admires you. It would mean a lot to him if you were involved.'

'I'll think about it. No promises though.'

'No promises.'

She leant over and gave me a kiss goodbye. Apart from the day when I'd met my mother it was the first time in a long while that a woman had kissed me. It felt better than it should.

I was halfway down the close stairs before I realised that I hadn't asked Johnny what his benefit was in aid of.

Berlin

Sylvie and I spent the rest of the afternoon and much of a long sober post-show night trying to light on the super-sexy twist we'd promised Ulla. It was morning by the time we'd sorted it out. We went through a private rehearsal then headed to our respective beds with the warm worn-out feeling that comes from a good evening's work.

Of course the cutting the lady in half trick was only a small part of the new act, but separating the woman's torso from her legs was a private nod to myself that I was moving on from the kind of second-rate penetration effect I'd performed at

214

Bill's club. There was a dramatic death-defying illusion destined for our finale, something I doubted the crowd at Schall und Rauch had seen before.

It was 9 a.m. and I was sitting on my hotel bed adding the last touch to a diagram and sipping a medicinal Grouse before finally getting my head down when the telephone rang. The voice on the other end was as brash as a barker in a penny arcade.

'William, I was expecting your fucking answerphone.'

'Hi, Richard, I was up all night rehearsing.'

'Good boy, well you can spare me three minutes.' I held the phone away from my ear while he coughed a phlegm-filled cough. 'How's things in der Fatherland?'

'Better.'

'You wowing them yet?'

'About to.'

'Glad to hear it 'cos I've got some good news for you.'

'What?'

'There's a scout travelling over on Saturday to take in your show.'

'Saturday?'

'Christ, don't drop dead of enthusiasm.'

'No, that's great news, Richard, it's just Saturday's the first night of the new act. I would've liked a chance to iron out any glitches that come up.'

'Don't worry, the adrenalin'll carry you through.' Richard hacked out another round of coughs and I wondered where he'd heard of adrenalin.

215

'Who's he scouting for?'

'TV, BBC3 to be exact, a late-night show. This could be what you've been waiting for.'

'So do you want me to meet him? Wine and dine him?'

'No, keep schtumm. He likes to go incognito. A lot of the big scouts are like that. But forewarned is forearmed. Save you screwing it up.'

'Thanks, Richard.'

'Don't mention it, son. Just thank me by keeping sober and avoiding making a balls up. This could be the big one. He was most insistent, no comics, no dancing girls, no singers, he only wants conjurers. This could have your name on it, Will.'

Glasgow

My trawl through the Mitchell Library's archives had revealed that one particular case was mentioned every time the murdered nightclub owner Bill Noon, or his father, Bill Noon senior, appeared in the newspapers. Bill had referred to it obliquely on the night we met and I'd read about it in the *Telegraph's* report of Sam and Bill's death, though its significance had been lost to me then.

On the morning of the Friday, 13th March, 1970, Mrs Gloria Noon had left her home at about 12.15 in the afternoon. She had never been seen or heard of again. There were no witnesses to her departure, but Gloria had spoken on the telephone to her sister, Sheila Bowen, at about midday. Gloria had asked Sheila for a recipe for pork and apple casserole. When Sheila phoned back a quarter of an hour later after searching out the recipe book there was no reply, though Gloria had been expecting the call.

Gloria's six-year-old son Billy went uncollected from school; her car lay untouched in the driveway. Gloria's makeup was spread out in front of her dressing-table mirror as if she had been interrupted in the act of applying it. Gloria had withdrawn no large sums of cash, nor did she pack any clothes, she had left her Valium and contraceptive pills in the bathroom cabinet. Her keys, purse and reading glasses were still in her handbag, which lay open on the bed she shared with her husband. Her passport lay undisturbed at the bottom of her underwear drawer. There was no sign of an accident or a struggle, no note; no woman was discovered wandering the local lanes with amnesia. Mrs Gloria Noon had simply disappeared.

Sheila told police that she and her sister had talked of more than recipes that morning. Gloria had finally decided to leave her husband, taking her young son with her. According to Sheila the boy was the only reason Gloria had stayed in her marriage.

It was confirmed that Gloria had been seen two weeks earlier by the casualty department of her local hospital, claiming to have fallen down the stairs. The doctor who'd examined her had written in his notes that he considered her injuries more consistent with an assault than a fall. Her sister claimed that Gloria had been beaten by her husband and that this beating, the most recent in a long series, was the reason Gloria had finally

217

decided to leave—that and the encouragement she'd received from her lover.

Gloria had never named the man she was leaving Bill senior for, fearing the danger he'd be in if her husband discovered his identity and knowing that divorce courts looked unsympathetically on women who indulged in extramarital affairs, even the wives of dubious businessmen who made easy with their fists.

'She wouldn't have done anything that interfered with her chance of getting custody of Billy,' her sister had insisted. 'And she would never have left him.'

But of course the affair had jeopardised Gloria's chance of custody. And she had most certainly left her son. The question was, had she left voluntarily?

If you could hang a man on hearsay, Bill Noon would have mounted the gallows in double-quick time. But he'd insisted that with the exception of his abandoned son he was the most confused and upset of anyone involved. He denied any knowledge of an affair and insisted that though they 'had their ups and downs like any married couple,' he knew of no plan to leave him. Gloria liked a drop, they both did, and once or twice he'd raised his hand but he'd never have seriously hurt her. The gin and not his fists were to blame for her fall and her bruises. He disputed his sister-in-law's account, accusing her of being jealous of Gloria's lifestyle and of actively wanting their marriage to fail. He poured scorn on the idea that his wife would confide anything in her sister. He even slandered the recipe for pork and apple casserole.

Though the newspapers recorded Bill Noon's

denials it was clear whose side they took, even after he had posted a substantial reward for news of his wife. Bill Noon stared out from their photos, photogenic as a Kray twin hard man, while Gloria's sister, Sheila, sat dignified in full suburban bloom, or was pictured working honestly and industriously in her husband's outfitting shop.

For a while Gloria was sighted almost as regularly as Lord Lucan. A holidaymaker thought he saw her walking along a beach in Majorca. She'd dyed her hair brown and was holding the hand of a thin aristocratic-looking man. She was seen on a bus in Margate, wearing a headscarf of the kind favoured by the queen. A hiker had passed Gloria walking along a cliff-top in Wales. She'd looked troubled and they'd thought of asking if she was OK. It was only later that it occurred to them who she was. What attraction coastlines had for the disappeared Gloria Noon was never explored in the press.

After a while the sightings of Gloria diminished, though over the years people continued to claim to have glimpsed her. Generally after the press had resurrected her story, something that happened whenever a respectable married woman went missing. Though, unlike Gloria, these women always seemed to turn up, in some form.

Gloria Noon had become her disappearance, a bundle of newspaper clippings, a police file, a chapter in true crime books and an entire Pan paperback, *The Friday the Thirteenth Vanishing*. The police denied her case was closed, but admitted there was little they could do with no evidence, no witnesses and no body.

The most spectacular resurrection of the

publicity surrounding the case had come with Bill Noon senior's remarriage twelve years after his first wife's disappearance. Several newspapers had run a copy of the wedding photo. Bill junior acted as best man. He stood at the front of the group photograph, handsome face stiff and unreadable. And if you looked closely, it was possible to spot a younger, thinner James Montgomery in the back row of the bravely smiling wedding party, grinning like a man who'd just come into a good thing.

*   *   *

I took all the clippings I had managed to get copied about the disappearance of Bill's mother and laid them across the floor of my room. Then I took out the map and the photograph that I'd filched from Montgomery and laid them side-by-side. I lifted the photograph and stared at the newspaper held in Montgomery's hand. The print was small, but it was still possible to read the headline and the date, 13th March 1970, the day of Gloria's disappearance. I looked again at the map and felt certain that this was the last resting place of Gloria Noon.

*   *   *

Bill had been nothing to me, Sam was a friend that I hadn't seen for a year and Gloria a woman who vanished when I was still a child. I didn't owe them any debt and nothing that I could do would bring them back. But maybe I held the solution to their deaths, and perhaps in helping to bring them justice I would find some peace of my own. Montgomery was out there somewhere, eager to get his hands on evidence that might damn him. Was I in mourning for what I'd done in Berlin? Or just a coward, hiding from a man who'd been playing dirty since before I was born? I'd been spending a long time on my decline. This could be my chance to redeem myself or go out Butch-Cassidy-and-the-Sundance-Kid-style, in a blaze of glory.

I left everything lying the way that it was, washed my face, locked the door, turned out the light and went to bed.

*   *   *

The cuttings were still splayed across the floor when I woke the following midmorning. I stepped over them, mindful not to stand on any of the photographs of Gloria and Bill Noon, the laughing wedding guests or the carefully coiffured sister, then fumbled in the dressing table drawer until I found an unopened pack of playing cards and slid away the red scarf I'd used to cover the mirror. I leaned in close and looked at myself properly for the first time in months. My face was drink-bloated and unshaven, my eyes puffy behind their glasses. I rubbed a hand across my bristles, wondering if the old William was lost forever, then pulled up a chair, slit open the pack and threw the jokers to one side. I shuffled the deck and started to perform some basic sleights of hand. My fingers were clumsy, but after a while they began to remember the familiar tricks and I knew that with practice they would regain their old knack. I shaved, showered and then went out to ring Johnny.

*　　　*　　　*

Eilidh sounded distracted.

'Oh, William, John's a bit busy, can he ring you back?'

'I'm calling from a phone booth.'

There was a smile in Eilidh's voice.

'That's novel these days.'

I looked out at the crowds of shoppers rushing along Argyle Street and realised it was a Saturday.

'I guess it is.' I paused, hoping she'd drag Johnny from whatever task he was caught up in. When she didn't I said, 'It's just to say I'll do the gig.'

'That's brilliant, William, he'll be delighted.'

I felt myself go gruff.

'Aye, well, he'll maybe not be so chuffed when he sees me; I'm a bit rusty.'

'Nonsense he's always going on about how brilliant you were when you were both at uni.'

I stored this nugget of praise away amongst my depleted stock.

'Johnny didn't tell me the kick-off time.'

'It's a week today, 3.30 in the Old Panopticon.'

'A matinee?'

The voice on the other end of the line sounded concerned.

'Is that a problem?'

I hesitated and then realised that it would make no difference to my purpose what time the show was at. 'No, not really, it just threw me that's all.'

222

'There'll be a lot of kids there, families, it should be fun.'

'I'll temper my act accordingly.'

Eilidh laughed.

'See that you do.'

Eilidh thanked me again and I realised she wanted to go. The pips sounded and I fired more change into the slot, holding her there.

'Johnny never said what the benefit was in aid of.'

'Did he not?' Eilidh's voice was bright. 'We're trying to raise funds for a charity catering for children like Grace.'

'Like what?'

It sounded flippant and inwardly I cringed.

'You really didn't talk much did you? Grace has Down's Syndrome.'

I felt a quick hit of pity, infused with embarrassment. The words were out before I knew I was going to say them. 'I'm sorry.'

'Don't be,' Eilidh's voice was serious. 'We consider ourselves blessed.'

Berlin

The three of us stood in the wings, Sylvie on one side of me trembling in a silky robe, Ulla on the other dressed in a close-fitting vest and tight leggings that had been severed at the knees. Both girls were wearing the same bottle-green fishnets and high shiny red sandals just as Sylvie had promised. Out on stage the clowns started to fling their buzz-saws around. I turned to Ulla.

223

'Ready?'

She nodded and I could sense her nervousness. I moved to help her into the hollow top of the table, but suddenly Kolja was beside her. He lifted her gently into his arms and deposited her safely in the compartment like some fairytale prince laying his new-won princess into their honeymoon bower. Sylvie leaned over to check something and her robe fell open. Beneath it she was almost naked. The green stockings were held up by a red satin suspender belt, which matched her high-cut shorts and the scarlet tassels, secured by mysterious means over her nipples.

Ulla made a noise somewhere between a sigh and a spit and Kolja smiled. He winked at me as if to ask, what could you do when women were around? Then leaned over and kissed Ulla quickly on the lips, ruffling her hair. I'd never suspected him of a sense of humour and would have liked him better for it if I hadn't noticed him meeting Sylvie's eyes as he rose out of the kiss.

Whenever cinema cameras go behind stage they show chaos. Half-dressed gaggles of showgirls tripping into departing acts, harassed stage managers pointing the odds with one hand and messing their hair into Bedlam peaks with the other. The reality probably doesn't look so different to the untrained eye. It's like watching a motorway from a pedestrian overpass. You wonder how the cars can snake from lane to lane without colliding, and yet when you're the driver the switch can be effortless.

The curtains dropped and the clowns ran off stage making lecherous faces at Sylvie as they passed. The prop-shifters swept away the debris, then moved the table behind the lowered curtain. Our music started up, Sylvie dropped her robe, I took her hand and we strode out in front of the curtains to greet the audience.

*   *   *

Something about the way the high heels made Sylvie's bottom stick out as she walked across the stage, spine straight, small breasts carried high, a diamanté tiara glinting from the top of her sleek head, made me think of a show pony. The crowd cheered. I turned her into a twirl and she stood sunning herself in their applause. I wondered if I was just a flesh bandit pimping a skin act, but there was no denying it was the best greeting I'd got in a long time.

Sylvie waited for the clapping to die down and our music to shift to a slower tempo, then handed me a deflated red balloon. I looked at her lithe body and held the balloon up to the audience displaying its limpness. They laughed and I raised it to my lips and started to blow.

The balloon expanded into a massive scarlet Bratwurst. I stopped, puffing theatrically, struggling to regain my breath, marvelling at the balloon's Priapic fullness, raising my eyes and looking at Sylvie's tits. The crowd belly laughed.

I raised the balloon back to my lips and kept on blowing. Sylvie covered her ears waiting for the explosion. Just when there was a danger of the crowd getting bored it burst, scattering red sparkles across the stage. I stepped back smartly, producing a bottle of champagne from its wreckage before the shreds of rubber had even hit

225

the ground. The crowd applauded, two champagne flutes were flung from the wings and I caught them, slick as any juggler. I'd opened the bottle, passed Sylvie a drink and had downed one myself by the time the applause faded.

Sylvie nodded to the remnants of burst balloon lying dead on the stage and grinned, 'That reminds me of last night.' I looked outraged and the audience laughed. Sylvie winked and said in a conspiratorial whisper that echoed to the very back of the room. 'Not for much longer though, just you wait until you see the big athlete in act three.'

'That's what you think.'

I pulled a wand from the inside pocket of my suit and pointed it towards the audience. There was a quick flash of red at the front of the stage and the music switched to a graveyard moan. Sylvie's hands flew to her mouth. The curtains behind us slid back to reveal the table where Ulla lay hidden. Before the audience had time to stare too closely, two of the ninjas jogged on, their features concealed by bandito scarves stretched black across their lower faces, each of them carrying one half of the sparkling blue cabinet. The first ninja handed me his half, I opened the lid and displayed its empty interior to the audience while he rolled the table centre-stage. I placed the box on top, exhibited the emptiness of its twin, then laid the two halves end to end. My ninja helpers slid out both boxes' fronts, fixing the two parts together, turning them into one long coffin.

Sylvie stood frozen.

I said, 'Remember the rumours about my first wife?'

Then, as if she'd suddenly realised what we were

226

about to do, Sylvie turned and tried to run towards the wings. The ninjas moved quickly. They grabbed my sexy young assis-tant and forced her high above their heads, ferrying her back to me. Sylvie's pleas for help cut across the room. Her body looked white against the black of the ninjas' costumes and the midnight-blue of the backdrop. She freed one leg and swung into an athletic turn, standing upright on one of her tormentors' shoulders for a split second, like an art deco figurine caught in the moment, but the ninjas regained their hold and pulled her down. I rubbed my hands as they lowered the kicking, screaming girl into the sparkling coffin, latching her in tight, her head and hands at the top, secured like a witch in the stocks, feet poking out through the holes in the other end.

Sylvie turned her face to the audience appealing to them. I forced fake champagne into her then twirled the table sickeningly fast until the top of her head was facing towards the audience. This was the girls' cue to do the fancy foot switch, while the bottom end of the box was out of sight. Sylvie cried for help, wiggling her hands, and I birled the table in the opposite direction so the audience could see Ulla's shoes kicking madly at the other end. I gave the table a final twist, laying the cabinet side-on to the audience, so they could see the whole arrangement now—Sylvie's frightened face and Ulla's kicking feet.

The lights dropped, leaving the stage in darkness save for one golden pool in the centre where the table lay. I got a sudden vision of Sylvie's half-naked curves lying above Ulla's svelte form. The thought of the women's closely packed

227

flesh sent a thrill through me that had been absent in rehearsals. I shook myself against the distraction of my own excitement, took a massive swig from the water in the champagne bottle and gave an evil cackle. One of the ninjas jogged on with a giant two-handed saw. We wobbled the saw between us, showing the audience its evil-looking teeth and then set to work, he at one end, I at the other, the only noise in the room the sound of metal eating through wood and Sylvie's petrified sobs. Ulla wiggled her feet frantically, the red shoes glinting as if they were desperate to separate themselves from the encumbrance of a body and begin a whirling, dancing life of their own.

The saw cut through the final layer of balsa, I bowed my thanks to the ninja and he ran off-stage, leaving the saw on the floor behind him, its discarded presence as much a part of the thrill as a centrefold's abandoned panties.

Slowly but slowly I approached the box; I hesitated for a beat, then reached out and gently separated the two sides. Sylvie's dark eyes were wide, her red mouth opened in a horrified silent scream, blood dripped from the box where the severed legs still danced.

The crowd roared, but I looked with horror at the cavorting red shoes. I shook my head then slammed the two sides of the box home, spinning the table until I got the signal that Sylvie and Ulla had regained their original places.

Sylvie cried, 'Have mercy.'

And the ninjas handed me seven long silver swords, unlatched the box and dragged her screaming into a new coffin, this time making her stand upright, sealing it shut while I sliced seven round, green watermelons in two, displaying the deep pink flesh of their insides to the audience, licking the last one lasciviously before I threw it into the wings. There was a drum roll and I thrust each of the blades into the box, pushing them hard, forcing against the resistance inside, until their sharp tips emerged, silver dripping red, from the other side. I crisscrossed the blades until it seemed no one could have hidden from their cuts, but when I slid them free and opened the door, instead of a punctured and bloody corpse there was Sylvie, triumphant and unscathed.

She said, 'Now will you free me?'

But behind us the ninjas were setting up a new device. A simple black-painted board, the same size and dimensions as a coffin. The board was decorated with a woman's curved silhouette, a silhouette formed of concentric black and red rings. A female-shaped shooting target with the bull's-eye roughly where the woman's mouth would be. Thick leather straps topped by metal buckles were attached to the figure's wrists and ankles. Sylvie turned, saw it and gasped, but once again the ninjas were too quick for my poor assistant. They secured her against the board and placed a clear, door-sized panel of glass between her and the audience. I took a revolver out of my pocket and stroked it gently.

'This is your last chance. If you escape this ordeal then I will let you go free. If not . . . well . . . it's been nice *knowing* you.'

Sylvie struggled against her bonds. I climbed off-stage and approached a table of men.

'Sirs, will you watch while I load my gun with six live bullets?' They stared warily at my hands while

229

I slotted the ammunition home, then each man nodded to show that the barrel was full. I handed the gun to the man nearest me. 'Sir, will you please hand this gun around your friends, I'd like you all to confirm that there is a bullet in every chamber.' The men passed the gun between themselves, weighing it in their palms, looking at the shells snug in their little hollows. Once more, each man nodded in turn. I said, 'Could you say it out loud please, so that everyone can hear you?'

And one by one they confirmed that, *Yes, the chamber is full.*

I turned to the man I had first accosted, a young blond boy with a clean-cut, intelligent-looking face.

'Thank you, sir. Now I'm going to ask if you could give the chamber a spin so that there is no way that I could have concealed a dud amongst the live bullets.' I handed the gun towards the man but he refused to take it. 'What's wrong? Don't you want to help me shoot my beautiful assistant?'

'No.'

The boy's smile was embarrassed. He shook his head shyly, aware of his friends' laughter, but unwilling to handle the weapon all the same. I held my hands out, gesturing casually as if I had almost forgotten that I was holding the gun.

'Don't laugh, this is a serious business, he has every right to refuse to help. Who knows?' I looked evilly around the room. 'He may be the only one of you who doesn't end the night on a charge of abetting a murder.' I looked at the revolver in my hand as if I had suddenly remembered it. 'Now, is anyone a little less squeamish than my young friend here?'

I scanned the audience, spotting Dix watching me, pale and intent from a centre table. His grey eyes, still as ice, caught mine and I faltered, but I had no need to jeopardise the illusion by appealing to someone I might have been seen with. I rallied myself and shouted, 'Anyone brave enough to help me out?' The young man's refusal had been exactly what was needed. The hilarity had gone from the room; in its place was a tension I hadn't felt in Schall und Rauch before.

Sylvie shouted, 'Don't help him.'

And a square-jawed man got to his feet, raising his hand in the air. I passed over the revolver and he gave the barrel three sharp spins, his face flushed. As he handed it back he whispered low enough that only I could hear, 'Shoot the bitch through the heart.'

I took the gun off him without faltering.

'Thank you very much, Sir.'

And walked into the centre of the audience, facing the stage where Sylvie stood shivering behind the transparent pane of glass. The prop shifters dragged on a huge padded mattress and placed it to her left.

I undid my tie, leaving its limp ends hanging down my white shirt, trying to look like a ruined man, then cast my gaze across the room and said, 'Love is a strange and fragile thing.' I lifted the gun and pointed it at Sylvie. She shrank against her board. I took a deep breath, squeezed the trigger and fired it, BANG, into the mattress, sending an explosion of stuffing into a small dark blizzard around the stage. 'I used to love that woman, but she took my love and . . .' BANG. The mattress took another hit and the smell of cordite filled the room. 'Ruined it.' I looked about the hall. 'It's enough to drive a man . . .' BANG, BANG, BANG. I dropped my voice to the low mild tone of the clinically insane. '. . . Mad.'

I turned, took aim, raised my arm and fired. The glass in front of Sylvie shattered, she jerked against the board and someone screamed. Then there was silence.

Sylvie stood intact with something clamped tight between her teeth. The ninjas jogged on and released her. She massaged her wrists then reached into her mouth, took out a bullet and held it high.

The crowd broke into noisy applause; I bounded on-stage to the accompaniment of laughter and hisses. We took our bows, the curtain descended and the lights came up for the interval.

*   *   *

Gina sat dizzyingly high above us at the suspended baby grand, her black hair spiked into a plume, her slim legs pumping against the pedals as she banged out a honky-tonk number. She shook her head with the melody and peered through her glasses, smiling at the party down below.

The theatre's seats and tables had been pushed around the side of the hall; a few couples had started to dance, but most people were still at the drinking stage. I leant by the bar listening to one of the clowns describe the new act his troupe were rehearsing, a mime gag that involved disguising him as a mechanical doll. It was an old ruse, but a good one.

If I'd known it was Ulla's birthday I would have

232

bought her a gift. The triumph of the evening's performance was soured by the missed opportunity. I swirled my drink around my glass wondering what I would have got her. Flowers? No, the clowns gave those to her all the time. Jewellery? Maybe too elaborate. Tomorrow I would walk along the Kurf ürstendamm and search for a modest but thoughtful present. Something Scottish? No, something chic but simple, something that would make her look at me in another way. I wondered what Kolja had bought her, perhaps a fancy frame and a new portrait of himself.

The party was mainly composed of people from Schall und Rauch, some still dressed in costume, others in street clothes, some half in, half out. They were performers, most of them in their twenties. I looked around the room and thought that maybe I should find a gym and try to get fit. Or maybe I should just join a library and find some good books to fill the long, lonely hours with.

Erhard gave Sylvie a hug and his twin Archard came up behind, enclosing her between their two tattooed bodies. My assistant looked like the dancer she was in a natty black cocktail dress whose skirt was all fringes, and a pair of satin shorts that made the most of her legs. Beside me the clown started to mime the new act; I laughed, watching Sylvie out of the corner of my eye as she smiled, showing her perfect American teeth, and wriggled out of the twins' embrace. I wondered if the rumours about the twins' sex life were true. It was an interesting thought.

I scanned the room looking for Ulla, realising that the party was getting busier as people drifted

233

in from other shows. Eventually I spotted her on the far side of the room amongst a small knot of well wishers, with Kolja smiling by her side. She'd swapped the high red shoes for a pair of sneakers but still wore the cut-off leggings and vest. They gave her the look of a scruffy principal boy. She laughed and looked up at Kolja. I took a sip of my drink and nodded to show that I was listening to the clown's description of the aluminium mask he hoped would fool the audience into thinking he was a mechanical man.

There was a light touch on my arm and I turned to see Nixie standing beside me.

'Hello, William.' Her voice was soft and hesitant. The clown gave me a wink, lifted his drink and went into the crowd. Nixie leaned up and kissed me gently on either cheek. 'Sorry.'

'Hey, no worries,' I grinned. 'It worked out OK in the end.'

She smiled. I could see the low neckline of her leotard beneath the gauzy yellow shirt she'd thrown on top. I hesitated; Nixie's English was equal to my German, but perhaps we could find other ways of communicating. Sylvie was chatting animatedly in the midst of a group of people I didn't recognise. She looked towards me, raising her eyebrows comically as she saw me leaning in to offer Nixie a drink. I ignored Sylvie's amusement and headed for the bar.

I was passing Nixie a chilled glass of white when I spotted a tall slim figure I knew walking into the hall. The hula girl raised her glass.

'Prost!'

Her blonde hair was soft and fluffy, her little body as tight and pneumatic as a high-school-movie cheerleader's. She looked wholesome and sweet and she liked me. I gave her a kiss, asked the barman for a glass of champagne and started to make my way across the room.

*   *   *

Zelda had swapped her sailorgirl costume for a sophisticated cowgirl look. Tight blue jeans and high-heeled western boots emphasised her long legs, her open-necked white shirt was crisp and cool, a simple gold lariat pointed from the hollow of her throat down into the crevice between her breasts. All she needed was a hat, a six-shooter and a donkey. I'd never really suited hats and my gun was with the rest of my props, but maybe I could help her out with the donkey side of things. She'd positioned herself by the stage and was standing on her own, glancing around the room, looking as if she wished she hadn't come. I slid up on her blind side and held out the glass of champagne.

'Drink?'

Zelda smiled.

'Thank you.' She took the glass and lifted it to her lips, leaving a trace of lipstick on its rim. 'I wondered if I would see you here.' I forced my face to stay straight, trying not to look too pleased. Zelda's voice was amused. 'I heard there was some trouble at the Nachtreview after I left.'

'Maybe a little.' I kept my voice casual. 'Is Sebastian with you?'

'No.' She shook her head laughing. 'He's angry with himself for letting Sylvie back.'

'It wasn't her fault, Zelda, a man started to

235

hassle her.'

'Hassle?'

'Harass.'

Zelda shrugged her shoulders.

'I wonder why.' She didn't wait for me to defend Sylvie any further. 'You didn't leave me a ticket.'

'I hope you didn't pay.'

'No,' she gestured vaguely to the room. 'I know people here.'

'It was the first evening, so not as slick as we will be.'

Zelda knew the performers' etiquette of false modesties, genuine insecurities and praise that was sometimes sincere, sometimes not, but was always welcome.

'You're very skilled.'

'I've always been good with my hands.'

Zelda shook her head, smiling.

'So I saw . . .' She looked out towards the dance floor, searching the crowd with her eyes. '. . . And you like the torture stuff?'

'No,' I grinned. 'No, it's all for the act. I'm . . .' I hesitated, not sure what I was going to say. 'I'm not into pain.' Zelda laughed again.

'Not for yourself perhaps, but you chop women in two, stick them full of knives then shoot them.'

There was an edge to her words that I hadn't expected. 'It's just an act, Zelda.'

'Yes?' She took another sip of champagne, looking at me over the rim of the glass. 'So as long as it's pretend that's OK?'

The conversation seemed to have snaked out of my control.

'I think so, yes.'

Zelda smiled.

'You and I see the world differently, William.'

'Perhaps you could educate me.'

'Do I look like a school miss?'

'No, but I imagine you've got the costume somewhere.'

A slim woman in black jeans, shirt and leather jacket that I recognised as one of the ninja prop shifters emerged from the press of people and slid her arm around Zelda. They kissed and Zelda lifted the champagne to her friend's lips. The dark girl took a tiny sip. Zelda smiled as if the off-duty ninja had just done something clever and the two girls leaned into each other. The ninja looked at me with mild unthreatened eyes. No one bothered to introduce me.

I turned to go. 'Have a good party.'

Zelda lifted her glass.

'Thanks for the drink. You were good, William. But you don't need women's blood to make you look talented.'

'Thanks for the advice.'

She shrugged.

'It comes free with every glass of champagne.'

High up on the baby grand Gina drove the keys into an up-tempo number. The dark girl put her arm through Zelda's, leading her onto the dance floor. Zelda looked back over her shoulder.

'Remember what I told you, strange people make for strange times.'

I said, 'Aye, aye.' Irritated by her white shirt, her smooth lipstick smile and the long legs stepping away from me. I turned to look for Nixie, wondering if I could regain ground, and saw Ulla moving slowly through the squeeze of bodies towards the office.

'Happy birthday.'

Ulla looked distracted but she gave me a smile. 'Thanks, William.'

'If I'd known I would have got you a present.'

'There was no need.'

She glanced nervously in the direction she'd been heading. The party was busy now and it was difficult to make headway without pushing through knots of people.

'Thanks again for helping us out.'

'You've thanked me already.'

'Sorry.' I grinned. 'What I really meant to say was . . .' I hesitated and Ulla looked worried. '. . . May I have this dance?'

Ulla laughed but her eyes still flickered away from me. 'I'm looking for Kolja.'

'He can dance with you anytime.' I turned my mouth down at the corners. 'I'm beginning to think German girls are unfriendly.'

Ulla sighed, and then smiled.

'OK, one dance.'

We moved towards the floor just as Gina switched from the up-tempo number she'd been playing into a German hit that I didn't recognise and whose beat I couldn't catch. Ulla was a good dancer, light on her feet with a nice synchronisation between her shoulders and hips. I lumbered as close to the rhythm as I could get, hoping my clumsiness was endearing. I wondered what kind of a dancer Kolja was, but couldn't imagine him sharing the floor with anyone else. The music shifted into another song, I kept dancing, but Ulla was determined.

'Thank you for the dance, William.' She smiled. 'But I'm worried Kolja may be unwell.'

'Nonsense,' I said, my feet still moving, hoping he'd been crushed under a giant prop, kidnapped by the Albanian mafia or maybe just disappeared. up his own arse-hole. 'He's the fittest man I've ever seen.'

I cast an invisible fishing line and started to wind its reel towards me.

Ulla refused to be hooked.

'Sometimes he does too much.' I wondered if Kolja was on steroids, but I stopped moving and stepped to one side, allowing Ulla to leave the dance floor. She squeezed my hand as she moved away. 'German girls are not always unfriendly, William, not if they're single. Nixie was looking for you earlier.'

I nodded, 'Yeah, thanks Ulla.' I turned away to hide my disappointment. I'd lost track of Sylvie, but that was hardly surprising. The floor was hoatching now. She'd probably found an attractive man to spend some time with. A sudden thought struck me and I moved quickly, ignoring the gasps and retaliating shoves of the party makers I forced aside in my panic to catch up with Ulla. At last I saw her brown ponytail bobbing in front of me and put my hand on her arm, halting her.

'I think I left my wallet in the office. If Kolja's in there I'll send him out to you.'

Ulla looked impatient. Her voice was firm.

'Nein . . . danke.'

She turned her back on me and walked on ahead. I hurried after, trying to think of something that might delay her, hoping I was wrong. We reached the office almost at the same time and I placed my hand across the door.

'I'll save you the trouble.'

239

Ulla pushed me away, walked into the room and turned on the light.

*   *   *

Kolja looked like an illustration from a Soviet poster expounding the health of communist ideology. A young pioneer, or a red-kerchiefed Stakhanovite. He stood straight and silent in the centre of the room, his broad chest flung out, muscular arms by his side. But the men in the posters had animated faces, full of joy at their role in the construction of the socialist nirvana. Kolja's face was serene, staring into the small mirror that was tucked amongst the framed pictures on Ray's wall. He turned his glazed eyes on us, a slight smile touched his lips then he shoved the source of his serenity from her knees and onto the ground.

Sylvie looked up at us from her position on the floor. Her eyes were glassy. She smiled unsteadily. Kolja started to button himself away; his mouth took on a grim set.

'Hey, William, Ulla . . . Happy birthday . . .' Sylvie wiped a gloss from her lips. 'You come to join the fun?'

There was a hiss as Ulla leapt at my assistant, wrestling her to the floor. Sylvie let out a sound that was halfway between a laugh and a groan. Kolja stepped neatly to one side and I bent into the fray. When I managed to pull the girls apart I could feel the scratch of a fingernail down the side of my face and Ulla had a bunch of Sylvie's sleek hair clutched in her fist. I shoved the struggling girl at her boyfriend and he put his hands on her shoulders, still smiling. I glanced at Kolja, unsure

240

of whether he was stoned or merely enjoying the sight of the two women fighting over him, then looked at Ulla's stricken face, and felt sorry for her humiliation. I managed to make my voice gentle.

'Can you not see she's out of her head?'

Ulla turned on me.

'You knew this was happening. You tried to cover for her. Your whore.' Her face screwed into a mask of grief; there was a keening in her shrill voice. 'You wanted me, so you sent her to make trouble.'

'No . . . I swear . . . I didn't know . . .'

My voice faltered against the accusation.

Sylvie was still on the floor.

'William?'

Her voice was thin and confused.

Ulla spat on Sylvie.

'She'd open her legs to a dog if it sniffed her.'

I looked at Ulla, and wondered what I'd seen in her.

'She's so drunk she can hardly see.' Sylvie looked at the spit glistening white against her lovely black dress as if wondering how it got there and I realised the truth of what I was saying. 'Into a bit of necrophilia is he, your athlete boyfriend? Look at her, she can hardly move.'

Ulla said, 'You disgust me.'

'Not as much as he disgusts me, your fucking boyfriend's no better than a fucking rapist.'

Kolja spoke for the first time. His voice was hesitant and it sounded like he had summoned up the total of his English vocabulary.

'It was nothing. It meant nothing, like a drink or a cigarette.'

Ulla saw what was going to happen and moved

to stop me, but she was too slow and too slight. I pushed her aside with my left hand, balled my right fist and hit Kolja square in the centre of his handsome weak face. The big athlete was caught by surprise. He lost his balance and fell against Ray's desk, which spewed a blizzard of files and documents onto the floor. Sylvie batted at the spray of papers as they drifted around her. Her voice was soft with awe.

'William, you just hit Kolja.'

I grinned at her.

'Aye, I did and you know what? I'm going to fucking hit him again.'

Ulla shouted something in German. I leaned in to pull Kolja upright, all the better to get a shot at him, and she leapt on me, clawing at my back. Kolja was beginning to rise from the desk of his own volition and suddenly I realised that if the athlete made it to his feet I was finished. I grabbed Ray's computer keyboard and slammed it into Kolja's face. The keyboard was too heavy to make a good weapon, but I stuck with it, amazed at how quickly the white keys became spotted with red, wondering if Ulla's screams really were in time to the offbeat rhythm of my assault.

It was a relief to hear the strong German voices of the men who pulled me off. I gasped for breath, not bothering to struggle against their hold, hoping I hadn't killed him. Then Kolja's fist crashed into my face. The sound went out of my ears and my eyes filled with red. I reeled against the person holding me, and would have fallen if they'd not braced against me. The pain was blinding. I waited for Kolja to take another shot, but it never came. A man I didn't know shouted something I didn't

242

understand and didn't bother to answer.

I spat blood and said, 'Fuck off the lot of yous, and take that fucking rapist scum with you or I'll fucking do him for good.'

It came out as a spray of spit and gore and I doubt anyone understood me but the room emptied anyway and Sylvie and I were left alone.

There was a silence and I found myself gazing at the photograph of Ray's granddad with his head inside the polar bear's mouth. A moment of triumph followed by decapitation, that's entertainment.

Sylvie looked up at me from the floor. The fringes of her dress were rucked around her waist; her red lipstick smeared across her mouth. She still wore the plaster and glass tiara, but it was sideways on now, a stupid gewgaw, not even a slipped halo. My assistant's eyes were wide, her voice small and distant as if she were talking to me from a long way off.

She said, 'What's so terrible about being called a whore?'

Glasgow

There isn't much between the magic you perform for adults and the type that you do for children. Once again, the difference is in the delivery, the patter, the flimflam, whatever it is that you want to call the chat and flourishes that distract the eye and make the audience want to indulge the conjurer's art.

I'd always looked down on children's

entertainers as a suspicious mix of arrested-development failures, half-arsed amateurs and prospective paedophiles. Now I was grateful that Johnny's gig was for a family audience. It would be as far from my disasters in Berlin as it was possible to get and still be conjuring.

I said goodbye to Eilidh, set down the receiver and stood for a second in the shelter of the phone booth wondering what to do next. There were a dozen pubs and a similar number of bookies within yards of where I was standing. I'd withdrawn the last of the money stashed in the wardrobe before I'd left my room. Over the previous months I'd frittered it on drink, resolved never to touch it, then frittered it again. I pushed the thought of a pint and a flutter out of my head and walked along the Trongate, past the born-again preachers, the animal rights activists, the *Big Issue* vendors, buskers, flower sellers and fake perfume boys until I found a cut-price opticians I'd noticed before. I went in and sorted out a supply of disposable contact lenses, then found a barbershop and had a haircut. I stepped freshly shorn into Princes Square and bought myself a flashy purple shirt that set me back a whack and a pay-as-you-go mobile phone that didn't. Finally, I broke away from the weekend shopping chaos and set off towards the Magician's Den.

*   *   *

Conjuring manuals are like recipe books, OK if all you want is a passable trick or an acceptable cake, but if you want to create something superlative then you must seek out people you can persuade to share their secrets with you. To do that you have to find the place where the masters hang out and maybe after a while they'll deign to notice you, and maybe a while after that, if you make yourself useful enough, they'll let a few tips drop your way.

I pushed open the door of the Den and heard the familiar bell ding news of my arrival into the backroom. Bruce had told me once that he considered his shop as dramatic as any stage.

'I give the customers a moment to soak up the ambience, the *strangeness* and then I make my entrance.'

Nothing seemed to have changed much. The long counter still stretched the length of the small sales area, displaying jokes and novelties beneath its glass top. The more expensive paraphernalia was at the furthest end, nearest to Bruce's cubbyhole, where he could keep an eye on it. High above the shelves were the rubberised masks, crones and old men, Boris Karloff creations, animals and politicians, including a set of American presidents stretching back all the way to Richard Nixon. Behind the masks hung framed replicas of ancient theatrical posters advertising Harry Houdini and his ilk, dressed in lion-skin togas or long combinations, battling with wild beasts, wrestling free of chains, tight-roping across impossible gorges. The velvet curtain, whose figured pattern concealed a small spy hole, drew to one side and out stepped Bruce McFarlane dressed in his brown shop coat.

'William, long time no see.'

It was three years since I'd last been in the shop, but Bruce didn't seem surprised. He was forty-five when I met him twenty-odd years ago, and a very old man to my ten-year-old eyes. He was nigh on seventy now, but I'd say he looked a little younger than he did then. I nodded up at the presidents past.

'Jimmy Carter, Bruce?'

'Ach, you never know, William, there's a lot of seventies parties on the go. Someone might want to go as the auld Peanut King.' He opened a flap in the counter. 'Didnae know when we were well off, eh?' He stuck his hand out and shook mine, holding my elbow with one hand while he grasped my palm with the other, the closest to a manly hug his generation ever got. He gave me a smile and I knew he was pleased to see me. 'Come away through and I'll stick the kettle on.'

The backroom was as unchanged as the main shop. This was where the real business was done, the trading and exchanges, the gossiping and boasting. I'd thought I'd find a few of the other conjurers in here having a Saturday morning gab, but I was pleased to see that apart from us and dizzying piles of stock the place was empty.

'All on your own?'

'Like the *Marie Celeste* in here today, William. There's a magic convention over Paisley way, I was going to go myself but my wee Saturday laddie's got exams coming up and his mother phoned to say he wasn't allowed out the house.' He shook his head. 'No like you, eh, William?'

I smiled.

'No, Mr McFarlane.'

'Aye, best wee Saturday laddie I ever had. Always on time and spent all your wages in the shop.' The kettle boiled and Bruce put a teabag, two sugars and milk into two mugs before adding water. 'But you're not here to reminisce are you?'

'It's always good to catch up . . .'

'But you've got a favour you'd like to ask.'

He passed me a mug and I took a sip; it was too sweet.

'Just a wee one.' I reached into my inside pocket and took out a small card I'd written while I was getting my haircut. 'I'm doing a charity gig . . .'

Bruce raised his eyebrows.

'Not like you, William.'

I ignored the gibe.

'See if I give you the details will you send folk my way? It's for a good cause.'

'Course I will.' He took a sip of his own tea, frowned and added another teaspoonful of sugar. 'Now, tell me what you're really after.' The bell pinged and Bruce cocked his head like a bright-eyed parrot that's just heard the lid of the cracker jar being unscrewed. He waited three beats then said, 'Excuse me a sec . . .'

I peeked through the hole in the curtain as he strolled down the counter to serve two ten-year-olds, treating them like maharajas. When he returned ten minutes later he was grinning.

'Fake dog poo.'

'Still your fastest seller?'

'From eight to eighty.' He laughed. 'It's a classic gag.'

'Aye, a fucking hoot.'

Bruce raised his eyebrows.

'You'll have to ditch that language if you're going into kiddie conjuring.'

'Sorry, I'll go and wash my mouth out with some of your special soap.'

Bruce laughed.

'Not as popular as it used to be, but still funny.'

'Not everything has the longevity of plaster of Paris poo.

'No,' Bruce shook his head sadly. 'It's a pity that.'

*   *   *

We sat drinking sweet tea and eating ginger biscuits, while Bruce filled me in on what had been happening in the Scottish magic scene. Genie McSweenie's rabbit had been kidnapped at a rugby club social and held to ransom—*it wasn't funny, William, the poor beast was traumatised;* Stevie Star had crashed his van on the way back from Perth; Peter Presto had moved to America to take a shot at the big time; and Manfred the Great had been exposed as a kiddie fiddler.

'I always thought there was something not right about him.'

Bruce dunked his gingernut into his tea and nodded then sat up straight. The tea-soaked end of the biscuit lost out to gravity and plopped into his mug.

'That reminds me . . .' he shook his head. '. . . See, that's what happens when you get to my age, bloody senility. There was a chap phoned a few weeks ago looking for you.'

'Yes?'

'English bloke, said he'd seen you somewhere and mislaid your number. I told him I didn't have a contact for you, but he sounded keen.'

Bruce looked worried; concerned I might have missed a gig or even my big break.

'Pushy even?'

'A wee bit, typical cocky cockney, you know the kind. I met a lot of them in the forces. Nice enough fellas once you get to know them but they think anything north of London's outer space.'

'Did he leave a number?'

Bruce's face brightened.

'He did indeed.' His mouth dropped again and he looked around the tiny backroom piled high with mysterious parcels. 'But where did I put it?'

*   *   *

I selected what I was going to need for Johnny's show while Bruce rummaged through the drawers and boxes that constituted his filing system, cooing over odds and ends he thought he'd lost, until eventually he found the scrap of paper he'd scribbled my name onto and a mobile number below.

'Bingo! I knew I had it somewhere.' Bruce looked at the props I'd assembled. 'You want me to wrap that lot up for you?'

'If you want.'

He shook his head, lifted a fluffy toy rabbit from the top of my pile and looked at me from between its long ears.

'Changed days, William, changed days. ' Bruce totted up my purchases and started to putting them into bags. He put on his best shopkeeper manner. 'Now, will Sir be requiring anything else?'

I told him and he shook his head.

'You always were a bloody pain in the arse, William, even when you were a kid.'

'A minute ago I was the best Saturday laddie you ever employed.' I grinned at him. 'Come on Bruce, it's in a good cause, wee Down's Syndrome kids. I'll get you a mention in the programme. The place'll be full of weans. Who knows how much fake dog shite you'll sell on the back of this.'

'The word is poo, William, we don't say shite in this shop.' His expression softened. 'Aye, go on then. But you can arrange the bloody transport yourself.'

*　　　*　　　*

I remembered an Internet cafe somewhere near George Square; I walked through the Saturday-afternoon shoppers until I found it, waited in the long queue to buy a coffee, keeping my head down, hoping I wouldn't meet anyone I knew, then rented time on a computer.

The author of *The Friday the Thirteenth Vanishing*, the book devoted to Gloria's disappearance, was a man called Drew Manson. He'd written three other books, all of them following the demise of unfortunate women, all of them out of print. I punched the title and author's name into a search engine and let out a low *Yes* when the hits appeared on the screen. I smiled a silent apology at the studious girl on the next computer and clicked on Manson's website. It had a clumsy homemade feel, but I was its thousand-and-fifth visitor. The most recent postings wavered between hurt and outrage. All of them lamented the lack of new editions of Manson's books, in the same faintly florid style. At the bottom of the page were an email address and an invitation to contact Manson with any new information relating to the crimes in his books. I might be a cynical bachelor

250

who'd forfeited all hope of romance, but I was growing to love the Internet.

I set up a new email account, VeritableCrimePublishing@hotmail.com, and sent Manson an invitation to meet and discuss the possibility of a new edition of his book in the light of Bill Noon's tragic death. Then I looked at the links from Manson's site. There were reviews of his books, some long-past festivals Manson had read at and the address for the website of the National Missing Persons Helpline. I clicked on the link and started to scroll through the images of the disappeared.

They were random faces, more young than old, though the old were there too, looking out from their photographs or hiding behind the faces of their younger selves in pictures taken decades ago. Long hippy hair, seventies mullets, eighties flat-tops, photographs so dated they'd make you smile, if they'd not been turned tragic by circumstance. The same skewed aspect clung to all of the images. The lost mothers and brothers, sisters, aunts, daughters, sons and uncles generally had a carefree air, caught at a family celebration or a party or maybe just the last photograph in the spool.

There were two photographs of Gloria Noon. The familiar image I'd come to know from the newspaper reports and a second, digitally aged one. The page flashed from one to the other: *young Gloria, aged Gloria, young Gloria, aged Gloria.* The images were imperfectly aligned and her shoulders moved up and down between the two, making it look like Gloria was shrugging as she smiled out from the screen of lost faces. Her resumé summarised the time and known circumstances of her vanishing. It said nothing about possible murder.

Even at my lowest I'd never totally vanished. I wondered how many of the disappeared were dead, how many had been coerced into leaving. I wondered if they even knew that they were missing, that there were people who loved them, desperate to forgive whatever they had done. But then who was I to jump to conclusions? Maybe some of them had committed acts too awful to be absolved.

I clicked to the next page and a warning that the following images might disturb me; I clicked again and the screen threw forth photographs of some of the found. There were only three of them. A woman washed up in the Thames, a youth discovered dead in Petersham Woods and an elderly man who had lain in the bushes in Richmond Park for a very long time before his skeletal remains were uncovered. All of them had lost their features to decay and the images on this page showed reconstructions of how they might have looked in life. The technicians who rebuilt these faces were more magician than I'd ever be. They crafted an illusion of flesh onto bare bone, dragging back the lost features of the dead. The technicians' skill was painstaking and exact, but the images were ghastly. The smiles of the missing people that had shone carelessly from the previous page were all gone. There was no glimmer of expression here, the skin was too smooth, the eyes too blank, the lips too set, no living face ever held such deathness. The missing may yet be alive, but one look at the remoulded faces of these three showed what their fate might be.

I closed the site. The dead and the missing weren't going to tell me anything, my search had to be through the living. I logged onto yell.com and started to search for Gloria's sister, Sheila Bowen.

*   *   *

There were several Bowens in the telephone listings but only one Bowen's & Sons Gents Outfitters. I jotted down the number then checked my new Veritable Crime email account. There was a welcome to the server and an offer to enlarge my penis and supply me with Viagra. Maybe my enlarged penis would be too big to keep up without help. There was no message from Mr Manson.

The Internet cafe resembled a large open-plan office where the dress code ranged from casual to scruffy-as-you-like. I sat for a second listening to the sounds around me, the clatter of computer keys and occasional exchange of muted conversation, the kind of ambience a busy newsroom might generate. I collected a fresh coffee then took out my new mobile, dialled Bowen's outfitters and asked to speak to Mrs Sheila Bowen. I expected the woman on the other end to say she was retired, dead, or too busy to come to the phone, but instead her voice became guarded.

It said, 'This is Sheila Bowen. Is it about Gloria?'

London

For a woman whose sister had disappeared without trace from her own home in the middle of the day, Sheila Bowen was remarkably lax about security. I gave her a big smile and one of the business cards that I'd had made in a machine at the railway station, identifying me as Will Gray, freelance journalist. She glanced at it casually then invited me in.

Sheila lived in one of a row of semi-detached houses built in the fifties to accommodate lower-middle-class commuters. Today it was probably worth a small fortune. She greeted me at the door, and then led me through to a lounge decorated in pale parchment shades. Her white blouse and cream slacks blended with the room. Maybe her sister had taken the coordinating colour scheme too far and simply faded into the wallpaper.

I had hoped she'd leave me alone to get my bearings while she made a pot of tea, but Sheila had obviously had faith in my punctuality, or maybe she'd simply wanted to occupy her nerves in a domestic task. A tray holding a teapot, two matching cups and what looked like homemade cake, was already waiting on the blond wood coffee table.

If we'd met socially I would have supposed Sheila Bowen a well-preserved, middle-class housewife whose only concern was finding the right shade of white for her hall carpet or keeping her husband's cholesterol down. The slim woman sitting on the ivory-coloured couch opposite me

254

was surprisingly unchanged from the photographs in the thirty-year-old newspapers I'd found in the Mitchell. Her hair was ash-gold, styled in soft fronds around a pale face that was remarkably unlined considering all the troubles she'd encountered. It seemed that I wasn't the only one who could create an illusion.

She started to pour the tea and I noticed that her hands were steady. There was a wedding band and a diamond eternity ring on her left hand, and a slim silver ring that looked cheap against her other jewellery on her right. She passed me my cup.

'You came all the way from Scotland?'

'I took the train down from Glasgow this morning.'

Sheila looked confused.

'Gloria never went to Scotland.'

'I know.' I smiled. 'I just happen to be based there at the moment.' I took a sip of tea. 'It's good of you to see me. Many unsolved cases like Gloria's are under review at the moment, but sometimes it needs a bit of outside pressure to get the police to reopen them.'

Sheila rubbed her thumb nervously over her chin and then folded her hands in her lap as if someone had told her it was an irritating habit.

'My husband's always said that they never shut cases like Gloria's.'

I leant forward putting a note of sincerity into my voice.

'He's right, they don't. But, as I'm sure your husband will tell you, the police are undermanned and overworked. Sometimes it doesn't hurt to have a bit of press attention.' Sheila nodded silently. 'I know it must still be very painful to talk about Gloria's disappearance even after all these years. Are you willing to give me a brief interview?'

Sheila looked at me.

'I'd walk barefoot into Hell to get my sister back, or even just find out what happened to her.'

'OK,' I smiled but there was no answering smile on Sheila Bowen's face. 'I'll get straight to the point. In all the press reports at the time of Gloria's disappearance, there seemed to be an underlying suggestion that it was her husband Bill who was responsible. Do you agree with them?'

Sheila Bowen looked over towards the picture of a Cotswold scene hanging above the living gas fireplace. It was a restful view across green fields to a little thatched cottage inside a neatly fenced country garden. It looked like the kind of place where nothing bad ever happened. There were even roses round the door. But who could guess what horrors might lie inside its rustic walls? At last Sheila met my gaze.

'Well, you're certainly direct.' She poured more tea into her cup then left it untouched on the table. 'This is difficult. There was a period after Gloria disappeared when I didn't . . . couldn't talk about her at all. I was suspicious of everyone, especially men.' She looked at her lap and began twisting the cheap silver ring on her right hand. 'But as time passed I began to realise that by shutting out memories of her I was denying the life that she had had. And by giving in to constant suspicion I was ruining my own life as well.' Shelia paused as if trying to order her thoughts. 'Her son's dead too, Billy.' I nodded to show that I already knew and she carried on talking, her voice

256

level. 'He was a sweet boy but after Gloria went it was hard to keep in touch with him.' She shook her head. 'There was a lot of bad feeling between his father and me after the investigation. I suspected him and he accused me of sending the police on the wrong track. It was hard to come back from that. Maybe I should have pressed more, but I wasn't in the best of health myself . . . then I got married. Jim hated to see me upset and it became easier to shut that part of my life up.'

'Perhaps you had to, to protect your own sanity.'

'That's what Jim said, but now I wonder; if I'd been around more, if I hadn't been so determined that his father was guilty, maybe Billy would still be alive.'

'You can't torture yourself with what-ifs. You did your best.'

'You and Jim should get together. That's exactly what he says. Jim's always wanted to protect me, he encouraged me to forget.' She took a sip of tea. 'When my children were young it was easy for a while. I was so busy. Then they began to grow up and I realised I was ready to talk about Gloria again, but by then no one was interested.' She looked into my eyes. 'You're the first one who's asked about her in a long while.' Sheila put her cup back on the table and straightened her back ready to get on with answering my question. 'Gloria's husband, Bill, was very handsome and compared to the family that Gloria and I grew up in, very comfortably off. Perhaps she should have asked a few more questions about where his money came from, but Gloria was young and pretty and wanted a good life. I never blamed her for marrying Bill.'

'But he hit her?'

Sheila looked at her feet again.

'I only saw evidence of it once.'

'The time Bill claimed Gloria had fallen down the stairs?'

Sheila nodded.

'Yes, and I believed her. Bill was in the nightclub business. You don't get anywhere in that world without knowing how to throw your weight around, and why should Gloria lie? Yes, of course I believed her.'

'I'm sorry. Some of these questions are going to touch on difficult ground.'

Sheila nodded and gave me a brave smile.

'Do you smoke?'

'Yes.'

'Then let's go outside and have a ciggy.'

We went through French windows onto a small terrace. Life had proved itself unreliable, but Sheila had managed to inflict order on nature. Her garden was an almost symmetrical arrangement of lawn and well-disciplined flowerbeds. There was a wrought-iron table and chairs beside us on the patio, but Sheila led me down the lawn, stopping occasionally to deadhead plants or pull a reckless weed from a border. Perhaps it was too chilly to sit outside or maybe she found it easier to talk of her sister without looking into someone else's eyes.

'Jim doesn't like me smoking, but an occasional one doesn't hurt and it sure as hell helps.' She laughed and for the first time I thought I could see a trace of her sister Gloria in her face. 'You want to ask about Gloria's lover.'

I nodded, relieved she'd broached the subject.

'Yes.'

258

'It always comes down to that in the end doesn't it? Sex.'

'It's a powerful force.'

'Is that what you call it? . . . He was very hush-hush, Gloria's amour.' Sheila pulled a brown-edged leaf from a bush and crushed it between her fingers. 'They never found him you know. It wasn't for the want of looking.' She opened her palm, looked at the crumpled leaf and then let it drop to the ground. 'He's never said so, but I know Jim thinks Gloria just made a lover up to make life a little more exciting.'

'And what do you think?'

'I think he was probably married.'

*   *   *

The rain that had threatened all day started to spit; Sheila and I moved back indoors, she glanced at her watch and I got the sensation that our interview was drawing to its end. I asked, 'If there was a lover do you think that Gloria would have left her husband?'

Sheila looked at me.

'I don't know and I've thought about it a lot over the years. That day has coloured everything since, even when I met Jim there was the shadow of it hanging over us. I used to think that she would have, but as I've got older I've wondered. She was devoted to Billy and his father wouldn't have let him go easily. Maybe if it was the love of her life, maybe then, but the maternal bond is the strongest one of all; I think it would have taken a lot of persuasion for her to jeopardise it.' She nodded towards a dresser where a group of framed photographs crowded together. 'I should know, I've got two of my own.'

I glanced at the photographs: two nondescript boys in school uniform, flanked by the graduation photographs of two nondescript young men, followed by the formal portraits of the same boys/men, balding now, wearing dark suits reminiscent of their school blazers. I wondered how many more pictures it would take to complete the set. To the right of the arrangement in a chased silver frame was a studio portrait of Gloria Noon.

I said, 'Do you mind?'

Sheila nodded her permission and I picked it up. 'She was a beautiful-looking woman.'

'Not just to look at, she was beautiful inside too.' She gave me the smile that was like Gloria's. 'It sounds silly, but sometimes I imagine that she's on a long journey around the world. I can picture her in Egypt or Turkey . . . Marrakech; always somewhere exotic, somewhere sunny.' She took the photograph from me and for the first time since we'd met I thought that she might cry, but instead she gave a short laugh. 'You know, if she came back now and said she'd just been on an extended holiday I might kill her myself.'

I watch Sheila's slim hands replace Gloria's portrait on the dresser and a second framed photograph caught my eye. I reached over and lifted it, keeping my voice as casual as I could.

'A family friend?'

'What made you say that?' Sheila's smile was warm. 'That's my husband, Jim.'

'Mr Bowen?'

'Bowen was my first husband's name. He died

260

two years before Gloria vanished.' She shook her head. 'Myeloid leukaemia, he lasted six months after the diagnosis. Gloria going would have hit me hard whatever happened but after Frank's death . . .' She shook her head, remembering. 'Well you can imagine, I thought that was going to be the end for me too. Then along came Jim.' She smiled again. 'He was part of the investigation team. I think deep down the rest of them just thought Gloria was an immoral woman who'd left her husband. Those were different times. But Jim never believed that. He kept on pushing and that was when I fell in love with him.' She smiled. 'I kept the name Bowen over the shop, Frank's grandfather was the founder and it would have been wrong to change it.' She smiled. 'That was how I knew that you were phoning about Gloria. No one calls me Bowen any more. I've been Sheila Montgomery since I married Jim.'

*   *   *

My mind was full of what might have happened had James Montgomery come home early and found me in his front room interrogating his wife. Part of me wished he had. What could he do with her there? But a larger part was relieved to escape.

I walked as swiftly as I could away from the Montgomery house, cursing suburbia's open streets, not daring to catch a train back in case I passed him en route to his home. Eventually I found a parade of shops and managed to catch a bus that would take me out of the district.

*   *   *

Back in central London I used a public email telephone to check my VeritableCrime inbox. Technology might have moved on but people were still pissing in phone boxes. I held my breath and tried to work out how to use the machine. The connection was painfully slow and I had time to read the details of a dozen women eager to dance, massage or generally entertain me. I wondered if they knew the risk they were taking.

The Viagra people had got back in touch and so had Drew Manson. He was keen to meet and had left a mobile number.

He answered on the third ring. I explained that I was heading off to a publishing conference tomorrow but would love to see him before I went, was he free for a late lunch? Mr Manson was free. He suggested a gastropub somewhere near Farringdon. I'd taken a dancer there once. The food had been expensive and she'd gone home for an early night saying she had to keep fresh for the next day's show. I hoped I'd have better luck with Mr Manson.

*　　　*　　　*

Drew Manson's author photograph showed a man in his thirties wearing spectacles of the kind favoured by David Hockney and an intense stare under a shock of dark hair styled in a manner popular with young intellectuals in the sixties. Manson looked up from the typewriter on his desk with a mixture of surprise and intellectual rigour on his blunt face, his right hand frozen above the keys in mid-strike as if he'd been surprised in the act of writing a very big word.

The clues were there in the sixties styling, the lack of computer and the publication date on the inside cover of the library book in my bag. But I wasn't prepared for the balding man in his sixties who walked into the pub, even though he was wearing the same glasses, or a close relative of them. I let him stand in the doorway for a second, looking around the pub with the controlled anxiety of a man who has attended many disappointments, but still harbours some hope, and then I stood up and went to meet him.

'Mr Manson?'

'Yes.'

His accent was how I imagined old-school Cambridge would sound and I was glad I'd decided to try for an intellectual look by wearing my own specs.

'William Wilson, thanks for agreeing to see me at such short notice.'

Manson looked self-consciously writerly. His trousers were a deep chocolate jumbo cord, his tie bore a monogram I didn't recognise, but would probably signal something to the initiated, and his tweed jacket was patched at the elbows. I wondered if he was the real thing or an old fraud. I started to go through the spiel about the new line in crime books that my very small, very newly established publishing house was hoping to reprint with updates on any developments since the original publication.

'I'm interested in the Gloria Noon case because of the recent murder of her son Bill.'

Manson nodded and made a hissing noise, sucking the air between his teeth like a man giving something serious thought.

The waitress came with our menus and Manson began studying his with the intensity of a shortsighted don assessing a borderline exam script. When the waitress returned he ordered, 'Steak, rare, with a green salad and a bottle of Barolo. I'll have a glass of Pouilly Fumé while we're waiting.' He watched as the girl bobbed off to the kitchen then turned to me, smiling patiently.

'Mr Wilson, I've listened to this with great interest but it's patently clear even to one of my failing abilities, that you've nothing whatsoever to do with publishing.' He gave me a mild look over his glasses, offering me the chance to contradict him. I sat silent and he smiled as if he approved of my lack of protest. 'Perhaps now lunch is safely ordered you'll do me the courtesy of telling me who you really are and what it is that you're after.'

I grinned.

'No flies on you, eh, Mr Manson?'

He gave me his donnish smile and I gave him my back-up story. It involved schooldays and Bill and I don't think he believed it any better, but he was satisfied that I wasn't writing a book, and perhaps there were enough contradictions in my pose to spark his curiosity.

Manson reached into his jacket.

'Right, as you've dragged me here on false pretences I think I'm entitled to claim some expenses from you.'

He laid his train ticket in front of me. I fished awkwardly in my pocket for the money to cover it then opened my wallet and added an extra tenner.

'Get a taxi from the station at the other end.'

He slid the note back across the bar-room table.

264

'The fare is sufficient thank you, and . . .' He took a sip of the Pouilly Fumé and nodded his head. '. . . Very good. I'm happy to discuss the Gloria Noon case with you, in return for one simple promise.'

'What?'

Manson's bookish aspect slipped slightly; there was a tinge of estuary to his accent now.

'That you share any new material you find with me.'

I hesitated, as if carefully considering his proposal. 'There's no guarantees I'll uncover anything new, but if I do I'll be happy to tell you all about it.'

'Good,' Manson took another sip of his drink. 'So we understand each other?'

I nodded and we sat in a silence that wasn't quite companionable, drinking our wine and tearing at the bread until the food arrived.

The waitress set Manson's steak down first then slid my ravioli in front of me and sprinkled it with Parmesan over its top. Manson looked at my lunch with distaste then lifted his knife and sliced into his steak. Blood seeped across the white plate, resisting mixing with the dark-brown gravy that pooled around the meat. Manson put the piece of steak in his mouth and started to chew, then he started to talk.

'Cases where the body remains unfound are always intriguing. In an instance like the unfortunate Mrs Noon's we know that she's probably deceased, and yet a scintilla of doubt remains. Maybe she simply walked away from an unsatisfactory marriage.'

'And her child?'

'It does happen.'

Manson speared a piece of broccoli, added a small roast potato to the fork and smiled tenderly at the arrangement before putting it in his mouth.

'I suppose it does, not often though.'

'More often than you might think, anyway,' he put a small piece of steak in his mouth and kept on talking. 'I wasn't saying that was what had happened, just that it's a possibility. No body, no certainty of death.'

'Like Lord Lucan.'

'Exactly.'

Manson's strong jaws set to work and I glanced away to avoid seeing the food churning between his teeth.

'What do you think happened in Gloria's case?'

'You read my book?'

'Yes.' I'd read it on the train down from Glasgow, half-disgusted by the ease with which I was drawn into the minutiae of Gloria's disappearance. It had told me nothing that the press reports hadn't. 'It was fascinating, but though the evidence pointed in certain directions you didn't come to any definite conclusions. I wondered what you thought had happened.'

'Off the record?'

'Sure.'

'Off the record I think Bill Noon killed his wife.' Manson slugged back the last of the wine. He smiled, savouring the vintage, or maybe the crime. I nodded to the waitress for a second bottle.

'How can you be sure?'

'Ah,' he held up his fork. 'I didn't say I was sure, I said that was what I thought had probably happened. There's a difference.'

266

'I take your point.'

'A crime boils down to three classic things— means, motive and opportunity. Bill Noon had all of these.'

'What about her lover?'

'The mysterious lover.' Manson pushed aside his empty plate and smiled as the waitress placed the second bottle on our table. 'Maybe he's on a beach in Acapulco drinking mai-tais with Gloria Noon, maybe he was a figment of her imagination, maybe he killed her or maybe Bill did him too.' I topped up his glass and he grinned. 'Of course that would assume that there was no one except Gloria who cared for him, because no one who fitted the bill was reported missing.'

'But he could have murdered her, disposed of the body and disappeared back to where he came from.'

'In theory, yes.'

'But unlikely?'

He shrugged.

'If you really were a publisher I'd spin you a line about the chapter I'd write about the possible lovers of Gloria Noon, all completely within the libel laws you understand, but no I don't think so.'

'So where's Bill Noon's motive if there's no lover?'

Manson knocked back more wine and levelled his stare at me.

'Doesn't every husband have a motive?'

'I don't know. I've never been married.'

'No,' he grinned. 'Me neither, but if I were . . .'

'You'd be divorced?'

'I was going to say I imagine I'd have a motive for murder.'

He laughed, serving himself more wine and I asked the question that had been in my mind ever since I'd seen the picture of the two men standing beside the loch's edge.

'Do you think that Bill Noon could have had someone helping him?'

Manson looked up sharply, half-cut but able to spot a lead when it was twitched in front of him.

'What makes you ask that?'

'It was just a thought. I saw a similar case a while back.'

Manson didn't bother asking me which case because he knew I was lying. His voice was hesitant; he put his glass on the table, though his fingers still touched its stem.

'It's not impossible; it would certainly make the disposal of the body easier. The main problem . . .' He smiled. 'Laying aside the usual difficulty of finding someone willing to help you get rid of your wife's dead body, the main problem would be finding someone you could trust to keep schtumm. If there's any trouble, or the possibility of a reward, they might grass you up to take the heat off themselves. Then there's the Raskolnikov effect. You mustn't underestimate the confessional instinct. It's very strong.' He took off his glasses, massaged his temples then looked at me, his small eyes pale and tired. 'But the basic fact is, the more people in on a crime, the more likely you are to be caught. Bill Noon would know that.' He belched softly. 'Unless you have evidence to the contrary I'd say you were barking up the wrong tree there, old mate. Bill Noon would have had to find an accomplice he could trust absolutely not to hand him in and one who wouldn't have an attack of

268

conscience, start boasting or get drunk and start blabbing to all and sundry.' He turned his gimlet eyes on me, and now he looked faintly like his author photo, though there was an insistent tone to his voice that was close to pleading. 'If you come up with anything, tell me. I'll give you a credit in the book.'

I told him he'd be welcome to whatever I found out. Drew Manson nodded, satisfied he'd got as good a guarantee as he was ever going to get from me. He replaced his glasses on his nose and looked around the bar in search of our waitress. She caught his eye and tripped prettily across the room towards us. Manson gave her a very unacademic glance and a smile that showed the traces of broccoli trapped between his teeth.

'That was delicious, darling.' He grinned. 'I think we're ready to see the dessert menu now.'

Berlin

I'd been leaning against the desk smoking a cigarette and watching Sylvie sleep when Ray knocked on his office door and put his head cautiously into the room. Ray's moustache looked sadder than I'd ever seen it, but his dark eyes were sharp as polished dice and his cheeks flushed. I ventured a smile, but there'd been a lot of calls on my charm recently and I could feel that my reserves had grown slim. Ray hesitated, then, satisfied that the violence was over, turned and said something soft to someone standing beyond my view. He nodded to say he'd be safe, then slid into the room and closed the door.

'William.'

He shook his head as if lost for words.

'Yeah, I know Ray, sorry.'

'No,' his voice was hard, 'I'm sorry. You were making a good act.'

I sucked the last draw from my cigarette and looked for somewhere to stub it out. Ray's computer lay askew amongst the mass of crushed paper on his desk, the key-board spattered with Kolja's blood. If there'd ever been an ashtray it was lost somewhere beneath the debris. I nipped the end of my fag with my fingers and put it in my pocket.

'Shit, Ray. I'm sorry about the mess.'

'Everyone's sorry, William. You, me, Ulla.' He nodded at Sylvie slumped on the chair I'd lifted her into. 'Her too probably, when she wakes up.'

The indignity of the moment made my speech formal. 'Is my engagement terminated?'

Ray nodded.

'We depend on . . ' He sought for an expression. 'Harmony . . . Ulla . . .'

'Ulla wants us out?' I hesitated, hoping he'd contradict me, but Ray nodded. I sighed. 'Yeah, I understand. Just pay me and I'll collect my stuff and go.'

Ray looked sadder than ever. He reached into his pocket, drew out a bundle of notes and peeled a couple off the top. He passed them to me.

'Someone will bring you your things.'

I looked at the hundred euros in my hand.

'Ray, this isn't what you owe me.'

'No, William.' The tide of red on Ray's face seemed to be gaining ground. 'It's not what I owe you. I spent money on advertising, travel, your new boxes, then . . .' He spread his hands out taking in the mess of his office and I remembered how he'd described it as his sanctuary. '. . . You try to destroy my theatre. I have to persuade Ulla not to call the police.' Sylvie stirred and I put my hand on her head. The theatre manager's voice was rising; it held the shrillness of a man not used to shouting. 'It is you who owes me.' The door to the office opened a sliver and Ray spat something short and sharp at whoever was on the other side then turned back towards the room. 'Be grateful I gave you any money at all. Let your English friend give you your fare home. You won't perform in Berlin again.'

'I put a lot of work into making the act perfect for Schall und Rauch.'

He shook his head and turned to leave.

'Someone will bring you your stuff.' He nodded towards Sylvie, averting his eyes as if it hurt him to look at her. 'Make sure you take her with you.'

'Ray,' I stepped away from the desk. 'I was relying on that money.'

'That is not my problem.' He looked me in the eye. 'Tidying this mess and finding someone who will take your place before tomorrow, calming my stage manager, keeping the police from my door, these are all my problems. You are simply one of my mistakes.'

*   *   *

At first I wasn't sure which twin it was who appeared in the office with my props case, then I saw the omega symbol on his wrist and knew it was

271

Erhard. He looked at Sylvie's half-slumped form and said, 'Kolja is a bastard.'

'He's a bastard with a job.' I lifted my props case. 'Can you give me a hand?'

Erhard glanced at Sylvie then at me.

'Sure.' He looked embarrassed. 'You should change.'

I laughed in spite of myself, but there was a bitter note to the laugh that made me stop.

'You could be right. Soon as I get home I'm going to give up hard drink and loose women and start studying moral philosophy.'

The acrobat nodded towards my case.

'Is there a fresh shirt in your bag?'

I glanced down and realised he hadn't been referring to my lifestyle. The front of my shirt was soaked with blood, Kolja's and mine, impossible to distinguish from each other, the same red merged on the no longer white cotton. I raised my hand to my face and felt the scab already crusting beneath my nose, becoming aware again of the pain where Kolja's fist had connected.

'No. I've not had time to do any laundry.'

The domestic detail seemed absurd and I giggled a little.

'Here.' Erhard pulled off his T-shirt and passed it to me. 'You sure?'

The young athlete nodded and I started unbuttoning my shirt. Erhard took it from me then got a bottle of clear liquid from Ray's desk drawer, poured some onto the stained cotton, and started dabbing the blood from my face. The alcohol stung. I winced and he placed his hand on my bare shoulder.

'It is necessary.'

272

I felt the heat of his naked chest close to mine. It was a strange sensation in the midst of a strange night. I took the ruined shirt from him and completed the operation myself then took a quick gulp from the bottle. The drink was some kind of schnapps. It was rough and strong and it made me feel better. I passed the bottle to Erhard and he screwed the lid back on without taking a pull.

I knelt beside Sylvie and whispered, 'Erhard's going to help me get you into a cab.'

She mumbled something I couldn't make out. I nodded to him and we hooked our hands gently under Sylvie's arms and helped her slowly along the back corridors to the stage door. Once, she looked up at Erhard and smiled dreamily like she wasn't sure where he had come from, but mostly she simply put one foot in front of the other, letting us support her, her head dipping gently under the weight of gravity. A bass beat reached us from somewhere deep within the theatre but we met no one during our slow progress to the exit. The stage doorman put down his newspaper and watched us with disapproving eyes. We ignored him and Erhard helped Sylvie and me leave Schall und Rauch for the last time. I stopped in sight of the main street.

'It's probably best if I take her from here. Cabs might start worrying about their upholstery if they see it takes two of us to hold her up.'

'OK.' Erhard stroked a hand across his tattooed chest. 'Good luck.'

'Thanks, I'm going to need it.'

He nodded.

'Will you go back to England?'

'Probably.' I remembered the scout Rich had

273

mentioned and tried to cheer myself up. Or maybe I was just trying to save a little bit of my dignity.

'My agent said there's TV interest back there. Something might come of it.'

Erhard rubbed his fingers together in the universal money gesture.

'So, soon all your problems will be over.'

I shook his hand and thanked him for his help; trying to push away the thought that the only time all your problems are ever over is when you reach your grave.

*   *   *

I slid Sylvie into one of the white Mercs idling at the cab-stand, marvelling that she could still walk in her high red shoes. The driver gave us a reluctant look, but I told him the name of the hotel and he turned on the ignition and swung slowly out of the rank. Perhaps money was tight for him too.

Sylvie woke in the cab and gave me a sweet smile, like a child drowsy from an afternoon nap.

'Don't worry, William, we'll find somewhere better. I bet there are some fancy cabarets in London.'

'I liked it at Schall und Rauch.'

Sylvie rested her head against my shoulder.

'You liked that uptight bitch.'

'Yeah,' I looked out at the shop windows shining brightly into the night. 'Yeah, I liked her too.'

*   *   *

The hotel was in darkness but this time I had a key

and let us in.

It was impossible to avoid my reflection in the hotel lift's mirrored walls. Erhard's T-shirt hugged my body, emphasising the gut that I'd been pretending didn't exist. A Hitler moustache of caked gore clung stubbornly to my upper lip, there was a cut on the bridge of my nose where Kolja's ring had caught me and my right eye was puffed half-closed.

The numbers above the elevator door climbed slowly towards four. Sylvie was awake now. She leaned against the opposite wall staring at her feet and I wondered if she was scared to see her reflection. I put my hand on her arm and she looked up at me.

'I'm too tired, William.' She smiled sadly, 'Let me sleep a while then we can do whatever you want.'

The lift pinged to a halt and she stepped into the corridor. Now she was sobering up Sylvie's walk seemed less assured. She stumbled, swore softly, took off one shoe, then the other and staggered flat-footed down the door-lined corridor towards my room. I strode after her.

'All I'm doing is giving you a bed for the night.'

Her stare was sharp and appraising, her mouth bent into a cynical Mona Lisa smile that made my palm twitch. 'Your bed.'

'You were comatose and I didn't have enough money to get you home.'

'Sure?'

'Christ, Sylvie, I'm in this mess because you decided to give that fucking pumped-up freak a blowjob.'

'You're in this mess because you decided to

275

smash him on the nose. If you'd kept your fists out of things all we would have had was a bit of embarrassment.'

I stopped at the door to my room and slid the keycard into the lock. The tiny light above the handle stayed a stubborn red.

'He's Ulla's boyfriend.'

'So then it was between her and him, or maybe her and me. It had fuck-all to do with you.'

I turned the card around, swiped it again and shoved. The door stayed firmly locked.

'He used you.'

'Maybe I wanted to be used. Face facts, William, you can't get it up so you don't want anyone else getting any.' I took her by the arm.

'You'd be the last girl I'd want to fuck. I'd be afraid my dick would go septic and fall off.' I felt my fingers digging into her flesh. She reached up and kissed me. Her breath was sharp, her lips salty. I thought of where her mouth had been and pushed her away. 'If I'd wanted to taste that big poof's muck I would've blown him myself.'

'Fuck you, William.'

'No, fuck you, you mad bitch.'

Sylvie turned away. I watched her walk slowly back down the corridor towards the lift then tried the card again. The lock glowed green. I pushed open the door, hesitated, then went in. It was the stench that hit me first. I half gagged, trying to place it, then suddenly I knew. It was my smell magnified a hundredfold. A dim slice of light shone in from the corridor. It wasn't much to see by, but it was enough to reveal the few possessions I'd brought to Berlin strewn around the shadows. My clothes had been dragged from the wardrobe, the duvet and pillows pulled from the bed. And somewhere, smashed amongst the debris, was a bottle of expensive after-shave that no longer smelt suave. I picked up the paperback novel I'd been reading. Its pages had been ripped from their cover. It was a shame. Now I'd never know how things worked out.

I pressed the light switch; there was a dull click but the room remained in gloom. It was a fitting end to the evening. I'd been beaten up, lost my job, alienated the girl I fancied, forfeited my money and fallen out with the only friend I'd made in the city. Robbery and a dead light bulb dovetailed perfectly. Way down the corridor I heard the lift doors breathe open then chime shut.

'Fuck, fuck, fuck.'

I snibbed the lock in the slim hope that Sylvie would decide to come back, then closed the door softly behind me and checked my watch. It was 3 a.m. All across the city people were snug in bed. Loved ones spooned together, rosy-cheeked children sucking their thumbs as they slumbered. I moved towards the window to let in whatever light the street offered, or maybe to watch Sylvie walking away. My foot hit against the whisky bottle lying on the floor and I bent over to pick it up, reminding myself that friends needn't always be flesh and blood. Perhaps something snagged the edge of my vision because I turned in the direction of the bathroom door just as it started to open.

Montgomery looked older, as if retirement wasn't suiting him. My waters shifted and I balled my fists, taking a step backwards. Montgomery shook his head sadly.

'You're a bloody mess.'

277

His voice was soft, concerned. My own voice sounded gruff, but more confident than I felt.

'A bit like this room then.'

'Yeah,' He smiled a melancholy smile. 'Sorry about that, I thought I could save us both a bit of bother.'

I sat down on the bed. 'Maybe I'm getting thick in my old age, but I'm still in the dark.' I looked at the unlit room and amazed myself by laughing. 'Obviously I'm in the dark. What are you doing here?'

Montgomery took a bulb out of his pocket and screwed it into the bedside lamp. A soft light showed up the full mess of the room.

'Better?'

I looked around at my scattered belongings. The ex-policeman had done more than search. His assault on my possessions had been furious. The duvet and pillows had been sliced open, coating the floor in a mess of foam and feathers. My jackets were shredded. The jaws of my suitcase gaped wide, its red lining slit and lolling, reminding me of the damage I'd inflicted on Kolja's face and making me wonder if I was about to taste my own medicine. I took a pack of cards from my pocket and started shuffling, giving my hands something to do.

'Not really, no, in fact I'm two seconds away from phoning your Berlin colleagues.'

'You're a disappointment, William. For a moment there, when you were straight about recognising me, I thought you were going to be a good boy.' Montgomery stood in front of me and I realised it had been a mistake to sit down. 'Where is it?'

'I've got perfect recall remember? Part of the job.' I squared the shuffle. 'It's an advantage in my game. For instance, I've memorised this entire deck in the time we've been talking.' I offered him the pack. 'Pick a card and I'll tell you the rest of the sequence. Then you can tell me what it is you're after.'

Montgomery knocked the cards from my hand; they scattered over my lap and onto the floor, like a cheap metaphor for my life.

'I asked you a question. Where is it?'

'Where's what?'

'What are you after? Money?' Montgomery's voice had lost its coolness. It was still low enough to stay within the bounds of the small room, but its tone was jagged. A spray of spittle landed on my face. 'You know damn well what.'

I hadn't got round to replacing my drowned mobile yet. I looked towards the toppled bedside table where the hotel phone should be. It was missing, ripped out of the wall, and probably tumbled amongst the rubble of my belongings. Somewhere down the corridor I thought that I heard the lift doors ping open. If I made a rush for it I might be able to get help. I shifted from Montgomery's shadow and started to get to my feet.

'You're barking up the wrong tree, pal. Whatever it is you've mislaid, it's nothing to do with me.'

Montgomery smiled, stepped to one side as if he were about to go, then turned suddenly, shoving me square on the chest. I sprawled back onto the bed and the policeman flung himself half astride me, his knee between my legs, hand at my throat,

279

gently pressing the cutting edge of a knife below my Adam's apple. I felt my flesh shift beneath the blade, not quite ready to yield my blood, but thinking about it. We seemed to lie there for a long time, though the red numbers on the radio alarm glowing from beneath a pile of my shirts stayed at 3.06.

'You are fucking trying my patience, Wilson.'

Montgomery's breath was warm against my face. My own was stuck deep in my chest, somewhere near my heart. I found it, exhaled slowly and tried to think of something soothing to say, something that might get him to take the knife away.

'You've searched the room, there's nothing of yours here.'

'Not here maybe.' The knife pressed down harder. I could see the blood climbing up Montgomery's face, but when he spoke the voice behind the whisper was calm. 'Are you a fan of the movies?'

I wondered what soundtrack played in his head while he acted the master villain. This was my cue to bound free, while he described the elaborate tortures in store. It worked in films, but I had Montgomery's full weight pinning me down, a blade at my throat and there was no unseen orchestra edging its way towards a climax. I swallowed, not liking the way my throat moved against the blade.

'Isn't everyone?'

'Quite right, they're a popular pastime. Did you see that film . . .' He paused as if searching his memory. 'What was it called now? It was by that young American guy, ugly git, total genius . . . *Reservoir Dogs*, that's it.' Montgomery smiled at me. 'You seen it? Fucking marvellous. They cut a guy's ear off.'

I stared into his eyes and spoke with as much command as I could muster.

'You *won't* cut my ear off.'

The knife regained its pressure and Montgomery leaned in towards me.

'Oh I will, and a lot more besides if I don't get what's mine.' He caught me between the legs, cradling my shrinking balls in his hand. 'Not much there but I dare say you'd prefer to hold on to the small portion God granted you.'

We lay there panting, his hand on my vitals, our faces strained, looking like an ugly scene from a very specialist porno movie. There was a slight movement on the right of my peripheral vision. I concentrated my gaze on Montgomery's and tried to avoid looking towards the not-quite-shut door as it slid slowly open.

Sylvie hadn't put her shoes back on; she edged silently across the carpet, her gaze on the bed, like a cat stalking a pigeon. I remembered I'd never yet seen a cat get to the kill. Maybe the thought made my eyes shift towards her after all or maybe the policeman simply felt the atmosphere change, because suddenly Montgomery gasped as if he had felt a hand on his shoulder and glanced towards her. Sylvie kicked the door shut and levelled my gun somewhere near the centre of our huddle.

'Having fun, William?'

For a second I wondered whose side she was on, but then I felt Montgomery's body tense.

'Not really my idea of a good Saturday night.'

'Hear that you old pervert?' Sylvie moved forward until the gun was squarely aimed at

Monty's torso, still staying far enough away to make it difficult for him to grab her. 'Be a dear and let go of his dick.'

Monty gave the blade another press and I thought he was going to call her bluff. But then Sylvie said, '*Now* please.' And maybe he sensed a strain of madness in her voice, because he raised his hands slowly in the air and threw the weapon beyond reach towards the far side of the room. 'Good boy, now kiss him goodbye and get to your feet.'

Monty said, 'You must be joking.'

'Just get off him.'

The policeman eased himself upright. His voice had regained its gentleness.

'It's not a real gun.'

I stood up holding a hand to my scratched throat, though it was a small wound in a night of pain. 'I'm afraid it is. Real bullets too.'

'We can check if you like.' Sylvie's voice was light, conversational even. She kept her eyes on Montgomery. 'No? Don't fancy that idea? Then reach slowly into your pocket and throw your mobile on the bed. Any funny business and I shoot.'

Her dialogue was pure movie gangster, but maybe that appealed to Montgomery because he did as she said.

'William, phone the police.' I looked blankly at her and she said, 'The number's 110.'

Montgomery started to talk quickly.

'This has nothing to do with you, darling.'

'Don't worry, I have a feeling William wants to talk to the police as little as you do, but as long as they're on their way we know you'll make yourself scarce. When they get here we'll say it was a simple break-in, unless you want to stick around and tell them different.'

Montgomery looked at Sylvie with a respect that was laced with frustration. I picked up his phone and dialled.

'I understand you want to protect your boyfriend, but he's not the plaster saint he makes himself out to be.'

He started to lower his hands.

'Any further and I'll shoot you in the stomach.'

The other end of the line picked up and I started to give the address of the hotel. Sylvie kept the gun level. I tried to think of the German word for emergency, failed and said, 'Schnell bitte.'

Montgomery smiled.

'You know I could take that off you don't you, darling?'

'I know the safety catch is off, I know that I'll press the trigger and I know it'll make one hell of a bang whether I hit anyone or not. You, on the other hand, know fuck-all.'

I said, 'Danke,' and killed the call. 'They're on their way.'

'Look, I went about this wrong. Your boyfriend's got something belonging to me.' Montgomery smiled, still holding his hands up to show he was no threat. 'Thirty-five years on the force,' he took a small step forward. His voice took on a hypnotic tone. 'I tend to get a bit impatient . . . go in like a bull in a china shop when there's no need . . . forget that sometimes softly, softly is better. It means a great deal to me. Sentimental reasons as much as anything else.'

'He's lying, Sylvie.'

283

Montgomery's voice was gentle.

'There could be a lot of money in it for you both.' He took another step. 'A *lot* of money.'

Sylvie's eyes locked with Montgomery's and I realised she still wasn't quite sober. The policeman took another step and I braced myself to go for the gun. Then Sylvie put her finger on the trigger, and a small smile touched her lips.

'Do you really want to test me?'

Montgomery took a step back and raised his hands a little higher.

'I guess I just did.'

A passing car broke the silence of the street outside. There were no sirens but it was enough to sever the spell. Montgomery turned to me.

'This isn't the end, Wilson. If I were you I'd be a sensible boy. I'm not going to let up.'

'Are you threatening him?'

'No, love, I'm making him a promise. Until I get what I want your boyfriend's the walking dead. You'll never know the day or the hour, but know this, I'll fucking swing before I'll let him away with it.'

'You've had your say, now scram.' Sylvie was in her element, Bonnie Parker and Patty Hearst all rolled into one. 'I'm going to keep pointing this gun at the door. Anyone walks through who isn't a member of the Berliner Polizei and they get a bullet in the guts.'

Montgomery hesitated, his gaze shifting between Sylvie and me. He said, 'You better get me what you owe me, Wilson, or you're a dead man.' Suddenly he smiled. 'Your agent tell you about the TV scout looking for you?' The realisation came before he said it. 'Sorry, chum, you just failed the audition.'

The policeman smiled again but there was a brittleness to the smile that belied the gag. The door closed quietly behind him, the latch clicking to, mild and gentle as his voice. I sunk onto the bed and put my head in my hands. Sylvie stood, legs apart, keeping her aim steady, looking like a female action hero towards the end of the movie. Her voice was level.

'William, go to the window and tell me when he leaves the building.' I concealed myself behind the curtain and looked down into the street. Sylvie asked, 'What was all that about?'

'My last chance to get on TV.'

'And I thought the dance world was tough. I'm not the prying type, Will, but I think you owe me an explanation.'

'I'll tell you back at your place.'

'You take a lot for granted, Wilson.' She sighed. 'OK, later.'

Later was fine. By the time later came I'd have made up something that sounded plausible. Or perhaps I'd have left Berlin. Or maybe I'd be lying snug on a satin mattress in a rosewood bed while my mother stroked my forehead and remembered the sweet boy I'd once been.

Outside it was dawn. After a minute or two Montgomery strolled across the road, all hint of menace gone, looking like the kind of man you might turn to for advice, a respectable middle-aged man with a sleep problem who liked to take the air in the early hours. He pulled up the collar on his jacket and glanced back at the hotel. Maybe he saw me, or maybe he just guessed I'd be watching. He made the shape of a gun with his

285

fingers, squeezed back the imaginary trigger and fired right between my eyes. I stepped behind the curtains. When I looked again he was gone.

'That's him.'

Sylvie breathed out, bent into a long stretch then straightened up.

'I guess you should have this.' She grinned and handed me my gun. 'It was naughty of me to put it in my bag, but I thought it might come in handy one day.'

'It did.'

'Yeah it did, didn't it? I was sure he'd spot it for a repro, but he was quaking in his unfashionable boots.'

'It's the real deal, Sylvie.'

Her face creased into an expression that the sight of me with a knife at my throat had failed to raise.

'It's what?'

'It's got to look good if the illusion is going to work.' I clicked the safety catch home, Sylvie's reaction making me glad the revolver was back in my possession. 'I told you, there's always a slim element of risk in the bullet trick, but believe me, you weren't in any real danger.'

'You bastard.'

Sylvie threw my ruined paperback at me, but it was a half-hearted gesture and for the first time that night I side-stepped a blow.

'I thought we'd decided we were on the same side?'

I opened the gun and checked the cylinder. It was empty. Suddenly I realised what a truly accomplished liar Sylvie was. Her skill had possibly saved my life. I put my arms around my rescuer, kissed her cheek and made a resolution never ever to trust her.

*   *   *

I woke up suddenly, grabbing my arm with the feeling that something small and quick had just run across it. I hit the bedclothes trying to kill it or flush it out, unsure whether there had been anything there at all, then lay back and looked at the ceiling. Day had slid back into night. Soon I would have to get up and face my old enemy the world; soon but not yet. Somewhere down the hallway a door shut. I wondered if it was Sylvie or Dix, or maybe some inhabitant of the apartment I hadn't met. After all, life was full of surprises.

I needed to work out how to get myself back to Britain. My credit card was long past fucked and my wallet nearly empty. I'd have to blag the fare from Rich or the British Consul or maybe my mum, though I wasn't sure she'd have the money.

I wondered if the hotel would come after me for damages and unpaid charges. Maybe there would be a stop at the airport. A hesitation when I handed over my passport then, *would you mind waiting here, sir?* Even if I made it home there would be the problem of a fresh start with no money. I'd packed in my flat in Ealing. New deposits and first month's rents were expensive. I was homeless, jobless and stuck in a foreign country, without even the stake for a reckless bet. I ran my hands down my body checking the damage. The pain was a comfort of sorts. *A skelped arse gives you something to cry over,* as my dad used to say.

287

All of this was just a way to avoid thinking about the envelope I'd sent unopened to my mother's for safekeeping. Would Montgomery think to search her out? He was a trained policeman. He was smart and plausible and ruthless. My mum would welcome him with a smile. Montgomery would pat the dog, step through the front door, then what?

I swung my legs out of bed. My clothes were a ruined heap. Sylvie's floral robe hung on the back of the door. I reached over and put it on. There was no point in trying to hold onto my dignity now.

Sylvie's voice sounded soft and serious through the living-room door. Dix's low rumble of reply was forceful, insistent. Sylvie said something harsh and Dix countered with a soft, measured response. It was an argument of sorts, but the words were beyond my reach. I concentrated, holding my breath to try and make out what they were saying, and realised that they were talking in German. I hesitated, not sure if I should knock, then pushed open the door, coughing as I entered the room.

Sylvie was curled up on the couch dressed in jeans and a scruffy T shirt, her body bent towards her sometime uncle who was leaning back in his usual seat. Dix's fingers still played with the gaffer-taped tear in the chair's arm, but he looked like a different man from the shabby dope smoker of that first long evening. Black trousers and a clean white shirt had taken the place of the stained joggers and distressed cardigan. His face was freshly shaved. He might even have lost weight. It suited him, except for around the eyes. They looked strained, as if lately he'd had too many worries and too little sleep.

I'd expected Sylvie to laugh at my getup, but her

face stayed grave.

'How you doing, William?'

'Rough.'

'I'll bet.'

I glanced at Dix, wondering how much he knew of our adventures and whether he'd blame me for putting Sylvie in danger. He nodded towards the couch.

'Let him sit next to the fire.'

Sylvie shifted along the sofa and I slid in between her and the gas fire.

'You're shivering.' Her face was still stern but her voice was gentle. She rubbed my arm. 'DTs or cold?'

'Knowing my luck, probably a new strain of black death.'

Dix looked at Sylvie.

'Coffee might help.'

I waited for her to say something smart, but she stopped massaging me, uncurled her legs and got to her feet.

I drew the robe closer and asked, 'Have you anything stronger?'

Dix's voice was final.

'Stick to coffee for a while.'

And at last Sylvie smiled.

'Watch out, he could become your uncle too.'

She gave my arm a last squeeze then went out, shutting the door after her. We sat in silence for a while then Dix asked, 'Still cold?'

'A bit.'

He reached to the back of his chair and threw a blanket towards me.

'Maybe shock too.'

'Thanks.' I pulled the blanket around my

shoulders. 'Aren't you going to ask what it was all about?'

'I told you before.' Dix's face was unreadable. 'I mind my own business.'

Sylvie came through with three mugs and set them on the table in front of us.

'I don't.'

Dix took his coffee without thanking her.

'But you don't like to tell everything either.'

'Who does?' Sylvie's voice was pointed. 'Not you, that's for sure.'

I sensed that they were going back to some earlier argument that had nothing to do with me and pulled out the line I'd prepared.

'Let's just say I owe some money. A lot of money.'

Sylvie put her cup to her lips and looked at me over its rim, raising her eyebrows.

'Your friend said it had sentimental attachments for him.'

Dix pulled back the piece of gaffer tape. 'A man can get sentimental about money.' He smoothed it down again and turned to me. 'There may be a solution to your problem. A way to make some money.'

Sylvie put her hand on my knee and opened her eyes wide as she stared deep into mine and said, 'An awful lot of money.'

Dix leaned forward, the strain in his eyes intensified by a spark of something else: excitement.

'Do you remember the night we were all together in the Nachtreview?' I nodded. There was little chance I would forget. 'That evening I said there were men who would be willing to pay a lot of money to see you play your Russian roulette with a live woman.'

'It's not Russian roulette. Roulette is a game of chance. What I do is a well-constructed illusion.'

'Sure.' Dix nodded impatiently. 'We know that, but we lead them to think otherwise.'

'And how would you manage that?'

Dix smiled.

'There are ways. In a business like this everyone has their role. You squeeze the trigger, Sylvie is the target and I convince them that they are seeing what they want to see.'

It was a philosophy I understood, the basis of every illusion and every successful con, but I held back.

'I don't know, it's too weird. Who are these people?'

'Weirder than what you do normally?' Dix's voice was soft, coaxing and I realised that I believed he would be able to sell the trick. 'What does it matter who they are? Sometimes it's better not to know these things. It's a lot of money. It could solve all your problems. Sylvie and I have discussed it. She's in and so am I, but we need you if it's going to work.' He looked me in the eye and smiled. 'What do you say, William?' The bathroom was cold, the towel the same shade of grey as when I'd seen it last, but the water was hot and foamed with scented bubbles. I eased myself slowly into the water, wincing as it made contact with my bruises, then shut my eyes and put my head beneath the surface. A whoosh of silence filled my ears, then above it the sound of the door opening. I surfaced, pushing my hair out of my eyes just as Sylvie stepped into the bathroom with a bundle of clothes over her arm.

'Dix said you could use these.'

'That's good of him.'

'Well,' Sylvie pressed the clothes to her chest and smiled sadly, 'he does need something from you.'

She placed the bundle on top of the toilet then sat on the edge of the bath and dipped her hand in the water, testing the temperature.

'Need?'

'You aren't the only one with debts to pay.'

Sylvie's face looked strained. I wondered again why she should care so much about Dix's needs, but smiled to lighten the mood.

'He's not going to come through here as well is he?'

'No,' Sylvie laughed. 'Why? Are you looking for company?'

'That's what the girls down Anderston way ask the punters.'

She flicked her fingers against the water's surface, splashing my face.

'I've no idea where Anderson Way is, but I get the idea you might be calling me a whore again.'

The splash was playful, but I thought there was real hurt behind the words. I caught her by the wrist.

'No, Sylvie, I'm sorry. I think you're brilliant.'

Her hand was tiny. I placed it on my chest. She held it there for a second, then scooped some bubbles from the top of the tub and rubbed them into my skin, brushing against my bruises. It felt sore and sad and good all at the same time. Sylvie looked down at my half-hardness emerging through the fading froth. She tugged my chest hair

292

teasingly and reached for the towel.

'You don't know what you want do you, William? A whore, a Madonna or just a good fuck.'

'And what do you want, Sylvie?'

'Nothing.' She looked away. 'Just to live.'

'Then you've got your wish.'

She shook her head.

'Who's the greatest person you can think of?'

'I don't know.'

'Just say someone. The first person to come into your head.'

'Einstein.'

'He's dead.'

'I know.'

She dropped her hand into the water again.

'All I want is to live while I'm still alive,' she grinned. 'Even if I die in the process.'

'A short life but a merry one?'

'You got it.'

Her hand slipped further beneath the water and brushed gently against my cock. I caught her wrist between my fingers and drew it away. Our eyes met.

'I don't need sex to be your friend.'

'No?'

'No.'

And I let go of her wrist, felt her fingers fasten around me, closed my eyes and allowed myself to be swallowed by the rhythm of her hand and the warm waves of bathwater that started to lap against my chest.

*   *   *

Afterwards Sylvie shook her hand clean in the bathwater. I caught her fingers again and held them to my lips. 'Thanks, Sylvie.'

She shook her head.

'You should relax, William, you're so formal, like a third-grade English teacher who's just been jerked off by his most promising student.'

The water had grown cold. I pushed the scum of my spunk away from me and started to get out of the bath.

'I wish I didn't feel you were talking from experience.'

Sylvie shrugged and shifted to the toilet seat. I wanted some privacy, but what had just passed between us stopped me from asking her to leave. She sat with Dix's clothes on her lap, and passed me the towel.

Her voice was soft.

'Has anyone ever died doing your bullet trick?'

'I've never shot anyone for real, no.'

'You know what I mean.'

'I told you before, it has its risks but they're probably no more than the odds of crashing on the motorway.'

'Midday or rush hour?'

'You were safe.' I wrapped the towel round my waist and sat on the edge of the tub, facing her. 'Magic is all about effects, if the trick doesn't look dangerous then who's impressed? The first man ever to die doing the bullet trick was beaten to death with his own gun.'

She laughed.

'And the second one?'

'I don't know, like I said, people try to make it seem more risky than it is. Some of the conjurers who supposedly died in the line of fire turned up in the next town, some of them never existed. Sometimes it's like the trick's reputation slays them. There was a conjurer in the Wild West who was killed when someone in the audience jumped up and shot him. Yeah, he was dead, but you couldn't really blame the trick. Another guy was shot by his wife, presumably she'd decided not to bother with the trouble of a divorce. None of that's going to happen to you.'

'And what about the ones who get it wrong?' I sighed.

'I guess the truth is that they just weren't careful enough. They didn't switch bullets properly or used faulty equipment.' I took her hands in mine and looked her in the eyes. 'The trick is safe if you do it right.'

'And you'll always do it right?'

'I wouldn't attempt it if I didn't believe that. Look,' I took a T-shirt from the top of the pile of clothes and pulled it over my head. 'You're right. I should have gone through the risks more carefully with you. I'm sorry. I guess I was just a bit gung-ho.'

'Gun ho.'

She passed me a jumper and I laughed.

'Yes, gun ho. I'll tell Dix its noho on his offer.'

'No, let's do it.'

'Why?'

'What's life without a risk or two?'

'Is anyone pushing you into it? Me?' I hesitated. 'Dix?' Her voice was impatient.

'No, you want to do it and I want to do it. And Dix certainly wants us to do it. So let's do it.'

'What makes you so sure I do want to do it?'

'I watched your face when Dix said he'd found someone who wanted us to perform a special show.'

It was true; Dix's news could solve my money problems, but it was more than that, it was a chance to perform, to go out on a high rather than slinking back to Britain with my tail between my legs.

'Then let's do it the other way round. This time you shoot me.'

Sylvie stared at me.

'Are you serious?'

'Serious as cancer. You're right, there is a risk and this time it's bigger. According to Dix we won't get to inspect the venue before we go ahead and we don't know who this creep is who's willing to pay a fortune for a command performance.' I slipped on a pair of boxers and pulled Dix's old jeans over them. 'So this time you shoot me. That way if there are any accidents it's no great loss.'

Sylvie grinned.

'You're good William, but when it comes down to it you're a shit liar. You know as well as I do that no one's going to pay big money to watch you getting shot. What they want is the chance to see a pretty lady take a bullet right between the eyes.' She stepped closer. 'Admit it.'

I took a comb from the washstand, wiped the condensation from the mirror and started to smooth back my wet hair. Sylvie pulled me round to face her.

'Admit you knew Dix and his audience of one wouldn't go for it or the deal is off, permanently.'

'OK,' I turned back to the mirror. She was right, for a man who made his living out of illusion I was a pretty crap liar. 'OK, I guessed it might be a possibility.'

'A possibility?'

I met her eyes in the mirror.

'OK, "possibility" might be a bit of an understatement.'

'William,' Sylvie shook her head as if mortally disappointed. 'You're just as bad as the rest of us.' She squeezed my waist as she pressed past me towards the hallway rubbing her groin briefly against mine. 'OK then, let's go out with a bang. But first you've got to reassure me by telling me exactly how the trick is done.' She held open the door for me. 'Tell Dix too, he'll enjoy it.'

So I followed her into the blood-red lounge, Dix passed me a beer, Sylvie phoned out for pizza and I explained the secrets of the bullet trick with all its complexities and variations. Sylvie was right. Dix did seem to enjoy it. He sat and stared and occasionally asked questions. All in all it was a pleasant evening, the last I was going to enjoy for a long time.

Glasgow

The van driver I'd hired to help take my equipment to Johnny's venue wasn't happy.

'I'm not meant to go along here, it's buses and taxis only.'

'And deliveries.'

'Deliveries until eleven, we're well past time.' He looked away from the road, giving me the full effect of his torn face. 'You're making me break the law.'

The driver was Archie, an old navy friend of my magic shop boss, Bruce McFarlane. He was bald, with three working teeth and a wrinkled face that had somehow shrivelled back in on itself. It was like being told off by a shrunken-headed tattooed baby.

'Aye well, I'll drop into St Mungo's on my way home and say a wee prayer for you.' Archie shot me a look that said he might just kick me and my junk out of his van and I backtracked. 'I didn't realise it was restricted, there'll be something on top for your trouble.'

'If I get a ticket it's your shout.'

'Fair enough.'

I grinned at him, but he was staring straight ahead, manoeuvring the van between the buses that were backed along the street. Eilidh had told me that the venue wasn't far along on the Trongate, but though I'd tramped the street countless times I couldn't remember ever noticing the Panopticon. I checked the numbers above the shops while the van eased its way through the traffic.

'Can you slow down a wee bit? We should be able to spit on it from here.'

'If I go any bloody slower we'll stop.'

I pointed to a space.

'You could pull in there.'

'It's a bloody bus stop.'

But Archie swung the van in anyway, muttering about blue meanies and bloody stupit cunts that didnae ken where they were going.

I slid back the passenger door and stuck my head out, looking for the hall.

'I'll just be a second.'

'If the polis come I'll have to mo—'

I slammed the door and ran along the pavement. The number Eilidh had given me belonged to a blue-fronted arcade that promised *Amusements, Amusements, Amusements* in pink neon swirls. The windows to the arcade were veiled behind elaborately pleated midnight-blue satin drapes. They made me think of a flashy funeral directors', the kind of concern that might have got Liberace's business. The space between the glass and the curtains was decorated with prizes the insurance company probably didn't require to be locked in the safe at night, oversized ornaments of liquid-eyed dogs, TVs and microwaves that retailed for around fifty quid in Tesco and huge fake-flower arrangements whose bulk was supplemented by multi-coloured feathers that had never seen a parrot. The bingo caller's voice reached out through the empty door into the street, above a clatter of mechanical whoops and bells.

Baby's done it, number two. One and five, fifteen. Key to the door, two and one, twenty-one, just your age, eh Lorna? Three and five, thirty-five, J Lo's Bum, seventy-one. Tony's Den, number ten. Blind eighty.

No one was shouting house. I glanced back to the van. Archie was making hurry-up gestures but there were no wardens in sight. I leaned through the open door to the arcade, into darkness punctuated by the flash of fruit machines, pinball and video games. For all of the noise it generated, the place wasn't very busy. A bouncer stood sentinel inside the doorway; in the gloom beyond him a few punters tried their luck on the machines or sat solemnly marking their bingo cards.

The bouncer gave me an appraising glance. Maybe he'd studied Zen or maybe he just knew that guys as big as him don't have to say anything to get guys like me to explain themselves. I said, 'I'm looking for the Panopticon, mate, ever heard of it?'

He nodded his head towards the ceiling.

'Upstairs.'

I stepped backwards into the street and looked towards the top of the building. Three huge storeys of what the early Victorians probably considered a Grecian façade, intersected by arched windows that decreased in size as the storeys rose.

The bouncer directed me to the goods entrance around the side, smiling mildly when I asked him if there was a lift.

I said, 'Never mind, it's all in a good cause eh?' And went back to the van, wondering if I could use that line on Archie.

But I was beginning to learn that although Archie moaned, he got the job done. He grumbled the full length of the dingy staircase, but it was only when we stepped from the landing into the auditorium that he almost dropped his end of the box.

'Bloody hell!'

If I'd have been first into the room I might have done the same. The mannequin was positioned so you didn't see it until you turned the corner from the stairs into the auditorium, then he was right in front of you, a whiskered Victorian decked out in frock coat and top hat. Eilidh hurried towards us.

'Are you OK?'

Archie's end of the box straightened up.

'You're all right, dear. He just gave me a bit of a start.'

Eilidh scruffed down nicely. Her hair was twisted into a loose half-knot and she wore an old checked work shirt over a pair of jeans that might have seen better days, but hadn't lost their fit.

'He has that effect on everyone. I'd move him, but we're being given use of the place as a favour and the management might go off us if we start shifting the furniture around.'

'Aye, you're right, dear, they management cu—kinds can be an awful trial.'

Eilidh nodded towards the brightly spangled, coffin-sized box that Bruce McFarlane had lent me.

'Is that for the stage?'

'Aye.'

She smiled apologetically.

'Then you've another flight to go yet, access is through the back stairs.'

Archie smiled at her.

'Never mind, dear.' He nodded towards me. 'This one could do with the exercise.'

Archie and I manoeuvred the box up the final staircase, and through a door that led straight onto the stage. We lowered it gently to the ground just as Eilidh came in behind us. Archie ran his hand over his head as if he'd forgotten he no longer had any hair and looked around.

'I remember my grandda talking about the music hall, but I've never been in it myself.'

Eilidh smiled.

'What do you think?'

'Aye, some place.'

The Panopticon was small by modern theatrical standards, a long room overhung on its left and right by high wooden balconies that I guessed used to house the cheap seats. Some old fruit machines, casualties from the amusement arcade below, stood sadly along the far wall looking like the Daleks' more frivolous cousins, their single arms raised in a greeting no one wanted to return. The building's eaves showed through its fractured ceiling, slanting into a peak that reminded me of an upturned boat. They gave the place a vaguely jaunty feel at odds with the otherwise Victorian atmosphere. The walls were the sallow brown that you find on the naked walls of old flats when you manage to peel back years of wallpaper. The floor was scuffed and unvarnished. There were no seats in place, but some metal chairs that looked like they would begin to pinch after a while were stacked along the back wall next to the fruit machines, waiting to be set in line.

It was clear that the Panopticon had been neglected for some time now, but there were signs that it was coming back to life. A pianola sat below the stage and a couple of glass-topped display tables containing artefacts from the music hall's heyday were pressed along the entrance wall. Above them hung old posters, playbills and programmes advertising forthcoming attractions that had taken their last bow a hundred years ago. It was far away from the sequinned edginess of Schall und Rauch, but I liked it that way. Something up on the balcony caught my eye; I started, then pointed towards it, saying to Archie, 'Someone you know?'

He followed my gaze.

'Jesus Christ.' Archie turned to me. 'You bugger.' Two more Victorian mannequins, a man and a woman, stood silhouetted in the gloom of the balcony. 'Give me the bloody heebie-jeebies they things.' He looked at Eilidh. 'I bet there's a few ghost stories about this place.'

'One or two.' She nodded down to the old pianola. 'Apparently George down there has been known to start playing all by himself, and a young soldier in a uniform from the Boer War has been spotted up on that balcony.'

Archie nodded his head sagely.

'Oh, come on,' I said. 'It's no wonder folk think they've seen a ghost with those waxworks up there. They're like something out of a Hammer Horror. The eye plays tricks on you, especially in an old place like this.'

'When you get to my age you begin to realise there's more in this world than can be explained.' Archie looked at Eilidh and me as if imparting some ancient wisdom. 'People don't just vanish when they die, they're all around us and sometimes we catch sight of them.'

A cold finger pressed into my neck bone then ran the length of my spine.

Eilidh said, 'Do you really believe that?'

'Aye, I do dear. You should go to the spiritualist church up on Berkeley Street sometime. It's amazing the messages that come through.'

'It's a pile of mince.'

I was surprised at my own vehemence. Archie bridled.

'We're all entitled to an opinion. I go there every Tuesday to see if the wife's got anything to tell me. It's a comfort.' He gave me a defiant stare, then turned to Eilidh. 'Do you mind if I go and have a look at your display, dear?'

'You're welcome.'

'Thanks.' He stropped off the stage muttering something that sounded suspiciously like *superior wee cunt* as he passed me.

When Archie was out of earshot Eilidh said, 'Poor old soul, he's lonely.' She gave me a compassionate look. 'How are you, William?'

I felt like saying *lonely* but settled for, 'Fine.'

Eilidh hesitated as if there was something else she'd like to add, then thought the better of it and said, 'I'll leave you to get on with things, while I make a start on setting up the chairs.'

I followed Archie's gaze as he watched Eilidh make her way to the back of the hall, then I went down to make amends.

'I shouldn't have said that just now. You're right, what do I know?'

'What does anyone know, son?' He gave me a sharp, shrewd look. 'Have you lost someone recently?'

My heart executed the familiar dip between fear, pain and shame, but my voice remained neutral.

'What makes you ask that?'

'Just a feeling.'

I kept my own counsel and handed Archie what I owed him, plus the promised extra. He counted it and smiled, tucking the notes safe in his jeans.

'Look at all this stuff.' He pointed to a tray in the cabinet filled with small objects, cigarette packets, buttons, ladies' brooches, a couple of rings, a silk commemorative poppy, old newspapers and programmes. 'See they old

304

Woodbines?' He smiled nostalgically. 'That's what I used to smoke when I was a boy.'

'It's true they stunt your growth then?'

'Cheeky bugger. They found all of this under the floor-boards in the gallery up there. Can you imagine it? Some poor woman loses an engagement ring or a fella drops a full pack of five, got to last him the whole night most likely, and that's that until a hundred years later.'

'I never realised you were interested in history, Archie.'

'Get to my age and you've got to be, son. What you call history's sometimes just yesterday to me.'

'Oh get off it, you're not that old.'

'Aye well, what I'm saying is, nothing vanishes for good. There's still traces of it somewhere, so don't close your mind. The dear departed often come back.'

'Like a packet of Woodbines?'

'Just don't close your mind, that's all I'm saying.' He grinned, showing me his missing teeth. 'She's a bit of all right that one; you could've been in there.'

'You're a dirty old man for a mystic.'

'That's the only reason I'm no trying to get in there myself, son.'

'Anyway you're wrong, she's married.'

'Ah.'

Archie gave me a look that said it wouldn't have stopped him in his prime.

'Her wee girl's one of the kids I'm doing the benefit for.'

'Ah right, I see.'

'And her husband's a friend of mine.'

'Aye, and you're an ugly scunner she wouldn't

look twice at. Here,' Archie took a fiver out of the money I'd just given him. 'Put that in the pot for the weans.'

'You don't have to.'

'I know I don't bloody have to. They get a hard deal they Down's kiddies, it's amazing what they can do given the chance.'

'Aye, I guess so.'

'I mean look at you. Bet your ma was told you'd never make it out your pram and here you are now.'

'Chatting to a turnip heid.' I shook my head and took his money. 'Cheers, you're a good man, Archie.'

'You'll not be saying that if I've got a ticket. I'll be back up these bloody stairs afore you can wave your wand and say fizzy fucking wizzy.'

*   *   *

After Archie had left I went up to the back of the hall where Eilidh was setting out rows of folding chairs. I had things to do but I dragged over a fresh stack and started to give her a hand.

'I thought I might catch Johnny today.'

'He'll be sorry to miss you. He's up to his ears in work, it's that time of year.'

'Exams?'

'Exams, essays, assessments.'

'It must be difficult to find time to spend together.'

'It's what you expect with a new baby.'

'And benefits to organise.'

Eilidh smiled.

'It's not the best timing but you know John, he

deals with things through action. Has to feel he's doing something.'

I picked a collapsed chair off my stack and hit its seat smartly with my hand, unfolding it and starting a new row in front of the one Eilidh had already begun.

'Looks to me like you're the one doing all the work.'

Eilidh paused; she looked straight at me to give her words emphasis.

'I'm not put upon.'

I placed a new seat next to the last.

'I never said you were.'

'You had that look, poor Eilidh all on her own again.'

I set another seat on the ground and held up my hands. 'Eilidh, I hardly know you and before I met you both in the pub that night it was years since I'd last seen John. I'm in no position to make assumptions.'

We worked without talking for a while, the only sound the scraping of chairs against the rough wooden floor until Eilidh said, 'The last time I saw you I said that every time we meet someone behaves badly. I guess I just proved my own point, sorry.'

I set up another chair.

'You must lead a pretty sheltered existence if you call that bad behaviour.'

'Perhaps I do.'

Eilidh unfastened another chair and wiped a hand across her face.

I hesitated then asked, 'Are you OK?'

'Yes, just a bit tired.'

'And staying up all night with fuck-ups like me

probably doesn't help.'

'It's my job. Anyway, it's only part-time.'

'I was hoping you'd say I wasn't a fuck-up.'

She laughed.

'Well, you're looking a whole lot better than you were a week or so ago.'

'I'm trying.'

It was my turn to look away.

Eilidh put her hand on my arm.

'What I mean is I don't think you're a fuck-up. Far from it.'

I asked softly, 'What do you think I am?'

'I think you're a bit of a chancer.'

Our eyes met. My lips tingled with the thought of what would happen if I kissed her. I thought of Johnny. Then there was a sound from the back of the building. I looked round and saw Eilidh's mother come through the door with a small child in her arms.

'Mum, you should have buzzed my mobile. I would have come down and got her. William, this is my mother, Margaret.'

Margaret's voice was on the edge of politeness.

'We've already met.'

'I was just giving Eilidh a hand with the chairs. Is this Grace?' Suddenly I felt awkward. 'I've not seen her yet.'

Margaret cradled the child close, her hand supporting its head.

'She's just dropped off.'

'Give her here, Mum, she's getting too big to carry any distance.'

Margaret kissed her granddaughter's crown and for a moment I thought she was going to refuse, but then she passed Grace to Eilidh.

'There was no way I could manage that buggy up the stairs, I told you when you bought it that it was too heavy.'

'I wanted something sturdy.'

The two women had the same strained look round the eyes and the same sharp defiant chins. There was no doubting they were mother and daughter. I said, 'I'll nip down and get the buggy for you.'

Margaret looked like she'd rather reject my offer, but Eilidh smiled gratefully.

'Would you mind, William? Then I can put her down in it.'

'No problem.'

*   *   *

When I returned, Margaret was sitting in one of the far rows of chairs with the baby on her lap.

'Thanks, William,' Eilidh's voice was low and amused. 'They're both knackered.'

We chatted a while about arrangements for the gig and then I said, 'Do you remember I asked you about old evidence?'

Eilidh nodded.

'Of course.'

'Well, if you had something like that who would you go to?'

'My lawyer, which in your case is me.'

Eilidh smiled. I thought again how beautiful she was and was tempted.

'I'd rather keep you out of it.'

'Then it's obvious, the police.'

'Sure, but is there anyone in particular? Especially if it was something a bit unusual.'

Eilidh raised her eyebrows.

'You're intriguing me, William.' She thought for a moment. 'You'd want someone experienced, but with a bit of imagination. After a while there's nothing policemen won't believe given the right evidence, they've seen so many odd things, but sometimes you find they can't be bothered. They've burnt out.' She paused. 'I'd probably go to Blunt, the guy who interviewed you the other week.'

'Why would I want to deal with that cunt?'

Margaret was too far away to hear our conversation, but maybe some instinct alerted her to the nature of it, or maybe she could lip-read swear words. She looked up in her chair and called over, 'Eilidh, have you almost finished?'

'Just a minute, mum.' Eilidh turned back to me. 'He is a cunt but he's a straight cunt. Take your lawyer's advice. If you won't show me, show Blunt. I happen to know he's back on nights this week.'

The voice came again from the back of the hall. 'Eilidh.'

'Whoops.' She took the buggy from me. 'I'd better go. Good luck.'

And she turned and ran towards her mother and child.

*   *   *

I waited a long time until Inspector Blunt walked into his local. He was alone, wearing the same tired suit and weary expression he'd worn the last time we'd met. He stepped up to the bar without looking at me, though I knew I'd been marked as soon as he came in. The barmaid set Blunt's drink

310

in front of him without waiting to be asked. I let him have his first swallow then joined him at the bar. Blunt looked at my not-so-fresh orange juice and asked, 'You signed the pledge?'

'No, I've made a resolution. No strong drink till after 8.30 in the morning.'

Blunt raised his pint to his lips.

'Aye, well, some of us have already done a full day's work.' He sucked the froth from his moustache. 'Been bedding down with any winos lately?'

'No. You?'

'Only the wife.' He pulled out his cigarettes and lit up without offering me one. 'I thought I said you weren't welcome round here.'

'If I listened to everyone who told me that I'd never leave the house.'

'That might not be such a bad thing.'

I lit my own cigarette.

'I've got something that might be of interest to you.'

'So come and see me in shop hours.'

'It's a bit delicate.'

'There are days I feel like a nurse at the clap clinic. Everyone wanting to show me their sores.' He looked at me through the smoke of his cigarette as if trying to make up his mind about something. 'Jesus Christ.' The policeman shook his head. 'OK then, what's the worst that can happen?' He laughed and I wondered if this was his first stop on the way home or if he had a bottle in his locker to ease the pain. 'Just give me a chance to order my breakfast.' Blunt leaned across the bar. 'Mary, goan throw us a packet of dry roasted over.'

'Not fancy a nice fry-up on the house, Mr Blunt?'

'Naw, hen, the wife'll have mine waiting when I get back.' He put the peanuts in his suit pocket, and straightened up muttering, 'Will she fuck.' He looked at me. 'Remind me of your name again.'

'Wiliam Wilson.'

'That's right. Down-among-the-dead-men Wilson. Right then, Mr Wilson, show me what you've got.'

'Can we go somewhere a bit more private?'

'As long as you promise not to slip into something more comfortable.'

We settled ourselves at a table with the kind of logistics favoured by teenage dope smokers, out of sight of the bar and away from the gents and the puggy machine. Blunt took another inch off his pint.

'Right,' he spanned his hand from the bottom of the glass to where the dark liquid ended. 'I'll give you this long.' I calculated it as two and a half seconds at his current rate of drinking, but there was no point in arguing. I reached into my pocket, took out a transparent plastic bag holding the envelope containing Montgomery's photographs and put it on the table. Blunt looked at the envelope, but made no effort to pick it up. 'Tell me about it.'

I started to regret not buying myself a short, but I took a deep breath and began.

'Twenty years ago a woman named Gloria Noon disappeared under mysterious circumstances. She never turned up, neither did her body. Her husband was chief suspect, but nothing was ever proven. This is a photograph that shows him with a

312

guy who was then a junior officer and is now a recently retired chief inspector in the Met. They're standing next to what I believe could be her grave. The policeman is married to the sister of the murdered woman.'

Blunt snorted.

'I don't know what I expected but it certainly wasn't that.'

'Will you look at them?'

'Hold your horses. A few questions first.' I nodded, trying to keep a lid on my impatience. 'Question number one, why land them in my lap?'

'I asked around, you've got a reputation for being straight.'

Blunt rubbed a hand over his face.

'And this is my reward I suppose? OK, question number two, what makes you think it's a gravesite?'

'I don't know, the look of the place, the two men standing there holding an edition of the newspaper from the day after she disappeared. That and . . .'

'And?'

'And the policeman in the photo is extremely eager to get a hold of it.'

'Oh lovely. Is this documented evidence?'

'No.'

'And how did you come across it?'

'I'd rather not say.'

'I see.' He paused, staring at me as he had probably stared at hundreds of men across tables in police interview rooms. 'OK, we'll come back to that if we need to. Why aren't you giving it to this eager detective?'

'I think it implicates him.'

Blunt looked at my untouched orange juice.

'Are you going to drink that?'

The sour liquid looked set solid inside the glass. 'No, probably not.'

'Well, get yourself a proper drink and another one of these for me while you're at it.'

I looked at the envelope and he said 'Leave that here, it'll be safe enough for the meantime.'

'No offence but I'm a conjurer by trade. I know how easy it is to make things disappear.'

I reached out to take it and Blunt put his glass on the envelope.

'Don't worry. It'll still be here when you come back.'

I tried to see what Blunt was doing from my position up at the bar, but we'd chosen our spot well and he was hidden from view. When I returned with the drinks he'd lit another cigarette, this time he offered me one.

'Where did you say this woman disappeared from?'

'Essex, it's near London.'

'I know where it is, and you presumably know it's not in my jurisdiction; there's nothing I could do with this except pass it on.'

'Aye, but at least then there would be a record. They'd be forced to investigate.'

Blunt took the head off his pint.

'Maybe so, maybe no.' He sighed. 'What your contact said about me being straight was right. I don't take bribes and I don't take bungs.' I looked towards the bar and he took another drag of his fag. 'I've got a tab, paid up every Friday on the dot. I do my best. Some people like it, some people don't, fuck them. But I don't go out of my way to make enemies. Accusing a well-respected officer in the largest force in the country of being an accessory to the murder of his sister-in-law is a sure-fire way to get yourself into trouble.' He turned, looked me full in the face and pushed the envelope back at me with the edge of a beer mat. 'I can't do anything, not on that.'

'But you're saying you think it looks dodgy?'

'I'm saying nothing.'

'But if I get more evidence you might be able to do something?'

Blunt drained the last of his pint.

'Gathering evidence is the job of the police.' He took a notebook and pen out of his pocket. 'What did you say the missing woman's name was?'

'Gloria Noon.'

Blunt wrote the name down and replaced the note-book.

'And the name of the inquisitive officer in the Met?'

'Montgomery, James Montgomery.'

I waited for him to jot it down and when he didn't asked, 'Aren't you going to put his name in your book?'

'I'm sure I can remember it.' Blunt shook his head wearily. 'This used to be a nice quiet pub.' He took out his wallet and rifled through it until he found a card. He checked to see there was nothing written on its back then passed it to me. 'Call if you have anything useful, don't bother otherwise. I'm not a sociable drinker, remember that in future.'

Berlin

It was two o'clock in the morning. Dix had looked at his watch so often in the rental car during our journey that I'd grown nervous about his driving. Now he glanced at it again while he fiddled with the heavy padlock to the door of the warehouse.

I could smell the odour of damp earth brought forth by the night. Close your eyes and you could be miles from the city in a freshly planted country garden, a new tilled field, or a cemetery ready for custom.

I asked, 'Who are these people?'

Sylvie pulled her long coat closer and stamped her red shoes against the ground, shivering. Dix threw her an impatient look, then turned the key and prised back the hasp.

'Would it make any difference if you knew?'

'Maybe.'

'It's too late for questions, William, just do as we discussed and it'll be payday.'

Sylvie wasn't the only one who was dressed up. Dix had revealed an unexpected showmanship, finding an outfit for me that would add a macabre touch to the proceedings. A black costume decorated front and back with a white glow-in-the-dark skeleton. There was a mask to go with it too, a grinning skull. The mask did a good job of hiding my bruises, but I'd been worried that my gut distorted the bones. Sylvie had reassured me.

'You look yummy, William. Death come to carry off my fresh young flesh.'

I'd pulled the skull over my face and stalked her

316

round the lounge, arms outstretched till Sylvie had let me scoop her, giggling and wriggling, onto the couch. I'd affected an aristocratic accent, Christopher Lee as Count Dracula.

'Your funeral bower, my dear.'

She'd mocked a faint and Dix had watched us with the indulgent smile of a miser reckoning money due.

The joke didn't seem so good now and the Halloween costume had lost its carnival air. Sylvie was as white as my fake bones. I put an arm around her but she pulled away impatiently.

'Let's just get this over with.'

'You don't have to go through with it if you don't want to.

Her laugh was harsh against the night.

Dix said, 'It'll be over soon. Less than an hour and we'll all walk away safely with cash in our pockets.'

Glasgow

Blunt needed more evidence before he could act and I had an idea of how I might get it. Like all the best tricks, it relied on a good grasp of psychology and a lot of finesse, but with the right assistance it could be simple.

I went back to the Internet cafe and checked up on flights from London. Then it was time to step into character and make a phone call. After that there was nothing much to do except hope and wait. I went back to my bed-sit, poured myself a drink, lay down on the bed and started working through the moves over and over again, until the homeward screech of buses drifted into the diesel growl of taxis and shouts of late-night drinkers. Eventually even they died away and I was left in silence, looking at the splash of light thrown by the streetlamp outside my window, wondering if Blunt would buy my scheme and if he did, whether it had any real chance of success.

Berlin

Sylvie was somewhere on the other edge of darkness. Dix and I stood side by side waiting for the signal. I sensed a movement and floodlights clicked on, searing white in the centre of the empty warehouse. A voice came from out of the firmament.

'OK, proceed.'

I'd expected German, but the words were English and the accents that came from the dark had an American twang. I looked at Dix.

'American?'

His voice held a hard edge of contempt.

'They still think Berlin is a place where they can get something they can't at home.'

I grinned and pulled the skull over my face, the whole thing making more sense now that I realised it was all the whim of a rich Yank with a taste for the exotic.

'Then let's oblige him.'

Dix put his hand on my arm.

'These are not holidaymakers who have wandered off the tourist trail.'

'What are you trying to tell me?'

'Sylvie knows her role. This is for her sake as much as mine. Just play your part and everything will be fine.'

I started to speak, but Dix put a finger over his lips and I heard the slow hollow sound of high heels striking against the wooden floor. Sylvie stepped out of the darkness into the floodlit centre of the warehouse. My poor victim looked magnificent. She wore a long silver robe that shimmered against the light; sparkles flashed from hair dark as coffin wood and her lips were painted a blood-red black that invited no kisses.

We waited for a beat of ten then Dix wrapped a black silk scarf across his face, nodded to me and strode forth, his footsteps brisk and full of business. He halted a foot away from Sylvie. She looked beyond him, ignoring his presence, and then dropped her robe, arching her back as if daring him to lay a finger on her, her naked body pale and magical against the pitch black. Dix stood frozen in place for a beat of ten while Sylvie stalked a full circle around him, like a half-tamed predator, not hungry but a killer by nature. I held my breath, wondering if they'd choreographed this earlier, or if Sylvie really was making her mind up about whether to go on. Then she stretched her spine like a show lion deciding to let its trainer live another day, and placed herself against the board. Dix immediately stepped forward and started to secure her, his fingers nimble and efficient, buckling the leather straps around her wrists and ankles, tugging at them to show they were firmly fastened.

I tried to push all other thoughts from my mind,

319

whispering a mantra over and over in my head, *concentrate, concentrate, concentrate . . .* and then it was my turn to walk into the light.

Glasgow

I decided to have my pre-performance drink in a bar beneath the railway arches because it was close to the Panopticon and I couldn't imagine any of the university buddies Johnny had recruited to help with the show dropping in for a quick one. The pub was tiny and cheap so it was never empty, but I was unprepared for the swarm of people busying it so early in the afternoon. I stood at the top of the small flight of steps leading down into the bar, taking in the press of green, the Celtic shirts and scarves, the sham-rocks and Jimmy hats, and realised it was St Patrick's Day. I hesitated for a second, wondering if the pub could accommodate another drinker, then a fresh group of men arrived and swept me down into the familiar odour of smoke, sweat and beer. I ordered a whisky even though every pint of Guinness came with a shamrock etched into the foam. Someone moved, I slid into a prime spot next to the cigarette machine and placed my drink on the ready-made shelf. St Patrick had chased the snakes out of Ireland. Maybe this was an omen that things would go well. But then it was a holiday to mark his death, so maybe it was a sign that the snakes always won in the end. The old man at the table next to me started to sing,

320

When I was a bachelor, I lived by myself
And I worked at the weaver's trade;
The only, only thing that I ever done wrong
Was to woo a fair young maid.

I wooed her in the summer-time,
And part of the winter-time too;

He turned and smiled a happy full-on denture smile and some old men joined in.

But the only thing that I ever did wrong
Was to keep her from the foggy, foggy dew.

The result was surprisingly melodic, when you considered that it was 2.30 in the afternoon and everyone seemed to be pissed. The aged singer had eyes the colour of forget-me-nots. They were soft and wet and happy with drink and memories. He cast his gaze around the room.

One night this maid came to my bed
Where I lay fast asleep.
She laid her head upon my chest
And then she began to weep.

'You're a dirty bugger, Peter,' shouted one of the drinkers. The old man smiled and tipped the heckler a wink, but he kept on singing.

She sighed, she cried, she damn near died.
She said, 'What shall I do?'
So I took her into bed and I covered up her head
Just to keep her from the foggy, foggy dew.

Behind my eyes a man covered a woman's ruined head with a clean white sheet. I put down my drink and went into the gents to splash water on my face. When I returned the song was over and someone had taken my place by the fag machine, but my drink was still there.

The barman squeezed by, collecting empty glasses. He handed the singer a half pint and a nip and said indulgently, 'There'll be no cut-price pensioner half'n'halfs if you lot get me shut down. Yous know I've no got an entertainment licence.'

An old drinker leant over.

'It's a dog licence he's needing with a voice like that.'

There was a burst of laughter, then someone on the other side of the room raised their voice and shouted, 'Give us a song, Ann.' The rest of the regulars took up the cry till even the men who'd only come for a St Patrick's Day bevvy joined in. The young barmaid shook her head shyly, but the drinkers kept up the demand, some of them banging the table with their pint glasses, chorusing *Ann, Ann, Ann* until the manager hurried back behind the counter and led the girl out in front. There was a call for hush followed by a shushing that threatened to descend into disruption, then the girl raised her face to the ceiling, closed her eyes and started to sing. Everyone else fell silent.

My young love said to me, 'My mother won't mind
And my father won't slight you for your lack of kind'
And she stepped away from me and this she did say:

322

'It will not be long, love, till our wedding day.'

Her voice was high and clear and pure. It should have made me think of green rolling hills and the white froth of a waterfall glinting against the sun, but instead I saw Sylvie strapped to the target as I walked towards her, masked in my Young Bones Wilson costume. She seemed to press her-self against the board. One of the sparkles in her hair caught the light and a bright prism glanced into my eyes, giving me a quick flash of the whole rainbow spectrum. It was an instant as fast as a bullet, then it was gone and there was just the frightened girl and the faceless audience watching from the dark.

As she stepped away from me and she moved
    through the fair
And fondly I watched her move here and move
    there
And then she turned homeward with one star
    awake
Like the swan in the evening moves over the
    lake.

I took the bullet from my pocket, gripped it between my finger and thumb and held it high in the air. Dix came out of the blackness, the scarf still hiding his features. He had a second man with him. The man wore a smart black suit over a black shirt and a latex mask of a red fox. The fox's wide smile was hungry, the eyes that glinted from its head an unnatural green that made me think of the damage a broken beer bottle can do.

323

The people were saying, no two e'er were wed
But one had a sorrow that never was said
And I smiled as she passed with her goods and
   her gear,
And that was the last that I saw of my dear.

The fox stared at the bullet for an age, turning it over in his hand, holding it close to his eye examining it until I lost track of time. Then at last he took the pen from Dix's hand and initialled the bullet along its edge, making sure he'd recognise it again. I handed Dix the revolver and he passed it to the fox, who examined it with the same intense thoroughness he'd used on the bullet. Then he gave the gun and bullet directly to me and stared through his green eyes as I placed the bullet into the revolver. That was the difficult moment, the point where I made the switch. And I managed it; I swapped the live bullet for its wax twin and loaded it into the chamber right before his suspicious eyes. He walked away and Sylvie and I were left facing each other in the bright white pool of light, surrounded on all sides by a blackness darker than deep space. I continued my mantra, *concentrate, concentrate, concentrate,* until her face lost its focus and became just a pale white thing, pressed behind glass, like a dead butterfly with a red marking at its centre.

Last night she came to me, my dead love came
   in.
So softly she came that her feet made no din
As she laid her hand on me and this she did say,
'It will not be long, love, 'til our wedding day.'

324

The pub broke into a racket of applause, rattling beer glasses and whoops. The barmaid bowed prettily and ducked behind the counter before she could be pressed into an encore. I wiped the sweat from my forehead and took another sip of my whisky. Then something made me look through the crush of bodies to the far end of the room, to where Inspector James Montgomery stood, still and sober amongst the revelry, with his eyes fixed on me.

*　　*　　*

The ex-policeman gave me a vague smile, the kind you might give a man whose face you recognise but can't quite place. I kept my own expression neutral and said, 'You're early.'

'Yeah, well I thought I'd arrive in good time, do a bit of sightseeing. I've never been to Scotland before.' He grinned. 'No wonder all you Jocks head down south.' Montgomery shook his head. 'What a dump.'

'Not like the classy joint you had your retirement do in, eh?'

'I'm not talking about this place, shithole though it is. I thought I'd make the most of my time up here; take in some of the sights. No offence but it's like going back fifty years.'

'No offence taken.'

The turns had ceased for a while and Dean Martin was belting out 'Little Old Wine Drinker Me' from the jukebox. He wasn't as popular as the barmaid, but he was going down OK and a few diehards were joining in the chorus. Montgomery laughed and put his arm around me like a man

325

enjoying a good joke and I felt something small and blunt press into my spine.

'Cumbernauld was the worst though. The conditions people live in there, especially the old folk, appalling. Quite frankly some of them'd be better off dead.'

My resolution to stay cool disappeared in a quick flash of heat. I hissed, 'You fucking go near my mother and you'll not live long enough to get what you're after.'

Montgomery wiped away a speck of spittle that had landed on his face.

'Touched a nerve did I?' He pressed a little further into my back. 'Must've done to make you start threatening a man who's holding a gun to you.' He grinned. 'You can't win, son. Just hand over what's mine and you never have to worry about me again.'

'I don't have it on me.'

'Then let's go and get it.' He smiled again. 'Shall I tell you a secret?'

'If you like.'

Montgomery put his face close to mine and whispered. 'Your mother isn't all you have to worry about.' His smile was small and sweet as a cupid's. 'I know all about your little German girlfriend.'

My voice was hoarse.

'How do you know?'

'Thirty-five years on the force has got to teach me something.'

My lips formed her name.

Sylvie.

'What do you know?'

Montgomery grinned.

'Oh, I know everything. What was her name again? Sylvie, that was it, wasn't it? She was quite something in that hotel room, eh? Too good for you, that's for sure.'

The sound of Sylvie's name on the lips of a policeman hit me in a dizzying wave of dread and liberation. The bitter release of fear made flesh made me laugh. The worst had happened, but I wasn't headed for a jail cell, not yet anyway. The balance of the deck had shifted. Up until now I'd wanted to free myself of guilt and Montgomery in one blow. But it seemed that he knew as much of my crime as I did of his. It was time for a reckoning and I was about to find out how far I was willing to go.

Most of the drinkers were too busy to notice Montgomery and me pressed together in the corner, but I'd spotted a squat man in a baseball cap staring at us. I threw him a look over the policeman's shoulder and he leered towards us.

'You a pair of fucking poofs?'

'I'm not, mate,' I made my eyes wide and honest. 'But I think this English git is, he won't leave me alone.'

The man raised his voice loud enough for the drinkers next to him to hear.

'That's the trouble with fucking faggots, they want to shove it down everyone else's throats.'

Montgomery twitched his wallet out of his pocket and flashed his ID, keeping a thumb pressed firmly over the part where it stated his name.

'I'm an inspector in the Metropolitan police force and this man is wanted on serious charges.'

'No problem, big man.' The punter took a step

327

back. 'I was only asking.'

I said, 'Your instinct's right enough though. He is a fucking poof, always up for Gay Pride duty, if you get my drift. Soon as we step outside he'll be trying to stick it in my arse.'

Montgomery kicked his toecap into the back of my heel shooting a stab of pain through my tendon, making sure that any thoughts I'd had of flight were over.

The punter said, 'I've nothing against poofs myself, like. I mean some of them are a good laugh . . . Graham Norton . . . Kenneth Williams . . .'

He faltered and I added, 'Noël Coward.'

The punter looked confused.

'I'm just saying, live and let live eh?'

Montgomery pulled out a pair of handcuffs and clicked me to himself. Someone in the crowd said, 'Oooh, kinky.' But the rest of the bar was silent. A pathway to the door had magically opened in the jam around us.

'Right,' the policeman's smile was grim. 'Let's go for a little walk.'

*   *   *

Argyle Street was busy enough with swarms of Saturday shoppers for two men walking closely side by side to go unnoticed. My bruised tendon shortened my gait, but Montgomery paced himself to my limp and our progress became more of a stroll. A father and son heading home after a couple of pints.

Something caught my eye. A small square of cardboard tagged to a lamppost and painted with sunny clowns and smiling faces. Bright red letters

328

announced the time and venue of Johnny's benefit in a careful, childish hand. In the sign's upper corner a moustachioed magician pulled a grinning rabbit from a top hat. I glanced at Montgomery, but his face was set straight, his eyes busy scanning the crowd. Homemade signs decorated with crayon, glitter and tinfoil shone from the rest of the lampposts leading to the Panopticon, my own version of the yellow brick road. There was nothing to do but hope that Montgomery wouldn't notice.

Moving towards us with the slow, unstoppable assurance of a Sherman tank was an elderly lady being pushed along in a wheelchair by her ancient husband. The wheelchair was strung with bulging carrier bags. They'd been doing their weekly shop, though why they'd left it to the busiest day of the week was beyond me. Maybe they just liked crowds. Montgomery stepped to the left of their path and I started to go with him, it was only at the last minute that I steered in the opposite direction, putting the wheel-chair between us.

'Christ Almighty, can yous no watch where you're going?'

The old man's breath was sharp and rasping. His skin was the grey-green of the cancer ward and he was carrying just enough weight to qualify as a hunger artist. His wife giggled. She had a pretty doll-like face plumped up with rouge and jolliness above a stack of quivering chins. Her legs were elephantine, the flesh cascading down into her unlaced sandshoes. Jack and Mrs Sprat. I wondered if they took turns in the chair. Her wobbling along his frailty one day, him struggling with her bulk the next. Love conquering all, except

329

poverty, disease and death.

I ignored Montgomery's jerk of the cuff and addressed myself to Jack.

'Sorry pal, it's my stag do, old Monty here's pinned me to him for a joke.'

'Aye,' the man's face was turning from green to beetroot with annoyance and high blood pressure. 'Fucking hilarious.'

The old lady tutted at the bad language and Montgomery tried to catch me by the scruff of my neck. I ducked out of his grasp, down towards the woman in the chair.

'Have you got a kiss for a condemned man?'

She laughed and landed me a smacker on the cheek enveloping me in her brandy breath. 'You're an awfy fella. I pity the poor lass that takes you on. You'll be the death of her.'

I said, 'If only you knew.' And reached into my pocket, grabbing a tenner. 'Here, have a drink on me the pair of you. For luck.'

'Keep your money, son, you'll need it yourself.'

The old woman shoved the note back, but Montgomery seized me and our bodies collided. This was my chance. The policeman had replaced his wallet in his inside pocket. His suit hung lower on the right than it did on the left. I guessed that was where he kept his keys. I only hoped that the one to the handcuff's padlock was amongst them. I dipped my fingers quickly, found the bunch and thrust them swiftly into my own pocket, uncertain whether I'd gained my release or merely access to the pale rooms far away where Sheila Montgomery had spent so many hours grieving for her lost sister Gloria.

The old lady shouted after us, 'Cheers son. And

you mind and look after that lassie of yours now.'

The old man shook his head and started to steer her down towards the Gallowgate.

*   *   *

I could feel Montgomery's unease growing as we climbed the Panopticon's dilapidated back staircase.

'What is this place?'

'I told you, it's where I store my gear.'

'What's wrong with a safety deposit box?'

'This is safe enough, and it doesn't cost anything.'

Montgomery snorted.

'Bloody Jock.'

I thought I heard the sound of laughter up above us and glanced at Montgomery to see if he'd noticed, but he was shaking his head.

'I don't like it.'

'I'm not exactly ecstatic myself. There's a gun at my back, cuffs on my wrist and a couple of sterling threats hanging over me.' I made my voice soft and reasonable. 'Do you not think I'm as eager to get this over with as you are?'

Montgomery stuck the gun firmly into my spine just as another wave of laughter floated through the corridor. He pulled up short.

'What was that?'

'Don't be so jumpy. It's the bingo hall down below. Saturday's their big day.' I grinned at him. 'What's wrong? Scared of ghosts?'

He shoved me forward.

'Let's just get on with it.'

I glanced at my watch. 'Aye, let's.'

331

And pushed open the door that led onto the stage.

*   *   *

Johnny's face broke into a mixture of confusion and relief when he saw me walking into the light, making no attempt to hide the handcuffs hooking Montgomery and me together. I nodded and he abandoned the half-hearted joke he'd been playing for time with, raising his hands in the air and shouting, 'Here's the man we've all been waiting for, the magnificent, the magical, William Wilson!'

There was a roar of applause from the audience and Montgomery turned to leave, but the cuffs that had held me prisoner now did the same for him. He put the hand holding the gun into his pocket and I wondered if any of the adults noticed.

I jerked him across the stage; all the months of drink and dreary bedsits falling from me. Energy climbed up my spine along my limbs and crackled on my fingertips. I was home again. I peeled my lips back into a William Wilson grin and shouted, 'Take a good look at this man's face. His name is Uncle Monty and he's a terrible villain.'

The audience laughed.

I said, 'Shout, "Hello Uncle Monty."'

Hello Uncle Monty!

The policeman tried to pull away but I wrenched him back, the wide smile on my face belying the pain jolting up my wrist.

'Look at his grumpy face. I don't think he heard you, girls and boys, shall we shout a little louder and see if we can get him to say hello?'

The kids knew the drill. They took a deep

breath of air, filled their little lungs to the top and bellowed *Hello Uncle Monty!*

I put my arm round Montgomery, leading him centre-stage, eager as an old dog in the vet's waiting room and whispered, 'Don't panic, you'll get your photo. This way I've got a witness or two who's seen us together.' I raised my voice again and shouted, 'Would you like to see some magic?'

Yes!

The hall was in full pantomime mode now. Montgomery still tried to edge us off stage, but I yanked him with me until we were level with the large bright box I'd borrowed from Bruce McFarlane.

'I'm sorry I was a little late. I had to go to the Magician's Den, a very special magic shop not too far from here, and buy some magic dust.' I reached into my pockets and sprinkled a handful of the glitter I'd filled them with that morning across the floor. It winked and blinked against the bright lights. 'Do you like that?'

Yes!

They were a very obliging crowd. I grinned and put my hand back in the pocket, but this time, instead of more glitter, I grasped the key and with one flourish unfastened the handcuffs, pulled Montgomery's jacket from his back and shoved him inside the box, shutting the door quick and latching it tight. I leant over to my props table and grabbed another padlock, fastening it for good effect. A banging came from inside the box.

'OK, boys and girls, mums and dads, aunties, uncles and hangers-on, now I'm going to show you what to do with bad men.' I sprinkled magic dust over the box and tapped it with an oversized wand,

333

reciting a traditional magical incantation, 'Abracadabra!'

The banging continued and Montgomery shouted, 'Let me out, Wilson!'

The crowd cheered and laughed.

'You know what, boys and girls? I think I'm going to need some help. Shout and stamp your feet as hard as you can if you're going to help me make the bad man disappear.'

The theatre exploded into an unholy din and I put my mouth to the box and whispered, 'Shut the fuck up and go with it or I swear to God, kids or no kids, I'll empty your gun into the box, pretend it's part of the act and dump this whole contraption in a loch. Now squash yourself up, it's about to get cramped in there.' There was no answer but the banging stopped. I turned back to the crowd. 'OK, at the count of three I want you to shout "Abracadabra!" One, two, three . . .'

Abracadabra!

'I'm not sure that was loud enough,' I shook my head. 'After all he is a very, very bad man. I think we should try it again.'

I made the kids shout three more times while I secretly slid in place the specially angled mirrored panels that would, if all went well, fling back a reflection of the box's interior, confusing the audience's eye enough to think it vacant.

I held my breath, kept the jacket containing the gun within reach and briskly opened the doors to the box revealing an illusion of pristine emptiness. I whacked my wand around inside, careful to avoid appearing in the mirrors myself then smartly slammed the door and bolted it shut. It got a round of applause but whatever the danger

334

involved, making an ugly man vanish never gets the same reaction as making a beautiful woman appear and I thought that for all my efforts the illusion fell a little flat.

*   *   *

Thirty minutes later the show was over, or just about to begin depending on your way of looking at things. I sat on stage in the empty theatre, staring at the box and smoking a cigarette. Regulations probably didn't allow smoking onstage, but there was no one around to stop me and I was planning on being very careful.

Montgomery had been quiet for so long I was beginning to wonder if he'd escaped. I'd had to abandon the room for a while after my set was through, pretending to leave with the crowd and encouraging Eilidh and John to go to the pub with the rest of the performers, before I could sneak back up into the auditorium.

But the padlock was still in place where I'd secured it and Bruce's box was undamaged, so the odds were that Monty was still inside biding his time, hoping to jump me when I set him free.

I thought about Sylvie and wondered how far I was willing to go. Was killing a bad man better than killing a good woman? Obviously. Did it matter whether you killed him because he was bad or because you wanted to save yourself? I didn't know. Could I set myself up as judge, jury and executioner? Maybe, if I was sure I was right. But how often had I been right?

The Panopticon felt eerie. Without the audience it was almost possible to believe in Archie's ghosts. I sent a small smile up to the balcony then made

335

sure my cigarette was dead and got up and unlocked the box.

* * *

I waited by the unlatched cabinet for ten minutes, willing myself not to look inside. My hand had just started to creep towards the door when Montgomery exploded out, bellowing towards me. But he was an old man, confinement had cramped his muscles and he wasn't much of a challenge.

I shouted, 'This is yours,' threw his jacket over his head and spun him round. He staggered to the far side of the stage then pulled the jacket free and went into its pockets. I held the gun in the air.

'Looking for this? Here, take it.'

I flung the weapon tumbling towards him. He caught it awkwardly and I held up the ammunition clip.

'Mind if I hold onto this for a while? If you get close enough you can always batter me to death with the barrel.' I kept my tone conversational. 'Is that what you did to Gloria? Stave her head in?'

'I never touched Gloria.'

'This photograph suggests otherwise.' I produced the envelope out of nowhere with a quick sleight of hand, then made it disappear again. 'Now you see it, now you don't.'

He took a step forward.

'That's mine.'

'Really?' My voice was mild. 'I thought it belonged to Bill Noon.'

Montgomery shook his head wearily.

'They were old Noon's not his son's. He had his and I had mine, whoever went first was to see his

336

copy destroyed.'

'An insurance policy?'

'Kind of.'

I'd guessed the ploy when I'd spoken with Drew Manson, but it was good to have it confirmed.

'So neither of you could get a sudden urge to confess or grass the other one up without sticking yourself in it. I suppose it was a good plan until one of you died suddenly and you got greedy and decided to blackmail young Bill.'

Montgomery laughed.

'Is that what he told you?' He looked at me incredulously. 'And you believed him?' He laughed again and shook his head. 'Why not, I suppose?' His voice became serious, like an instructor explaining a basic point to a particularly dull student. 'The night you nicked it I had just paid a lot of money for that picture.' He repeated the phrase, stressing the point. 'A lot of money. All I wanted was to go home and do to that photo what I'd done to my own one as soon as I'd heard Bill's dad had snuffed it: burn it and get shot of the whole sorry business. Thirty years with that hanging over me, never a day, an hour even, when I didn't think of it. But Bill wanted to torment me. If he'd stuck me in it I would have understood. She was his mother after all. But he didn't want that. He wanted to torture me. A big party, the whole squad, strippers and me sitting with evidence of the crime that ruined my life and could still send me down, burning a hole in my pocket. Then . . .' Montgomery started to laugh at Bill's audacity, 'then he stole it back.'

'And you killed him and his boyfriend.'

'No, things got out of hand. His boyfriend dived

in. Bill and I would have worked it out somehow, but his little nancy had got hold of a gun from somewhere. He aimed it at me, Bill went to stop him and the thing went off. He saw what he'd done and turned it on himself. It was nothing to do with me. There was blood everywhere, a fucking forensic man's wet dream.'

I was certain that I could hear the lie in his voice but asked, 'So why didn't you call the police? An ambulance?'

Montgomery was indignant.

'Be reasonable, can you imagine? That would have gone down a storm wouldn't it? Anyway, there was no point. They were dead already. I just wanted to get what I'd come for then get out. I tore that office apart.' Montgomery shook his head as if he was still amazed. 'He got his revenge all right. It was only later, when I thought through the night, that it became obvious what had happened. Then I knew I had to find you.' He smiled softly. 'It took a while, but I got you in the end.'

'Do you think so?'

'Look,' the policeman's voice was reasonable. 'It was a long time ago. I'm a different man from the one I was then. I've made a different life. You can understand that. Everyone makes mistakes.' He reached into his pocket and pulled out a wedge of notes. 'I can pay, name your price.'

'Absolution.'

'What?'

I pointed up towards the balcony where the pair of mannequins stood.

'Up there.'

Montgomery shook his head.

'You forget, Wilson, I've been dealing with

villains for thirty-five years.'

A soft whisper came from above.

'James.'

Montgomery birled round. A third figure had joined the Victorian couple. It stood silhouetted against the shadows, and then stepped down to the edge of the balcony. She was ghost-pale, her eyes set like stabs of jet, lips so blood-less they were almost absent. Her ash-gold hair seemed faded to white and she wore a loose cotton dress that could have been a shroud.

Montgomery's voice was hoarse with dread.

'Gloria?'

Sheila Montgomery raised her head and stared out at us like vengeance made flesh.

'How could I be Gloria? Gloria's dead.'

The policeman gasped for air. For a second I thought he might collapse, but then slowly his breaths grew longer and he regained his voice.

'He's a crook, Sheila.' Montgomery looked at me. 'He's trying to set me up.'

'In that case he's done a good job. I saw the photograph, Jim, the one you're so eager to buy. It was taken years ago.' She gave a bitter laugh. 'Setting you up in his pram was he?'

'No . . . he . . .'

The policeman faltered.

'I just heard you admit to standing by while Billy died, tell me what else you've done or I'll think the worst.'

'I never wanted you anywhere near any of this.'

Sheila's voice was faint.

'Near what?'

'This.' Montgomery spread his hands vaguely. 'I swear . . . I never touched her.'

'But you knew her? You knew Gloria?'

There was silence as the policeman searched for an excuse and failed. I wondered if there was a release in surrendering to the truth, but if there was, no sign of it appeared on his face. Montgomery looked ten years older than the man I'd first seen in Bill's club. He sighed and said, 'Yes, I knew her.'

Sheila gasped and I realised that until then, despite the photograph I'd shown her, she'd been unconvinced of her husband's involvement. Montgomery took a step forward, looking up at the gallery like an aged ruined Romeo.

'I swear, as soon as I met you I knew the affair with Gloria had been nothing. She was nothing compared to you.'

Sheila shouted, 'You think I'm upset about that? You think I care about that? About the sex? You think I'm jealous of Gloria?' She gripped the balcony and fought for composure. 'What did you do, Jim?'

Montgomery talked on, as if he hadn't heard her, or as if he'd been preparing his speech for a long time.

'We were young . . . Gloria was bored . . . she thought it was funny to seduce a policeman . . . to have lovers on both sides of the law. I was naïve . . . unsophisticated . . . easily flattered.'

Sheila's voice was shrill.

'You're blaming her? A dead woman?'

Montgomery whispered.

'No . . . no . . . I . . .'

'Tell me Jim or so help me God I'll throw myself off this balcony. Did you and Bill Noon kill my sister?'

340

'No!' James Montgomery looked away from his wife, out into the empty stalls. 'No, I never killed her. It was Bill. He knew she'd been mucking around and he lost his temper. She fell down the stairs. Nobody meant it, it just happened. I was in the wrong place at the wrong time and he made me help him.' His voice was cracking now. 'He made me.'

'And young Bill?'

'I swear I had nothing to do with that.' He took another step forward. 'I never touched Gloria. All I did was help dispose of her body and I've been paying for it ever since.'

Heavy footsteps sounded across the stage. Montgomery looked at me, then towards the wings where the tall figure I'd been hoping to see all night was walking towards us.

'No, you haven't.' Blunt was as scruffy as ever, but his voice was strong and sober. 'You've been avoiding it. But you'll start paying pretty soon.'

Montgomery looked at Blunt blankly, then he saw the uniformed policemen behind him and realised what was happening. He edged backwards across the stage.

I said, 'There's nowhere to go, Monty, you've got to face them.'

James Montgomery took a last step back. Sheila gasped and I reached out to grab him. Our fingers touched and then he tumbled beyond my grasp. It was as fast and as sure as gravity. The feel of his hand was still upon mine even as I saw him twisting awkwardly and heard the sickening thump.

There was a clatter of police boots and a cackle of radios on the back stairs as the uniforms ran the

341

slow route down. Blunt walked across the stage and looked into the audience pit.

'He'll live.'

The sound of Sheila Montgomery's sobbing drifted down from above. Blunt made his way wearily down into the stalls and started to recite the police litany.

'James Montgomery, I am arresting you on suspicion of murder. You do not have to say anything but it may harm your defence if you do not mention now anything you later rely on in court. Anything you do say will be given in evidence . . .'

I sank to the floor, put my head in my hands and shut my eyes.

Berlin

Sylvie's red lips mouthed something that might have been *I love you* or *Don't do it* or *Do it quick.* My consciousness shifted and I saw us both caught in a tableau. Sylvie afraid but determined, her pale skin shining as if it were drawing all the light in the warehouse towards her, and me in my ridiculous costume, right arm raising the gun level with my shoulder. Somewhere in the dark the stranger and Dix were watching, waiting for me to go through with the trick, and somewhere far off so was I; still sure the wax was in the chamber, but wondering what it was that I'd missed. I lowered the gun and took a step towards Sylvie. Scared as she'd looked, her fear had been nothing to the terror that suddenly shadowed her face.

'Come on, dear,' her voice shook with the effort of calm. 'Why don't you show them our William Tell act?'

And I realised that the die was cast. I had been tempted with money and performance pride but something worse than humiliation would happen if I rejected the challenge now.

I slid from my position on the outside, back into myself, breathed deeply, raised my arm, slowly took aim, squeezed the trigger and fired. The glass shattered and the target flew backwards into the centre of an explosion of noise and red.

I sank to the floor, into the warmth of my own piss, putting my head in my hands, feeling a thousand shards of glass rain down on me, scattering across the floor like diamonds spilled by a careless hand.

*   *   *

I crouched there, hearing nothing but the repeat of the blast exploding over and over in my ears. After what seemed like a long time Dix touched my shoulder.

'Here,' his voice was gentle. 'Swallow, you'll feel better.'

I kept my eyes on the ground unable to run towards the red blur at the edge of my vision and asked, 'Did I kill her?'

'Shhhh.'

Dix prised open my mouth and slipped a pill beneath my tongue. I swallowed then hunched back on the floor, letting darkness claim me. He was right, oblivion was better than the knowledge of what I'd done.

343

Consciousness brought the sharp tang of disinfectant. My first thought was that they weren't making hospital beds any softer. But when I forced open my eyes I lay curled in a square of sunlight beneath the warehouse's skylight. The shadows of pigeons roosting in the roof above crawled across me. One touched my face; I winced and raised a hand to bat it away though it was nothing.

I thought of Sylvie. The vision of her ruined body dropping to the floor flashed into my mind in bloody Technicolor. There was a sudden pain in my gut and I twisted into it, heaving deep dry sobs whose echoes were my only replies. Above me the birds launched into the air, their wings beating out a fractured rhythm; I thought of the sound a pistol makes and groaned.

I'm not sure how much time passed before I managed to raise my head, but I know it was a long interval between that first move and struggling to my feet. Someone had covered me with my raincoat. I pulled it on and stumbled like a three-day drunk to the spot where Sylvie had fallen. The warehouse was huge and empty, a transitory space where things were stored then moved on, where women were shot then disappeared and shattered conjurers stood and wondered what to do next.

Someone had done a good job. There was no sign left of my crime, except for a patch on the floorboards that was cleaner than the rest, where traces of blood and tooth would still be stored, if you knew how to look. I got down on my knees and traced my fingertips across it. The boards were

344

rough and unpolished, their surface still vaguely damp.

My hand went into my pocket feeling for the gun, but instead of hard metal my fingers closed around a stiff paper package. I drew it out and looked at a large bundle of euros, more cash than I'd ever seen. I stared blankly at the money then put it back in my pocket, fastened my coat and stepped out into the open air, walking a long way until I felt straight enough to hail a cab. The door to Sylvie and Dix's flat was open, the place abandoned. I'm not sure how long I stayed there, sitting on Dix's chair, pulling at the gaffer-taped tear in its arm, wondering what had happened and what to do, waiting for the police to arrive. But some time after it had become clear that no one was going to come for me, I found myself on a flight home to Glasgow.

London

It felt good to be back in London. A friend of Eilidh and John's had a studio apartment he'd wanted to let in a hurry. Johnny had given me a reference that dispensed with the deposit and I'd managed to cobble together a month's rent. After dumping my few things in the flat my next stop was Rich's office.

I braced myself for Mrs Pierce's disapproval but there was a young woman at the desk. Slim and dark, with short black hair framing a pixie-like face.

She called Rich on the intercom and he buzzed

me straight through.

'Bloody hell, I thought you were dead or in jail.'

'Neither.' I sat on the visitors' chair. 'What happened to Mrs Pierce?'

'Retired, said she had no desire to work past sixty.' Rich looked disgusted. 'I don't know what's happening, William, used to be you got loyalty, now what do you get? Women who work for you for forty years then suddenly want to spend time with their grandchildren. I ask you.' He looked at me. 'Oh I get it, what you mean is, who's the sweet young thing sitting out front?'

'My womanising days are over.'

Rich smiled like he'd heard it all before.

'That says a lot about why you've been off the map. I'll tell you what my old dad, God rest his soul, told me. He said, *Don't go for the good-looking ones Richie, they'll only give you grief.* He was right. My mother was an ugly woman, God rest her, and Mrs Banks . . . have you met my wife?'

I shook my head. 'No.'

'Well, Mrs Banks is what they used to call homely, but she's a wonderful woman, William, a good mother, good cook and . . . well . . . Take my advice, find a woman who thinks she's lucky to have you and she'll treat you like a king.'

'I'll give that serious thought. In the meantime I was wondering if you've got anything in my line.'

Rich blew through his lips.

'Nada. Summer season starts in a couple of weeks and I'll more than likely manage to scrape something up for you then if you're still looking but right now trade's as dry as Mrs Pierce without her HRT.' I raised my eyebrows and he said, 'Crude, I know, but that woman left me in the lurch. Been threatening to go for years, then suddenly she's off. Unbelievable.'

He took a cigar out of his desk and started to unwrap it. 'Is that the best you can do?'

Rich shrugged.

'I told you, it's quiet. You know the drill. Work up something good and come and see me in time for the Summer Season casualties. Bound to be some lushed-up comedian hits the skids and needs replacing.'

I shook my head.

'Always the bridesmaid.'

'They also serve who only stand and wait, William.'

'Christ, if I ever end up as a waiter I'll saw myself in half and disappear up my own jacksie.'

'If you learn how to do that get in touch but in the meantime . . .'

'Cheerio?'

'You always did catch on quick.' He picked up the phone. 'Rozena, Mr Wilson's on his way out now. Don't let him chat you up, he's got no money and fewer prospects.' He put the phone down. 'My accountant's daughter, I promised him she wouldn't lose her virginity on the premises.'

I said, 'You've nothing to fear from me.'

'It's not my virtue that I'm worried about, son.'

I closed the door just as his phlegmy laugh descended into coughs.

*   *   *

Rozena put an arm over the file she was reading but too slowly for her to hide that it was mine.

'Interesting?'

347

'It confirms what Mr Banks said. No job, no prospects, but reading between the lines I'd say you know your way around.'

'Only because I've been around for a long time.'

'Long enough to give a girl a guided tour?'

It was the kind of offer that only comes once or twice in a lifetime. She smiled and I saw how even her teeth were. A lot of book balancing had gone into making that perfect smile. I lifted the file, looked at my own grinning face clipped to the right-hand corner, slid the photo from the folder and put it in my pocket. If I ever came back to the office I'd replace it with one that looked like me.

I said, 'There's a tour bus leaves Marble Arch every half-hour, I've heard they give a good commentary.' And went out into the sunshine.

*　　　*　　　*

Back out in the street my phone beeped. I flipped it open and read the new text.

Gt yr arse up2 Glesga by 25 June you've got a wedding 2go2—Johnny

I texted back A OK and replaced the phone in my pocket. I wasn't the best man but that was all right, when was I ever?

*　　　*　　　*

I caught the underground to Tottenham Court Road then walked into Soho. I was making a new life. That meant no avoided streets and no-go areas, and that meant facing up to the past.

Maybe I was half aware of the clatter of high heels and the scream of giggles gaining on me from behind as I approached my destination. But if I thought about it at all I probably imagined it was the sound of a couple of teenage shop-girls released from the prison of their counters and making the most of their lunch hour. Then someone hooked my left arm in theirs and an instant later a second person put an arm around my shoulder, hugging me into a squeeze. I jarred to a halt.

Shaz giggled.

'Remember us?'

It was a moment before I regained enough breath to reply.

'How could I forget?'

Jacque looked at me.

'Did we give you a fright?'

'Maybe a wee bit.'

The girls laughed. Jacque's hair was cut short and streaked three different shades of blonde. Shaz's dark curls were perhaps a trifle longer. But otherwise the Divines looked unchanged from when I'd seen them last, except of course that they had their clothes on.

'You're both looking great.'

They chimed *thanks.* Nobody complimented me on my weight loss, but perhaps they hadn't noticed.

Jacque let go of my arm.

'That was one weird night wasn't it? You know Bill was shot?'

'Yeah, I heard.'

'Lucky we were well clear by that time.' Shaz shook her head. 'He always was an oddball.'

'Was he?'

'Oh for sure, way out in cuckoo land.'

Jacque giggled.

'He was off the cuckoo map.'

Shaz joined in.

'Way out in the cuckoo sea.'

'Without a cuckoo paddle.'

I broke in before they could stretch the fantasy further. 'It's good to see you looking so well . . .'

Shaz cut me off.

'Ah no, you don't escape us so easily.'

She caught hold of my left arm again and her girlfriend took my right.

'Come and have a drink.'

'I was heading somewhere.'

Jacque nipped my wrist.

'A couple of exotic dancers not good enough for you anymore?'

'It's not that . . .'

'What then?'

I wanted to say I couldn't be trusted around women, but the explanation would be too long and too strange so instead I smiled and said, 'OK, where do you fancy?'

Jacque giggled.

'That's why we came chasing after you. There's something you've got to see.'

Shaz looked at her watch.

'And if we're quick we'll just be in time.'

*   *   *

After Montgomery's arrest I had expected to find myself back in the cells en route for extradition to a German jail, but Sylvie's name was never mentioned. Eventually, during one of the long debriefing and drinking sessions that took place

350

between Blunt and me, where some of the liberties we'd taken were edited out of our recollections, I steeled myself and said, 'Montgomery threatened my mother.'

'The guy was desperate and ruthless, not a good combination.'

'It got him pretty far up the police ranks.'

Blunt gave me a look.

'It doesn't matter what line you're in, the bosses generally feature a couple of successful psychopaths.'

'Is that right?'

He nodded.

'Makes sense when you think about it, explains why all bosses are cunts.'

I nodded and took a sip of my beer.

'He also threatened a lassie I was friendly with in Berlin. I wondered if he mentioned her?'

'Nah, he's not going to drop himself in it is he? Was it nasty?'

I thought back to our encounter in the pub beneath the railway arches.

'He said, "I know all about your little German girlfriend."'

'Typical con talk. He knew you had a girlfriend so he threatens her as a matter of course. Maybe he knows where she lives or works, maybe not. But he brings her up and you go into a panic. It's an old trick.'

'I thought . . .'

'What?'

'I guess I didn't think. I just reacted.'

Blunt snorted.

'Aye well, some women have that effect. Make you imagine all sorts of daft things.'

I'd nodded and downed the rest of my pint.

*   *   *

The trial filled the papers for weeks. Montgomery had admitted to helping dispose of Gloria Noon's body, but still maintained her death had been an accident. Gloria and he had been having an affair for six months before Bill Noon had got wise and made a point of coming home early. Montgomery stuck to his story, maintaining that Noon had caught them together and Gloria had fallen down the stairs in the ensuing argument, hitting a fatal blow to her head. He'd panicked and he and Bill had disposed of the body, pooling their gangster/police expertise to ensure Gloria would never be found. It was their shared experience of crimes and villains that decided them to take the photograph as insurance.

Montgomery described their controlled fear, how he and Bill senior had become uneasy allies and hatched a plan, waited till dark then driven through the night before slipping Gloria's weighted body into the country park lake. Then they'd kept on driving, forced to stick together until the shops opened and they were able to lodge the film in a distant quick-developing chemist's. He and Bill had sat together in silence, deep beneath the earth in an underground car park, until the prints were ready. Then they'd taken a copy each and burnt the negative together.

The bond between them had been formed that night. Maybe it was a union forged in blood and taboo, or maybe they were simply greedy men who each found an ally on the other side. Because after that evening neither man seemed able to leave the other quite alone, and the jury heard how many of Bill senior's scams and undertakings had benefited from Montgomery's influence.

There was no one left to dispute Montgomery's story. He admitted a lot in the hope that a show of honesty and contrition would validate his denial of involvement in Gloria's death. But the Crown charged him with murder and the jury agreed.

The evidence regarding Bill and Sam's deaths was inconclusive. Montgomery was right, the scene had been a forensic man's wet dream and now that they knew to look, his fingerprints and DNA were all over the place. But Montgomery had never denied being in Bill's office when the shots were fired, though he vehemently refuted pulling the trigger. At the very least, he had watched the two men die and made no attempt to call for help. That was enough to convince the jury of his ruthlessness and he was found guilty on two more counts of murder, though Eilidh thought Montgomery's defence might succeed in getting them over-turned on appeal.

Whatever the truth, James Montgomery was going away for a very long time to a place where policemen were welcomed with a special kind of glee. There would be no family visits and no one waiting for him if he ever came out. It was justice of a sort, but I kept thinking of his fading wife and wondering if she could ever reconcile the price paid for discovering her sister's fate.

*   *   *

The Divines stopped in front of a building I knew

well, though I'd only visited it once before.

Shaz grinned.

'Recognise it?'

'You've got to be kidding me.'

'No joke, William.'

We'd unknowingly had the same destination in mind, but if I'd not been led there I might easily have walked past. Bill's old club was no longer the blank-faced dive where we'd met on that first night. It had undergone a paint job and a glowing peppermint-green sign proclaimed it *BUMPERS*.

Jacque looked admiringly at the building's fresh facade.

'And who do you think the new management are?'

I shook my head.

'I can honestly say I've not got a Scooby.' The Divines' excited smiles registered. 'You?'

They chorused *Yes!* Jacque caught me by the elbow.

'Come on, William, or you'll miss your treat.'

The doorman smiled at the women then put his broad body in front of me.

'Are you a member, sir?'

'It's all right, Dave, he's with us.'

Dave looked unsure, but he stepped out of the way and let me through. The lounge where I had performed my act and the girls had danced for the policemen was transformed. Banks of purple couches now grouped around its edge and where the mirror ball had half-heartedly rotated, a massive crystal chandelier shimmered from the ceiling. Airbrushed photographs of big-breasted women with wet, open mouths hung around the walls in oversized gilt frames. I thought that the models looked mildly pained, as if they had eaten something that disagreed with them. But all of this decoration was merely an adjunct to the room's focus: a mirrored stage pierced by a silver pole.

'No offence girls, you've done a grand job, but I'm not sure this is my kind of place.'

'It never was, William,' Shaz nodded to a waitress. 'But wait till you see this, it's right up your street.'

*   *   *

I'd thought I'd seen her face before and been mistaken so many times that I had learnt not to trust my senses. But when she stepped out from the darkness I knew that this time she was for real.

She strode across the small stage wearing a smart black business suit edged with white cuffs, raising her hands palm out, showing they were empty, then conjured forth a red silk handkerchief from nowhere. Her slender fingers folded the silk in on itself and made it disappear. She held her hands up once more as if amazed by their emptiness. Her eyes opened wide as she ripped off the white cuffs one by one and threw them behind her, then repeated the trick, conjuring the red square from nothing. Her smile was bright and daring as she moved with the music, slowly peeling off her conservative jacket, flinging it in the same direction as the cuffs, revealing a lacy black bra beneath. Once again the handkerchief suddenly appeared between her fingers. She waved it in the air, folded it away, then looked down at her skirt, raising her eyebrows cheekily as she slid down its zip, dropping the skirt to the floor and kicking it off-stage. Now she was wearing nothing but her underwear and shoes. The red hanky was relentless. It appeared again in her hand and once more she folded it into extinction. The trick was simple, something a precocious six-year-old could master, but I was mesmerised. I shook my head, a smile working its way across my face as her bra and knickers each hit the deck in turn and she stood before us naked. I got to my feet, ready to applaud, but she wasn't finished yet. The naughty magician glanced down at herself, put her hand towards her sex and once more drew forth the red scrap of material. She flung her hands in the air, made the hanky vanish for the last time and bent into a bow. There was a dismal mid-afternoon round of applause from the half-empty tables. I got to my feet, started clapping my hands as hard as I could and cheered. Shaz and Jacque smiled at me, pleased I'd enjoyed their joke. They couldn't know that it wasn't the handkerchief trick I was applauding, but another more spectacular illusion. Sylvie looked in my direction and our eyes met.

*   *   *

We were the only people in the dressing-room. Sylvie cleared a space amongst the discarded fragments of costumes—the used tissues, abandoned makeup, kirby grips and hair-brushes —and pulled herself up onto the counter with her back to the mirror. I drew up a chair and sat opposite her. The sign above Sylvie's head said *NO SMOKING*. She took a pack of cigarettes from her robe and offered me one. I sparked both of us up. She inhaled and gave me a smile through

356

the smoke.

'So, William, mad at me?'

I thought for a long moment, keeping my eyes on her face.

'I should want to kill you.'

Sylvie pulled the lid from a can of hairspray, flicked her ash into it and gave the smile that had dazzled me in Berlin. It was still worth seeing.

'I guessed you'd wash up in London.'

'Is that why you came here?'

'Perhaps.'

'Perhaps?'

Sylvie shrugged.

'It's a small world, smaller business. I guessed we'd run into each other sooner or later.'

Disbelief caught in the back of my throat.

'You guessed we'd run into each other?' She drew on her cigarette and her eyes narrowed against the smoke.

'You could of found me William, if you'd cared to look.' She laughed and held her hands out, indicating the tawdry room. 'Seek and you shall find.'

'Have you any idea of what you did to me, Sylvie?' I shook my head, stumbling for words. 'Christ, I don't know what to ask first. Why or how? How? How did you manage it?'

Sylvie smiled wearily.

'Smoke and mirrors, auto-suggestion. I primed you, planted the seed that everything was going to go wrong, then when Dix set off the effect you believed it. You were on your knees and in shock practically before I hit the deck.'

'I still don't understand. Why Sylvie? Did I do something to deserve it?'

357

She looked at her feet and wiggled her toes.

'Do you think we get what we deserve? No, you didn't deserve it. It was necessary. The show was the price Dix had to pay to clear his debts.'

'Then why not let me in on it? I thought I'd killed you.' I added emphasis to my words. *I thought I was a murderer.* Have you any idea how horrible that feels?'

'I guess not.' She raised her head. 'Sorry, William, your reaction was central to the effect.' She smiled. 'You couldn't have faked it.'

My voice was bitter.

'No, I guess not.'

Sylvie sighed.

'Dix got out of his depth. The men he was in debt to wanted to make a tape that would recoup what he owed and punish him at the same time.' She leant over and touched my hand. 'You were the opposite of a murderer and I was grateful . . . very grateful. I made Dix leave you a whole bunch of money.'

I slid my hand from under hers.

'Money I thought was covered in your blood.' Sylvie looked at her feet again and I asked, 'So Dix made on the deal?'

Her voice took on a brittle, jaunty tone.

'You know Dix, always an eye to an angle. For every official watcher there'll be others in the wings, for every video there'll be a dozen copies.'

The thought of the episode captured on countless tapes, trapped in the worldwide web, sweated over by an infinite audience of nameless viewers struck me. The realisation must have shown in my expression because Sylvie said, 'Don't worry, the only face on show is mine.'

I forced my voice calm.

'How is Dix?'

Sylvie looked away.

'He's fine.'

'A rich man?'

She smiled.

'You know money, it has a habit of evaporating.'

'Hence . . .'

I looked around at the dressing-room.

'Yes,' she smiled. 'Hence.'

'So,' I asked the question I'd wanted to know the answer to even in the first shock of our reunion, 'Dix is here with you?'

Sylvie nodded.

I said, 'Send him my regards.'

'You are mad at me, William.'

I shrugged.

'No, I'm not mad. I was, but I'm not now.' I got to my feet. 'Take care of yourself, Sylvie.'

She took a last drag and looked at me. For a second I thought she might ask me to stay, but instead she stubbed her cigarette out in the makeshift ashtray and gave me her special smile, the one that could have had them cheering all the way to the gods.

'You too, William.'

I closed the door of the dressing-room and walked out of the club, into the late-afternoon bustle of Soho.

Sheila Montgomery once said that if her sister turned up alive and well she would be tempted to kill her for all the pain she had caused. I knew now that wasn't true. The revelation of Sylvie's betrayal hurt, but it didn't hurt as much as when I thought I'd killed her. I'd entered the club a murderer and left it absolved. That had to be worth a celebratory drink.

There was a decent pub close by that kept the racing on TV all afternoon. I turned the corner and started to walk towards it, the memory of Sylvie's smile shining sweet and sad in my head.

Acknowledgements

For permission to reprint, acknowledgement is made to the following:

'Raftery's Dialogue With the Whiskey' from *A Look In The Mirror and Other Poems* by Padraic Fallon. Published by Carcanet Press Limited, 2003.

'In the Heat of the Night'. Words by Alan and Marilyn Bergman, music by Quincy Jones © 1967 United Artists Music Company, Inc. © Renewed and assigned to EMI U Catalog Inc. Lyrics reprinted by permission of Alfred Publishing Company, Inc. All rights reserved.

'Don't Tell Mama' from *Cabaret*. Words by Fred Ebb and music by John Kander © 1966.

'Those Were the Days My Friend'. Words by Mary Hopkin © 1968.

Every effort has been made to trace and contact copyright holders. If there are any inadvertent omissions we apologise to those concerned, and ask that you contact Canongate Books at 14 High Street, Edinburgh, EH 11TE, so that we can correct any oversights as soon as possible.